FARRAR
STRAUS
GIROUX

BY MARGUERITE YOURCENAR

NOVELS AND SHORT STORIES

Alexis ou le traité du vain combat, 1929;
in English, *Alexis,* 1984
La nouvelle Eurydice, 1931
Denier du rêve, 1934; revised edition, 1959;
in English, *A Coin in Nine Hands,* 1982
Nouvelles orientales, 1938; revised edition, 1963, 1978;
in English, *Oriental Tales,* 1985
Le coup de grâce, 1939; in English, *Coup de Grâce,* 1957
Mémoires d'Hadrien, 1951; in English, *Memoirs of Hadrian,* 1954
L'oeuvre au noir, 1968; in English, *The Abyss,* 1976
Comme l'eau qui coule, 1982;
in English, *Two Lives and a Dream,* 1987

POEMS AND PROSE POEMS

Feux, 1936; in English, *Fires,* 1981
Les charités d'Alcippe, 1956
Blues et gospels, 1984; photographs by Jerry Wilson

DRAMA

Théâtre I, 1971
Théâtre II, 1971

ESSAYS AND AUTOBIOGRAPHY

Pindare, 1932
Les songes et les sorts, 1938
Sous bénéfice d'inventaire, 1962;
in English, *The Dark Brain of Piranesi,* 1984
*Discours de réception de Marguerite Yourcenar
à l'Académie Royale belge,* 1971
Le labyrinthe du monde I: Souvenirs pieux, 1974;
in English, *Dear Departed,* 1991
Le labyrinthe du monde II: Archives du nord, 1977;
in English, *How Many Years,* 1995
Le labyrinthe du monde III: Quoi? L'éternité, 1988
Mishima ou la vision du vide, 1980;
in English, *Mishima: A Vision of the Void,* 1986
*Discours de réception à l'Académie Française
de Mme M. Yourcenar,* 1981
Le temps, ce grand sculpteur, 1983;
in English, *That Mighty Sculptor, Time,* 1992

THE ABYSS

THE
ABYSS

MARGUERITE
YOURCENAR

TRANSLATED FROM THE FRENCH

BY GRACE FRICK IN COLLABORATION

WITH THE AUTHOR

FARRAR, STRAUS AND GIROUX

NEW YORK

Library of Congress Cataloging-in-Publication Data
Yourcenar, Marguerite. / The abyss.
Translation of *L'oeuvre au noir*. / I. Title.
PZ3.Y897AG / [PQ2649.08] / 843'.9'12 / 76-72

CONTENTS

PART ONE

THE WANDERINGS

Nec certam sedem, nec propriam faciem, nec munus ullum peculiare tibi dedimus, o Adam, ut quam sedem, quam faciem, quae munera tute optaveris, ea, pro voto, pro tua sententia, habeas et possideas. Definita ceteris natura intra praescriptas a nobis leges coercetur. Tu, nullis angustiis coercitus, pro tuo arbitrio, in cuius manu te posui, tibi illam praefinies. Medium te mundi posui, ut circumspiceres inde commodius quicquid est in mundo. Nec te caelestem neque terrenum, neque mortalem neque immortalem fecimus, ut tui ipsius quasi arbitrarius honorariusque plastes et fictor, in quam malueris tute formam effingas . . .*

–Pico della Mirandola, *Oratio de hominis dignitate*

I have given you, O Adam, no fixed abode, and no visage of your own, nor any special gift, in order that whatever place or aspect or talents you yourself will have desired, you may have and possess them wholly in accord with your desire and your own decision. Other species are confined to a prescribed nature, under laws of my making. No limits have been imposed upon you, however; you determine your nature by your own free will, in the hands of which I have placed you. I have placed you at the world's very center, that you may the better behold from this point whatever is in the world. And I have made you neither celestial nor terrestrial, neither mortal nor immortal, so that, like a free and able sculptor and painter of yourself, you may mold yourself wholly in the form of your choice.

THE HIGHROAD

YOUNG HENRY Maximilian Ligre was making his way toward Paris, taking the long journey in short stretches.

The bones of contention between King and Emperor were nothing to him; what counted was that the peace signed only a few months back was already fraying away, like a garment the worse for wear. Everyone knew that Francis of Valois still cast amorous eyes upon Milan, much as a rejected lover continues to ogle his lady fair; report had it, on good authority, that the French King was quietly working to assemble and equip a wholly new army on the Duke of Savoy's frontiers, to send it to Pavia, of course, to regain his lost spurs. For Henry Maximilian, however, Italy was composed of snatches of Virgil mingled with less poetic accounts from his merchant and banker father, who had traveled there. Thus the youth imagined, beyond mountains sheathed with ice, long lines of horsemen descending to vast and fertile realms, beautiful as a dream, with russet plains and bubbling springs where white flocks came to drink; with cities carved like jewel caskets, overflowing with gold, spice, and finely wrought leather, each one rich as a warehouse but stately as a church. There would be gardens full of statues and great rooms piled high with precious manuscripts; gentlewomen in silken raiment would be waiting to welcome the victorious young Captain. Every sort of dainty would be offered to eat, and every conceivable refinement would be practiced in the art of love. On massive silver tables vials of glass from Venice would glow with mellow malmsey.

Only a few days ago he had left his family home, without regret, and his future there in Bruges as a merchant's son. For he had listened one evening to a lamed sergeant who was boasting of his service in Italy in the time of Charles VIII; the man had acted out his deeds of daring, and had described the girls and the sacks of gold he had managed to lay hands on during the pillage of the cities. Henry Maximilian had paid him a tankard of wine at the tavern for his swaggering, and on reaching home had decided that it was time for him, in his turn, to see and feel the delectable rounds and curves of this world. He hesitated briefly, this would-be High Constable, as to whether to enlist with the Emperor's troops or with those of the King of France; finally he staked the decision heads or tails: the Emperor lost.

A maidservant spread the news of his preparations for departure. At first, Henry Justus Ligre administered a few sound whacks to his prodigal son; then, mollified by the sight of his younger boy, toddling in long skirts between leading strings across the parlor rug, he jocosely wished the elder "wind aft" among those scatterbrained French. Partly out of paternal affection, but more out of vanity, to prove to himself how far his power extended, he promised himself to write in due time to his agent in Lyons, Master Muzot, to recommend this unruly son to Admiral Chabot de Brion (who was heavily indebted to the Ligre bank). To no avail, therefore, had Henry Maximilian shaken the dust of the family countinghouse from his shoes: not so easily does one cease to be son of a man who makes prices rise and fall, and who lends money to kings. As for the budding hero's mother, she stuffed his pockets with food, and privately slipped him money for the journey.

In passing through Dranoutre, where his father owned a manor house, he persuaded the steward to let him exchange his horse, which was already limping, for the finest courser in the banker's stable; but he sold the creature on reaching Saint-Quentin, partly because so splendid a mount made his reckoning grow as if by magic on the innkeeper's slate, and partly because the rich trappings set him apart, preventing his savoring to the full all the highway's pleasures. In order to make his coins hold out (they were sliding through his fingers quicker than one might have supposed), he ate with carters at wretched inns, sharing their fare of rancid bacon and dried pease, and sleeping at night in the straw; but the economies thus made on the cost of better lodgings were cheerfully lost at cards, or in standing to rounds of drinks. From time to time some kindly widow on an isolated farm would offer him food, and her bed.

He kept to his love of letters, too, for he had weighed himself down with small parchment-bound volumes purloined (in advance of his inheritance) from the library of his uncle, Canon Bartholomew Campanus, a discerning collector of books. At midday, resting in a meadow, he would laugh aloud at some joke in Latin, from Martial; or in more meditative mood, beside a pond, while spitting idly into the water, he would dream of some wise and discreet lady to whom he would dedicate life and soul in sonnets of Petrarchan vein. Often he lay half asleep, boots pointing upward toward the sky, like two church spires; round about him the tall oat blades made a company of halberd bearers, clad in jerkins of green, and a poppy became a fine lass in a rumpled skirt. Sometimes the young giant dreamed amorous dreams, embracing the earth. But a fly would awake him, or perhaps the deep drone of a village bell; with bonnet cocked on one ear and wisps of straw in his tawny hair, Henry Maximilian, long and angular of face (all nose), ruddy from sun and cold water, would rise again and set forth, blithely pursuing his way toward glory.

Exchanging pleasantries with the passers-by, he kept informed of the news. From the time of his stop at La Fère a pilgrim had been preceding him on the road, just beyond hailing distance and walking fast. The jovial Fleming, tired of having no one to talk to, speeded his pace to accost the traveler with the familiar request: "Pray for me, an you will, at Compostela."

"You guess rightly," replied the brown-hooded figure, "that is where I am bound." As he turned to give this answer, Henry Maximilian recognized him as his cousin Zeno. Slim as ever, he seemed to have grown a head taller since their last escapade together, at the autumn Fair. The handsome face, though always pale, looked haggard now, and there was something almost fierce in his headlong gait.

"Well met, cousin!" exclaimed Henry Maximilian joyously. "Canon Campanus has been waiting for you in Bruges all winter; the Rector Magnificus at Louvain is tearing his beard out because you have not come back, and here you reappear at the turn of a lane, like one whom I shall not name."

"The Mitered Abbot in Ghent found a post for me," Zeno explained guardedly. "How is that for a respectable protector? But you? Tell me why you are here, playing the vagabond along the roads of France?"

"Perhaps you have had something to do with it," replied the younger of the two travelers. "I took off from my father's countinghouse just as you did from the School of Theology. But now that you have jumped from Rector Magnificus only to fall back upon Mitered Abbot . . ."

"Laugh if you will," the clerk bade him. "One always has to begin as somebody's famulus."

"Shouldering a harquebus is better than that," declared Henry Maximilian.

Zeno cast a disdainful glance at his young cousin. "Your father is rich enough to buy you the best company of halberdiers in all Emperor Charles's armies," he scoffed, "that is, if the two of you think that bearing arms is fit occupation for a man."

"The halberdiers my father could buy have about as much appeal for me as the prebends of your abbots do for you," Henry Maximilian retorted. "And then, besides, it is only in France that ladies are well serviced."

But the jest fell flat. The captain-to-be stopped to buy a handful of cherries from a peasant, and the wayfarers sat down on a grassy bank to eat. The younger one, looking askance at the pilgrim's habit, observed, "You are wearing the dress of those fools."

"Yes," Zeno admitted. "I was tired of books for fodder. Give me a text that moves; let me see thousands of figures, Roman and Arabic; characters running sometimes from left to right, like those of our scribes, and sometimes from right to left, as in manuscripts from the East; blank spaces which spell plague or war, rubrics traced in blood. And everywhere signs and symbols, with here and there stains even stranger than symbols . . . What better garb than this for journeying unseen? . . . I can roam the world no more remarked than an insect on the pages of a psalter."

"Well and good, perhaps," said Henry Maximilian, whose attention had wandered. "But why to Compostela? I hardly see you sitting among those fat monks, singing through your nose."

"Bah!" the pilgrim protested. "What are those dolts and sluggards to me? But the Prior of the Jacobins at Leon practices alchemy. He has corresponded with our good uncle, Canon Campanus, that simpleton who sometimes treads forbidden ground without knowing what he does. The Abbot of Saint Bavon, in his turn, has written to the Prior and has disposed him to impart his knowledge to me. But I must hurry, for he is old, and I fear lest he soon forget his learning, and die."

"He will feed you on raw onions, and will set you to skimming his brew of copper laced with sulphur. Not for me, thank you! I mean to win better rations at less expense."

Zeno rose, without reply, so Henry Maximilian, spitting the last of his cherry pits into the road, continued: "The peace is tottering, friend Zeno. The princes are grabbing up countries like drunkards in a tavern snatching each other's plates: here Provence, this honey cake; there Milan, as choice a bit as eel pie. From such a fine feast I can surely pick up some crumb of glory."

"*Ineptissima vanitas*," the young clerk exclaimed impatiently. "Aren't you old enough yet to know what is merely wind in men's mouths?"

"I'm sixteen," proclaimed Henry Maximilian. "In fifteen more years we shall see if perchance I'm a second Alexander. In thirty years we'll know if I'm equal or not to the defunct Julius Caesar. Why should I spend my life measuring out cloth in a shop in Woolmarket Street? One wants to be a man."

"I am twenty now," Zeno reckoned. "At best I can count on some fifty years for study before this cranium of mine becomes an empty skull. You can have your hazy dreams, friend Henry, and your heroes out of Plutarch. For me it's a matter of being more than a man."

After an interval Henry Maximilian said, "I'm heading for the Alps."

"And I," said Zeno, "for the Pyrenees."

Then they fell silent. The road, bordered by poplars, stretched out level before them, opening to them a fragment of boundless universe; the adventurer seeking for power and the adventurer in quest of knowledge strode forward together, side by side.

It was Zeno who resumed the discourse. "Look there," he

said, pointing ahead, "beyond this village, other villages; beyond that abbey, other abbeys; and after the fortress, more fortresses still. And each of these castles of stone and each wooden hut has its structure of fixed ideas or flimsy, ill-based opinions superposed above it within which fools stay immured, but the wise find apertures for escape . . . Beyond the Alps, Italy. Beyond the Pyrenees, Spain. On one side, the country of Pico della Mirandola; on the other the land of Avicenna. And farther still, the sea, and beyond the sea and its vast expanse, Arabia and the Morea, India and the two Americas. Everywhere valleys where herbs may be gathered, rocks where metals hide, each symbolizing a single moment in the Great Transmutation; everywhere magic formulas, placed between the teeth of the dead; gods each with his promise; and multitudes of men, each deeming himself the center of the universe . . . Who would be so besotted as to die without having made at least the round of this, his prison? You can see, friend Henry, I truly am a pilgrim. The way is long, but I am young."

Henry Maximilian spoke with awe. "The world is so big."

"The world *is* big," Zeno echoed gravely. "May it please the One who perchance Is to expand the human heart to life's full measure."

Once more they walked on in silence, but not for long. Henry Maximilian, struck by a remembrance, burst out laughing. "Zeno," he exclaimed, "your comrade Colas Gheel, you know, the beery fellow, your sworn brother by the rites of Saint John? Well, he has left my father's factory (where they are starving, anyhow); he's back in Bruges, walking the streets, chaplet in hand, mumbling paternosters for the soul of his beloved Thomas, the one who went off his head because of your machines. Gheel calls you the Devil's helper, and a Judas, or the Antichrist. As for his friend Perrotin, no one knows where he is; Satan must have carried him away."

For a moment an ugly grimace disfigured the young clerk's face, making him look old. "Rubbish, the whole lot of it.

Enough of these ignorant fools. They are what they are, mere raw stuff for your father to turn into gold, for you to inherit someday. Don't speak to me of machines or of broken necks, and I'll say nothing to you of foundered mares, taken on credit at the horse trader's in Dranoutre, or of girls in trouble, or whole hogsheads of wine that you staved in last summer."

Henry Maximilian, offering no reply, began vaguely to whistle a soldier's tune. The conversation came to an end after that, except for some talk about the state of the roads and the price of lodgings.

§

They separated at the next crossroads. Henry Maximilian kept to the highway, but Zeno chose a less traveled route. Suddenly the younger one turned in his footsteps and caught up with his comrade again, taking the pilgrim by the shoulder to say, "Cousin, you remember Vivine, that meek little girl that you used to protect while the rest of us scamps tried to pinch her bum when we raced past her leaving school? Well, she loves you; she claims that she is bound to you by a vow, and has lately refused the proposal of an alderman. Her aunt slapped her hard and put her on bread and water, but she held out. She'll wait for you if need be, she says, till Judgment Day."

Zeno stopped abruptly. A shadow of indecision crossed his face, but vanished like the merest vapor passing over burning coals. "Never mind," he said sharply. "What is there in common between me and that stubborn child? Someone awaits me elsewhere. I'm going to him." And he resumed his pace.

Henry Maximilian, astonished, asked, "Who? That old man, the Prior of Leon?"

Zeno turned around, then replied, "*Hic Zeno.* Myself."

ZENO'S BOYHOOD

T W E N T Y Y E A R S earlier Zeno had come into the world in Bruges, in the Ligre household. His mother, Hilzonda, was sister to Henry Justus Ligre. His father, Alberico de' Numi, was a princely young prelate, descendant of an ancient family of Florence.

Messer Alberico de' Numi, while still a youth, added luster of his own to the court of the Borgias. Ardent, handsome, with boyish long hair, he took part in the bullfights held in the square in front of Saint Peter's, and between bouts liked to talk horses and war machines with Leonardo da Vinci, Caesar Borgia's engineer at the time. Later on, in the somber glow of his twenty-two years, he was one of the few young noblemen upon whom Michelangelo bestowed his passionate friendship, an honor almost like a title. He had some adventures which ended in drawn daggers; he began to collect ancient statues and gems; a liaison with Julia Farnese, kept discreet, proved to be no hindrance to his fortunes. He earned the favor of the Pope and his son in the affair of Sinigaglia (where he helped to draw enemies of the Holy See into the ambush in which they perished), and was virtually promised the Bishopric of Nerpi. But the sudden death of the Holy Father retarded this promotion. Such a reversal, or possibly some cross in love (the secret of which was never known), threw him for a year or two, body and soul, into a life of austerity and study.

He was suspected at first of covert ambitions, but actually his impetuous nature had been seized with a frenzy of asceticism. He was said to be living at Grotta Ferrata, in the abbey of the Greek monks of Saint Nilus. There, secluded in one of the harshest and loneliest regions of Latium, he was working, in meditation and prayer, on his translation into Latin of *The Life of the Monks of the Desert;* only at the express order of Julius II, who valued his keen intelligence, was he induced to accept the post of Apostolic Secretary at the League in Cambrai. Almost immediately upon his arrival at the sessions, his voice carried more authority in discussion than that of the legate himself, and the interest of the Holy See in dismembering Venice (a matter on which he had scarcely reflected ten times in his life) now absorbed him entirely. At the banquets given during the course of the negotiations, Messer Alberico de' Numi, draped in scarlet like a cardinal, made the most of that inimitable presence which had won for him the epithet "the Unique" from the courtesans of Rome. It was he who in the midst of heated controversy, with surprising ardor and Ciceronian eloquence, persuaded the ambassadors of Emperor Maximilian to adhere to the Papal cause. But then when his mother (a hard-driving Florentine) wrote to remind him of certain credits due her from the Adornos of Bruges, he decided to recover these sums at once, so urgently did he need them to further his career as a prince of the Church.

He settled in Bruges at the home of Henry Justus Ligre, his business agent in Flanders, who offered him hospitality. This corpulent Fleming was enamored of everything Italian; he even imagined that he might have had a Genoan forebear, some trader to whose blandishments an ancestress had lent willing ears during one of those temporary widowhoods which the wives of merchants must endure. Messer Alberico de' Numi did not succeed in collecting his money, being paid only in new notes drawn on the Herwarts of Augsburg, but he evened the score by letting his host bear the cost of his dogs and falcons, and his pages. The Ligre mansion, flanked by the great warehouses, was regally maintained: the fare was sumptuous, the wines better still; and although Henry Justus read nothing but the registers of his cloth manufactories, he prided himself on possessing books.

Much of the time the merchant was off and away, traveling by hill and by dale to Tournai or to Court at Mechlin (where he advanced funds to the Regent); or to Antwerp, where he had just entered into partnership with the venturous Lambrecht von Rechterghem for the pepper trade, and for other foreign commodities; and in France to Lyons, where he usually preferred to settle his banking transactions in person at the Fair of All Saints' Day. So he often entrusted the governance of his household to his young sister Hilzonda.

Messer Alberico de' Numi fell promptly in love with this maiden of slender features and small tapering breasts; clothed in heavily brocaded velvets, she seemed almost to be supported by those stiff skirts; the jewels she wore on feast days would have roused envy in an empress. Her eyes were a pale gray, and the delicate lids had a tint of rose; the lips, slightly full, seemed always about to send forth a sigh, or to begin a prayer or a song. If one longed to disrobe her, perhaps it was only because it was hard to imagine her nude.

One snowy evening, which made more welcome the thought of warm beds in well-closed chambers, a maidservant bribed for the occasion introduced Messer Alberico into the bathing room, where Hilzonda was brushing her hair with bran; the long waving tresses fell around her like a cloak. The young girl covered her face but, without struggle, yielded her body (smooth and white as an almond newly blanched) to the eyes, lips, and hands of the lover. On that night the young Florentine drank at the sealed fountain, tamed the young twin roes, and taught the willing mouth how to play love's play. At dawn a Hilzonda won over at last, gave herself wholly to him; in the morning, scratching with the tips of her nails at the frosted windowpane, then using the diamond of her ring, she etched her initials on the glass, interlacing them with those of her lover, thus recording her happiness in that thin, transparent substance, fragile, to be sure, but hardly more so than the flesh itself, or the heart.

Every pleasure of place and season served to enhance their felicity: the intricate music of the day, which Hilzonda played on the small water organ, her brother's gift; wines strongly spiced, and chambers kept warm; boating on canals still blue from the melting snow, or long days of riding, when May came, through fields in flower. Messer Alberico spent some exquisite hours (even sweeter, perhaps, than those afforded him by Hilzonda) searching the peaceful monasteries of the Lowlands for ancient, forgotten manuscripts. The Italian scholars to whom he wrote of these discoveries thought to see in him a new flowering of great Ficino's genius. At eventide the two lovers, sitting by the fire, would gaze together on a gem brought from Italy, an amethyst whereon were carved Nymphs clasped by Satyrs, and the Florentine would teach Hilzonda the words of his country which denote the art of love. He composed a ballade for her in the Tuscan tongue. Indeed, the verses that he dedicated to this daughter of merchant lineage would have been fit for the Shulamite maid of the Canticles.

Spring passed and summer came. One day he received a letter from his cousin Giovanni de' Medici, written partly in code and partly in that facetious tone with which Giovanni seasoned everything (whether politics, learning, or love). The missive provided Messer Alberico with details of intrigue in the Curia and in Rome from which he had cut himself off by this stay in Flanders. After all, Julius II was not immortal. Despite the imbeciles and paid supporters already committed to that wealthy ninny Riario, the wily Medici was preparing, well in advance, for his own election by the next conclave. Messer Alberico was aware that his several discussions with the Emperor's bankers had been no sufficient excuse to the present Pontiff for such undue prolongation of his absence; his career would depend from this time on, therefore, on this cousin so well launched toward the Holy See! As boys, the two had played together on the terraces of Careggi; later on, Giovanni had introduced Alberico into his small, choice coterie of men of letters, all of them playing something of the buffoon, with a trace of the pander, too. Now Messer Alberico could see his way toward manipulation of this man (subtle, but soft and pliant as a woman); he would help him push his way to Saint Peter's throne; then, keeping somewhat in the background, while awaiting greater things, he himself would become the ruling force of the reign. He took only an hour to arrange for his departure.

Perhaps he had no soul. Perhaps his sudden ardors were only the overflow of incredible physical vigor, or possibly, magnificent actor that he was, he was always trying the effect of new modes of feeling. Or was all this only a succession of poses, each violent and superb, but arbitrary, like those assumed by Michelangelo's figures on the vaults of the Sistine chapel? Lucca, Urbino, Ferrara . . . Those pawns on his family chessboard suddenly obliterated for him all thought of these flat landscapes of green turf and water where, for a brief interval, he had deigned to live. Speedily he stacked his fragments of ancient manuscripts in coffers, together with the drafts of his love poems, and, booted and spurred, wearing leather gloves and a hat of felt, looking more than ever the cavalier and less than ever a churchman, he went up to Hilzonda's room to tell her he was leaving.

Hilzonda was with child. She knew it, but did not tell him. She was far too tender to lay any obstacle in the path of his ambitious designs, but was also too proud to take advantage of an avowal which her slender waist and unswollen womb did not as yet confirm. She would not have liked to be accused of lying, and even less to seem to importune. But months later, having given birth to a male child, she supposed that she had no right to leave Messer Alberico de' Numi in ignorance of this, their son. She hardly knew how to write, so spent hours composing a letter, rubbing out word after word with her finger; after finally completing the page, she confided the missive to a merchant from Genoa whom she knew to be reliable and who was leaving for Rome. Messer Alberico never replied. Although the merchant assured her when he came again that he had delivered the message himself, Hilzonda preferred to believe that the man she had so loved never received it.

Her brief period of bliss, followed by brusque abandonment, had given the young woman a surfeit of both delight and disgust; weary of her body and its fruit, she seemed to extend to the child the same reprobation she felt for herself. Inert in the bed of her confinement, she looked on with indifference as the maids swaddled that brown little mass in the glow of embers on the hearth. Since bastardy was a common occurrence, Henry Justus could easily have negotiated a profitable marriage for his sister; but the memory of the man she no longer loved was enough to turn Hilzonda away from whatever heavy burgher might have come, with benefit of clergy, to lie beside her under the eiderdown, sharing her pillow. She wore, with the same indifference, the splendid attire which her brother had ordered for her, cut and sewn from the costliest stuffs; but out of rancor toward herself rather than from remorse, she would go without wine and delicacies, or a good fire, and often without clean linens. She went punctually to Mass and the other offices, but evenings, after supper, if some guest of Henry Justus were denouncing the debaucheries of Rome and Papal extortion, she would stop her lace making the better to hear, sometimes mechanically breaking a thread, only to reknot it again in silence. Then, perhaps, the men would deplore the silting up of the port, which was driving trade from Bruges to other places more accessible to ships; everyone ridiculed the engineer Lancelot Blondeel, who claimed that this malady of gravel could be cured if channels and ditches were dug. A few gross pleasantries might make the round of the company, then someone would begin a tale, already told twenty times, of an avid mistress or a cuckolded husband; or of a seducer hiding in a wine vat; or else of scheming merchants cheating each other. Hilzonda would quit the room and go into the kitchen to see that the remainder of the food was properly put away, but would throw no more than a glance at her son, greedily suckling there at a servant's breast.

§

One morning Henry Justus, on returning from one of his travels, presented a new guest to her, a gray-bearded man so grave and simple in manner that the sight of him made one think of a wholesome wind, fresh from a sunless northern sea. This Zeeland merchant, Simon Adriansen by name, was a God-fearing man. The approach of age, and a wealth which was said to have been honestly acquired, conferred upon him the dignity of a patriarch. He had twice been left a widower: two fruitful wives had successively shared his house and his bed before going to lie side by side in the family tomb along a wall of the church of Middelburg; his sons, in their turn, had each made a fortune. Simon was one of those men whose desire takes the form of paternal solicitude toward women. Deeming Hilzonda sad, he made it his habit to go and sit beside her.

Henry Justus felt a lasting gratitude to him, for Simon's fortune had helped him through difficult straits; he respected the older man to the point of refraining from drinking too much in his presence. But wines were a great temptation to the Flemish host. They made him loquacious, and he did not long conceal from his guest the misfortunes of Hilzonda.

One winter morning as she sat working at lace under a window in the great hall, Simon Adriansen approached and said solemnly, "Someday God will erase from the hearts of men all laws which are not the laws of love."

She seemed not to understand, so he began anew: "Someday God will accept no other baptism than that of the Spirit, and no other sacrament of marriage than that which is tenderly consummated by our bodies."

Hilzonda, at these words, began to tremble. But this man so austere, and yet so gentle, sought to tell her of the breath of a new truth which was passing over the world, and of the lies implicit in any law which complicates God's handiwork; the time was coming, he said, when loving would be as simple as believing. His discourse was as full of pictures as the pages of a Bible, and he mingled parables with reminiscences of Saints who, according to him, had held against the tyranny of Rome. Speaking only slightly lower, but looking first to see if the doors were closed, he admitted that he was still hesitating to make a public confession of faith in Anabaptism, but privately he had repudiated the Church's outworn pomp, its vain ceremonies and deceiving sacraments. To judge from Simon's account, the Righteous in every age are victims, but are privileged, too, for they form a small band immune from the crime and folly of this world; sin is only belief in false doctrines; for the chaste in heart all things of the flesh are pure.

After that, he spoke to her of her son. Hilzonda's child, conceived outside the laws of the Church, and even against them, seemed to him especially designated to receive, and someday transmit, the gospel of the Poor in Spirit and of the Saints. Simon saw a mysterious allegory in the love of the young virgin, so quickly seduced, for the handsome Italian demon with an archangel's face: Rome was the Whore of Babylon to whom the innocent maiden had been vilely sacrificed. Sometimes the credulous smile of a visionary passed over his face, ordinarily so strong and firm, and his calm voice would take on the rather peremptory tone of one who wants to convince himself, frequently even at the cost of self-deception. But Hilzonda was aware only of the quiet kindliness of this stranger. While everyone around her up to this time had expressed mere derision or pity, or else coarsely familiar indulgence, Simon, when he spoke to her of the man who had left her, would always say, "Your husband." And he would gravely remind her that every union is indissoluble before God. Listening to him, Hilzonda regained serenity. Though sad, still, she could hold her head high again. The Ligre mansion, which the family pride in maritime commerce had blazoned with a ship, was now as familiar to the Dutch merchant as was his own dwelling. He came every year, Hilzonda's friend, and she was waiting for him; hand in hand they would speak together of the true spiritual church that was to replace the Church.

§

One autumn evening some Italian merchants brought them news. Messer Alberico de' Numi, already named cardinal at the age of thirty, had been killed in Rome during an orgy in one of the Farnese vineyards. The popular lampoons of the day accused Cardinal Giulio de' Medici of this murder, because he was known to be displeased by the influence which his relative had acquired over the Holy Father.

Simon disdained to comment upon these vague rumors, emanating, as he put it, from the Roman sewer. But a week later they were confirmed in reports received by Henry Justus. From Hilzonda's apparent tranquillity it was impossible to conjecture whether, when alone, she wept or rejoiced at this ending.

"You are a widow now," Simon said at once, speaking in that tone of tender affection which he invariably reserved for her. But contrary to the expectations of her brother, he left for Zeeland again the next morning.

Six months passed before he returned, coming on the accustomed date, and only then did he ask Henry Justus for her hand. Her brother bade him enter the great hall where Hil-

zonda was again at her lace. Sitting down beside her, he began, "God has given us no right to make his creatures suffer."
Hilzonda paused in her work, resting her hands upon the
fragile web; her long fingers quivering on the unfinished
tendrils brought to mind uncertain patterns of the future.
Simon continued: "How then could God have given us the
right to make us suffer, ourselves?"

The fair young woman looked up at him with the gaze of
an ailing child. He spoke again. "You are not happy in this
house, full of vain laughter. My house is a house of peace and
silence. Come with me."

She accepted. Her brother, for his part, was delighted.
Jacqueline, his dear wife, whom he had married shortly after
Hilzonda's trouble and chagrin, was always complaining
loudly of having to take second place in the family, standing
lower, she protested, than a priest's bastard and a whore; and
his father-in-law, Jean Bell, a wealthy trader of Tournai,
made use of such grievances to delay due payment of the
dowry. In truth, although Hilzonda neglected her son, a gift
of the merest bauble to the child engendered in a legitimate
bed made for war between these two women. From this time
on blond Jacqueline could have her fill of embroidered bonnets and bibs for her lusty Henry Maximilian, and on feast
days could let him crawl all over the tablecloth, trailing his
feet in the plates.

In spite of his aversion to the ceremonies of the Church,
Simon consented to let the marriage be celebrated with a degree of pomp since, to his surprise, such proved to be Hilzonda's desire. But in the evening, privately, when the bridal
couple had retired to their nuptial chamber, he readministered
the sacrament in his own way, breaking the bread and drinking the wine with his chosen mate. At this man's side Hilzonda revived like a stranded vessel released by the rising tide.
Free now of reproach, she savored the mystery of these law-
ful pleasures, and the way in which the elderly man, leaning

over her shoulder, caressed her breasts, as if love-making were a form of benediction.

Simon had intended to take full charge of Zeno. But when Hilzonda pushed the child toward that bearded and wrinkled face, where a wart seemed to tremble at the lips, he screamed and struggled furiously to escape from his mother's hands, and from her rings, which hurt his fingers. He ran away, but they found him again that same evening, in the woodshed at the far end of the garden; he was ready to bite the jovial valet who pulled him out from behind a pile of logs. Simon, despairing of taming this wild wolf cub, had to desist and leave him in Flanders. Furthermore, it was clear that the presence of the child added to Hilzonda's sorrow.

§

Left to his uncle, Zeno was destined for the Church. The surest way for a bastard son to live at ease and accede to honors was to take orders, Henry Justus reasoned. And besides, it seemed to him that that mania for learning which early possessed the boy, and the expenditure of ink and candles burning till dawn, were tolerable only in an apprentice priest; so he turned the young student over to his brother-in-law, Bartholomew Campanus, a canon of Saint Donatian, in Bruges. This scholar, worn by prayer and by long study of ancient writers, was so mild that he already seemed old, at barely thirty. He taught the youth Latin and the little that he himself knew of Greek and alchemy, and attempted to satisfy his pupil's curiosity for the sciences with Pliny's *Natural History*. The Canon's cold, bleak study was a refuge where the boy could escape the voices of traders discussing English cloth, or Henry Justus's trite wisdom; likewise, he could avoid the caresses of chambermaids eager to try this green young fruit. Here he was liberated from the poverty and servitude of childhood; these books and this master dealt with him as with a man. He loved this room lined with books, and the goose-quill pen and inkwell of horn, tools for further knowledge; and he welcomed the enrichment to be gained from learning such things as that rubies come from India, that sulphur unites with mercury, and that the flower called *lilium* in Latin is *krinon* in Greek and *susannah* in Hebrew. But later on he perceived that books lie and speak folly, just as men do, and that the Canon's prolix explanations pertained often to facts which did not exist, and which therefore did not need to be explained.

His elders were concerned about the company he kept: his favorite companions during those years were the barber-surgeon Jan Myers, a skillful man without equal for bloodletting and for cutting kidney stones (but who was suspected of dissecting dead bodies), and a certain weaver named Colas Gheel, a roisterer and a braggart, with whom Zeno passed hours (which, he was warned, might better be employed in study and in prayer) combining pulleys and winches. This big fellow was a solid mass of muscles. Sprightly in spite of his size, he spent freely the money he did not have, a veritable prince in the eyes of the apprentices whom he treated on days of kermis. Beneath his sandy mane and fair skin was housed a mind with a practical turn, but also with its chimeric twists: he was forever sharpening, readjusting, simplifying, or complicating something.

Cloth-weaving manufactories in the cities were shutting down each year; Henry Justus, who boasted of keeping his shops open out of Christian charity, was profiting from the dearth of employment by periodic paring of wages. Thus his anxious weavers, only too happy to have a livelihood, of sorts, and a bell to call them daily to work, were constantly threatened with vague rumors of closing; they spoke piteously of having soon to swell the bands of beggars who, in these times of soaring prices, took to the roads and, in their turn, were frightening the burghers. Colas dreamed of easing their toil, and their distress, by the use of mechanical looms such as were being tried out in great secrecy here and there, in Ypres and

Ghent, and in France at Lyons. He had seen some designs, rough sketches of which he relayed to Zeno. The student rectified the proportions and waxed enthusiastic over plans and models, turning what had been only Colas's zest for these new engines into an obsession which both of them shared. Squatting side by side on their heels, and bending over a heap of old iron, they never tired of helping each other suspend a counterweight or adjust a lever, or assemble gears and take them apart again; endless discussions took place about the position of a bolt or the greasing of a track. Zeno's ingenuity went much beyond that of Colas Gheel's slow brain, but the artisan's thick hands had a dexterity that astonished the Canon's pupil, who was here experimenting for the first time with something other than books.

"*Prachtig werk, mijn zoon, prachtig werk,*" the foreman would say, with ponderous approval, putting his brawny arm around the youth's shoulders.

In the evening, after preparing the next day's lessons, Zeno would rejoin his comrade, on the quiet; he would signal by throwing a handful of gravel on the windowpane of the tavern, where the factory foreman often lingered somewhat too long. Or else almost stealthily he would thread his way into the corner of the empty warehouse where Colas lived with his machines. The great room was dimly lit by a candle, set for fear of fire in a basin of water on the table, like a small lighthouse in the midst of a tiny sea. Thomas of Dixmude, who acted as factotum to the foreman, would amuse himself by jumping, catlike, on the shaky frames, or by walking overhead in the dark of the rafters, balancing a lantern or a mug of ale. Gheel would laugh very loud at these antics. Then, sitting on a board and vaguely staring about him, he would listen while Zeno held forth, running on from Epicurus' atoms to the squaring of a cube, and from the nature of gold to the nonsense of proofs offered for the existence of God, the whole evoking a low whistle of admiration from his auditor. These men in their leathern jackets afforded the student what the grooms of stable and kennel offered to the sons of lords of the manor: a world cruder but freer than his own, because at a humbler level, far from precepts and syllogisms. Through them he came to know the reassuring alternation between heavy labor and idle ease, the human warmth and smell of bodies, the language of oaths, allusions, and proverbs, as secret as the jargon of workers' brotherhoods, and activity not limited to bending over a book with pen in hand.

The student claimed that from the workshop and the barber-surgeon's laboratory he was attaining means to confute or confirm the assertions of his schoolbooks: he regarded Plato, on the one hand, and Aristotle, on the other, as if they were ordinary merchants whose weights and measures had to be verified. Titus Livius could be dismissed as a mere babbler, and Caesar, however great he had been, was dead. Although Canon Campanus had been nourished on the marrow of Plutarch's heroes conjointly with the milk of the Gospels, the boy had gathered from those worthies only one thing: that their audacity of mind and body had taken them as far and as high as continence and fasting are said to do in helping good Christians reach Heaven. According to the Canon, sacred wisdom and its profane sister supported each other; so, when the day came that he heard Zeno deriding the pious reveries of *Scipio's Dream*, he realized that his student had inwardly renounced the consolations offered by Christ.

Nevertheless, Zeno enrolled in the School of Theology at Louvain. His ardor and his avidity for learning amazed everyone; this new arrival, capable of sustaining any thesis whatsoever on a moment's notice, acquired extraordinary prestige among his fellow students. Those young bachelors lived high and well; they invited him to their banquets, where he drank only plain water; and he found the brothel girls about as tempting as is a plate of spoiled meat to an epicure. Admittedly, he was handsome, but his curt tone made him feared; the dark fire of his eyes both attracted and repelled. There were wild rumors about his birth, none of which he troubled to refute. Followers of Nicholas Flamel were quick to discern a preoccupation with alchemy in this student who hugged the fire, always sitting to read beneath the very hood of a chimney: a small group of the more inquiring and restless spirits opened their ranks to welcome him to their midst. But before the end of term he had grown disdainful of the Doctors in their fur-lined robes, bending over full plates at the refectory table, stolidly content with their dull and cumbrous learning. The students were no better, a boorish, noisy lot, firmly decided to seek no instruction beyond what was needed to snap up a sinecure; poor devils, whose ferment of ideas was no more than a rush of blood to the head and would pass with the passing of youth. Little by little this same disdain was extended even to his cabalist friends, addled brains, swollen with wind and stuffed with words which they did not understand, and which they spouted forth in mere formulas. He came bitterly to the conclusion that none of these people on whom at first he had counted was advancing further in thought or in act than he, or even so far.

He was living on the topmost floor of a house with a priest in charge; a notice hanging in the stairway ordered the lodgers to attend evening service, and forbade them, under threat of a fine, to bring prostitutes inside, or to void anywhere but in the latrines. But neither odors nor soot from the hearth, nor the housekeeper's shrill voice, nor the walls scribbled by his predecessors with Latin ribaldries and obscene drawings, nor the flies lighting on the parchment before him could distract him from his calculations, this mind for which everything in the world was a phenomenon or a sign. Up in his garret the bachelor passed through those doubts and temptations, those triumphs and defeats, those tears of exasperation, and also those joys of youth which maturity is apt to belittle or forget, and which he himself only half remembered thereafter.

Inclined by his tastes toward the sensuous passions least commonly felt, or least commonly avowed, requiring as they do concealment, and often lies, or, on the contrary, defiance, this young David at grips with the Goliath, Scholasticism, thought to find his Jonathan in an indolent blond fellow student, who, however, took himself off quickly enough, abandoning so tyrannical a comrade in favor of associates more versed in wines and in dice. Nothing appeared to outer view of this secret intimacy, wholly a matter of bodily presence and contact, and as hidden as are the entrails and the blood; the only effect of its termination was to plunge Zeno deeper than ever into study.

Later, there was the embroideress Jeannette Fauconnier, also blond, a capricious lass, as bold as a page boy, well accustomed to trailing a pack of students at her heels; the young clerk paid court to her for an entire evening with his teasing and taunting. When he boasted before the others that he could win the favors of this girl, if he wished, in less time than it takes to gallop from Market Square to Saint Peter's, a brawl ensued that turned into a small battle. Zeno was wounded. The fair Jeannette, desiring to appear generous, bestowed a kiss upon her detractor which came, as the jargon of the time had it, from the very portal of the soul. Finally, toward Christmas, when Zeno had forgotten everything about the escapade except for a scar across his cheek, the seductress crept into his lodging house on a moonlight night, stealthily mounted the creaking stairs, and slipped silently into his bed. The smooth, lithe body, so versed in love play, took Zeno by surprise, as did the dove-like throat and low-voiced cooing, and her laughter stifled just in time to keep from waking the housekeeper, asleep in the next garret room. Tempering his delight, however, was the fear of the swimmer who plunges into a cooling but treacherous current.

For several days he was to be seen insolently strolling beside the fallen maiden, braving the Rector's tedious sermonizing; he seemed to have developed an appetite for this mocking and fickle siren. Nevertheless, hardly a week passed before he threw himself once more into his books. He was blamed for abandoning the girl so soon, after having lightheartedly compromised for her sake his chance for the honors of *cum laude* throughout a whole term. Furthermore, his comparative indifference to women made people suspect him of commerce with a succubus.

THE LEISURES OF
SUMMER

THAT SUMMER, shortly before the August harvest, Zeno returned as he did each year to put himself out to grass, as it were, at the Ligre country home. But this time it was not at Kuypen, as before, in the property which Henry Justus had always owned near Bruges; the banker had become proprietor of the domain of Dranoutre, between Oudenaarde and Tournai, with its ancient manor house newly restored after the French troops had left. The place had been renovated in the style in vogue, complete with stone plinths and caryatids. For the corpulent Ligre was investing more and more in landed estates, those properties which attest, almost arrogantly, to a man's wealth—and in case of danger can qualify him as a burgher of more than one town. In the region of Tournai, he was rounding out the holdings of his wife Jacqueline, piece by piece; near Antwerp he had just acquired the domain of Gallifort, an imposing complement to his bank in Place Saint-Jacques, which he now directed in partnership with Lazarus Tucher. His posts and possessions multiplied: he had become High Treasurer of Flanders; he owned a sugar refinery at Maastricht, and another in the Canaries; he was farmer of customs for Zeeland and held the monopoly for alum in the Baltic. Jointly with the Fuggers he had taken a mortgage on a third of all revenues of the Knights of Calatrava. Thus he was moving more and more among the mighty of this world. After Mass at Mechlin the Regent herself offered him his portion of blessed bread, from her own hands. The Lord of Croÿ (in his debt for the sum of thirteen thousand florins) had recently consented to stand godfather to the merchant's newborn son; a date had been set with His Excellence for the baptismal festivities, to be held in his château at Roeulx. The great financier's two daughters, Aldegonde and Constance, were little maids still, but they would have titles someday, just as they already had fine long trains to their skirts.

His cloth manufactory at Bruges was an outmoded enterprise for Henry Justus; it competed, too, with his own importations of German velvets and of brocades from Lyons. So for cheaper operation he had newly established a few rural workshops in the low open country around Dranoutre; the municipal regulations of Bruges would not hamper him here. He had ordered installation of some twenty mechanical looms constructed in a previous summer by Colas Gheel, from Zeno's designs. The merchant had taken a notion to try out these workmen of wood and metal, who neither drank nor brawled, did each the work of four men, and did not take advantage of the rise in food costs to ask for an increase in wages.

§

On a cool day when there was already a touch of autumn in the air, Zeno went on foot to visit one of these weaving factories, at Oudenove. The countryside was overrun with men out of work; scarcely ten leagues separated the pompous splendors of Dranoutre from the village of Oudenove, but the distance might well have been as far as from Heaven to Hell. Henry Justus had housed a small group of artisans from

Bruges, together with their foremen, in an old, half-repaired shed at the entrance to the village. This dormitory was fast becoming a shambles. Zeno caught only a glimpse of Colas Gheel there, dead drunk that morning; a pale, morose apprentice from France, by the name of Perrotin, was washing up Gheel's porringers and tending his fire. Thomas, who had recently married a girl of the region, was parading up and down the village square in a jacket of red silk, bought for his wedding day. A sharp, hard little man, a certain Thierry Loon, who had been abruptly promoted from reel winder to foreman, showed Zeno the machines, finally set in operation. The weavers, however, had come to detest them almost at once, after having founded extravagant hopes upon them for greater gain with less toil.

But these frames and weights had ceased to interest the young clerk; now he had other problems at heart. Thierry Loon continued to talk. He spoke of Henry Justus with obsequious respect, but kept cautiously glancing at Zeno while deploring the scanty food, the ramshackle houses of wood and plaster hastily put up by the merchant's stewards, and the longer hours than at Bruges, where the working day was governed by the municipal bell. The little fellow regretted the past, when artisans, secure in their privileges, could set the independent workmen a-hanging, and could hold their own even against kings. Not that he had anything against the new inventions; they were clever, these cages where each worker could operate two levers and two pedals at the same time with feet and hands. But the pace was too rapid; it left the men exhausted, and the complicated gear called for more care and attention than their poor fingers and noodles could muster.

Zeno suggested a few adjustments, but the new foreman seemed to find them of little account. He was, in fact, thinking only of how to rid himself of Colas Gheel, to whom he referred disdainfully as a spineless sop, a muddler whose crazy contraptions would finally end only in extorting more work from the men, while increasing the general unemployment.

And worse, this great ox had caught religion, like mange, as soon as he was cut off from the comforts and pleasures of Bruges; in his drinking bouts he was taking the contrite tone of a preacher in the public square. The ignorant, quarrelsome lot of them disgusted the student; by comparison, the Doctors at Louvain, decked out in ermine and furbished with logic, regained prestige in his eyes.

§

Zeno's talents for mechanics were held in low esteem in the family, who looked down upon him as a penniless bastard, though at the same time vaguely respecting him for his future calling as a priest. At the supper hour in the great hall the young clerk had to listen to a fuddled Henry Justus eructing old saws on the proper mode of conduct in life: always keep clear of maidens, lest they get with child, and of married women, too, lest some husband stab you; likewise avoid widows, they devour a man; look well to your revenues, and say your prayers. To all such coarse-grained wisdom Canon Campanus raised no objection, accustomed as he was to expect no more from the human soul than the little which it consents to give. One day at table there was talk of a witch whom the harvesters had caught in an act of malice, pissing in a field of grain already half rotted by torrential rains, and on which she hoped to invoke a further downpour. They had burned her alive, without any form of trial. The guests made merry over this sibyl who thought she could summon the waters but had ended on hot coals. Meanwhile, the Canon was proffering an explanation: when man punishes the wicked with death by fire, the agony lasting but a moment, he is only following God's example. God condemns them to the same torment, the same, but eternal.

Such conversations never interrupted the copious evening meal. Jacqueline, whose blood had been warmed by summer, was favoring Zeno with as many enticements as an honest wife could offer. Ample Flemish matron that she was, her recent confinement had made her prettier still; vain about her complexion and white hands, she retained the luxuriance of a peony. The Canon appeared not to notice her low-cut bodice, or how her blond locks brushed the young clerk's neck as he bent to his book before the lamps were brought in—or the startled anger of the student contemptuous of all women. For Bartholomew Campanus, indeed, every daughter of the race of man was both Eve and Mary, she who yields to the serpent and she who gives her milk and her tears to save the world. So he merely lowered his eyes and passed no judgment.

Zeno, indignant, would quit the room, stalking across the leveled terrace with its newly planted trees and pretentious balustrades, to reach the fields and pastures. Beyond the billowing rows of haycocks stood a hamlet, its low roofs half hidden; but the time had passed when he could have stretched out with farmhands beside the Saint John's Day fires, as he used to do at Kuypen, on that clear night which marks the opening of summer. Nor on cool evenings would they still have made room for him at the forge, on the bench where some of the rustics, always the same few, sat drowsily in the welcome heat, swapping their bits of news midst the drone of the season's last flies. Everything served to set him apart from them now; their slow local speech, their thinking (hardly less slow), and the fear which a lad naturally inspires who knows Latin and can read portents in the stars.

Sometimes he lured his young cousin, Henry Maximilian, into nocturnal jaunts. He had only to descend to the court and whistle softly to awaken this comrade, who would climb over the balcony, still half immersed in the heavy slumber of youth, and smelling of his horse and of sweat after the long exercises of the day just ended. But hope of tumbling a wench at the roadside, or of swigging claret at the inn with carters for boon companions, would rouse him quickly enough. The two of them would take off through the fields, helping each other to jump the ditches and heading, perhaps, for a gypsy campfire or the reddish gleam of some distant tavern. Coming home, Henry Maximilian would brag of his exploits, but Zeno kept his to himself.

Most foolish of these pranks was the one in which the Ligre heir stole by night into a horse trader's stable in Dranoutre and painted two mares pink. In the morning their owner took them for bewitched. Then one fine day it was discovered that for one such outing Henry Maximilian had spent some gold ducats filched from old Justus; father and son, half in play, half in earnest, came to blows and had to be separated, like a bull and its offspring in a farmyard, charging each other.

But, for the most part, Zeno would take off alone, at dawn, his notebooks in hand, going far into the back country, seeking whatever he might learn from direct contact with the nature of things. Thus for hours at a time he would examine stones, weighing them and studying their rough or polished contours, their coloration from rust or mold, all of which tell a tale and testify as to the metals which have composed them, the waters which long ago precipitated their substance, and the fires which have coagulated them into the shapes we see. Insects would often escape from beneath the stones, strange creatures from some animal inferno. Seated, perhaps, on a hummock he would gaze at the plains, undulating under gray skies, and swollen here and there by long ranges of sandy hills; he would dream then of times gone by when the sea had filled these great spaces where grain was now growing, and had left on them, in receding, the shape and imprint of waves. For everything suffers change, both the form of the world and what Nature produces in its motion, each moment of which takes centuries. Or again, his attention suddenly fixed and furtive like that of a poacher, he would turn to the beasts which run, fly, or crawl in the depths of the woods, to study exactly what traces they leave behind them, their rut and mating, their nourishment, their signals and their stratagems; and the way in which, when struck with a stick, they die. He was drawn by a certain sympathy toward the reptiles, calumniated as they are by man's superstition or fear; he marveled at their cold, cautious, half-subterranean nature, enclosing in each of their earthbound coils an ancient, mineral-like wisdom.

One evening during the hottest part of the dog days a farmer had a stroke, and Zeno, fortified by past instructions of Jan Myers, undertook to bleed the man rather than wait for uncertain aid from the village barber. Canon Campanus found such action indecent; Henry Justus, agreeing emphatically with the Canon, openly regretted the ducats he was spending to pay for his nephew's studies, all wasted if the young fellow was going to pass his life between a lancet and a basin. The clerk bore these remonstrances in haughty silence, but from that day on he prolonged his absences. Jacqueline concluded that he was dallying with some farm girl.

§

Once, taking bread with him for several days' time, he ventured as far as the Forest of Houthuist. Its woods were the last of the lofty trees such as grew there in pagan times; strange counsels might be read from their leaves. Looking up to contemplate the green mass of foliage and needles, Zeno fell back into those alchemical speculations which he had begun in the School, or rather, in defiance of the School; in each vegetal pyramid above him he could read secret hieroglyphs of ascending forces: the sign of Air, which bathes and feeds those fair sylvan entities; the sign of Fire, the virtuality of which they have already within them, and which perhaps will destroy them one day. But he knew that these rising forces were balanced by forces descending underground: beneath his feet the blind but sentient race of roots was tracing, in the dark, that same pattern of twigs infinitely dividing in the sky; cautiously these roots were groping their way toward some mysterious nadir. Here and there a leaf turned yellow too soon revealed, beneath its green, the presence of metals from which it had formed its substance, and on which it was now operating a transmutation. The force of wind had left the great tree trunks aslant, much as destiny bends a man. The young clerk felt as free as an animal of the wood, but equally threatened, too. Poised like a tree between earth and sky, he, too, felt bowed by forces which were pressing upon him, and would do so until his death. The word *death*, however, was still only a word for this young man of twenty years.

At dusk he came upon the track of a cart on the moss, weighed down as if by a load of felled trees; soon after, the smell of smoke guided him through the dark to the hut of some charcoal burners. There were three of them, a father and two sons, executioners all, with trees for victims; both as masters and servitors of the fire, they made the igneous element slowly consume the damp wood and change it, hissing and quivering, into coals which forever retain their affinity with fire. The men's ragged garments were hardly distinguishable from their grimy bodies, almost Ethiopian in their coating of ci..ders and sweat. The father's white hair and the long blond manes of his sons were startling to see above their sooty faces and bare black chests. These three solitaries, as detached from the world as if they were hermits, had nearly forgotten the life of their times, or else had never known anything about it. It mattered little to them who might be reigning in Flanders, or whether it was the year 1529 after Christ's Incarnation. Snorting more than actually speaking, they welcomed Zeno much as animals of the forest acknowledge the presence of another creature. He was well aware that they could have killed him, just to have his clothes, instead of accepting a portion of his bread and sharing with him their soup of herbs. Late in the night, half suffocating in their smoky hut, he rose to take his customary observations of the stars and stepped out into the cinder yard, which glistened in the dark as if white. The charcoal pyre was dully burning, a geometric structure as perfect as any beavers' dam, or hive of bees. Across this red field a shadow passed back and forth: the younger of the two brothers was keeping watch on the incandescent mass. Zeno helped him to separate with a crow whatever small logs were burning too fast. Vega and Deneb above sparkled between the treetops, but stars lower in the sky were hidden by the trunks and branches. The young clerk called Pythagoras to mind, and Nicholas of Cusa, and a certain Copernicus, whose theories, recently expounded, had been ardently welcomed or else violently contradicted in the School; a feeling of pride came over him at the thought of belonging to this restless but industrious race of man, he who tames fire and transforms the substance of things, and who scans the paths of the stars.

On departing, he left his hosts with no more ceremony than he would have quitted the woodland deer, taking to his way again hurriedly, as if the goal he had set for himself were very near, but also as if he must hasten in order to attain it. He realized that he was consuming his last portion of freedom, and that in a few more days he would have to resume his college bench in order to assure himself of a post later on, perhaps as secretary to some bishop, assigned to compose smoothly cadenced sermons in Latin; or perhaps as incumbent of a chair in theology, where it would be best to let nothing fall upon the ears of his auditors other than what was fully sanctioned and approved. In his youthful innocence he supposed that no one before him had ever felt so bitter about entering the clerical profession, or had carried either hypocrisy or revolt so far. For the moment, however, the only morning offices to be heard were the woodpecker's drill and the blue jay's cry of alarm. A thread of steam rose delicately from animal droppings on the moss, traces of the passage of some nocturnal creature.

Once back on the highroad he came again upon the noise and turmoil of his times. A troop of peasants were running excitedly with pails and pitchforks in hand to put out a fire. A large, isolated farm had been set burning by one of those Anabaptists who were cropping up everywhere, mingling their hatred of the rich and powerful with a special form of love of God. Zeno could feel no more than disdainful pity for such visionaries as these; they were jumping from a rotting ship to one that was equally leaky, and from an age-old folly to a wholly new madness. But his aversion for the complacent opulence with which he was surrounded put him, in spite of himself, on the side of the poor. A little farther along his way he met with a weaver out of work who had taken to begging in order to seek out a livelihood elsewhere; Zeno envied the wretch for being less bound than himself.

FESTIVITIES AT
DRANOUTRE

ONE EVENING when he was coming home like a weary hound after several days' absence, the manor house was so illumined with torches that it appeared to him from a distance all ablaze. For a moment he thought it had been set on fire, like the farm he had recently passed. The road was crowded with heavy carriages. Then he recalled that Henry Justus was hoping for a visit from royalty, and had been negotiating for it for weeks.

The Treaty of Cambrai had just been signed. People called it the "Paix des Dames," because two princesses had taken upon themselves the task of healing, as well as they could, the wounds of the time. Canon Bartholomew Campanus compared these ladies in his sermons to the Holy Women of Scripture. The Queen Mother of France had at first been delayed in departing from Cambrai, fearing the inauspicious conjunctions of the stars, but had now at last returned to her palace of the Louvre. The Regent of the Low Countries, the Emperor's aunt, was to stop for one night on her way to Mechlin at the country estate of her High Treasurer. Accordingly, Henry Justus had invited the notables of the region, and had bought, right and left, a store of rare viands and supplies of candle wax. He had asked the Bishop to send his musicians from Tournai, and had ordered a divertissement prepared in classical style, in the course of which Fauns clad in brocade and Nymphs in smocks of green silk were to offer a collation of marchpane, frangipane, and sweetmeats to Her Highness, Madame Marguerite.

§

Zeno hesitated to enter the great hall, fearing that his worn and dusty garments and unwashed, sweaty body could lose him his chance of advancement among the great of this world. For the first time in his life, flattery and intrigue seemed to him arts in which it would be good to excel, and the post of private secretary or tutor to a prince appeared preferable to that of a college pedant, or of a village barber-surgeon. Then the arrogance of a twenty-year-old prevailed, together with the assurance that a man's fortune depended upon his own nature, and upon the good will of the stars. He went in and sat down on the hearth; the great mantel had been festooned with green boughs for the occasion, and from beneath it he gazed at this human Olympus around him.

The Nymphs and Fauns, dressed in classic garb, were the offspring of nearby farmers now grown rich, or of country gentry with whom the High Treasurer had been lenient about loans; beneath the wigs and the paint and powder of the young masquers Zeno could recognize their thick blond hair and blue eyes, and under the puffed tunics, where they were slit or gathered high, he could see the rather heavy legs of the girls, some of whom had tried tenderly to beguile him beside a haystack. Henry Justus, looking more pompous and even more apoplectic than usual, did the honors of the household, with all the luxury a merchant's home affords. The Regent, a round, dainty little woman, dressed in black, had the melancholy pallor of a widow, and the compressed lips of a careful housekeeper who not only surveys the linen and the leftover food but also watches over the State itself. Her panegyrists exalted her piety and her learning, and the chastity which had kept her from a second marriage, leaving her to the sad austerity of widowhood. Her detractors, on the other hand, accused her under their breath of loving women, though agreeing that such a taste is less shocking in a lady of rank than is the parallel inclination in men; for it is better, they said, for a woman to assume the role of a man than for a man to play a woman's part. The Regent's attire was sumptuous but severe, as befits a princess who owes it to herself to give every external indication of her sovereignty, but who is little concerned to dazzle or to charm. As she nibbled at sweets she lent an obliging ear to Henry Justus, who was mingling a few wanton jests with his courtly compliments; for a pious woman who is not a prude can listen unabashed to the free discourse of men.

Wines from the Rhine and Hungary and France had already been served. Jacqueline unhooked her bodice, of cloth of silver, and ordered her younger son to be brought to her; he was not yet weaned, she said gaily, and was thirsty like the rest of the company. Henry Justus and his wife loved to exhibit this new child, who made them feel young themselves.

The bare breast showing between the folds of fine linen delighted the guests. "There's no denying that that child has sucked a good mother's milk," Madame Marguerite said lightly, and she asked what name he bore.

"He has not yet been christened, only baptized," the mother explained.

"Then call him Philibert," said Madame Marguerite, "after my lord who is now with God."

Henry Maximilian, who was seated nearby and drinking too much, was boasting to the maids-in-waiting of the feats of arms that he would accomplish when he should come of age. Madame Marguerite commented, "Alas, in these unhappy times he will not lack for battles."

Within herself she was wondering if the High Treasurer

would accord the Emperor that loan at twelve percent which the Fuggers had refused, and which would serve to pay for the expenses of the last campaign, or perhaps of the next . . . for one knows what peace treaties are worth! Just one small portion of those ninety thousand crowns would suffice to complete her chapel at Brou, in Bresse, where she would go, one day, to sleep beside her prince until Judgment Day. In the time it took to raise a gilded spoon to her lips, Madame Marguerite in a fantasy saw again the young man whom she had laid to rest, yes, now more than twenty years ago: naked, his hair wet with the sweat of fever and his chest swollen with the humours of pleurisy, he was nevertheless fair as the Apollos of ancient Fable. Nothing consoled her for that loss, neither the pretty ways of the Green Lover (her parrot from the Indies), nor her books, nor the sweet face of her tender companion, Madame Laodamia; nor affairs of state, nor God, who is the support and confidant of princes. But the image of the dead husband went back into memory's chest of treasures; the spoonful of sherbet spread its cool taste over the Regent's tongue, and she regained the place at table which she had never left, with Henry Justus's red hands upon the crimson cloth, the gaudy finery of Madame d'Hallouin, her lady-in-waiting, the nursling still held on the hostess's bosom, and over yonder, on the hearth, a handsome youth of haughty mien, paying no heed to the guests as he ate.

"And the one over there," she asked, "who keeps company with the embers?"

The banker, displeased, replied, "These are my only sons," and pointed to Henry Maximilian and to the babe on its embroidered sheet. But Bartholomew Campanus, in a low voice, told the Regent the story of Zeno's mother, taking the occasion meanwhile to deplore the heretical paths into which Hilzonda had strayed. Madame Marguerite then entered with the Canon into one of those discussions, resumed every day by the pious and cultivated persons of the time, as to which is more important for salvation, faith or works, even though such idle debate never served to resolve the problem, or to prove the inanity of posing it. At this moment there was noise at the door; timidly, but in a single push forward, a throng of artisans entered.

They were weavers who had come to Dranoutre with a costly gift for Madame, the presentation of which was to have been a part of the entertainment. But a brawl had arisen two nights before in one of the workrooms and had transformed the intended procession almost into a riot. Colas Gheel's entire dormitory had come to ask for pardon for Thomas of Dixmude, who was threatened with the gallows because he had taken a hammer to the mechanical looms so newly mounted and finally put in operation. The disordered band, their numbers swollen with discharged workmen from other regions and with vagabonds encountered on the way, had spent two days in covering the few leagues that separated the manufactory from the merchant's country estate. Although Colas Gheel had injured his hands in trying to defend his machines, he was nevertheless in the front ranks of the petitioners. In that changed face with the mumbling lips Zeno scarcely recognized the solid Colas he had known when he himself was sixteen. When a page came to offer the clerk some comfits, Zeno detained him, holding him by the sleeve, and learned from him that Henry Justus had refused to hear the grievances of the malcontents; but they had been allowed to sleep in a meadow, fed by whatever the cooks had thrown to them. The servants had kept guard all night on the pantries and the silver, the wine cellar and the haystacks. But the poor wretches seemed as docile as sheep led to shearing; they doffed their bonnets on entering the hall, and the meekest of them dropped to their knees.

Colas Gheel was intoning: "Pardon for Thomas, my comrade! Pardon for Thomas, whose reason was unsettled by my machines. He is too young to hang on the gibbet!"

"What?" cried Zeno. "Do you defend this rascal who has

wrecked your work and mine? Your fine Thomas so liked to dance: let him dance now in the sky."

This altercation in Flemish, uncouth to the ears of the small group of maids-of-honor, made them burst out laughing. Disconcerted, Colas looked vaguely round about him to find the speaker, and crossed himself on beholding at the fireplace no other than the young clerk whom he used to call his brother by the rites of Saint John. "God tempted me," he declared, weeping, and holding up his bandaged hands, "me who played with those winches and pulleys like a child. A devil showed me figures and proportions, and all unawares I built a gibbet with a rope hanging down." And as if in presence of the Evil One, he drew back a step or two, leaning on the scrawny shoulder of his apprentice Perrotin.

A small man, as quick in his motion as mercury, whom Zeno recognized as Thierry Loon, slipped through the crowd to the Princess to present her with a petition. Distractedly, as though her attention were fixed elsewhere, she handed it over to a gentleman of her suite. The High Treasurer pressed her, obsequiously, to move into the adjoining gallery, where musicians were making ready for a concert of instruments and voices for the ladies.

Madame Marguerite rose, concluding the conversation with the Canon which she had been careful to maintain throughout the disturbance. "Every traitor to the Church is sooner or later rebellious to his ruler," she said, thus condemning the Reformation for its challenge to authority. At this moment a few of the weavers, directed by the glances of Henry Justus, came forward to present the august widow ceremoniously with a knot of pearls embroidered on black velvet to form her monogram. Extending her jeweled hands, she graciously accepted the artisans' gift.

The merchant host, escorting his guest to the music room, said to her, half humorously, "You see, Madame, what we stand to gain by keeping factories open, out of pure charity, when they are already operating at a loss. These yokels bring you disputes to settle which a village judge would dispatch with a word. Were it not that I have so much at heart the renown of our velvets and our brocades . . ."

Drawing her shoulders in slightly, as she always did when the weight of public affairs descended upon her, the Regent gravely insisted upon the need to check insubordination in the people, especially in a world already troubled by conflicts between rulers, by the advance of the Turks, and by heresy, disrupting the Church. The Canon had gone to whisper to Zeno, inviting him to come nearer to Madame; but Zeno did not hear. A noise of chairs scraping and of instruments being tuned was already mingling with the interjections of the cloth-workers.

"No," said the merchant, closing the door of the gallery behind him and taking his stand before the men like a herd dog before cattle. "No pity for Thomas. His neck will be broken just as he broke my looms. Would you like to have someone come to your homes and smash your bedsteads?"

All hope for Thomas thus ended, Colas Gheel let forth a bellow, like a bull being bled.

"Silence, fellow," the fat merchant commanded, contemptuously. "Your concert spoils the music being served up to the ladies."

Meanwhile, like a good cantor conducting a choir, Thierry Loon was heading the other malcontents. On their behalf he pleaded: "You are learned, Zeno! Your Latin and your French sound better than our Flemish voices. Explain to those folk that our piles of work are increased while our pay is cut down, and the lint from these engines makes us spit blood."

"If those machines take hold in the Low Country we are done for," said a ribbon weaver. "We're not made for bobbing between two wheels like squirrels in a cage."

The man of affairs now began to temper his severity with a semblance of gruff good will, like sugar added to harsh, new-vintage wine: "Do you think I'm so fond of novelties, like a Frenchman? All these wheels and clappers together are worth

less than the arms of good men. Do you take me for an ogre?
Now, no more threats, and no more whining about fines for
cloth you spoil and for knots in the thread; and no more
foolish demands for higher wages, as if money was as cheap as
dung—then I'll put these looms aside for the spiders to use!
Your contracts will be renewed for the coming year at the
same wage as last year."

"At the same wage as last year!" quavered a voice which,
however, was already less defiant. "At last year's wage, when
today an egg costs more than a hen did at last Saint Martin's
Day Fair! Better to take to the roads with a staff in hand."

"Thomas be hanged and let me have my job again,"
shouted one of the itinerant weavers, whose chirring French
dialect made him sound fiercer still. "Farmers have turned
their dogs on me, and in the cities the burghers stone us. I'll
take a straw pallet in a dormitory rather than sleep in a ditch."

At this, Zeno burst out indignantly: "These looms that you
cry fie upon would have made my uncle a king, and all the
rest of you princes. But there's no one here but a rich bully
and foolish paupers."

A sound of commotion rose from the court, where the rest
of the throng, looking up to the tall windows, could see only
the festal candelabra and the tops of the towering pastries. A
stone was hurled through the azure ground of an armorial
pane: the merchant speedily took cover from the shower
of blue hail, but pointing to his nephew, who was still at the
corner of the hearth, he called in derision to the men, "Save
your stones for that mooncalf there! The simpleton made you
think you could stand idle while a bobbin, all by itself, does
the work of four pairs of hands. I lose my money in this
venture, and Thomas loses his neck. Oh, the fine schemes of a
noodle who knows nothing but his books!"

The companion of the fire merely spat without further
reply.

"When Thomas saw the loom working day and night and
doing all alone the work of eight hands," resumed Colas

Gheel, "he said nothing, but he trembled and sweated like one a-feared. They laid him off one of the first when they cut down my band of apprentices. And those reels kept on a-creaking, and the iron arms kept on weaving the cloth all alone. And there was Thomas just sitting at the far end of the dormitory with the wife he had taken last spring, and I could hear their teeth chattering as if they were cold. I understood then that our machines are a scourge, like war, or like the high price of victuals, or like cloth from abroad . . . So my hands have deserved the blows that fell on them . . . And I say that a man must simply work, as his fathers have done before him, and be content with his two arms and ten fingers."

"And what are you yourself," Zeno exclaimed in sudden fury, "if not a machine ill-greased that they use up and throw out as rubbish; and one who engenders more such, alas? I took you for a man, Colas, and what do I see here but a blind mole! Dumb brutes, all of you; you would have neither fire, nor candle, nor cooking spoon if someone had not invented them for you. You would even take fright at a bobbin if you were shown one for the first time! Go back to your dormitories to rot there, five or six to the same blanket, and die there at work on your ribbons and velvets as your fathers have done before you!"

At this point the apprentice Perrotin armed himself with a tankard left empty on a table and charged on Zeno, but Thierry Loon seized him by the wrist; he yelped out a volley of threats in his sharp Picardy jargon as he wriggled like a grass snake to get free. Henry Justus, however, had dispatched one of his major-domos down below, and now suddenly announced in a booming voice that they were open-ing some casks in the courtyard to drink to the Peace. Im-mediately there was a rush of men from the hall, sweeping Colas Gheel along with them, still gesticulating with his two bandaged hands; Perrotin managed to make off, shaking him-self from the grip of Thierry Loon. Only a stout few remained where they were, taking counsel together on how best to augment their wages in the next contract by at least a few meager pence. Thomas and his anguish were wholly forgotten. Nor did they think, either, of appealing again to the Regent, who was comfortably installed in the adjoining room. For the merchant-banker was the only power that these artisans knew and feared; they saw Madame Marguerite only from afar, just as they saw only confusedly, in a blur, the silver dishes, the jewels, and the ribbons and cloth (which they themselves had woven) whether worn on the bodies of the persons present or lining the walls.

Henry Justus laughed to himself over the success of his harangue and his largesse. This uproar had lasted, all told, no longer than the time it takes to sing a motet. Those mechanical looms, to which he attached very little importance, had just now served as a bargaining point, and without great cost to him; they could be put in operation again in the future, perhaps, but only if, by some misfortune, labor should mount excessively high in cost, or should be in short supply. As for Zeno, his presence in Dranoutre was about as welcome to the merchant as a burning brand in a barn; he could take his wild projects elsewhere, and his fiery eyes, which so excited the women. In a moment or two, Henry Justus would be able to vaunt himself before Her Highness for knowing how to keep the populace in hand in these troubled times, appearing to cede on an issue while actually never giving way.

From a window recess Zeno was watching the figures below, shadows dressed in rags intermingled with the guards and valets of Madame. Torches fixed in the walls of the court served to light the festivities; Zeno could make out Colas Gheel in the crowd, with his reddish-blond hair and his white bandages. Pale as that linen itself, and lying against a barrel, he was greedily drinking down the contents of a large mug. "He swills his beer while his Thomas sweats with terror in prison," said the clerk disdainfully. "And to think that I loved this man . . . Race of Simon Peter!"

"Peace," said Thierry Loon, who had stayed at his side. "You don't know what fear and hunger are." And nudging Zeno with his elbow, he continued: "Drop Colas and Thomas, and think about the rest of us from now on. Our men would follow you as thread follows the shuttle," he whispered. "They are poor, ignorant, and stupid, but they are many; they are active and stirring like worms, and as avid as rats that smell cheese . . . Your looms, if they belonged to them alone, would please them. Setting fire to a country mansion is a beginning that can end by taking over whole cities."

"You're drunk yourself, with dreams. Off with you. Go drink with the others!" said Zeno, cutting him short and quitting the hall. He plunged into the stairway, now deserted.

On the landing, in the dark, he bumped into Jacqueline; she was coming back up, quite out of breath, and holding a bunch of keys. "I have locked the door to the wine cellar," she gasped. "One never knows." And seizing Zeno's hand to prove to him that her heart was beating too fast, she implored him, "Stay with me, Zeno! I'm afraid."

"Console yourself with the soldiers of the guard," the young clerk answered harshly.

The next day Canon Campanus looked for his pupil in order to tell him that Madame Marguerite, before re-entering her coach, had inquired about the student's knowledge of Greek and Hebrew, and had shown an interest in admitting him to her household staff. But Zeno's room was empty. He had left at daybreak, according to the valets. The Regent's departure was retarded somewhat by a steady rainfall of several hours' duration. The weavers had taken off for Oudenove, not too dissatisfied with what they had finally obtained from the High Treasurer, an increase in their wages of a penny per florin. Colas Gheel was sleeping off his beer under a tarpaulin. As for Perrotin, he had disappeared in the early hours of the day. It was known later on that he had gone about that night launching threats everywhere against Zeno. He had also bragged a great deal about his skill in knife play.

DEPARTURE
FROM BRUGES

V I V I N E C A U W E R S Y N lived with her uncle, Curate of the Church of Jerusalem, in Bruges. Her small room in the rectory was paneled with polished oak, and contained a narrow white bed, a pot of rosemary on the window-sill, and a missal on a shelf; everything was clean, neat, and peaceful. Daily, at the hour of prime, this self-appointed little sacristan would enter the church in advance of the first worshippers, all women, and before the beggar had resumed his good place in the corner of the porch; shod in felt she would trot across the paving stones of the choir, emptying and refilling the flower vases, and carefully shining the candelabra and silver ciboria. Her pale cheeks and sharply pointed nose, together with a certain clumsiness, never inspired anyone to make those lively remarks which naturally follow upon the passage of a pretty girl; but her Aunt Godelieve always tenderly compared her fair hair to the gold of well-baked buns, or of the blessed bread given after Sunday Mass, and all her demeanor was housewifely and devout. Her ancestors, etched in burnished brass along the walls, were doubtless content to behold her excellent behavior.

For she was of good family. Her father, Thibault Cauwersyn, former page to Madame Marie of Burgundy, had been one of the litter bearers bringing his young Duchess, mortally wounded, back to Bruges, midst the tears and prayers of her retinue. The memory of that fatal hunt stayed ever with him; all his life long he kept a tender respect for that mistress so quickly gone, a feeling akin to love. He traveled far; he served in the suite of Emperor Maximilian at Ratisbon; he came back to die in Flanders. Vivine remembered him as a big man who used to take her on his leather-clad knees and sing, in a voice laboring for breath, ancient, melancholy ballads in German. Left an orphan, she was reared by her Cleenwerck aunt, a good woman, enormously fat, who was sister and housekeeper to the Curate of the Church of Jerusalem. Aunt Godelieve was noted for her soothing syrups and exquisite preserves. Canon Bartholomew Campanus liked to frequent a house so full of the odor of Christian piety and delectable cookery. He introduced his young pupil to the household, too. The aunt and niece fairly stuffed the boy with cakes burning hot from the oven; they washed his knees and hands when they were skinned by a fall or perhaps in a fight; and they confidently admired his progress in the Latin tongue. Later on, however, during the student's rare visits to Bruges from Louvain, the Curate would refuse him the door, sensing an evil aroma of atheism and heresy from that quarter.

But Vivine had learned one morning from a woman peddler that Zeno had been seen spattered with mud, and wet through, going in the rain toward the laboratory of Jan Myers, so she waited quietly for him to come to see her in the church.

He entered without a sound, by the low side door. Vivine, her arms still full of altar cloths, ran to meet him with the artless solicitude of a little servant.

"I am leaving, Vivine," he said. "Make a parcel of the note-

books that I have hidden in your cupboard, and I will come
to fetch them at dusk."

"Just look at you, my friend," she exclaimed.

He must have floundered during the storm in the mud of
the Lowlands, for his boots and his garments were caked with
it to the knees. It seemed also that he had been stoned, or that
he had fallen, for his face was one great bruise, and the hem of
a sleeve was streaked with blood.

"It's nothing," he said. "A scuffle. I've already forgotten the
thing." But he let her sponge the spatters and the mire with a
wet cloth as well as she could. Vivine, though distressed,
thought him as beautiful as the somber Christ of painted
wood lying near them under an arch, and she worked over
him as zealously as an innocent little Magdalene.

She proposed to take him to Aunt Godelieve's kitchen to
clean his garments and feed him with waffles, which would still
be warm.

"No, I'm leaving, Vivine," he repeated. "I'm going away to
see if ignorance and fear, stupidity and hypocrisy reign elsewhere as they do here."

Such vehement talk frightened her, but then so did everything out of the ordinary. Yet this manly anger and the former
schoolboy's tempests were all one to her; the mud and darkened bloodstains served only to remind her of the Zeno who
used to come back disheveled from street fights, he who had
been her dear friend and sweet brother when they were some
ten years old. Tenderly she admonished him: "How loud you
are speaking in the church!"

"God hardly hears," he replied bitterly.

He did not explain whence he came or whither he was
going, or from what affray or foul play he had escaped; or
what particular aversion drove him from a doctoral existence,
furred with ermine and laden with honors; or what secret
aims impelled him to go, unequipped and alone, along doubtful
roads overrun with men coming back on foot from the war,

and with homeless vagabonds. Their like was prudently given wide berth by the Curate and Aunt Godelieve returning together with the servants from a visit to their small farmhouse not far from town.

"The times are so bad," murmured Vivine, repeating the usual laments of household and marketplace. "And if once again you meet with a ruffian . . ."

"Who tells you that I will not be the one to get the better of him?" Zeno demanded, with some heat. "It is not so difficult to dispatch someone . . ."

But Vivine insisted further: "Christian Merghelynck and my cousin Jean de Behaghel, who study in Louvain, are getting ready also to go back to the School. If only you were joining them at the Swan Inn . . ."

"Let Christian and Jean wear themselves pale and thin, if they choose, over the attributes of the Divine Person," the young clerk interrupted in disdain. "And if your uncle the Curate, who suspects me of atheism, is still worried about my opinions, will you tell him that I profess my faith in a God who is not born of a virgin, who will not rise on the third day, but whose kingdom is of this world. Do you understand me?"

"I shall repeat it to him without understanding it," she answered gently, but without even trying to keep in mind those statements all too abstruse for her. "And since my Aunt Godelieve locks the door at curfew and hides the key under her mattress, I shall leave your notebooks on the stoop with some food for you on your way."

"No," said he. "This is a time of vigil and fasting for me."

"Why is that?" she asked, searching vainly to recall what Saint was honored just then in the calendar.

"I am prescribing it for myself," he answered more lightly. "Have you never seen pilgrims preparing for departure?"

"As you will," she said, tears choking her voice at the thought of that strange journey. "And I, I shall be counting the hours and the days and the months, as I do each time during your absence."

"What ballad is this that you are reciting to me?" he asked with a shade of a smile. "The road that I take will never pass by here again. I am not of those who turn back in order to see a girl once more."

"Then," said she, raising her obstinate little brow to confront him, "I will go someday to you, instead of you coming to me."

"Labor lost," he rejoined, entering into this rhythmic exchange as in a game. "I'll forget you."

"My dear lord," Vivine answered gravely, "people of my family lie here under these stones, and their motto is on each of their pillows, *Plus est en vous*. There is more in me than to pay back forgetfulness with its like."

She remained standing before him, a small wellspring of pure but insipid water. He did not in the least love her; this rather simple child was surely the slightest of the ties attaching him to his brief past. But a faint pity came over him, mingled with some pride at being regretted. Suddenly, with the impetuous gesture of a man at the moment of departure who gives or tosses away, or, on the contrary, dedicates some object in order to placate unknown powers (if not to liberate himself from them), he drew off his small silver ring. He had won it in playing "Capture the Ring" with Jeannette Fauconnier, and now dropped it like a penny into Vivine's outstretched hand. He was expecting never to come back, so this slip of a girl would have nothing more from him than the alms of a little dream.

§

At nightfall he went to fetch the notebooks on the sheltered doorstep and took them to the house of Jan Myers. They consisted, for the most part, of extracts from pagan philosophers which he had copied in great secrecy during the time of his studies in Bruges, despite the supervision of the Canon, and which contained a certain number of blasphemous opinions on the nature of the soul and the nonexistence of God. There were also some quotations from the Church Fathers attacking idolatry, but he had altered them so as to show the inanity of Christian ritual and worship. Zeno was still young enough to attach great importance to these first liberties taken by a schoolboy. He discussed his projects for the future with Jan Myers, who counseled study at the School of Medicine in Paris, which he himself had attended, though without going so far as to sustain a thesis and earn a square bonnet. Zeno, however, was all afire for more distant travels.

The barber-surgeon deposited the student's notebooks carefully in the closet where he kept his used bottles and his supply of linen for lint and bandages. The clerk did not notice that Vivine had placed a small sprig of eglantine between the pages.

THEY SAID...

I T W A S learned later on that Zeno had first passed some time in Ghent, with the Mitered Provost of Saint Bavon's Cathedral, who was engaged in alchemy. Next he was thought to have been seen in Paris, on Woodhouse Street, where medical students dissect corpses in secret, and where skepticism and heresy take hold like an ague. But some people, whose word could well be trusted, affirmed that he earned his diplomas from the University of Montpellier; others contradicted this, saying that he had never done more than enroll in its celebrated School of Medicine, and had forgone titles on parchment in favor of practical experience alone, disdaining both Celsus and Galen. He was supposedly recognized in Languedoc in the person of a magician and seducer of women, but was also reported, at about that same period, to be in Catalonia, wearing a pilgrim's habit and coming from Montserrat, sought after for the murder of a young lad. They said that this affair took place in a hostelry frequented by a dubious lot, sailors and horse traders, usurers suspected of Judaism, and Arabs only half converted.

Because it was known, vaguely, that he was given to speculation on physiology and anatomy, the rumor about the assassinated boy (signifying no more for crude or credulous minds than an instance of magic, or of sinister debauch) was interpreted by the more learned as the story of an operation intended to transfuse new blood into the veins of a rich Hebrew patient. Later still, folk who had returned from long journeys (with lies even longer than their travels) claimed to have seen him in Barbary, or in the land of the Agathyrsi, or as far to the east as the court of the Great Dairi.

About the year 1541, a new recipe for Greek fire, used by the Pasha Khaireddin Barbarossa in Algiers, seriously damaged a small Spanish fleet, and this deadly invention was laid to Zeno's account; it had enriched him, everyone said. A Franciscan monk on mission in Hungary had met a Flemish physician there, in Buda, who was careful to withhold his name: undoubtedly, that was Zeno. It was known also, on reliable authority, that he was called into consultation by Joseph Ha-Cohen, private physician to the Doge of Genoa, but that he had insolently refused to succeed to the post when that Jew was sentenced to exile.

Since audacities of the intellect are assumed (often rightly) to be accompanied by audacities in carnal pleasure, idle conjecture credited him with exploits no less daring than his works; hence diverse tales were told about him, varied, of course, according to the predilections of those who diffused (or invented) reports of his adventures. But, of all these bold practices and procedures, everyone agreed that most shocking was his lowering of the noble calling of physician by applying himself to the vulgar art of surgery, thus soiling his hands with pus and blood. What could endure if a restless mind chose to defy professional decorum and propriety in this way?

After a long eclipse, he was believed to be seen again at Basel, during an epidemic of black plague; a series of cures on his part, remarkable beyond all expectation, won him the reputation of a miracle worker during those years. Then,

once more, talk and stir about him died out. The man seemed
to fear lest glory become his trumpeter.

§

Toward 1539 a short treatise in French reached Bruges, under
the imprint of Etienne Dolet in Lyons, and bearing Zeno's
name. It gave a minutely detailed description of the tendinous
fibers and valvular rings of the heart, and was followed by a
study of the role probably played by the left branch of the
vagus nerve in the behavior of that organ. Zeno asserted in this
study that the pulse beat corresponds to the moment of the
systole, contrary to the opinion taught in the Schools. He
discoursed also on the fact that the arteries shrink and thicken
in certain ailments caused by the wear and tear of age. Canon
Campanus, who had little knowledge of such matters, read
and reread the short treatise, almost disappointed to find nothing in it to justify the rumors about impiety now surrounding his former pupil. It seemed as if any practicing physician
would have been capable of composing a book like that,
which was not even adorned with fine quotations in Latin.

The Canon caught sight of the barber-surgeon Jan Myers
rather often in town, mounted on his faithful mule; he had
become more and more a surgeon and less a barber as the years
had brought him increasingly into esteem. This Myers was
probably the only inhabitant of Bruges who might reasonably
be suspected of receiving news from time to time of that
student turned master. The Canon was sometimes tempted to
approach this man of humble estate, but it seemed hardly
fitting that the first overtures should come from a dignitary
of the Church, and the fellow had the reputation of being
mocking and sly.

Each time that some chance brought him an echo of his
former scholar, the Canon would go promptly to the house of
his old friend, the Curate Cleenwerck. They would talk of
Zeno together of an evening, in the Curate's parlor. Some-

times Aunt Godelieve or her niece would cross the room, carrying a lamp, or a plate, but neither one took the trouble to listen, not being accustomed to heed the conversation of two churchmen. Vivine had passed the age of girlish love affairs; she still kept the slender ring, engraved with a flower device, in a box together with some glass pearls and a few needles; but she was aware that her aunt had serious plans for her. While the women folded the tablecloth and put away the dishes, the Canon would go over and over again with the Curate those thin shreds of information which, in proportion to the whole life of Zeno, were what the fingernail is to the entire body. The ageing Curate would shake his head, expecting only the worst from that mind wild with curiosity, empty learning, and pride. The Canon, for his part, would feebly defend the student whom he had formed. Little by little, however, Zeno ceased to be a person for them, or even a visage, a soul, a man living somewhere on one point of the world's circumference; he became a name, then less than a name, a faded label on a jar where were slowly molding a few incomplete and dead memories of their own past. Though they talked of him still, the truth was that they had forgotten him.

DEATH

IN MÜNSTER

SIMON ADRIANSEN was growing old. He sensed it less from his fatigue than from a kind of deepening serenity. He was experiencing something of what a sea pilot feels who has become hard of hearing and catches the tempest's roar only confusedly, but continues, with the same skill, to gauge the currents, the winds, and the tides. All his life long Simon had been rich, mounting from less to greater wealth; gold fairly flowed into his hands. He had quitted his family home in Middelburg for a house built to his order on a newly constructed embankment in Amsterdam, once he had obtained the concession for the spice trade in this port. In this dwelling adjoining the Weepers' Tower were assembled, as if in a strong coffer, treasures from overseas, arranged in goodly order. But Simon and his wife, withdrawn from such splendor, lived on the topmost storey in a small, bare chamber, like a ship's cabin. All their luxury served only to solace the poor, for whom the doors were always open, bread always baked, lamps always alight.

These ragged wretches numbered not only insolvent debtors, and the sick whom crowded hospitals refused to nurse, but also starving actors, sailors besotted with drink, and jailbirds gathered up from the pillories, still bearing whip welts on their backs. Like God, who desires that all should walk freely on His earth and enjoy His sun, Simon Adriansen did not choose his guests; or rather, in disgust of man-made laws, chose those who were supposed to be the worst. Clothed anew in warm garments by the host's own hands, these waifs would sit shyly at his board. Musicians concealed in the gallery above would pour down upon them a foretaste of Paradise; Hilzonda would don magnificent robes to receive them, thus enhancing the value of her alms, and would serve the soups into their plates from a ladle of silver.

Like Abraham and Sarah, or Jacob and Rachel, Simon and his wife had lived in peace for twelve years. Nevertheless, they had their sorrows. Several infants born to them, though tenderly nursed and cherished, died one after the other. Each time, Simon would bow his head and say: "The Lord is Father. He knows what is best for children." This truly pious man taught Hilzonda the sweetness of resignation. But some of the sadness remained. Finally a daughter was born who survived. From that time Simon lived with Hilzonda only as a brother.

His vessels sailed from the farthest coasts back to the port of Amsterdam, but Simon's thoughts were fixed on that great voyage which inevitably ends for us all, rich or poor, by shipwreck on an unknown shore. The navigators and geographers who pored with him over maps, preparing charts for his use, were less close to him than these adventurers on their way to another world, preachers in rags and tatters, prophets scoffed at and tossed in blankets on the public square, a certain baker, Jan Matthyjs, who saw visions, and one Hans Bockhold, a mountebank whom Simon had found one evening half frozen at the door of a tavern. This Bockhold used the cajoleries of a Fair booth to serve the Kingdom of the Spirit. Among these men, and most modest of all (hiding his great theological learning and voluntarily laying aside his critical faculties in order to let divine inspiration descend on him unimpeded), was Bernard Rottmann in his old fur-lined cloak, he who was once the dearest to Luther of all his disciples. But now Rottmann abhorred and reviled that man of Wittenberg, so falsely called "righteous" as he sat in comfort between truth and error, holding with the poor, but also ready to run with the rich.

The arrogance of these Saints, and the impudent way in which they contemplated stripping the burghers of their wealth and the magistrates of their titles, to redistribute them as they saw fit, had drawn down public indignation upon them. Threatened with immediate expulsion or death, the Just held meetings in Simon's house in order to take counsel together like mariners on a foundering ship. But hope dawned in the distance, like a sail: Münster, where Jan Matthyjs had succeeded in implanting himself after driving out its Bishop-Prince and its aldermen, had become the City of God. There, for the first time on earth, the lambs had a refuge. In vain were the Imperial troops planning to take that Jerusalem of the disinherited; the poor of the whole world would rally round their brothers; there would be bands going from city to city, pillaging treasures shamefully amassed in the churches, and overturning the idols; plump Martin would be bled to death in his den in Thuringia, and likewise the Pope in his Rome.

Simon listened to these assertions, stroking his white beard the while; as a man accustomed to high risks, he was inclined to accept, undaunted, the prodigious dangers of this pious adventure. Rottmann's serenity and Hans's jests relieved him of his last doubts, reassuring him as once did a captain's cool mien, and the gaiety of a lad aloft, when one of his ships was weighing anchor during the season of storms. With a confident heart he watched his shabby guests departing one evening, pulling their bonnets down on their brows and drawing

their worn woolen scarves close around their necks as they
went off together in the mud and the snow, ready to trudge
along side by side to that Münster of their dreams.

One night in February, just before a cold dawn, Simon
mounted to the chamber where Hilzonda lay straight and
motionless in her bed, lighted by a faint night lamp. He spoke
to her in a low voice and, after making certain that she was
not asleep, sat down heavily on the foot of the bed to tell her
of the meeting in the small room below, talking as a merchant
does with his wife in going over the reckonings of the day.
Was she not weary, too, of living in one of these cities where
money, flesh, and vanity parade absurdly in the public square,
where men's toil seems to be solidified into brick and stone, or
useless clutter, on which the Spirit no longer breathes? As for
himself, he was proposing to abandon his house and possessions in Amsterdam, or rather, to sell them (for why should
one squander holdings which rightly belong to God?), in
order to go, while there was still time, to settle in the Ark
which Münster had become. That city was already full to
bursting, but their friend Rottmann would be able to find
them a roof and provisions. Simon was giving Hilzonda a
fortnight to consider the project. Exile and destitution, possibly death, awaited them there, but they had also the chance
to be among the first to welcome the Reign of Heaven.

"A fortnight, wife," he repeated. "But not an hour more,
for the time grows short."

Hilzonda raised herself on her elbow, her eyes suddenly
open wide and fixed upon him. "My husband, the fortnight is
already passed," she replied, with a kind of quiet disdain for
all that she was thus leaving behind.

Simon praised her for being always a leap ahead of him in
their progress toward God. His veneration for his companion
had not succumbed to the routines of daily life. Deliberately
this elderly man overlooked the imperfections, shadows, and
defects, which were nevertheless visible on the soul's surface,
in order to retain from the persons of his choice only what

they were, possibly, at their purest, or what they aspired to become. Thus, under the grotesque exteriors of the prophets whom he sheltered, he could see the Saint in each one. Touched from the time that he had first met her by Hilzonda's limpid eyes, he took no notice of the rather sly curve which was forming at the sad lips. To his mind this woman, though grown thin and weary, remained truly a Great Angel.

§

The sale of the house and furnishings was the last of Simon's successful transactions. As always, his indifference in matters of money served him in good stead, sparing him both the errors due to fear of loss and those which come from too great haste to reap a profit. These voluntary exiles were treated, as they left Amsterdam, with all the respect which the rich enjoy, in spite of everything, even if, shockingly, they take the side of the poor. A river barge brought them as far as Deventer, whence they continued by coach through the Gelderland hills, now a-shimmer with new young leaves. In Westphalia they stopped at the inns to taste the smoked ham of the region; for these city folk, the whole journey to Münster took on the aspect of a country excursion. A servant named Johanna accompanied Hilzonda and the child; Simon revered her because she had once endured torture for the sake of her Anabaptist faith.

Bernard Rottmann received them at the gates of Münster amidst a confusion of carts, sacks, and barrels. The preparations for siege were not unlike the disordered activity of certain days just before a festival. While the two women took down the clothing and a cradle from the coach, Simon was listening to Rottmann's explanations. This Grand Restitutor was calm; like the crowd whom he had indoctrinated (all busy dragging through the streets supplies of vegetables and firewood from the neighboring countryside), he was counting upon help from God. But, he continued, Münster needed money. Even more, it needed support from the humble people, and from the malcontents and the outraged who are scattered throughout the world, and who are only awaiting the new Christ's first victory in order to shake off the yoke of all idolatries. Simon was rich, still; he had payments due him at Lübeck and in Elbing, and as far away as Jutland and distant Norway; he owed it to himself to recuperate these sums, which belonged only to the Lord. Furthermore, as he traveled he would be able to transmit the message of these Saints in revolt in Münster to the hearts of the pious everywhere. His reputation for being a man of good sense, and of wealth, like his garments of whole cloth and fine leather, would win him auditors where a ragged preacher would have no access at all. This rich convert was the best possible emissary from the Council of the Poor.

Simon fell in with these views. It was important to act fast so as to escape the ambushes of the princes and the prelates. Hastily embracing his wife and daughter, he set off at once, drawn by the freshest of the mules which had just brought him to the Ark's doors. Only a few days passed before the gleam of halberds could be seen upon the horizon. The troops of the Bishop-Prince soon encamped around the city, but without attempting an assault; they were ready to stay for the time it might take to reduce these wretches by hunger.

Bernard Rottmann had settled Hilzonda and her child in the house of the burgomaster, Knipperdollinck, who had been the earliest protector of the Pure in Münster. This giant of a man, placidly cordial, treated her like a sister. Under the influence of Jan Matthyjs, who kneaded and shaped this new world as he formerly did his bread in a cellar of Haarlem, everything in daily life was changing to something different, becoming easy and simple. Here the fruits of the earth belonged to everyone, just as did the air and the light of God; so those who had linen, dishes, or furniture carried them into the street for others to share. All of them, loving each other with rigorous affection, helped each other, corrected and spied on each other, to warn everyone of his faults; civil laws were abolished, as were the sacraments; blasphemy and carnal sins were punished by hanging; the women, half veiled, glided here and there like tall, restless angels, and the sobbing of public confession was heard on the square. The small citadel of the Just, encircled by the Catholic troops, lived in a very fever of God. The spur to their courage was the open-air preaching held each evening. Bockhold, the favorite Saint, pleased them all with his sermons, for he knew how to season the gory images drawn from the Apocalypse with jokes from the actor's trade. Mingled with the shrill voices of the women, imploring aid from their Father in Heaven, rose the groans of the sick and of those first wounded in the siege, who lay on these warm summer nights under the arcades of the square. Hilzonda was one of the most ardent among the worshippers: standing tall, elongated like a flame, the mother of Zeno would denounce the ignominies of Rome. Her eyes, filled with frightful visions, would cloud with tears; suddenly collapsing like a too slender taper and sinking to the ground, she would weep in tender contrition, and in the desire to die.

The first official mourning was for the death of Jan Matthyjs, killed while leading thirty men (and a host of angels) in a sortie attempted against the Bishop's army. Immediately after this disaster, Hans Bockhold was proclaimed Prophet-King; wearing a royal crown and mounted on a horse irreverently caparisoned with a chasuble, he took office on the open space before the church. Soon a platform was erected where the new David sat enthroned each morning, rendering decisions without appeal on matters both terrestrial and celestial. A few felicitous excursions, which had overturned the Bishop's kitchen tents and produced a booty of pigs and hens, were occasion for a feast on this platform, accompanied by the music of fifes; when the enemy's kitchen boys, taken prisoner, were forced to prepare the viands and then were killed by the pommeling and kicking of the crowd, Hilzonda laughed with the rest of the company.

Gradually a change was taking place in the souls of these folk, like the almost imperceptible transformation of a dream, at night, into a grim nightmare. Ecstasy was giving the Saints the reeling walk of drunkards. The new Christ-King ordered fast upon fast for the sake of husbanding the provisions stacked everywhere in the city's lofts and cellars; sometimes, however, if a keg of herring stank too strongly, or if spots of mold appeared on the butt of a ham, the hungry could have this spoiling food to stuff themselves. The new King's decisions were endorsed by Bernard Rottmann without a word. Worn out and sick abed, he contented himself with preaching to the people assembled under his windows about Love, which consumes all the dross of the earth, and about waiting for the Coming of God's Kingdom. The office of burgomaster had been abolished and Knipperdollinck had been solemnly promoted from it to that of executioner; this fat man with the thick red neck seemed perfectly at home in the exercise of his new duties, as if he had always secretly dreamed of being a butcher. There was killing a-plenty: the King had the cowardly and the lukewarm put away before they could infect the others: in any case, each death made for economies on rations. Executions were a topic of conversation in the house where Hilzonda lived, much as the price of wool used to be in Bruges.

For humility's sake, Hans Bockhold allowed himself to be called John of Leyden (his native city) in the earthly assemblies, but used also another name, ineffable that one, in the intimacy of his close followers, for he felt within him a superhuman strength and ardor. Seventeen spouses bore witness to this inexhaustible vigor of God: the burghers were pushed by fear, or by vanity, to loose their wives to the living Christ, just as they had handed over their gold coins; likewise, harlots from the lowest brothels schemed for the honor of serving the King in his conjugal pleasures.

He came to Knipperdollinck's house to converse with Hilzonda. She blanched at the touch of this small man, whose eyes were so bright and whose exploring hands were pulling down the edge of her bodice as a tailor would do. She remembered, though not wishing to recall it, that in the time of Amsterdam, when he was still only a famished actor at her table, he had seized the chance to stroke her thigh as she bent over him with a plate in hand. She yielded now with disgust to the kisses of that wet mouth, but disgust changed to ecstasy; decency's last restraints fell from her like mere rags, or rather, like that dead skin which is scraped off in a steam bath. Held under that hot breath, Hilzonda ceased to be, and with her went all the past fears, scruples, and vexations of that Hilzonda. The King, lying close beside her, admired her slender body; its slightness, he said, seemed to make the blessed forms of woman stand out the better, the long sloping breasts and the rounded belly. This man accustomed only to bawds, or to matrons devoid of grace, marveled at her exquisiteness: her delicate hands resting on the soft hair of her mount of Venus reminded him of a lady's hands reposing casually on a fur muff, or on a curly lapdog.

He recounted for her the story of his life: he had known, from the age of sixteen, that he was God. He had had a seizure in the shop of the tailor to whom he was apprenticed, and had actually entered into Heaven during his outcries and his drooling. Another time, after he had been driven from the shop, he had felt this trembling (which is God within) while he stood in the wings of a traveling stage, where he played the role of buffeted clown. Then again, in a barn where he had known his first girl, he had understood that God *is* the stirring flesh and the naked bodies for which neither poverty nor riches exist, this flood of life, bearing within it death also, and running like angels' blood. He recited all this in the pretentious jargon of an actor, sprinkling it here and there with the grammatical errors of any peasant's son.

A few evenings later he led her to a seat at the banquet table among the wives of Christ. The starving mob was pushing against the tables hard enough to break them down, imploring the King's blessing and snapping up the chicken's neck or leg bones which he deigned to throw them. The young Prophets, who served as bodyguards to the King, used their fists to keep the crowd at a respectful distance. Divara, the reigning Queen, who came from a house of ill fame in Amsterdam, was placidly chewing her food, revealing her teeth and tongue at every mouthful; she had the air of an indolent, healthy cow. All of a sudden the King would raise his hands to pray, his face embellished by a theatrical pallor touched with rouge on the cheekbones. Or he might breathe into the face of a fellow diner to communicate to him the breath of the Holy Spirit. One night he made Hilzonda go into the back room, where he lifted her robes to show the young Prophets how white and pure is the naked Church. A fight broke out between the new Queen and Divara, who was proud to be only twenty; she called Hilzonda an old woman. The two of them ended flat on the pavement, pulling out each other's hair by fistfuls, but the King restored harmony by taking them both to his bosom that night.

§

From time to time a burst of activity would arouse these crazed, stupefied souls. Hans decreed immediate destruction of the belfries and towers, and of all city gables which rose proudly higher than the others and thus flaunted the ideal of equality which ought to prevail everywhere in the presence of God. Squadrons of men and women, followed by shrieking children, rushed to climb the towers; armfuls of slate and showers of brick were plumped to the ground, injuring not only the heads of the passers-by but also the roofs of houses below. On the pinnacles of Saint Maurice's Church the wreckers could only half loosen the brass figures, so they left them suspended awry between earth and the heavens. In the former dwellings of the rich they tore down some rafters, thus making holes for the rain and the snow to fall through.

One old woman complained that she was freezing alive in her room thus opened to the four winds, and accordingly was pushed out of the city gate. The Bishop refused to receive her in his camp; for a few nights thereafter she was heard crying in the moat. Toward evening the workers would cease their toil and remain sitting on the battered roofs or walls with their legs hanging out over empty space; they would lean backward to scan the sky above for signs of the Lord's Coming, so eagerly awaited. But the red in the west would grow pale, and one more evening would turn first to gray and then to dark; the weary demolishers would descend again to the interior of their hovels to lie down and sleep.

§

A restlessness which was close to gaiety impelled the people to wander in the streets alongside the crumbling buildings. Or from the top of the ramparts they would look both with interest and with fear out onto the open countryside, to which they had no access, like passengers watching a dangerous sea surrounding their ship; their nausea from hunger, too, was like the sickness felt on venturing out to sea. Hilzonda came and went, constantly, by the same alleys, the same vaulted passageways, and the same stairs mounting to the towers, sometimes alone but sometimes pulling her child along by the hand. Famine's bells were ringing in her vacant head; she felt light, and swift as the birds ever wheeling between the church spires; she was faint, but only as a woman is who is about to swoon in love's play. Sometimes, breaking a long icicle from a beam overhead, she would open her mouth to suck at its coolness. The people around her seemed to be in the same dangerous state of euphoria: in spite of the quarrels breaking out over a hunch of bread or a rotten cabbage, a kind of tenderness flowing from the heart fused these wretched and starving creatures into a single mass. For some time now, however, the discontented had dared to speak out, and those who were merely halfhearted were no longer executed, for they were too numerous.

Johanna reported to her mistress the sinister rumors which were beginning to circulate about the kind of meat being distributed to the people. Hilzonda ate the food without seeming to hear. There were some who bragged of having partaken of hedgehogs and rats, or worse still; in the same way, certain burghers who passed for austere were suddenly boasting of acts of fornication which seemed impossible for such skeletons and phantoms as they had now become. Privacy was no longer sought for relieving the needs of a sick body. The general fatigue was too great to permit interment of the dead, but the freezing cold kept the corpses, stacked in the courtyards, from decomposing and giving off odors. No one spoke of the threat of plague, though cases would doubtless occur with the first warm days of April; there was no hope of holding out so long as that. Nor did anyone mention the enemy's work in preparing their approach, methodically filling in the moats, nor the imminent assault, which was thought to be quite close. Indeed, the faces of the faithful had taken on the sly expression of hounds who seem not to hear the crack of the whip behind their ears.

Finally one day, Hilzonda, standing on a rampart, saw a man beside her raising his arm to point out something. A long column was advancing over the uneven surface of the plain; lines of horses were picking their way through the muddy thaw. A joyful cry burst forth and fragments of hymns arose from enfeebled chests: were not these the Anabaptist armies recruited in Holland and in Gelderland whose arrival Bernard Rottmann and Hans Bockhold were always announcing, Brothers coming to rescue Brothers? But these regiments were soon seen to be fraternizing with the Bishop's troops which encircled Münster. As the March wind flapped the banners of the host, someone spied among them the pennant of the Prince of Hesse; that Lutheran, then, was joining the idolaters to annihilate the people of the Saints. A few of the besieged managed to overturn a block of stone on the top of the wall, letting it fall to crush several soldiers working with pickaxes at the foot of a bastion; and a sentry's shot laid a Hessian courier low. The attackers responded with a volley from the harquebuses which caused several deaths, but after that no one attempted anything more. The expected assault did not take place that night, or on the nights following. Five weeks went by in total lethargy.

Bernard Rottmann had long since dispensed his last provision of edibles and the contents of his phials of remedies. The King, as was his custom, continued to throw handfuls of grain to the people through the window, but without releasing the rest of his reserves hidden under his floor. He slept a great deal: he passed thirty-six hours in cataleptic slumber before going a last time to preach on the almost empty square. He had already renounced, sometime ago, his nightly visits to Hilzonda's dwelling. His seventeen spouses had been ignominiously chased away, and in their stead was a mere girl, hardly nubile yet, who stammered somewhat and had the gift of prophecy; he called her tenderly his white birdling, and the dove of the Ark. Hilzonda felt neither sorrow nor discontent, and no surprise, at being abandoned by the King; the boundaries between what had and what had not been were fading for her; it seemed that she no longer remembered having been taken by Hans as a beloved. But nothing, to her mind, was illicit: she came to the point of waiting late into the night for Knipperdollinck to return, curious to try to stir that great mass of flesh; he passed her by, however, muttering without looking at her, concerned with other matters than women.

The night that the Bishop's troops entered the city, Hilzonda was awakened toward midnight by the screaming of a sentry, stabbed. Two hundred halberdiers, guided by a traitor, had been let in through a postern gate. Bernard Rottmann, one of the first to hear the alarm, rushed from his sickbed into the street, his shirttails flapping grotesquely against his scrawny legs; he had the good fortune to be killed by a Hungarian mercenary who had not understood the Bishop's orders to bring back all leaders of the rebellion alive. The King, surprised in his sleep, fought from room to room and from corridor to corridor with the courage and the agility of a cat hunted down by dogs; at daybreak Hilzonda saw him pass on the square, stripped of his theatrical trappings and naked to the waist, bent double under the whip. He was seen being kicked into the great cage where he used to shut up the discontented and the lukewarm until they were judged. Knipperdollinck, half stunned by blows on the head, had been left for dead on a bench. All day long the heavy tread of soldiers echoed through the city; this rhythmic sound signified that in the stronghold of folly common sense again ruled in the likeness of these men who sell their lives for fixed pay, who eat and drink at the hour set, who steal and rape on occasion, but who have somewhere an old mother, a thrifty wife, and a small farm where they will come back to live, when crippled and aged; who go to Mass when they have to, and who believe, moderately, in God. Executions were resumed, though decreed this time by legitimate authority, approved equally by the Pope and by Luther. These ragged creatures with haggard faces and gums gangrened from starvation were only disgusting vermin in the eyes of the well-fed soldiery, and could therefore easily and justly be stamped out.

When the first upheaval had subsided, a criminal tribunal was set up on the square before the Cathedral, at the base of the platform where the King had held hearings. Those designated for death were vaguely aware that the Prophet's promises were being fulfilled for them, though otherwise than they had expected (as is always the case with prophecies): their world of tribulation had come to an end; they were passing effortlessly into a vast red sky. Only a few of them cursed the man who had drawn them into this wild dance of redemption. There were those who knew deep within themselves that they had long since desired to die, much as the too taut rope surely desires to break.

Hilzonda awaited her turn until evening. She had put on the finest dress which was left to her, and had fastened her braids with pins of silver. At last four soldiers appeared; they were honest brutes, merely doing their duty. She seized little Martha's hand as the child began to cry, and said to her: "Come, daughter, we are going to God."

One of the men tore the child away and tossed her toward Johanna, who caught her in her arms and held her to her black-bodiced bosom. Hilzonda followed the executioners without speaking further, walking so fast that they had to hasten their steps. In order not to trip over her long, billowing gown, which gave her the appearance of walking on waves, she held up its folds of green silk with both hands. Arrived at the platform, she could recognize, though confusedly, people she knew among the dead bodies; one of them was a former Queen. She let herself drop on that heap, which was still warm; and offered her throat to the sword.

§

Simon's journey was turning into a road to Calvary. His principal debtors dismissed him without paying, for fear of filling an Anabaptist pocket or beggar's bag: the cheats and the misers poured forth remonstrances. His brother-in-law Justus Ligre declared that on such short notice he could not repay the large sums which Simon had invested in his bank in Antwerp; he felt certain, anyhow, that he could take better care of the possessions of Hilzonda and her child than one so benighted as to make common cause with the State's enemies. Simon, dispirited, went out again like a rejected mendicant through the carved and gilded door (rich as a reliquary) of that trading and banking house which he had helped to found. He failed equally in his mission to solicit donations: only the very poor, and few of them, were willing to bleed themselves for their Brothers' gain. Two different times he was questioned by ecclesiastical authority, and had to pay money in order not to be imprisoned; thus, to the end, he continued to be the wealthy man protected by his florins. Of the meager sums collected on this journey, one portion was stolen by an innkeeper in Lübeck at whose house he had fallen ill, suffering a stroke.

His state of health thereafter obliged him to travel by short stages, so he did not arrive in sight of Münster until two days before the assault. All hope of getting inside the besieged city proved vain. He was received with ill grace, though not molested, in the camp of the Bishop-Prince, to whom he had formerly been of service, and managed to find lodging in a farm very near the moat and gray walls which concealed Hilzonda and the child from his view. He took his meals at the farmwife's scoured wooden table, together with a judge (summoned in anticipation of the ecclesiastical trial which would soon open), and a military officer of the Bishop, billeted there; to these were added several refugees from Münster itself, who never wearied of denouncing the follies of the Faithful and the crimes of the King. But Simon would lend only half an ear to such traitors' talk vilifying martyrs. On the third day after the fall of Münster, he finally obtained permission to enter the city.

He walked with effort along the streets patrolled by troops, resisting both the sun and dry wind of a June morning and uncertainly seeking his way in this city known to him only by hearsay. Under an arcade of Great Market Square, he recognized Johanna sitting on a doorstep, with the child on her lap. The little girl wailed when this stranger drew near to kiss her; Johanna curtsied in servant fashion without saying a word. Simon pushed open the door, noting its broken locks, and went through the empty rooms of the ground floor, then those of the upper storeys.

Returning to the square, he walked in the direction of the esplanade where the executions had been held. A length of green brocade was hanging down from the platform; from this trailing cloth he recognized Hilzonda at some distance, caught under a pile of dead bodies. Without staying to examine further that corpse from which the soul had already been freed, he went back to join the housekeeper and the child.

A milk vendor passed down the street with his cow and pail and stool, crying his milk for sale; a tavern was reopening in the house across the way. Johanna used the few farthings which Simon had given her to fill some pewter goblets. Fire soon crackled on the hearth, and the clink of a spoon could be heard in the hands of the child. Domestic life was slowly beginning again around them, little by little filling this devastated house much as a mounting tide spreads again over a shore where driftwood lay scattered, along with treasures from shipwrecks and crabs from the ocean's depths. The servant prepared Knipperdollinck's bed for her master in order to spare him the fatigue of climbing the stairs again. At first she answered only by dour silence to the old man's questions as he slowly consumed his warmed beer. When at last she spoke, what she poured forth was a torrent of filth reeking both of the kitchen sink and of Biblical obscenity: for this severe old Hussite, the King had never been more than a low vagabond, such as are fed belowstairs but dare to sleep with the master's wife. When she had said it all, she set herself to scrubbing the floor with a clatter of brushes and pails, and great rinsing and slapping of cloths.

Simon slept little that night, but contrary to what his servant supposed, the feeling which was most poignant for him was neither indignation nor shame; it was that more tender sorrow which is called compassion. As he struggled to breathe in the warm night air, he found himself thinking of Hilzonda as of a daughter whom he might have lost. He blamed himself for having left her alone to cross this hazardous strait, but then told himself that each of us has his lot, his particular portion of the bread of life, and of death, which belongs only to him, and that it was right that Hilzonda should have eaten of this bread in her own way and at her appointed hour. This time, too, she was ahead of him: she had passed first through death's terrors.

He continued to approve the Faithful in their stand against the Church and the State which had crushed them; to be sure, Hans and Knipperdollinck had shed blood, but what else could be expected in a world of blood? For more than fifteen centuries the Kingdom of God on earth, which John and Peter and Thomas were to have seen in their lifetime, with their own eyes, had been lazily put off till Judgment Day by the cowards and the tepid-hearted, and by the contrivers. The Prophet had dared to proclaim, right here and now, that Kingdom which is of Heaven. He was pointing out the way, even though by mischance he himself had taken the wrong road. For Simon, Hans remained a Christ in the sense that every man is capable of being a Christ, and his follies seemed less ignoble than the cautious sinning of the Pharisees and the sages. It did not shock the bereaved husband to learn that Hilzonda had sought in the King's embrace what he himself had long since been unable to give her: these Saints, left wholly to themselves, had tasted to the point of abuse that bliss which comes from the union of two bodies; but doubtless such bodies, freed as they were from worldly ties and already dead to everything external, had known in their mating a more ardent and tender form of spiritual union.

The beer was relaxing the aged man's constricted chest, helping him to this merciful mood, in which fatigue, too, played a part, as did a sensuous and almost passionate kindness. Hilzonda at least, he told himself, was now in peace. In the light of the candle burning at his bedside he watched the flies wandering over the covers; flies abounded in Münster at this moment, and these, perhaps, had lighted on that fair face; he felt no disaccord with such decay. But suddenly he was gripped by the thought that the interrogators were torturing the flesh of the New Christ every morning with pincers and red-hot iron, and his stomach turned; chained to this ludicrous Man of Sorrows, he fell back into this hell of our human bodies, destined to so little joy and to so much woe; he suffered with Hans much as Hilzonda had known pleasure with him. All that night, under the sheet and in that room where, absurdly, comfort reigned, he stumbled, with anguish, against the image of the King alive in his cage on the square, just as a man with a gangrened foot keeps striking the afflicted member involuntarily at every turn. In his prayers he no longer distinguished between the pain which was slowly contracting his heart (tearing at the shoulder muscles and on down to the left wrist), and the pincers so savagely applied to Hans in the thick of his arm, and around the sensitive breasts.

As soon as he had gained enough strength to walk a few steps, he dragged himself to the King's cage. The citizens of Münster had tired of the spectacle, but a few children, pressing tightly against the bars, persisted in throwing things inside (pins, horse dung, sharp ends of bones) on which the captive was forced to walk barefooted. Guards pushed this rabble away, though with lenience, as former guards had done in the banquet hall; Monseigneur von Waldeck was anxious to keep the King alive up to the date set for his execution, planned for midsummer at the earliest.

When Simon arrived they had just put the prisoner back in his cage after a session of torture; he was still trembling, crouched in a corner. His cassock and his sores gave off a fetid odor. But the little man had retained his quick eye, and the engaging voice of his days as an actor.

"I cut, I baste, I sew," the condemned one chanted. "I am only a poor apprentice-tailor . . . Garments of skin . . . The hem of a robe without seam . . . Do not cut into the work of . . ." He stopped short, casting about him the furtive glance of a man who desires to safeguard his secret and yet, at the same time, to divulge it in part.

Simon Adriansen brushed the guards aside and succeeded in passing his arm between the bars. "God keep you, Hans," he said, holding out his hand.

§

He returned to his house exhausted, as if coming back from a long voyage. Since he had last been out-of-doors great changes had taken place, gradually restoring Münster to its usual dull aspect. The noise of Church music filled the Cathedral again. The Bishop had reinstalled his mistress a step or two from the episcopal palace, but this discreet woman, the fair Julia Alt, caused no scandal. Simon took all this with the indifference of a man who is about to leave a city, and consequently is no longer concerned with what goes on there. But his gentleness of old had dried up like a spring. As soon as he re-entered the house, he burst out in fury against Johanna, who had forgotten to procure him a pen and bottle of ink, with paper, as he had ordered. When these objects were assembled, he employed them to write to his sister.

He had not communicated with her for nearly fifteen years. The kindly Salomé had married Martin Fugger, a younger son of the powerful banking family of Augsburg. Martin, after being disadvantaged by his relatives, had made a fortune on his own, and had lived in Cologne since the beginning of the century. Simon wrote to ask them to take charge of his child.

Salomé received this letter in her country home at Luisdorf, where she was supervising in person the spreading and bleaching of the household laundry. For once abandoning the care of the sheets and the fine linens to her servants, she ordered her coach without even asking the banker's advice (he counted for little in these matters), and stacking it high with provisions and coverlets, she set off for Münster across a region desolated by the recent Tumults.

She found Simon in bed, his head supported by an old coat folded in fours which she replaced at once with a cushion.

With that obtuse benevolence of women who try to reduce sickness and death to an anodyne series of minor ills, no more important than what could be soothed by maternal care, the visitor and the servant launched upon an exchange of views concerning the diet, the bedding, and the commode. The cold gaze of the dying man had taken in his sister, but Simon made use of his invalid state to delay for some moments the fatigue of habitual greetings. Finally he raised himself and exchanged the usual kisses with Salomé. After that he recovered his businessman's precision long enough to enumerate the assets which would come to Martha, and those which it was essential to recuperate for her as soon as possible. The notes and bonds were folded in a waxed canvas within reach of his hand. His sons, established one in Lisbon, one in London, and one at the head of a printing plant in Amsterdam, needed neither his bits of worldly goods nor his benediction: he was leaving the whole of his possessions to Hilzonda's child. The old man seemed to have forgotten his promises to the Grand Restitutor and was conforming again to the customs of this world which he was quitting and which he had ceased to try to reform. Or perhaps in so doing, and thereby renouncing principles dearer to him than life itself, he was tasting to the end the bitter pleasure of total resignation.

Salomé petted the child as she exclaimed with tender pity over her thin little legs. She could not utter three sentences without calling for aid upon the Virgin and all the Saints of Cologne: Martha would be reared, Simon realized, by idolaters. That was hard, but not harder than the mad rage of some folk and the torpor of others, not so hard as old age, which prevents the husband from satisfying his mate, or so hard as to find dead, on one's return, those whom one had left behind alive. He tried to think of the King in his cage of agony, but the torments of Hans no longer signified to Simon, today, what they had meant for him yesterday; they were becoming bearable, just as this pain in his chest was becoming bearable, and would die with him. He prayed, but something told him that the Eternal no longer asked him to pray. He made an effort to recall Hilzonda's face, but the beloved visage was no longer distinct. He had to go further back, to the period of their mystical marriage in Bruges, of the bread and the wine shared in secret, the low bodice half revealing the long, pure breasts. That image, too, faded away; but he saw his first wife again, that good soul with whom he used to enjoy the cool of evening in his garden at Flushing. Salomé and Johanna, hearing a great sigh, rushed to the bedside, frightened . . . He was buried in the Church of Saint Lambrecht after a High Mass.

THE FUGGERS OF
COLOGNE

THE FUGGER family of Cologne lived in Saint Gereon Square, in a small, unpretentious house where everything was arranged for comfort and repose. The odor of cakes and cherry brandy was always in the air.

The long repasts were composed with art, and Salomé liked to linger afterward at table, drying her lips with a fine damask napkin. She liked, too, to encircle her ample waist and sizable, rosy neck with chains of gold, and to wear substantial stuffs (their wool almost reverently carded and woven so as to retain something of the soft warmth of the living ewe). Her guimpes, though not stiff or prudish, were cut discreetly high at the bosom, attesting to her modesty as an honest wife. She played the small portable organ in the parlor with strong, solid fingers, and when she was young had sung both popular madrigals and Church motets in her fine, flexible voice; for she enjoyed such interlacings of harmonies, just as she liked her embroideries.

But food and meals always came first with her: the liturgical year, piously observed, was matched by a culinary year, by the season of cucumbers or preserves, and by the advent of fresh herring or cream cheese. Martin was a small, thin man who never grew fat, in spite of the rich fare which his wife set before him. Formidable as he was in business affairs, this mastiff became a mere harmless spaniel at home, where his utmost daring consisted of repeating bawdy tales at table, for the benefit of the maidservants.

The couple had only one son, Sigismund, who had embarked at the age of sixteen with Gonzalo Pizarro for Peru, where the banker had large sums invested. They had given up hope of seeing him again, since things had taken a bad turn in Lima in recent years. A daughter, still quite young, had softened that loss for them; Salomé used to tell gaily about this belated pregnancy, attributed by her in part to prayer at Novenas, and in part to the effect of a caper sauce! This child was almost the same age as Martha; the two cousins shared the same bed and the same toys, the same salutary spankings, and, later on, the same singing lessons and adornments.

Burly Justus Ligre, Flanders's wild boar, and the spare Martin, the weasel of Rhineland, sometimes rivals but often conniving together, had kept watch on each other for more than thirty years, exchanging advice from afar, and alternately supporting or working against each other. Each one valued the other at his true worth, a thing which simpletons dazzled by the wealth of these two could not do, no more than could the kings whom these bankers served and made use of in turn. Martin knew, almost to the penny, the current value of the fabrics, the workshops and shipyards, and the lordly domains, as well, in which Henry Justus had invested his fortune; the Flemish merchant's taste for gross luxury provided the German banker with matter for many a good story, as did two or three obvious tricks, always the same, which enabled old Justus to extricate himself when in difficulty. On his side, Henry Justus (good servitor though he was of the Regent of the Low Countries, dutifully lending what sums she needed for purchases of paintings from Italy, or for her charitable foundations) would rub his hands with glee on learning that the Elector Palatine or the Duke of Bavaria were pawning their jewels at Martin's, and were begging him for a loan at a rate of interest worthy of the Jewish usurers. The Antwerp banker had only praise, though not without a touch of mocking pity, for this rat who was discreetly nibbling away at the world's substance, instead of visibly bolting it down, this puny little man so scornful of conspicuous, tangible, confiscable riches, but whose signature at the foot of a page was worth more than that of the Emperor Charles V.

These two financiers, each so respectful of the ruling powers of their time, would have been astonished had they heard themselves declared a greater danger to the established order of things than the infidel Turk, or the peasants in revolt; with that absorption, characteristic of their ilk in affairs of the moment, and in detail, they did not even suspect the disturbing power inherent in their small notebooks and their bags of gold. And nevertheless they had to smile, from time to time, as they sat behind their respective counters, perhaps watching the stiff figure of some knight trying to hide, under haughty airs, his fear of being refused; or the dignified profile of some bishop hoping to finish the towers of his cathedral at not too great cost. To others the glory of clanging bells and booming cannon, of prancing horses and women nude or draped in brocades; these two held to this solid stuff, both shameful and sublime, openly reviled but adored and brooded over in secret (like private parts, seldom spoken about but always in mind), this yellow substance without which Madame Imperia would never yield, even in a king's bed, nor could My Lord Bishop pay for the jewels in his miter—GOLD, the lack or abundance of which decides whether the Cross will, or will not, wage war upon the Crescent. These moneylenders did, indeed, know themselves to be Masters, not of Arts, but of Realities.

§

Like Martin with his son Sigismund, Henry Justus had been disappointed in his elder son, Henry Maximilian. Nothing had been heard from that soldier of fortune for ten years, except for a few requests for money and for the arrival of a volume of verse, in French, which he had doubtless hatched out somewhere in Italy between campaigns. Nothing but trouble could come from that quarter, for sure. The more reason, therefore, for the merchant-banker to keep close watch on his younger son, to avoid further mistakes. As soon as this lad, Philibert (a child after his own heart), was old enough to slide the beads of a counting board correctly into place, the father sent him to learn the finer points of banking under Martin the Infallible. Philibert at twenty was already fat; a certain rusticity was visible under the manners he had so carefully acquired; his small gray eyes gleamed through narrow slits between eyelids always half closed. As son of the High Treasurer of the Court at Mechlin, he could well have played the prince; instead, his forte lay in tracking down errors in the clerks' calculations. Early and late, in an ill-lighted back room where copyists were ruining their eyesight, he spent his time verifying the D's, M's, X's, and C's which were combined with L's and I's to form the figures. For Martin disdained Arabic numeration, though he did not deny its utility in long columns of addition. The German banker grew to like this taciturn youth, and when asthma or twinges of gout made him think of the day when his appointed time should come, he could be heard to say to his wife, "This big booby will be my successor."

Philibert seemed wholly absorbed by his registers and his ink scrapers. But there was irony in his glance; sometimes in reflecting upon his employer's affairs he would go so far as to say to himself that, following Henry Justus and Martin, there would one day be Philibert, the clever man, more astute than the one and more ferocious than the other. For certainly it was not he who would have assumed Portugal's debts in return for a scant interest rate, sixteen deniers to the pound, due quarterly at each of the four great Fairs of the year.

He came on Sundays to the household gatherings, held in summer in the arbor and in wintertime in the parlor. An ecclesiastic of rank would be there, quoting Latin; Salomé, playing backgammon with a neighbor's wife, would pronounce upon each good move with some Rhenish proverb; Martin, who had had the two girls learn French (so becoming to women), made use of it himself when he had occasion to express anything more elevated or more intricate than ordinary, workaday matters. There would be talk of the war in Saxony, and of its effect upon the discount rate, of the spread of heresy, or according to the season, of the grape harvest or of carnival.

The banker's right-hand man, a solemn Swiss from Geneva, named Zebedee Cret, was the butt of many jokes because he abhorred pipe smoking and wines. This fellow Zebedee did not wholly deny that he had left Geneva after a scandal (he had directed a gambling house, illegal there, as was his manufacture of playing cards); but he laid his infractions of the law at the door of his former friends, libertines who were now justly punished, and he did not conceal his desire to return someday to the sheepfold of the Reformation. The prelate would protest against any such intention, shaking a warning finger (adorned with an amethyst ring), and someone would teasingly quote from the light, lewd verse of Théodore de Bèze, that fair youth so favored by the irreproachable Calvin. As to the wisdom of Zebedee's projected return to Geneva, there would be discussion about how favorable or unfavorable the Consistory now was to banking and trade, but no one was really surprised that he, a burgher of that city, should be willing to subscribe to the dogmas promulgated by its magistrates. After supper Martin would take a guest aside into an alcove, perhaps some imperial councilor or a secret envoy of the French King. But the Parisian envoy would soon propose gallantly to rejoin the ladies.

When Philibert would begin to play his lute, Martin's daughter, Benedicta, and her cousin Martha would rise hand in hand. Madrigals from *The Lovers' Book* told of lambs and flowers, and of Dame Venus, but these popular airs of the time also served for the words of hymns sung by the Anabaptist or Lutheran rabble whom the churchman had been denouncing in his sermon that very morning! Unintentionally Benedicta might substitute a verse of a psalm for some couplet of a love song, and Martha would then anxiously signal to her to stop. The two girls would sit down again side by side, and no other refrain would be heard that evening, save for that of the bell of Saint Gereon sounding the Angelus. Fat Philibert, who had a talent for dancing, would sometimes offer to show some new steps to Benedicta; at first she would refuse, but later assenting, would take a childish delight in this pastime.

§

The two girls loved each other with the pure love of angels. Salomé had not had the heart to separate Martha from her nurse, Johanna, and the old Hussite had instilled in Simon's child her own fear of God, and her austerity. The ordeal of Münster had made of Johanna, outwardly, an old woman like all the others who take holy water in church and kiss the *Agnus Dei*. But deep within her subsisted the hatred of all Satans in brocade vestments, of golden calves, and of worldly idols. This aged and feeble creature, whom the banker had never bothered to distinguish from the other toothless women who scoured his porringers belowstairs, was perpetually muttering to everything an eternal *No*. To take her word for it, in this house, so redolent of comfort and well-being, evil brooded everywhere, like rats teeming in the soft down of a bed puff: it was hiding in the tall chest of Dame Salomé's chamber and in Martin's strongbox, in the tuns of the wine cellars and in the rich sauce at the bottom of the pots; in the frivolous noise of the Sunday concerts, as well; in the apothecary's scented pills and in the relic of Saint Apollina which cures toothache. The old servant did not dare to attack outright the Mother of God in her niche on the stairway, but was heard grumbling about the oil burned for nothing in front of dolls of stone.

When Martha had reached sixteen, Salomé was alarmed to see her teach Benedicta mere disdain for the peddler's boxes filled with costly finery from Paris or from Florence, and to cry *fie* upon Christmas, with its hodgepodge of music, new garments, and goose stuffed with truffles. For this good woman, Heaven and earth alike were free of problems: Mass was an edifying occasion, a spectacle, and a pretext for wearing her short fur cape in winter and her silk jacket in summer; Mary and the Child, Jesus on the Cross, God in His cloud all sat in glory in Paradise, and on the walls of churches; one learned by experience which Virgin was most apt to grant a prayer in a given case. In domestic crises the Prioress of the Ursulines, who was good at advice, was readily consulted, though this did not keep Martin from jeering at nuns. It is true that the sale of indulgences had unduly swollen the Holy Father's money bags, but the practice of drawing upon the credit of Our Lady and the Saints in order to cover a sinner's deficits was as logical as the transactions of any banker. Salomé attributed Martha's peculiarities to a sickly disposition; it would have been monstrous to suppose that a maiden so delicately bred could have perverted her young companion, the two of them putting themselves on the side of miscreants, such as are condemned to be mutilated and burned. Nor could she believe that in order to involve themselves in the Church's quarrels they would forsake that modest silence which is proper to young girls.

Johanna could do no more than denounce to her young mistresses, in her somewhat crazed voice, the paths of error. Saintly but ignorant, and therefore incapable of recourse to the Scriptures (of which she could repeat only a few fragments learned by heart in her Dutch dialect), she was not the one to point out the true way. As soon as their intelligence had been developed by the liberal education which Martin had given them, Martha secretly seized upon those books which speak of God.

Lost in the forest of sects and dogma, and terrified to be without a guide, Simon's child feared to renounce ancient errors lest she fall into others, anew. Johanna had not hidden her mother's infamy from the orphan girl, nor the pitiful ending of her father, duped and betrayed. Martha knew, therefore, that in turning their backs on Rome's aberrations, her parents had only engaged themselves further along a road which did not lead to Heaven. This carefully protected young maiden, who had never yet gone down to the street unaccompanied by a servant, would tremble at the thought of joining a band of sniveling exiles and fanatic outlaws wandering from city to city, despised by respectable people, and ending their days on a bed of straw, whether in prison or at the stake. Roman idolatry was Charybdis for her, but revolt, dire poverty, danger, and abjection were her Scylla.

It was the pious Zebedee who drew her, cautiously, from this impasse; under her promise of secrecy, the circumspect Swiss lent her a work of John Calvin which she read at night, by candlelight, taking as many precautions as other young girls might do to decipher a love letter. Thus was presented to Simon's daughter a faith cleansed of all error, exempt from any weakness, strict even in its liberty, in short, rebellion transformed into law. According to Zebedee, virtues taught in the Gospels went hand in hand in Geneva with bourgeois prudence and wisdom; those who indulged in dancing (behind closed doors), hopping about like pagans, were flogged till the blood ran; gluttonous brats who impudently sucked their barley sugar or their candied almonds during sermons were chastised in the same way; all dissidents were banished; gamblers and lewd persons were punished by death; atheists were condemned, and rightly so, to be burned. Far from yielding to the lascivious impulses of his blood, like fat Luther marrying a nun on leaving the cloister, the layman Calvin had waited a long time before contracting a chaste marriage with a widow; instead of battening at princes' tables, Master John astonished his guests, at his house in Canons' Close, by his frugality; his everyday fare was only bread and fishes, as in the Gospel (in his case, speckled trout of Lake Leman, which, however, were very choice).

Martha had indoctrinated her companion, who followed her in all things of the mind, although well ahead of her in matters of the spirit. Benedicta was a child of light; a century earlier she would have entered a cloister, to know there the joy of living entirely in God; but the times being what they were, this lamb had found her green grass and salt and pure water in the Evangelical faith. At night, in their unheated chamber, Martha and Benedicta, scorning the appeal of eiderdown and pillows, would sit side by side rereading the Bible in lowered voices. Their cheeks, touching each other, seemed no more than the surface where two souls join. Martha would wait at the end of each page for Benedicta and, if the younger girl should fall asleep during the sacred reading, would gently twitch her hair. Meanwhile, Martin's household, benumbed with solid comfort, was sunk in heavy slumber. Like the lamp of the Wise Virgins, alone in the hearts of two silent girls in a chamber on high burned the cold ardor of the Reformation.

Nevertheless, Martha herself did not yet dare to abjure, openly, the Papist depravities. She invented pretexts for avoiding Mass on Sundays, but her lack of courage weighed on her like the worst of sins. Zebedee, however, approved of such circumspection: Master John, he said, always warned his followers against any unnecessary scandal, and would have blamed Johanna for blowing out the lamp at the feet of the Virgin, on the stairway. A certain delicacy of feeling kept Benedicta from wounding or disturbing her family, but Martha appalled Salomé in refusing, on All Saints' Eve, to pray for her dead father; wherever he might be now, said

Martha, he had no need of Aves from her. Her aunt could not understand such harshness; how could one refuse a poor soul the small charity of a prayer?

§

Martin and his wife had long intended that their child and the Ligre heir should marry. They spoke of it when abed, lying tranquilly between sheets carefully tucked in by the servant. Salomé would count on her fingers the pieces of the trousseau, the marten pelts, and the embroidered coverlets. Or, fearing that Benedicta's modesty might make her resistant to the joys of marriage, she would try to recall the recipe for an aphrodisiac salve which families used on the wedding night to anoint young brides. As to Martha, some prominent merchant of Cologne would be found, or even a nobleman, one heavily indebted, for whom Martin would generously cancel the mortgages encumbering his lands.

Philibert paid the usual compliments to the banker's heiress. But the cousins wore the same ornaments and the same bonnets, so he mistook one for the other, and Benedicta seemed to delight in provoking such errors. He would swear aloud at this, for the daughter was worth her weight in gold, but the niece would bring no more than a handful of florins, at the most.

When the contract was more or less drawn up, Martin called his daughter into his office to set the date of the wedding. Benedicta, showing neither gaiety nor sadness, but cutting short her mother's tender effusions and embraces, went back up to her room to sew with Martha, who, that night, proposed flight: a boatman would perhaps consent to take them to Basel, where doubtless some good Christians would help them on to the next stop. Pensively Benedicta poured the sand from the inkstand out onto the table and began to trace the furrow of a river in it with her finger. As day broke, however, she passed her hand slowly over the surface to efface the whole design; when the sand was smooth again

on the polished tabletop she rose, Philibert's pledged bride,
and sighed: "No, I am too weak to run away."

After that the orphaned cousin no longer spoke to her of
fleeing, contenting herself with pointing to the verses which
treat of abandoning one's family in order to follow the Lord.
The cold of dawn forced them to take refuge in their bed.
Lying chastely embraced in each other's arms, they consoled
themselves in weeping together. Then sheer youth gained the
upper hand: they began to make fun of the small eyes and fat
cheeks of the bridegroom.

The suitors proposed to Martha were no better: Benedicta
made her laugh in describing the rather bald merchant, and the
impoverished gentleman tightly encased in his rattling armor
on days of tournament; or the burgomaster's son, a fop
decked out in his plumed bonnet and striped codpiece, like a
puppet sent from France to serve as a tailor's model. Martha
dreamed that night that Philibert, that worldly Sadducee, that
Amalekite of uncircumcised heart, had stolen Benedicta away
in a box, which was then left to drift alone on the river Rhine.

§

The year 1549 opened with rains which washed out all the
seeds planted by the vegetable farmers; the swollen Rhine
flooded cellars and set quantities of apples and barrels still half
full of garden produce afloat on the gray waters. In May the
strawberries in the woods spoiled while still green, as did the
cherries in the orchards. Martin had soup distributed to the
poor on the steps of Saint Gereon; the burghers were moved
to offer this kind of alms not only out of Christian charity but
also in fear of riots. Such woes, however, were only forerun-
ners of a more terrible calamity: plague from the Orient entered the Germanys by way of Bohemia; it traveled slowly,
to the sound of bells ringing, like an empress. Bending over
the drunkard's glass, blowing out the scholar's candle as he
sat at his books, assisting the priest at Mass, hiding like a flea
in the shift of a whore, the plague brought to each and all alike

an element of insolent equality, a harsh and dangerous ferment of adventure. The air was filled with the insistent clamor of the death bell, like the call to some sinister festival: the idlers gathered below the belfries never wearied of watching, high above, the figure of the bell ringer now crouched low, now suspended tall, pulling with all his strength upon the rope of his great drone bell. The churches were never empty, nor were the taverns.

Martin barricaded himself in his office as he would have done against a robber. According to him, the best preventive was to drink in moderation a fine Johannisberg of good vintage, to avoid harlots and tavern companions, not to sniff the street odors, and especially not to inquire about the number of deaths. Johanna continued to go to market and to come downstairs to empty the rubbish; her face, seamed with scars, and her foreign dialect had ill-disposed the neighbors toward her from the beginning, and now in these pernicious times their mistrust turned to hatred; people spoke of witches and malevolent sowers of the plague as she passed. Whether or not she admitted the fact, the old servant secretly rejoiced at the coming of God's scourge: this horrible joy could be read in her face. In vain did she take on dangerous chores which the other servants refused to perform for Salomé, who was gravely stricken; her mistress, groaning, would push her away, as if the maid had been bringing a scythe and an hourglass instead of an earthenware hot-water bottle.

On the third day Johanna no longer appeared at the patient's bedside; Benedicta took over the duty of making her mother swallow the remedies, and of replacing the rosary which Salomé continually let fall. Benedicta loved her mother, or, rather, did not know it to be even conceivable that she might not love her. But she had suffered from Salomé's stupid and vulgar piousness, from her endless prattle about the neighbors, and even from her merriment, like that of an old nurse who likes to recall to grown children the days of their lisping, their chamber pots, and their swaddling clothes.

Shame for her unavowed impatience in the past only increased Benedicta's zeal now as bedside attendant. Martha brought the trays and the stacks of linen, but managed never to enter the room. They had not succeeded in obtaining the help of a physician.

§

On the night following Salomé's death Benedicta, sleeping beside her cousin, felt in her turn the first approach of the malady. She burned with thirst, which she tried to allay in imagining the Biblical stag drinking at the spring of clear water. A slight, convulsive cough racked her throat, but she restrained it as much as she could in order to let Martha sleep. She was already afloat, her hands joined in prayer, ready to escape from the canopied bed to mount into a vast and luminous Paradise, where God dwells. The Evangelical hymns had been forgotten; the friendly faces of the Saints reappeared, between the bed curtains; high in the heavens Mary extended her arms from the trailing blue folds of her cloak, and her gesture was repeated by the fair, chubby Child with the rosy fingers. Silently Benedicta deplored her sins: a dispute with Johanna on the subject of a torn collar, smiles in response to gallant glances of youths passing under her window, a desire to die which was due partly to inertia, partly to impatience to reach Heaven, and partly because there was no longer any need to choose between Martha and her parents, and between two ways of speaking to God. When the first light of morning came, Martha cried out in fright at the sight of her cousin's face, already ravaged.

Benedicta had gone to bed naked, as was the custom. She begged that they would keep her fine chemise ready, freshly pleated, and made some futile efforts to smooth her hair. Martha, with a handkerchief over her nose, attended her, confounded by the horror which she felt for this sickened body. An insidious damp was spreading through the chamber, and the stricken girl felt cold; in spite of the season, already full summer, Martha lighted the stove. In a hoarse voice, exactly as her good mother had done the evening before, the sufferer asked for a chaplet; Martha passed her one, held out at her fingertips. Suddenly, noting with childish glee her companion's terrified eyes peering from above the linen soaked in vinegar, Benedicta said gently, "Don't be afraid, cousin. The fat gallant who dances so gaily will be yours." And she turned toward the wall as she usually did when ready to sleep.

The banker stayed tightly closed in his chamber; Philibert had returned to Flanders to pass the month of August with his father; Martha, abandoned by the servants, who feared to come upstairs, called down to them to summon at least Zebedee (who had delayed his departure for his native city for a few days in order to cope with the rush of business matters). He was willing to risk mounting to the landing, and showed proper solicitude. The physicians of the city, he said, were either worn out or were stricken themselves, or else were firmly decided not to contaminate their regular patients by visiting the plague victims; but there was talk of a learned doctor who had, indeed, just arrived in Cologne in order to study the pestilence and its effects at first hand. Zebedee would do what he could to persuade this man to attend upon Benedicta.

Such help was long in coming. Meanwhile the young girl was sinking. Martha, braced against the doorjamb, kept watch on her from a distance. At intervals, however, she would draw near to the patient to make her drink something, though holding the glass with a trembling hand. Benedicta could hardly swallow now, and the liquid ran down on the covers. From time to time her short, dry cough could be heard, so like the bark of a small dog that Martha, refusing to believe that an animal cry could come from that delicate mouth, looked down each time, in spite of herself, to see if the barbet of the household was at her heels. Finally she sat down on the landing in order not to hear it. For several hours she fought against the terror of a death which was in progress under her very eyes, and struggled even more against the dread of being infected, in her turn, by pestilence, just as one is by sin. This was no longer Benedicta, but an enemy, an animal, a dangerous object which one should be careful not to touch. Toward evening, unable to bear it any longer, Martha went down to the entrance door to watch for the physician's arrival.

§

When he came, at last, he entered without ceremony, simply asking if this were the Fuggers' house. He was a thin, tall man, hollow-eyed, wearing the red robe of those practitioners who had agreed to attend the plague victims, and who therefore had to renounce all visits to ordinary patients. His dark complexion gave him the aspect of a foreigner. He mounted the stairs rapidly; Martha, on the contrary, slowed her pace, even though against her will. Standing in the alcove beside the bed, he drew back the sheet, exposing the thin body, shaken with spasms, upon the soiled mattress.

"All the servants have left me," Martha faltered, trying to explain the state of the bed linen.

He replied with a vague inclination of the head, being occupied in delicately palpating the lymph glands of the groin and the armpits. The poor child was babbling or singing feebly between brief fits of hoarse coughing; Martha thought that she could recognize a fragment of some frivolous song mingled with a ballad about the visit of the good Jesus.

"She is wandering," said Martha, as if annoyed.

"Yes, of course," the physician replied, his attention elsewhere.

He let the sheet fall back in place and took the pulse, almost routinely, at the wrist and at the base of the throat. Then he measured out some drops of an elixir into a spoon and inserted it dexterously into the corner of her mouth.

"Don't ask too much of your courage," he admonished Martha, observing that it was only with repugnance that she supported the sick girl's head. "You do not need to hold her head or her hands just now." With a small ball of lint he wiped away some reddish matter from the patient's lips and threw it into the stove. The spoon and the gloves which he had used followed the same course.

"Shall you not lance the swellings?" Martha asked, fearing that the hard-pressed physician might omit some essential procedure, but especially hoping to keep him longer at the bedside.

"No, surely not," he replied in a low tone. "The lymphatic vessels are hardly swollen as yet, and she will go, probably, before they become too big. *Non est medicamentum* . . . Your sister's vital force is at its lowest. The most that we can do is to diminish her suffering."

"I am not her sister," Martha protested suddenly, as if this specific information excused her for trembling especially on her own account. "My name is Martha Adriansen, not Martha Fugger. I am her cousin."

The physician gave her only a glance, absorbed as he was in observing the effects of his remedy. The patient, now less agitated, seemed to smile. He counted out a second dose of the elixir, to be given that night. Though he held out no hope, this man's presence transformed what had been a chamber of horror for Martha, since dawn, into an ordinary room again. When he was once more on the staircase, he removed the mask which he had worn, as was required, at the patient's bed. Martha followed him to the bottom of the stairs. "You say that your name is Martha Adriansen," he commented suddenly. "In my youth I knew a man, then already elderly, who had that name. His wife was called Hilzonda."

"They were my parents," Martha replied, as if against her will.

"Are they still alive?" he asked.

"No," she answered, lowering her voice. "They were at Münster when the Bishop took the city."

The street door, with locks as complicated as those of a strongbox, had to be manipulated. As the physician opened it, some air penetrated into the oppressive but richly furnished vestibule. Outside, it was gray and rainy in the dusk. "Go back upstairs," he said at last, with some kindness, but coolness, too. "You seem to be fairly robust, and the plague is claiming few new victims now. I advise you to wear below your nostrils some linen soaked in alcohol or wine (I have little confidence in vinegars) so that you can watch over this dying girl to the end. Your fears are natural and reasonable, but shame and regret afterward are also hard to bear."

She turned her head away, her cheeks afire, then searched in the purse which she wore at her belt and decided, finally, on a gold piece. The gesture of paying re-established the distance between them, elevating her well above this vagabond who passed from city to city, earning his pittance at the bedside of one plague-ridden victim after another. The physician put the coin into the pocket of his robe without examining it, and departed.

Left alone, Martha went to look in the kitchen for a vial of alcohol. The room was empty; the servants were doubtless at church, mumbling litanies. She found a slice of meat pie on a table and ate it, slowly, trying deliberately to renew her strength. As a precaution she forced herself also to munch a little garlic. When she had summoned enough courage to go back upstairs, Benedicta seemed to be asleep, but the boxwood beads moved from time to time between her fingers. After the second dose of elixir she was better, but a new crisis at dawn brought the end.

§

On that same day Martha watched her interment together with that of Salomé, in the cloister of the Ursulines; it was as if Benedicta lay sealed under the weight of a lie. No one would ever know how close she had been to taking the straight and narrow path into which her cousin was urging her, the two of them making their way toward the City of God. Martha felt despoiled, betrayed. The cases of plague were becoming rare, but out of precaution, as she walked along the nearly deserted streets, she continued to gather the folds of her cloak closely about her. The beloved girl's death had only increased Martha's furious desire to stay alive, and not to surrender either her identity or her possessions, becoming merely one of those cold bundles which are placed beneath the pavings of a church. Benedicta had died assured of her salvation by Paternosters and Aves; Martha had no reason for such confidence for herself; it seemed to her sometimes that she was one of those whom divine decree condemns before their birth, and whose very virtue is a form of obduracy displeasing to God. And what virtue, anyhow, was in question? In presence of the scourge she had proved to be a coward; it was not certain that in presence of executioners she would prove more faithful to the Lord than in time of plague she had been to that innocent girl, whom she had thought to hold so dear. More reason still to delay as long as possible that verdict from which there can be no appeal.

She turned at once to the matter of engaging new servants that very evening, since those who had fled the pestilence either had not returned or had been dismissed as soon as they came back. She had everything washed and scoured and then had the floors spread with aromatic herbs, mingled with pine needles.

It was during this great cleaning that they discovered that Johanna had died, neglected by everyone, in her servant's garret. Martha had no time to mourn for her. The banker reappeared, appropriately afflicted by these bereavements, but resolved to organize his life as a widower peaceably, with some good housekeeper of his choice, one not talkative or noisy, and not too young, but not too distasteful, either. No one, not even he, had ever suspected that his excellent spouse had tyrannized over him all his life long. From this time on, he alone would be the one to decide upon his hour of rising, the time for his meals, and the day on which he would take his purgative; and no one now would interrupt him if he happened to be telling a chambermaid, at some length, the story of the girl and the nightingale.

He was anxious to rid himself of this niece whom the plague had made his sole heir, but whom he did not care to see presiding across from him at his table. He procured a dispensation to allow a marriage between cousins-german, and the name of Martha replaced that of Benedicta on the marriage contract.

When Martha learned of her uncle's projects for her, she went down to the office where Zebedee busied himself. The Switzer's fortune was made: since war with France was bound to come soon, the clerk was to be installed in Geneva and would serve Martin from this time on as a straw man in his transactions with his royal French debtors. Then, too, while the pestilence was raging, Zebedee had made certain profits on his own account which would enable him to reappear in his native country as a respected burgher whose youthful peccadilloes had been forgotten. Martha found him engaged talking with a Jewish moneylender who dealt in day-to-day loans, and who was discreetly buying for Martin the furnishings and other assets of those who had died in the recent disaster. All the opprobrium which such lucrative commerce might evoke would fall back upon this Hebrew, if necessary. On perceiving the heiress at his door, Zebedee dismissed the man.

"Take me for wife," Martha said to the Calvinist brusquely.

"Hold, softly now," he replied, searching about for some lie.

Zebedee was already married, having wed in his youth a girl of low estate, a baker's daughter of the quarter of Pâquis. He had been intimidated by her tears and by the family's outcry as a consequence of the sole amorous indiscretion of his life. Long ago their one child had died in convulsions, and from that time Zebedee had paid a meager allowance to his wife, managing to keep her and her weeping at a distance . . . But one does not commit the crime of bigamy with lightness of heart.

"Believe me," he said, "you would best leave your servitor in peace, and not buy at such great price a tuppence worth of what you will later regret. Are you so eager as all that to see Martin's money go for repairs of convents and churches?"

"Must I live to the end of my days in this land of Canaan?" was the orphan girl's bitter reply.

"A worthy woman makes Justice reign even in the house of the Wicked," retorted the clerk, who was quite as well versed as she in the style of the Scriptures.

It was plain that he did not care to quarrel with the powerful Fugger family. Martha hung her head; the clerk's prudence and foresight were providing her with the very reasons for submission which she had unconsciously sought. For this austere maiden had an old man's vice, that of loving money for the security which it affords, and for the respect and consideration which it can procure. God himself had marked her out to live among the great of this world; she was fully aware that a dowry like hers would increase her authority tenfold as a wife. Besides, the uniting of two fortunes is a duty which no sensible girl would shirk.

§

She was anxious, nevertheless, to avoid all deceit. In her first meeting with the Fleming after their betrothal, she said to him: "Possibly you do not know that I have embraced the holy Evangelical faith." Doubtless she was expecting some reproach.

But her unresponsive husband-to-be confined himself to nodding a kind of assent, and saying: "If you will excuse me, I have a great deal to do. Questions of theology are very difficult." And never did he speak of her avowal again. It was hard to tell if he was singularly subtle, or only obtuse.

A CONVERSATION
IN INNSBRUCK

CAPTAIN HENRY Maximilian was watching it rain in Innsbruck. The Emperor had installed himself here in order to keep an eye on the Council of Trent, which, like all assemblies set up to decide something, was threatening to end without result. At Court one heard nothing but theology and canon law; hunting on muddy mountain slopes hardly tempted a man accustomed to chasing stag on Lombardy's fertile plains; so the Captain, watching the stupid, everlasting trickle on the windowpanes, gave himself over to the pleasure of swearing, silently, in full Italian fashion.

He yawned the whole day through. To this Fleming the glorious Emperor Charles seemed a kind of melancholic madman, and the pomp of the Spanish Court appeared to him as cumbersome as those polished coats of mail under which one sweats on days of parade, and which any veteran soldier would gladly exchange for a leathern jacket. In choosing a military career Henry Maximilian had not counted on the boredom of the periods off-season, so he was waiting, grumbling, until this worm-eaten peace should give way to war. Happily, the Imperial repasts included many a capon and roast of venison, as well as eel pie; he ate enormously, by way of distraction.

One afternoon, he had seated himself in a tavern and was working to put into a sonnet the fair breasts (like new white satin) of his Neapolitan mistress, Vanina Cami. He thought that a Hungarian officer brushed him with his saber in passing, so accordingly he sought to pick a quarrel. Such disputes, which always ended in swordplay, were part and parcel of his character, as he saw it, and moreover were as necessary to one of his temperament as fisticuffs are to an artisan, or clog fights to a peasant. But this time the duel, begun with insults in mock Latin, stopped short; the Hungarian was only a craven who took refuge behind the ample figure of the tavern hostess: everything ended in a fracas of crying women and broken dishes, and the Captain, disgusted, sat down again trying once more to polish his quatrains and tercets.

But his rhyming mood had passed. The slash on his cheek hurt, though he did not want to admit it, and the handkerchief which he had tied around his head in guise of a bandage (and which had quickly become blood-spotted) gave him the ridiculous air of a man afflicted with toothache. Faced with a plate of goulash, he lacked the heart to eat.

"You ought to see a surgeon," said the tavernkeeper.

Henry Maximilian replied that in his opinion all surgeons were asses.

"I know a clever physician," said the host, "but he is peculiar, and does not wish to tend anyone."

"That's just my luck," the Captain answered lightly.

The rain had not stopped. Standing on the threshold, watching the streaming gutters, the tavernkeeper suddenly remarked, "Speaking of the Devil . . ."

A man dressed for protection from the cold in a long brown cloak, and appearing to stoop somewhat under its hood, was hurrying down the street (which was now almost a brook). Henry Maximilian exclaimed, "Zeno!"

The man turned around. The two of them scrutinized each

other across the open street shelf where pastries and trussed chickens were piled. Henry Maximilian thought that he detected an anxiety on Zeno's features akin to fear, but the alchemist, on recognizing the Captain, seemed reassured. He took one step down into the room, asking, "Are you wounded?"

"Yes, a scratch," his cousin replied. "Since you have not yet gone to the alchemists' heaven, pray give me some lint, and a drop of vulnerary water, for you seem to lack water from the Fountain of Youth." His jest was bitter, for it was singularly painful to him to find how much Zeno had aged.

"I treat no patients now," said the physician. But his mistrust had been allayed. He stepped farther into the room, holding ajar the door behind him, which was slamming in the wind. "Pardon me, Henry, my friend," he continued. "It's good to see your face again. But I have to protect myself from importuners."

"Who doesn't?" said the Captain, thinking of his creditors.

"Come to my place," the alchemist proposed, after some hesitation. "We shall be more comfortable there than in this tavern."

They went out together. The rain was now driving in gusts. It was one of those times when air and water are in mutiny, and seem to turn the world into one vast, melancholy chaos. The Captain thought that the alchemist looked tired and worried. Stopping before a low building, Zeno pushed open the door with his shoulder. "Your innkeeper has rented me this abandoned forge, where I live more or less protected from the curious," he explained, "but his charge is very high. It is he who makes gold."

The room was obscurely lighted by the reddish glow of a small fire, on which some preparation or other was cooking in an earthenware pot. The anvil and tongs of the blacksmith who had previously occupied this wretched structure gave the somber interior the aspect of a torture chamber. A ladder led to a loft where doubtless Zeno slept. A blunt-nosed, red-

haired servant boy was pretending to busy himself at something in a corner. Zeno dismissed him for the day, after having
told him to go first to fetch something to drink. Then he began
to look for some linen. When he had applied the bandage, he
inquired, "What brings you to this city?"

"I am here to play the spy," the Captain replied very
simply. "Marshal Strozzi and his French master have entrusted me with a secret mission pertaining to Tuscan affairs;
the fact is that Strozzi is angling for Siena. He chafes under
his exile from Florence, and hopes someday to regain the
upper hand there. I am supposed to be trying the different
baths and cataplasms and cuppings of the Germanys, but I pay
court here to the Nuncio, who is too close to the Farneses
to like the Medicis, and who in his turn pays court to Caesar,
though hardly with zeal. One can as well play at this game as
at tarot."

"I know the Nuncio," said Zeno; "I am, to some degree, his
physician, and to some degree his alchemist; if I chose to do so
I could melt his money for him in my small charcoal stove.
Have you noticed that men with goat-shaped heads like his
are partly faun and partly ancient Chimaera? Monsignor turns
out licentious little verses, and dotes on his pages. If I had the
talent for it, I should have much to gain in playing his pander."

"And what am I doing here if not pandering?" exclaimed
the Captain. "That is what they all do: some procure women,
or other things, some traffic in Justice, and some in God. The
least dishonest are still those who sell flesh, and not hazy
ideas. But I don't take my small trade and its wares seriously
enough, these cities already sold ten times over, these pock-
marked loyalties, and these opportunities already passed by
and rotten. Where a true intriguer would be filling his pockets,
I manage at most to pay expenses for my inns and my post
horses. We shall both die poor, you and I."

"Amen," was Zeno's response. "Sit down."

But Henry Maximilian remained standing near the fire, the
steam rising from his damp garments. Zeno took a seat on the

anvil, bending forward, hands between his knees, to watch the blazing brands.

"Still the companion of the fire, aren't you, Zeno?" Henry Maximilian observed. The young redhead brought the wine and then took himself off, whistling. The Captain poured himself a drink, and continued: "Do you remember how the Canon of Saint Donatian used to worry about you? Your *Prognostications of Things to Come* will have confirmed his darkest fears; as to your discourse on the nature of blood (not that I've read it), it must have seemed to him more worthy of a barber than of a philosopher; and your *Treatise on the Physical World* will have made him weep. If some mischance brought you back to Bruges, he would exorcise you!"

"He would do worse than that," said Zeno, with a wry grimace. "Nevertheless, I have been careful to wrap my thought in all the usual circumlocutions, with a capital letter here, and a Name there; I have even been willing to load my sentences with a weighty paraphernalia of Attributes and Substances. Such verbiage is like our shirts and our hose: they protect the wearer, but do not keep him from being tranquilly nude underneath."

"No, they do prevent it," the soldier objected. "I have never looked at an Apollo in the Pope's gardens without envying the god for offering himself to view just as his mother Latona made him. One is at ease only when free, and hiding one's opinions is even more bother than covering one's skin."

"Mere stratagems of war, Captain!" rejoined Zeno. "We philosophers live among them as you warfaring men do among your mines and trenches. One ends by pluming oneself on underlying meanings which alter the whole, like negative signs placed inconspicuously before columns of addition; by risking a more pointed expression here and there, one contrives to give what amounts to a wink of the eye, or to removal of the vine leaf, or perhaps to a momentary dropping of the mask (even though it be tied back again at once, as if nothing had occurred). By such means we sort out our readers: the fools take us literally; other fools, thinking us more stupid than themselves, abandon us; those who stay with us make their way in the labyrinth of our books, learning to jump the obstacle, the lie, or to go around it. I should be greatly surprised if the same subterfuges are not to be found even in the most sacred texts. When read thus, every book has a hidden meaning."

"You exaggerate man's capacity for hypocrisy," said the Captain with a shrug. "Most men think too little for two such layers of thought." Filling his glass, he added meditatively, "Strange as it may be, the Victorious Caesar Charles believes at this moment that he wants peace, and his Christian Majesty thinks that he does also."

But Zeno pursued his idea. "What is error, and its sequel, lie, if not a kind of *Caput Mortum*, an inert matter without which truth would be too volatile, and could not be mixed and ground in human mortars? . . . Mere dull logicians exalt whoever thinks as they do, and raise a hue and cry against their opponents; but if they meet with thinking truly different in essence, it escapes them entirely; they no longer see it, no more than a snarling beast continues to see some unaccustomed object (if it cannot be eaten or torn to shreds) when it is placed on the floor of his cage. By such means one could make oneself invisible."

"*Aegri somnia,*" protested the Captain, "I do not follow you."

"Am I Servetus, that donkey," Zeno continued, but now with vehemence, "to risk being burned by slow fire on a public square because of this or that interpretation of a dogma, when I have in hand studies far more important to me, my work on the diastolic and systolic movements of the heart? If I say that three make one, or that the world was saved in Palestine, can I not inscribe within these words a secret meaning, and thus even spare myself the humiliation of having lied? Certain cardinals (I know some of them) have managed in this way, and that is what some learned doctors have done who are now supposed to be wearing halos in Heaven. I write the three letters of the august Name as others do, but what meaning should I give to that word? The Whole, or the Regulator of the Whole? What Is, or What Is Not, or What Is-in-Not-Existing, like the void and dark of night? Between the Yes and the No, between the *Pro* and the *Contra*, there are thus immense subterranean spaces where even the most threatened of men can live in peace."

"Your censors are not so thick-witted as that," Henry Maximilian warned him. "Those Lutheran burghers at Basel and the Holy Office in Rome both understand you well enough to condemn you. In their eyes you are only an atheist."

"They think that whoever is not like them is against them," Zeno replied, and his voice was bitter. Filling a goblet in his turn, he drank avidly of the sour German wine.

The Captain reverted to a lighter mood. "Thanks be to God!" he said gaily, "bigots of all varieties will not stick their noses into my little love verses. I have never exposed myself to anything but the simpler dangers: wounds at war, fevers in Italy, pox from whores, vermin at inns, and creditors everywhere. As for the doctoral or priestly rabble, tonsured or not, I seek them out about as much as I would go hunting porcupine. I did not even refute that blockhead Robortello of Udine, who thinks that he finds errors in my version of Anacreon. He is only a dunce in Greek, and in all languages. Like anyone else, I like science, but it's little to me whether the blood goes up or down in the cavous vein; it's enough to know that when we die it grows cold. And if the earth turns . . ."

"It does," Zeno interposed.

"Well, if the earth turns, I hardly care about that at this moment when I am walking on it, and I shall care less still when I come to lie in it. As to matters of faith, I'll believe what the Council decides, *if* it decides anything, exactly as I shall eat, this evening, whatever the innkeeper scrambles together. I take my God and my time as they come, even though I should have preferred to live in the days when Venus was worshipped. I don't even wish to deprive myself on my deathbed, if my heart so bids me, of turning toward Our Lord Jesus Christ."

"You are like a man who is willing to believe that there is a table and two benches in the next room, if he is told so, because the matter is of no moment to him."

"Friend Zeno," said the Captain, by way of reply, "I find you here, thin and haggard, harassed, and wearing a doublet so old that my valet would disdain it. Is it worth the trouble of toiling for twenty years' time to get no further than doubt? Doubt will grow by itself, anyhow, in any well-stocked pate."

"Yes, incontestably worth it," Zeno affirmed. "Your doubts and your faith are but bubbles of air on the surface, but the truth which condenses within us, like the salt deposed in an alembic during a hazardous distillation, is beyond explanation and all limitation of form; it is both too cold and too burning for human utterance, too subtle for the written word, and more precious than writings can be."

"More precious than the August Syllable?"

"Yes," said Zeno, but he lowered his voice, in spite of himself.

At this moment a begging friar knocked at the door; thanks to the Captain's generosity, he went away fortified by a few pennies. After his departure the Captain came to sit near the fire; he, too, spoke in a low tone. "Tell me instead about your travels," he whispered.

"What is there to tell?" asked the philosopher. "I will not speak to you of the mysteries of the East, for they do not exist, and you are not a simpleton to be amused by descriptions of the Gran Signor's Seraglio. I learned rapidly that the differences of climate of which so much is made signify little in comparison with the fact that everywhere man has two feet and two hands, a virile member and a belly, a mouth and two eyes. People attribute voyages to me that I have never made, and I have credited some to myself by way of subterfuge, in order to be peacefully elsewhere than they supposed me to be. For example, I was said to be already in Tartary when actually I was quietly experimenting at Pont-Saint-Esprit, in Languedoc.

"But let us go further back: shortly after my arrival in Leon, my Prior was driven from his abbey by his monks, who accused him of Jewish leanings. It is true that his old head was full of strange formulas, taken from the *Zohar*, concerning the affinity between metals, celestial hierarchies, and the stars. I had learned at Louvain to despise such allegories, disgusted as I was with those exercises where facts are made into symbols, and these, in turn, are built upon as if they were facts. But no one is so mad as to lack his share of wisdom: my Prior, by dint of simmering his alembics, had discovered for himself certain ways of proceeding, secrets which he passed on to me. After Leon, the School of Medicine at Montpellier taught me almost nothing: for the doctors there, Galen had become an idol to whom they sacrificed Nature itself; when I attacked certain of his notions (which the barber Jan Myers already knew to be based on the anatomy of the monkey, rather than on that of man), my learned colleagues preferred to believe that the human spine had changed since the time of Christ rather than charge their oracle with laxity or error.

"There were nevertheless some fearless souls at Montpellier . . . We were short of corpses for study, the general prejudices being what they are. A physician called Rondelet, as comically rotund as his name, lost a son from an attack of purple fever, a young student of twenty-two with whom I had often gone collecting herbs in Grau-du-Roi. He died a day after. In that room impregnated with vinegar, where we dissected this dead youth, who had ceased to be either son or friend and was now only a fine specimen of the human machine, I had the feeling for the first time that the arts of mathematics and mechanics, on the one side, and the Great Art, alchemy, on the other, apply to our study of the universe only those same truths which our bodies teach us; for in our bodies is repeated the structure of the Whole. I realized then that an entire lifetime is not too long for examining and comparing this world in which we dwell and the world which we ourselves are. The lungs are the bellows which keep the coals ablaze; the phallus is a weapon of propulsion; the blood in its intricate course through the body resembles water in the small channels of a garden of the East; the heart (according to which theory you follow) is the pump or the furnace, the brain the alembic wherein a soul is distilled . . ."

"We are falling back into allegory," said the Captain, interrupting him. "If you mean by all that that the body is the most solid of realities, then say so."

"No, not exactly," Zeno explained. "This body, our kingdom, sometimes seems to me to be made of a fabric as loosely woven and as evanescent as a shadow. I should hardly be more astonished to see my mother again (who is dead) than to come upon you around a corner as I did, your face grown older and its substance recomposed more than once in twenty years' time, with its color altered by the seasons and its form somewhat changed, but your mouth still knowing my name. Think of the grain that has grown and the creatures that have lived and died in order to sustain that Henry who is and is not the one I knew twenty years ago.

"But to come back to the travels . . . Pont-Saint-Esprit was not always a bed of roses. The townsmen peeked from behind their shutters to spy on the new physician, and the Eminence on whom I was counting left Avignon for Rome . . . My chance came, however, in a different form, with a renegade Frenchman whose trade it was to keep the royal stables of France in supply from Algiers; this worthy bandit broke a leg almost on my doorstep, and in exchange for my care offered me passage on his tartan. I am still grateful to him for that. There in Barbary my work in ballistics won me the friendship of His Highness, and also gave me the opportunity to study the properties of naphtha, combining it with quicklime to construct rockets which could be shot from the ships of his fleet.

"*Ubicumque idem:* rulers want engines to protect or increase their power; the rich want gold, so are willing to pay (for a time) for the cost of our stoves; the ambitious, and the cowardly, too, seek to know what the future holds for them. I coped with all that the best I could. The greatest windfall, after all, was some enfeebled doge or an ailing sultan: there was money for me, and good dwellings, one in Genoa near San Lorenzo, one in Constantinople in the Christian quarter of Pera. The tools of my trade were provided me, and with them that most precious and rarest of all aids, the license to think and to act as I chose.

"But then would arise the envious intriguers or the whisperings of fools, accusing me of blaspheming their Gospel, or their Alcoran; next, some plot at Court in which I could readily be implicated; and finally the day would come when it was better to spend one's last gold piece to buy a horse or hire a boat. I have had twenty years of such minor crises, which in books are called adventures. I have taken some chances, too, in the practice of my art, killing some patients but curing others by the same excess of daring. But their gains or relapses were of interest to me chiefly as confirmation of a prognosis on my part, or as proof of the value of a method. Knowledge and contemplation are not enough, friend Henry, if they are not transmuted into power, so the unschooled are right in judging us to be adepts of a white or a black magic. To make the ephemeral endure, to advance or retard the ordained hour, to master the secrets of death in order to battle against it, to avail oneself of natural remedies so as either to help or to thwart Nature, to dominate man and the world and to make them over, or perhaps even to create them . . ."

Here the Captain broke in. "There are times," he observed,

with melancholy, "when, on rereading my Plutarch, I have told myself it's too late, man and the world have had their day."

"Illusion and mirage," said Zeno. "Those Golden Ages you cherish are like Damascus or Constantinople, beautiful from afar; but you have to walk in their streets to see the lepers and the dead dogs. Your Plutarch tells me that Hephaestion persisted in eating, like many another victim of fever, when told to fast, and that Alexander drank like a German mercenary. Few bipeds, from Adam's time down, have been worthy of the name of man."

"Still, you are a physician . . . ?" the Captain questioned.

"Yes," replied Zeno, "among other things."

"You're a physician," the Fleming persisted, ". . . but I suppose that one tires of sewing men together, just as one does of ripping them apart. Don't you weary of rising by night to attend on this miserable lot?"

"*Sutor, ne ultra* . . ." was Zeno's reminder. "I take pulses and examine tongues; I study urine, not souls . . . It is not for me to decide if a miser stricken with colic deserves to live ten years more, or if it is a good thing that a tyrant should die. We still have something to learn from the dullest or the most despicable of our patients, and corruption from their sores is not more offensive than what runs from the wounds of a clever man, or a just. Each night passed at the bedside of anyone sick, no matter who, confronts me with questions as yet unanswered: whether or not suffering has a purpose, whether Nature is benevolent, or, on the contrary, indifferent, and whether or not the soul survives the shipwreck of the body. Once it had seemed to me possible to explain the mysteries of the universe by the system of analogies, but then such explanations appeared to teem, in their turn, with new chances for error in that they tended to attribute to Nature, obscure and unfathomable as it is, a pre-established plan such as others attribute to God. I am not speaking of mere doubt: doubting is something different; I was only carrying my investigation through to the point where each idea gave way, as it were, in my hands, like the coil of a spring being forced out of shape; as soon as I mounted the ladder of an hypothesis, I could feel that indispensable IF crashing under my weight . . . "Paracelsus and his system of signatures had once seemed to me to open a triumphal way to our art, but in practice they led us back to village superstition. Nor did the study of horoscopes seem to me so useful as before for the choice of remedies and prediction of fatal accidents; granted that we are made of the same stuff as the stars, it does not follow that they determine us, or can influence us. The more I think of it, the more our ideas, our idols and our so-called holy practices, and those of our visions which supposedly are ineffable, all seem to me to be engendered merely by the stirrings of the human machine, exactly as is the wind from our nostrils or from our netherparts, and as is our sweat and salty water from tears, or the white blood passed in love, or the muddy excrement of the body. It enraged me to think that man should so waste his own substance in construction of theories that were almost always pernicious, and should speak of chastity before having examined the whole machinery of sex; that he should debate the question of free will instead of pondering the thousand obscure reasons which, for example, cause you to blink if I suddenly point a stick at your eyes; or that he should talk of Hell before having looked more closely into the question of death."

"I know what death is," said the Captain, yawning. "Between the shot from the harquebus that felled me at Ceresole, and the dram of brandy that resurrected me, there is a black hole. I owe it to the sergeant's gourd that I'm not in that hole, still."

"Yes, I grant you that," the alchemist concurred, "though there is much to be said for the concept of immortality as well as against it. What the dead lose first of all is motion, then heat, and next, more or less promptly, according to the agents to which they are submitted, their form. Would it then be only the soul's form and motion, but not its substance, which are abolished in death . . .?

"I was in Basel, at the time of the black plague . . ."

Henry Maximilian interrupted him to say that he himself was living in Rome at that time, and that the plague had caught him at the house of a courtesan.

"I was in Basel," Zeno continued. "I may explain that at Pera I had just missed meeting My Lord Lorenzo de' Medici, the tyrannicide, him whom the people call Lorenzaccio in derision. In his impoverished condition he was playing the go-between like you, friend Henry, and had managed to be sent by France on a secret mission to the Sublime Porte. I had long wanted to meet that truly great prince. Four years later, when I passed through Lyons to deposit my *Treatise on the Physical World* with the ill-fated Dolet, my bookseller, I met Lorenzo in the back room of an inn, sitting lone and melancholy at a table. It so happened that during his stay there he was attacked by a Florentine assassin, hired for the purpose; I tended him as best I could, and we had the time to discuss the follies of the Turks, and our own. Hounded though he was, he planned to return to his native Italy in spite of the risk that he ran there. Before we parted, he made me a gift, a Caucasian page whom he had received from the Sultan himself, and he had from me in exchange a poison on which he could depend (should he fall into enemy hands), in order to die without dishonor, and in the style which had been his all his life. He had no occasion, however, to try my tablet; he got himself dispatched in Venice, in a dark alley, by the same murderer who had failed to kill him in France.

"But I had his servant, still . . . You poets, you have made love into a vast lie; what falls to our lot in loving always seems less fair than those rhymes of yours, joined like two mouths pressed together in a kiss. And yet what other name is there for that flame which leaps anew, like the Phoenix, from its own consumption, for that passion to see again each evening the face and the body from which one parted at morning?

For certain bodies, my friend, are refreshing, like water, and we might well ask ourselves why those that are most ardent refresh us most. So, as I was saying, Aleï came from the East, like my unguents and my elixirs; never once, however muddy the German roads or how smoky our lodgings there, did he reproach me by seeming to regret the gardens of the Gran Signor, and their fountains playing in the sun . . . Above all, I relished the silence to which the difficulties of language reduced us. I can read Arabic, but can speak only enough Turkish to ask my way; Aleï spoke Turkish and a little Italian; of his native speech only a few words came back to him, in dream . . . After so many impudent, noisy servants hired previously by ill luck, I had at last come upon this sprite or sylph, such as the common voice attributes to us alchemists as our familiar aides . . .

"One somber evening in Basel, however, the year of the pestilence, I found my servant in my room stricken with that scourge . . . Do you hold beauty dear, friend Henry?"

"Yes," said the Fleming, "women's beauty. Anacreon is a good poet, and Socrates a very great man, but I cannot see why they forgo those tender, rosy curves of flesh, those ample bodies so pleasingly different from our own, where we enter like conquerors coming into a city festively decked for us and flower-strewn. If such delight be a lie and the welcome deceive us, what matter? The pomades, perfumes, and curls, which a man wears only to his shame, I enjoy through womankind. Why should I go seeking hidden alleys when before me lies an open road whereon I can make my way with honor? Fie upon those cheeks which turn rough so soon, more appealing to the barber than to the lover!"

"For my part," Zeno replied, "I value most this delight rather more secret than any other, a body like my own reflecting my pleasure, agreeably dispensing with all that paraphernalia which is added to love-making by courtesans' smirks and conceits of the Petrarchists, or by Madame Livia's embroidered chemises and the demure guimpes of

Madame Laura. Such intimacy does not try to justify itself, hypocritically, by perpetuation of the human race; it is born of desire, but passes with its passing, and if any element of love is mingled therein, it is not because I have been disposed toward it, in advance, by the cheap love songs of the day.

"I was living that spring in a room of an inn on the Rhine, in time of high water; the roar of the torrent was so loud that we had to shout to make ourselves heard, and I could barely catch the tones of the long viol that my servant used to play for me when I was tired (for music has always seemed to me both a festivity and a specific). But one evening there was no Aleï waiting for me, lantern in hand, near the stable where I kept my mule. Friend Henry, I suppose that you have seen statues injured by picks and shovels, or half decayed in the earth, and have deplored their fate, cursing Time for so maltreating beauty. But still I can imagine that the marble, wearied with keeping human guise so long, might rejoice in turning simply to stone again . . . Living creatures, however, fear the return to a formless substance . . .

"At the very threshold a fetid odor gave me warning, as did the mouth, striving to suck in water but vomiting back what the throat could no longer swallow; blood was spurting from the infected lungs. But that which we call the soul subsisted, and the eyes were still those of a trusting dog who never doubts that his master can come to his aid . . . That was certainly not the first time that my juleps proved futile, but up to then each death had been little more than the loss of a pawn in my game as a physician. Furthermore, after long years of combating His Black Majesty, a kind of obscure complicity is formed between us; it is thus that a captain finally learns to know and admire the enemy's tactics. The moment always comes when our patients perceive that we know Death too well not to resign ourselves to what is inevitable for them: while they are still pleading with us and struggling, they read in our eyes a verdict which they would fain not see. One has truly to cherish someone before he can realize how monstrous it is that a living being should die . . .

"My courage failed me, or at least that impassibility which we physicians must have. My calling seemed to me vain, a view which is almost as absurd as to hold it sublime. Not that I could share his suffering: quite the reverse, for I knew that I was wholly incapable of imagining, for myself, the pain in which that body was writhing before my very eyes; my servant was dying as if in the depths of a wholly different realm. I called for help, but the innkeeper was careful to avoid coming to my aid. I lifted the corpse from the bed to place it on the floor, there to await the gravediggers whom I would summon at daybreak; then I burned the straw mattress, by handfuls, in the stove. The world of inner being and the external world, the microcosm and the macrocosm, were still the same for me as in the time of dissections at Montpellier, but those great interlocking wheels turned now in a total void; their fragile mechanisms no longer enthralled me . . .

"It shames me to admit that the death of a valet sufficed to produce in me so dark a revolution; but one grows weary, friend Henry, and I am no longer young; I am more than forty. I was tired of my business of patching bodies: it repelled me to think of going each morning to take the pulse of Monsieur the Alderman, to reassure Madame the Bailiff's wife, or to hold the urinal of Monsieur the Pastor up to the light to examine it. I promised myself that night to treat no one from that time on."

"The host of the Golden Lamb told me about this fantasy of yours," said the Captain gravely. "But you are treating the Nuncio's gout, and here on my cheek is your bandage and your plaster."

"Six months have now gone by," said Zeno, as he traced some figures in the ashes with a half-burned stick. "Curiosity takes the upper hand again, as does the desire to use what talent one possesses, and also the wish to help, if at all possible, those engaged with us in this strange adventure. The vision of utter darkness is behind me. By never speaking to anyone of these things, one forgets them."

Henry Maximilian, rising, moved to the window and remarked, "It's still raining." And raining it was, incessantly. The Captain drummed on the windowpane, then suddenly turned back to his host, inquiring, "Did you know that they say that Sigismund Fugger, my kinsman of Cologne, has been mortally wounded in battle in the land of the Incas? They say that he had a hundred women captives, a hundred bodies of coppery hue with incrustations of coral, their long braids oiled and scented with spice. When he saw that he was going to die, he ordered the hair of all those prisoners cut for him and spread upon a bed. Then he asked to be laid thereon, to breathe his last upon this fleece redolent of cinnamon and sweat, and the odor of women."

"It is hard to believe that those beauteous tresses were free of vermin," the philosopher commented wryly, and then added, in anticipation of some irritable gesture from the Captain, "I know what you are thinking. Yes, I have at times tenderly combed the lice from dark curls."

The Flemishman continued to walk aimlessly about, less for the purpose of unstiffening his legs, it seemed, than for shaking off some grim thoughts. "Your mood is catching," he admitted, coming back finally to take a place on the hearth. "The story you recounted just now makes me brood over my own life. I am not complaining, but everything has turned out differently from what I had believed. I know that I lack the makings of a great strategist, but I have observed at close range those who are supposed to be such, and they were certainly far from what I expected. By preference I have spent a good third of my time in the Peninsula; the weather is better there than in Flanders, but the food is worse. My poems are not worth surviving the paper on which my bookseller prints them (at my cost, when by chance I have the means to offer myself, as others do, a frontispiece and a florid title page).

The laurels of Hippocrene are not for me; I shall not go down through the centuries bound in calfskin. But when I see how few people read Homer's *Iliad* I accept more lightly my lot of being so little read. There have been some Ladies who have loved me, but they were rarely the ones for love of whom I would have laid down my life . . . (But when I look at myself—what arrogance to suppose that the beauties for whom I sigh might want me . . .) Take Vanina, now, in Naples, who is more or less my wife; a good-natured girl, but her odor is not one of ambergris, and her coils of red-gold hair are not wholly her own.

"I have gone back to spend some time at home; my mother is dead, God rest her!—the good woman was sweet on you. My father is down in Hell, I suppose, with his sacks of gold. My brother received me well enough, but after a week I knew that the time had come to depart. Sometimes I regret that I have not engendered some legitimate children, but none of my nephews appeals to me as a son. I have ambitions, like anyone else, but when some mighty one of the moment refuses me a commission, or a pension, what a joy it is to quit the antechamber without having to thank My Lord, and to stroll the streets as I please, with my hands in my empty pockets . . . Pleasure I have had in plenty, and I thank God that every year brings its full contingent of nubile girls, and that new wine is made each autumn. I sometimes think that I shall have had the good life of a dog basking in the sun, with not a few street fights and a bone or two to gnaw. And nevertheless I rarely part from a mistress without a slight sigh of relief, like a schoolboy coming out from school; and I do believe that I shall utter a sigh of the very same kind at the hour of my death.

"You were speaking of statues; I know few pleasures more exquisite than that of contemplating the marble Venus which my good friend the Cardinal Caraffa keeps in his gallery in Naples: her white body is so beautiful as to cleanse the heart of every profane desire, and makes one want to cry. But if I try to look upon her even half of a quarter hour, neither my eyes nor my mind can still see her. Friend, in almost every earthly thing there is some sediment, or some aftertaste, to disgust you with the whole, and the rare objects which happen to have some portion of perfection are themselves mortally sad. Philosophy is not my strong point, but I often say to myself that Plato is right, and Canon Campanus also. There must exist, somewhere, something more perfect than ourselves, an absolute Good whose presence overpowers us, but which we cannot do without."

"*Sempiterna temptatio*," Zeno agreed. "I often say that nothing in the world, if not a divine order, or a strange whim of matter to outdo itself, explains why I strive each day to think a little more clearly than the evening before."

He remained seated, head lowered, in the damp dusk. The glow of the hearth cast a reddish reflection on his hands, which were stained with acids and marked here and there by pale scars from burns; one could see that he was looking attentively at those strange prolongations of the soul, those great tools of the body which serve for contact with everything else.

"Praise be to me!" he exclaimed at last, in a kind of exaltation which Henry Maximilian could have recognized as that of the Zeno of yore, in the elation of mechanical construction, those dreams shared with Colas Gheel. "Never shall I cease to marvel that this flesh sustained by its vertebrae, this trunk joined to the head by the isthmus of the neck and disposing its members symmetrically about itself, contains and perhaps even produces a mind which makes use of my eyes in order to see and my movements in order to touch . . . I know this mind's limitations, and know that it will not have time to go further, or the strength, if by chance enough time be accorded to it. But this mind *is*, and, in this moment, it is the *One who Is*. I know that it makes mistakes, goes astray, and often wrongly interprets the lessons which the world doles out to it; but I know, too, that it has within itself the capacity to recognize and sometimes to rectify its own errors.

"I have traversed at least one part of this sphere where we are; I have studied the fecundation of plants and the point at which metals fuse; I have observed the stars and have examined the inside of bodies. From this brand that I lift here I can deduce a concept of weight, and from these flames the concept of warmth. What I do not know, I know full well that I do not know, and I envy those who will eventually know more; but I know also that, exactly like me, they will be obliged to measure, weigh, deduce, and then mistrust the deductions so produced; they will have to make allowance for the part which is true in any falsehood, and likewise reckon the eternal admixture of falsity in truth.

"I have never clung blindly to some idea for fear of the perplexity into which I should fall if I let it go. I have never seasoned a truth with the sauce of a lie in order to digest it more easily. I have never misrepresented the views of my adversary to get the better of him more readily, not even the views of Bombastus during our debate on antimony (though he showed no gratitude for my restraint). Or perhaps, yes: I have caught myself in the act of such misrepresentation, and each time reprimanded myself as if I were scolding a dishonest valet; I could trust myself again only after promising myself to do better. I have dreamed my dreams, but I do not take them for anything more than dreams. I have refrained from making an idol of truth, preferring to leave to it its more modest name of exactitude. My triumphs and my dangers are not the ones that people suppose: there are other glories than fame and other fires than those of the stake. I have almost attained to the point of distrusting words. I shall die a little less witless than I was born."

"All that is very well," said the soldier, yawning again. "But the general rumor credits you with more substantial success: they say that you are making gold."

"No," replied the alchemist, "but others to come will make it. It is just a matter of time and of adequate tools to complete the experiment. What are a few centuries?" "Exceeding long, if one has to pay the score at the Golden Lamb," answered the Captain ruefully. "Making gold will possibly be as easy someday as blowing glass," Zeno continued. "By dint of biting well into the substance of things, we shall finally come to the hidden reasons for affinities and for discords . . . A mechanical spit or a self-filling bobbin do not amount to much, perhaps, and yet a chain of such small inventions could take us farther than Amerigo Vespucci and Magellan went in their voyages. I am wild when I consider that man's inventiveness has not gone beyond his first wheel for a cart, the first potter's wheel, or the first forge; there has hardly been any effort to diversify the uses of fire from the time that it was stolen from the heavens. And nevertheless, it would suffice merely to apply oneself seriously in order to deduce from a few simple principles a whole series of ingenious machines capable of increasing man's wisdom or his power, such as engines to produce heat by their motion, and pipes through which to convey fire, just as some now convey water, thus utilizing the systems of ancient hypocausts and Oriental steam baths for smelting and distillation . . . Riemer in Ratisbon believed that study of the laws of equilibrium would give rise to construction for both warfare and peace, of chariots moving in air and swimming under water. Your gunpowder, which has reduced the exploits of Alexander to the rank of child's play, was born in this way from the cogitations of a brain . . ."

"Hold on!" Henry Maximilian interjected. "When our forefathers lighted a fuse for the first time, one would have thought that this invention loudly acclaimed would turn the art of war upside down, and would reduce the fighting by killing off all fighters. But nothing of the sort came of it, thank God! We do more killing than before (though, on second thought, I doubt this), and my hardy fellows use harquebuses instead of crossbows. But the same old courage and the old cowardice, the old stratagems, disciplines, and insubordination are what they always were, and with them remain the same arts of advancing, retreating, and holding one's ground, and of terrifying the opponent while appearing not to be terrified oneself. Our military men are still copying Hannibal and poring over their Vegetius. We continue, as ever, to drag along behind the arses of our teachers."

"Yes, an ounce of inertia outweighs a bushel of wisdom, I've long known that," Zeno said with resentment. "I am fully aware that for our rulers science is only an arsenal stocked with expedients less important to them than their tournaments and their regalia, and their bestowal of titles. And yet, friend Henry, here and there in different corners of the earth I know five or six poor beggars even madder and more shorn of possessions than I, and more under suspicion, who secretly aspire to a power more awesome than the Emperor Charles will ever have. If Archimedes had had a point to stand on outside the world, he would have been able not only to lift up our sphere, as he boasted that he could do, but to make it fall back again into the abyss, like a cracked shell . . . And frankly, when I saw the bestial ferocities of the Turks in Algiers, or again, on beholding the furies and follies which run rampant everywhere in our Christian kingdoms, I have sometimes said to myself that the attempt to organize and instruct our human race, and to equip and enrich it, is perhaps only a makeshift in this universal disorder of ours; and that some Phaeton could one day set fire to the earth of his own accord, rather than do so by mischance. Who knows but what some baneful comet will emerge one day from our alembics? When I see how far our speculations carry us, friend Henry, I am less surprised that they burn us alchemists at the stake."

And suddenly rising, as if to depart, he said, "I've had word that they are after me again, more than ever, for having published my *Prognostications*. Nothing has been decided against me yet, but I can expect some alarms soon in the days to come. I rarely sleep here in this forge; it is better to look for a less likely shelter for the night. Let us leave together, but if you fear being spied upon, you would be wise to separate from me at the door."

"What do you take me for?" the Captain asked, making show of more nonchalance, perhaps, than he actually felt. He buttoned up his jacket, cursing the while at those meddlers who stick their noses into other people's business.

Zeno put on his cloak, now nearly dry. Before leaving, the two men shared the wine that was left in the bottom of the pitcher. The alchemist closed and locked the door, hanging the massive key beneath a beam where the valet would find it. The rain had ceased and it was growing dark, but feeble gleams from the setting sun were still reflected upon the fresh snow of the mountain slopes, visible beyond the gray slate of the city rooftops. Zeno kept scanning the shadowy alleyways as he walked.

"I'm short of pelf," said the Captain. "But if, considering your present difficulties . . ."

"No, my friend," the alchemist replied. "In case of danger the Nuncio will provide me with money to pack off. Keep your wherewithal to lighten your own troubles."

A coach escorted by guards plunged at full speed into the narrow street, doubtless carrying some important personage to the Imperial castle of Ambras. The two of them had to hug the wall in order to make way. The fracas passed, Henry resumed thoughtfully: "In Paris, Nostradamus predicts the future, yet practices undisturbed. What do they have against you?"

"He admits that he does so by means of aid from on high, or from below," the philosopher answered, wiping the splashes of mud from his face with the back of his sleeve. "Those Gentlemen of the Sorbonne apparently find a bare hypothesis, with none of that trapping of his of angels or demons in singing cauldrons, more impious . . . And then, the quatrains of that Michael of Notre Dame, though I do not deride them, hold the attention of the crowd by announcing general calamities and deaths of royalty. As for me, the present worries of King Henry II move me too little for me to try to calculate their outcome . . .

"In the course of my travels a certain notion came to me: as a result of wandering over roads in space, always knowing, when Here, that a There was awaiting me (although I was not yet there in that other place), I wanted to venture, in my own way, upon roads in time; to fill the gap between the absolute predictions of the astronomer and the somewhat less definite prognosis by the physician; to risk, though with utmost caution, the coupling of premonition and conjecture; to trace on that part of the continent of time where we do not yet dwell the map of oceans and lands already emerging . . . I wore myself out in the attempt."

"You will end like Doctor Faustus of the puppet shows at the Fair," the Captain interposed, for a joke.

"No, far from it!" the alchemist protested. "Old wives' tales, these stupid stories of pact and perdition concerning the learned Doctor. A true Faustus would have other views on the soul and on Hell."

They did little more now than try to avoid the puddles; they walked along the quays, since Henry Maximilian had taken lodgings near the bridge. Suddenly Henry asked, "Where will you pass the night?"

Zeno darted a suspicious glance at his companion, then answered circumspectly, "I don't yet know."

Silence fell again; each had exhausted his store of talk. But soon Henry Maximilian stopped short before a shop window, where a jeweler was working late into the evening, his candle placed behind a great bowl of water to magnify the light; pulling from his pocket a small notebook, the Captain began to read aloud:

" ' . . . *Stultissimi, inquit Eumolpus, tum Encolpii, tum Gitonis aerumnae, et praecipue blanditiarum Gitonis non immemor, certe estis vos qui felices esse potestis, vitam tamen aerumnosam degitis et singulis diebus vos ultro novis torquetis cruciatibus. Ego sic semper et ubique vixi, ut ultimam quamque lucem tanquam non redituram consumarem, id est in summa tranquillitate . . .'*

"Let me translate this," he added, "for I believe that for you mere pharmacist's Latin has driven off the other. This old rascal Eumolpus addresses to the two minions, Encolpius and Gito, a discourse that I have judged worthy of inscribing in what I call my breviary:

" 'Fools that you are,' said Eumolpus, recalling the woes of Encolpius and those of Gito, and especially the tender ways of the latter. 'You could be happy, but still you lead a wretched life, inflicting upon yourselves each day a torture worse than that of the day before. For my part, I have lived each day, everywhere, as if it were to be my last, that is, *in utter tranquillity.*' Petronius," he went on to explain, "is one of my patron saints."

Zeno, moved to warm approval, commented, "The beauty of the thing is that your author does not even imagine that the dying day of a sage might be lived otherwise than in tranquillity. We shall try to remember this when our time comes."

Their street ended in a turning which brought them in front of a chapel brightly lighted for celebration of a Novena. Zeno made ready to enter.

"What are you going to do among those bigots?" the Captain inquired.

"Have I not explained that to you already?" was the reply. "Make myself invisible." And so saying Zeno slipped behind the leather curtain suspended across the doorway.

Henry Maximilian paused for a moment, then went on; but he came back again, retracing his steps, before finally departing for good, whistling his tune of old:

> *"Nous étions deux compagnons*
> *Qui allions delà les monts.*
> *Nous pensions faire grand chère . . ."*

On returning to his lodgings, he found a message from Sieur Strozzi terminating the secret mediations on Sienese affairs. Henry Maximilian surmised that the wind was veering in the direction of war; or perhaps he had been ill-represented to the Florentine marshal, and His Excellency had thus been persuaded to employ another agent. During the night the rain began again, then turned to snow. The next day, after his bundles were made, the Captain set out in search of Zeno. The houses, draped in white, suggested faces that hide their secrets under the uniformity of the cowl. Henry Maximilian was pleased to go again to the Golden Lamb, where the wine was good. The host, on bringing him something to drink, told him that Zeno's valet had come very early that morning to return the key and pay the rent due for the forge. Toward noon, an officer of the Inquisition, sent to arrest Zeno, had ordered the innkeeper to lend him a hand. But doubtless some devil, said the innkeeper, had warned the alchemist in time. Nothing more unusual had been found at the forge than a heap of glass phials, all carefully broken.

Henry Maximilian rose hurriedly, leaving on the table the change from his silver piece. Some few days later he reached Italy, traveling through the valley of the Brenner.

THE CAREER OF
HENRY MAXIMILIAN

A T T H E Battle of Ceresole Henry Maximilian had performed brilliantly. There, as he liked to say, he had exerted as much ingenuity to defend a few tumbledown huts of the Milan countryside as great Caesar had done to conquer the world. His good cheer was appreciated by his General, Blaise de Montluc, for it heartened the men. He had spent his life serving, alternately, the Very Christian King of France and His Catholic Majesty of Spain, but of the two nations the gay French were more to his taste. As a poet, he blamed the weakness of his rhymes upon his campaign responsibilities; as a captain, however, he explained his tactical errors by the fact that poetry was brewing in his brain; in any case, he did creditably in both professions, though in combination they did not make for wealth.

Roaming the length of the Peninsula had left him no illusions about the Italy of his dreams: he had learned to distrust the Roman courtesans, after once having paid them their due by getting himself clapped; and he had learned to discriminate in melons, as well, choosing them from Trastevere's stalls and tossing their green rinds casually into the Tiber. He knew that the Cardinal Maurizio Caraffa considered him hardly more than a rough soldier, of some intelligence; in time of peace the most that he could expect would be the alms of a poorly paid post as captain of the palace guards. His mistress in Naples, Vanina, had extracted from him a goodly sum for a child which perhaps was not his at all; but never mind. A sinecure would have been offered him readily by Madame Renée of France, whose ducal palace in Ferrara was the veritable Refuge of the Disinherited, but she welcomed there any and every sort of ragged wretch provided that they would indulge with her in the thin, sour wine of Calvinist Psalms; the Captain had no use for people like that.

He tended to live more and more with his humble foot soldiers, and just as they did, putting on the same patched jacket again each morning with the pleasure of finding an old friend, and cheerfully admitting that he washed only when it rained; he shared with his motley band, made up of soldiers of fortune from Picardy, mercenaries from Albania, and banished Florentines, their rancid bacon and their moldy straw, and also the affection of the yellow cur which followed the troop. But this rude life was not without its subtler joys. He still kept his love of those resounding, ancient names which add to the merest strip of wall in Italy the golden glimmer, or the vestige of purple, of some great memory. And he liked to stroll the streets, sometimes in sun, sometimes in shade, and to address a pretty girl in good Tuscan, expecting either a kiss or a volley of insults; or to drink at the fountains, shaking the drops from his thick fingers over the dusty paving; or he might decipher a fragment of a Latin inscription, seen from the corner of his eye as he absent-mindedly pissed against a boundary stone.

From his father's vast opulence he had inherited no more than a few shares of the sugar refinery at Maastricht, but revenue from that source rarely found its way to his pocket; he had also received one of the smallest of the family estates, a certain property in Flanders called Lombardy, the very name of which was ludicrous to a man who had walked every inch of the true Lombardy. The capons and the cords of wood from this domain, however, went into his brother's ovens and woodsheds. Henry did not care about that, for, at the early age of sixteen, he had freely and gaily renounced his rights as an elder son in exchange for the soldier's mess of pottage. The brief, ceremonious letters which he received from time to time from this brother, on the occasion of a death or a marriage, always ended, to be sure, with offers of service in case of need; but Henry Maximilian knew very well that the writer, in formulating such offers, was aware that the elder son would not take advantage of them. Furthermore, Philibert Ligre seldom failed to allude to the enormous obligations and expenditures required of him in his position as member of the Council of the Low Countries, to the extent that finally it was the Captain, being free of all cares, who seemed the rich man of the two, while he who was laden with gold appeared to be the man in straitened circumstances, in whose coffers one would have blushed to dip.

Only once had the soldier of fortune returned to his home. He had been much exhibited there, as if it were a matter of making it known to all and sundry that the prodigal was, after all, presentable. The very fact that this confidant of Marshal Strozzi was practically without visible employment, and without exalted rank, conferred a kind of luster upon him, as if he were becoming worthy of notice just because of his obscurity. The few years' advance that he had over his younger brother had made of him, he felt, a relic of another age; he seemed to himself naïve beside this younger man, so cautious and so cool. Shortly before Henry Maximilian's departure Philibert confided to him that the Emperor, who had baronets' crowns to distribute for the asking, would gladly append a title to the domain of Lombardy if, hereafter, the military and diplomatic talents of the Captain were put solely to the service of the Holy Empire. The soldier's refusal offended them all: even if he disdained, for his own sake, to drag such a tail behind him, as he said, the title would have added to the family glory. He replied in advising his brother to put the family glory "you know where." He had quickly had enough of the magnificent carved interiors of the domain of Stenberg, which his younger brother now preferred to Dranoutre, the more old-fashioned of the two; the paintings at Stenberg, all on mythological subjects, seemed of coarse workmanship to this man accustomed to the best in Italian art. He had had his fill, too, of the sight of his sullen sister-in-law, with her trappings of jewels, and of the troop of sisters and brothers-in-law established in the manor houses of the district, with their brats of children barely held in leash by trembling tutors. The petty quarrels and intrigues, and the mawkish compromise on the faces of these folk, made him value anew the society of rowdy soldiery and their women followers, where at least one could swear and belch at ease, and where even the worst are but surface scum, and not the underlying dregs.

From the Duchy of Modena, where his comrade Lanza del Vasto had found him employment (the extended peace being too much for his purse), Henry Maximilian kept an eye on the results of his past negotiations for affairs in Tuscany: Strozzi's agents had finally persuaded the Sienese to revolt, out of love of liberty, against the Imperial troops; so these patriots had promptly saddled themselves with a French garrison to defend themselves against His Germanic Majesty. Henry took service again under Monsieur de Montluc, for a siege was a windfall not to be forgone. The winter was severe: cannons on the ramparts were covered each morning with a thin coat of frost; the scant rations of olives and leathery sausage repelled the French appetites. Monsieur de Montluc never appeared before the citizens until he had rubbed his hollow cheeks with wine, like an actor putting on rouge before going onstage, and he tried to conceal the yawns induced by hunger behind his carefully gloved hand.

Henry Maximilian proposed in burlesque verses to put the Imperial Eagle itself on the spit. Actually, the whole affair was only artifice and theatrical repartee, such as is found in Plautus, or in comedies at Bergamo. The Eagle would once again devour some Italian states, mere barnyard fowl, after having struck a few good blows here and there at the presumptuous Gallic cock; some brave folk would lose their lives, whose calling it was to do so; the Emperor would order a *Te Deum* sung for the victory over Siena; and new loans, negotiated as expertly as a treaty between two sovereign princes, would further subject His Majesty to the House of Ligre (which, for that matter, had been going discreetly under another name for some years now); or else the Emperor would borrow from some rival bank in Antwerp or Germany. Twenty-five years of war and armed peace had taught the Captain what goes on behind the scenes.

But this man of Flanders, even though ill-nourished, delighted in the laughter and the games, the gay and elegant processions in which Sienese noblewomen paraded on the public square, disguised as nymphs and Amazons in petticoats of pink satin. The ribbons and the painted banners, the skirts agreeably lifted by the blast of wind at the corners of the somber streets (like trenches between the high houses), all served to cheer the troops and even the burghers, though these to a lesser degree, troubled as these merchants were by the stagnation in business and the high cost of foodstuffs. The gentlemen of the garrison were enraptured: the young Cardinal of Ferrara extolled the Signora Fausta to the skies, although the north wind, from over the mountains, raised gooseflesh on her beauteous bare shoulders; Monsieur de Ternes, however, thought the prize should go to Signora Fortinguerra, who, from the top of the ramparts, boldly displayed her long slender limbs, like Diana's, to the enemy below; Henry Maximilian held out for the blond braids of Signora Piccolomini, a proud beauty, but one who freely enjoyed the pleasurable state of widowhood.

He had been smitten by this goddess with one of those

consuming passions which come in maturity. During bragging sessions or exchanges of confidence, the warrior did not refrain from assuming the discreet victorious air of a successful lover, but everyone knows the small worth of such awkward pretensions, accepting them as a comrade does in order to be listened to with equal charity when the day comes for boasting about his own fictitious conquests. Henry Maximilian knew well enough that the fair one joked about him with her other suitors. But he told himself that he had never been handsome, and was now no longer young; sun and wind had given his countenance the overbaked tones of Sienese bricks. Seated on a stool at his mistress's feet, a timid, even bashful lover, it would sometimes occur to him that these feints and maneuvers of sighs, on the one side, and coquetry, on the other, were not less idiotic than those of two opposing armies; and that, after all, he would have preferred to see her in the embrace of a young Adonis, the two of them nude, or enjoying some amorous intimacy with a maidservant, than to force upon her exquisite body the distasteful weight of his own. But at night, as he lay under his thin blanket, he would recall abruptly some slight movement of the long, bejeweled hand of his beloved, or a way that she had, unique with her, of smoothing her hair; and relighting his candle, he would set to work at some intricate stanzas, spurred by sorrow and jealousy.

§

One day when the cupboards of Siena were even barer than usual, if that were possible, he ventured to present to his blond Nymph some slices of a ham rather ill acquired. The young widow was lying on her couch, protected from the cold by a quilt, and playing in absent fashion with the golden tassel of a cushion. At sight of the treasure she sat up straight, her eyelids suddenly quivering, and swiftly, with a motion almost furtive, she leaned toward the donor and kissed his hand. The wave of ecstasy which came over him was greater than anything which the utmost abandon of this same beauty might have given him. He quietly withdrew in order to let her eat.

§

He had often wondered what would be the manner and the circumstances of his death: a shot from a harquebus, perhaps, which would leave him broken and covered with blood, nobly carried high on the broken shafts of captured Spanish lances, regretted by princes and bewept by his comrades at arms, and finally buried under an eloquent inscription in Latin in the floor along a church wall? Or a sword thrust during a duel in honor of some lady? A knife stab in a dark street? Or a recurrence of the pox of yore? Or even surviving beyond the age of sixty to die of an apoplexy in some castle where he would have found a place as stablemaster, there to end his days?

Once when he lay ill with malaria in Rome, and was shivering on the pallet of an inn only a stone's throw from the Pantheon, he had consoled himself for having to die in that fever-ridden land by reflecting that, after all, the dead are in better company there than elsewhere. He had peopled those curving vaults, visible through his small window, with eagles and with fasces turned upside down, with veterans in tears, and with torches lighting the funeral procession of an emperor who was not he himself, but a kind of eternally great man in whom he had a part. Through the ringing bells of tertian fever, he thought that he had heard the piercing fifes and sonorous trumpets announcing to the world the Prince's death; in his own body he had felt the fire which devours the hero and carries him to the heavens.

Such deaths and imagined obsequies were his true death and his real burial. He died in the course of a foraging expedition during which his cavalrymen tried to storm a poorly guarded barn some short distance from the ramparts; Henry Maximilian's horse was frisking gaily on the earth with its carpet of dry grass; the cool air of February on the sunny hillside was good to breathe in after the windy, dark streets of Siena. An unforeseen attack from the Imperial forces scattered the troop, which turned back toward the walls; Henry Maximilian pursued his men, swearing loudly at them the while. A bullet struck him in the shoulder, and he fell, hitting his head against a stone. He had time to feel the shock of the fall, but not death itself. His charger, freed of the rider's weight, pranced in the fields until a Spaniard caught it to lead it thereafter, mincing its way, toward the Emperor's camp. Two or three German mercenaries divided the arms and the garments of the dead man. In the pocket of his jacket was the manuscript of his *Blazon of Woman's Body;* this collection of playful and amorous sonnets from which he had hoped for a little glory, or at least for some success among the ladies, ended in the bottom of a ditch, buried with him under a few shovelfuls of earth. A motto in honor of Signora Piccolomini, which he had scratched more or less well on the marble rim of the Fontebranda, did remain for a long time visible.

ZENO'S LAST
JOURNEYS

I T W A S one of those periods when the human mind gets entrapped, in a circle of flames. On escaping from Innsbruck, Zeno had lived for a while in seclusion at Würzburg with a former student and follower. This Bonifacius Kastel practiced alchemy in a small house on the bank of the Main, where the turbid green of the water reflected on the windowpanes. But the immobility and lack of activity weighed on the fugitive, and besides, Bonifacius was assuredly not one to court risk very long for a friend in danger. So Zeno moved on into Thuringia, and later made his way to Poland; there he took service as a surgeon in the forces of King Sigismund, who was preparing, with Sweden's help, to drive the Muscovites from Kurland.

At the end of his second winter in that campaign, his zest for new climes and new flora led him to embark for Sweden with a certain Captain Guldenstarr, who presented him to Gustavus Vasa. The Swedish King was looking for a physician who could soothe the miseries accumulated in his aged body from the damp of past encampments and from those cold nights when, in the adventurous days of his youth, he had slept on the ice in order to evade his enemies. He suffered, too, from the effects of old wounds, and from the French disease. Zeno won favor by compounding a cordial to counteract the monarch's fatigue after he had celebrated Christmas with his young wife (his third) in his white castle at Vadstena. All that winter, high up between the lake's frozen plains and the cold sky, peering from the recess of a tall window, the philosopher would compute the positions of such stars as might bring good or bad fortune to the house of Vasa. He was aided in this task by the heir to the throne, young Prince Erik, for whom these dangerous sciences held an unwholesome attraction. In vain did Zeno remind him that the stars, though they influence our destinies, do not determine them; and that our lives are regulated by the heart, that fiery star palpitating in the dark of our bodies, suspended there in its cage of flesh and bone, as strong and mysterious as the stars above, and obeying laws more complicated than the laws which we ourselves make.

But Erik was of those who prefer to receive their destinies from without, whether out of pride, finding it meet that the heavens themselves should take concern for his fate, or whether from indolence, so as not to be obliged to answer for the good or evil which he bore within him. He believed in the stars much as he prayed to the angels and the Saints, in spite of the Reformed faith in which his father had reared him. As a mentor tempted to exert some influence upon the soul of a future king, Zeno tried the effect of instruction or advice here and there; but ideas from others sank and were lost, as in a marsh, in that young brain a-doze behind the pale-gray eyes.

When the cold became too intense, the philosopher and his pupil would draw near the huge fire held captive under the chimney's hood, and Zeno would marvel each time that the domesticated daemon who gave out this beneficent heat, and docilely warmed the pot of beer set low in the cinders, should be one and the same as that flaming god who makes the round of the sky. There were evenings when the Prince did not come, spending his time with his brothers drinking in taverns and wenching, and the philosopher would then rectify the prognostics, if they proved ominous on such nights, merely shrugging his shoulders.

In June, a few weeks before Saint John's Day, Zeno had leave given him so that he might go to the Northland to observe for himself the effects of the long polar day. Traveling sometimes on foot and sometimes in small boats, he wandered from parish to parish, conversing with the help of the pastors as interpreters, since the use of Church Latin still survived among them. Often he collected recipes of value from the village healers, women who knew well the virtues of herbs and forest mosses; or from the nomads who treat their sick by baths and fumigations, and by interpretation of dreams. When he returned to the Court at Uppsala, where his Swedish Majesty was opening the autumn Assembly, he found that the King had been turned against him through the jealous contriving of a German colleague. The aged monarch was fearful lest his sons make use of Zeno's computations to calculate too closely how long their father would live. Zeno thought to count on the help of the heir apparent, of whom he had made a friend and almost a disciple, but when he met Erik by chance in the corridors of the castle, the young Prince passed by without seeing him, as if the philosopher had suddenly acquired the faculty of becoming invisible. Zeno took off in secret, embarking on a fishing boat of Lake Malar, by means of which he reached Stockholm; from there he took passage for Kalmar, then sailed for German shores.

For the first time in his life, he felt the strange need of retracing his steps, as if his existence were moving along a pre-established orbit, like that of the circling stars; so he stayed only a few months in Lübeck, although he practiced there with success. He had conceived a desire to have his *Pro-theories* published in France. In this treatise, on which he had worked at intervals throughout much of his life, he was not concerned to set forth a particular doctrine but wished to establish a classification of men's opinions, indicating both their chance and deliberate interlocking, and their concealed tangents or their underlying relationships. At Louvain, where he stopped in transit, no one recognized him under the name of Sebastian Theus, which he had fashioned for himself. Masters and students had changed there more than once, like the atoms of a body which is constantly in process of renewal, but which keeps to the end the same lineaments, even to the same moles; what he heard, on venturing into a lecture hall, did not seem to him markedly different from what he had listened to formerly with irritation, or, on the contrary, with ardor. He did not trouble to visit a cloth manufactory recently established on the outskirts of Oudenaarde; machines much like those which he had constructed in his youth together with Colas Gheel were functioning there to the satisfaction of all concerned. But he listened with interest to a detailed description of their mechanism given him by an algebraist of the faculty. That professor, who was an exception in not disdaining practical problems, invited the learned stranger to dinner, and kept him overnight in his house.

In Paris he was received with open arms by the Italian Ruggieri, whom he had met previously in Bologna. This man-of-all-work for Queen Catherine was seeking a safe and dependable assistant, someone sufficiently compromised to be at his mercy in case of danger, but who would help him prescribe for the young princes and predict their future. He conducted Zeno to the Palace of the Louvre to present the physician to his mistress, with whom he spoke rapidly in their native tongue, not without much bowing and scraping, smiling ingratiatingly the while. The Queen surveyed the stranger, playing her sparkling eyes to their best advantage, just as she liked, in gesticulating, to make the diamonds on her fingers flash their fires; her hands, white and soft from pomades, and slightly puffy, moved over the black silk of her lap like marionettes.

But when she spoke of the fatal accident which had caused the death of the late monarch three years before, it was as if she were drawing crêpe down over her face. "Would that I had better comprehended your *Prognostications*, some time ago, when I saw in them only calculations on the term of life commonly accorded to princes! We could perhaps have saved the former King from the spearhead which made a widow of me . . . For I believe," she added graciously, "that you are not without having had some part in that work, reputed to be dangerous for those of feeble intellect, and which is credited to a certain Zeno."

"Let us speak as if I were that Zeno," said the alchemist. "*Speluncam exploravimus* . . . Your Majesty knows as I do that the future is big with more events than it can bring forth into the world. It is not impossible to hear some of them stirring deep within the womb of time. But only the ultimate occurrence determines which of these larvae is viable, and can come to full term. I have never trafficked in premature deliveries, whether of joys or of catastrophes."

"Did you depreciate your art thus in presence of His Swedish Majesty?"

"I find no reason to lie to the cleverest woman in France," Zeno replied.

The Queen smiled, but Ruggieri, alarmed to see a fellow worker rate their science so low, protested: "*Parla per divertimento. Questo honorato viatore ha studiato anche altro che cose celeste; sa le virtudi di veleni e piante benefiche di altre parti che possano sanare gli ascessi auricolari del Suo Santissimo Figlio.*"

"I can drain an abscess, but cannot cure the young King," said Zeno laconically. "I have seen His Majesty, from a distance, in the gallery at the hour of audience: it takes no great skill to recognize the cough and sweats of a consumptive. Happily, Heaven has given you more than one son."

"May God conserve him for us!" the Queen responded, mechanically crossing herself. "Ruggieri will install you in the

King's service and we shall count on you to alleviate at least some part of his ills."

"And who will alleviate mine?" The philosopher's tone was bitter. "The Sorbonne threatens to have my *Protheories* seized; it is just now being printed by a bookseller in Saint Jacob Street. If my writings are burned on the public square, can the Queen keep the smoke from rising to disturb me in my garret in the Louvre?"

"Those Gentlemen of the Sorbonne would take umbrage at any attempt on my part to meddle in their quarrels," was the evasive reply of the woman from Italy.

Before dismissing the visitor, she inquired at length about the health of the King of Sweden (the state of his viscera and of his blood), for she sometimes thought of negotiating a marriage between one of her sons and a princess of the North.

§

As soon as they had visited the afflicted young King, the two men left the Louvre together and followed along the quays. As they walked, the Italian poured forth a flood of Court anecdotes. Zeno, preoccupied, interrupted him to say, "You will take care that the compresses are applied to that poor child for five days straight running."

"Shall you not go back yourself?" asked the Italian in surprise.

"Indeed not!" was the reply. "Don't you see that she will not lift a finger to help me from the peril in which my books have put me? I am not ambitious for the honor of being apprehended while in the service of royalty."

"*Peccato!*" exclaimed the Queen's factotum. "Your gruffness pleased her." And suddenly stopping short in the thick of the crowd, he seized his companion by the elbow to say, lowering his voice, "*E questi veleni? Sara vero che ne abbia tanto e quanto?*"

"Don't make me think that popular opinion is right to accuse you of expediting the death of the Queen's enemies?"

"Ah, they exaggerate," said Ruggieri, playing the buffoon. "But why wouldn't Her Majesty have her arsenal of poisons just as she does her harquebuses and her mortars? Remember that she is widowed, and a foreigner in France, that she is considered a Jezebel by the Lutherans and Herodias by our Catholics, and that she has five young children on her hands." "God keep her!" was the atheist's mechanical response. "But if the time ever comes for me to employ poisons, it will be for my own welfare, not for that of the Queen."

§

Nevertheless, he took up residence with Ruggieri, whose babble seemed to amuse him. From the time that his first printer, Etienne Dolet, had been strangled and his body publicly burned for his subversive opinions, Zeno had not published anything more in France. It was therefore with the greater attention that he oversaw the printing of his book in the shop on Saint Jacob Street, correcting a word here and there, or an idea which lay back of the word, eliminating something obscure, or sometimes, on the contrary, and to his regret, adding an obscurity as a precaution. One evening at the hour for supper (which he took alone at Ruggieri's while the Italian was busy at the Louvre), Master Langelier, his printer for this book, came in a state of great agitation to tell him that definitely an order had been given for seizure of the *Protheories;* they were to be destroyed by the hand of the executioner. The merchant deplored the loss of his goods, on which the ink was hardly yet dry. Possibly, he suggested, a dedicatory epistle to the Queen Mother could mend matters at the last minute. So all that night Zeno wrote, deleted, and wrote anew, then deleted again. At dawn he rose from his chair to stretch and yawn; then he threw his pages into the fire, and with them the quill which he had been using.

It was easy enough to assemble his few garments and his doctor's chest, the remainder of his luggage having been cautiously stored in Senlis, in the loft of an inn. Ruggieri was snoring in his second-floor room, in the arms of some girl. Zeno slipped a note under his door, announcing his departure for Provence. Actually, he had decided to go back to Bruges, there to be utterly forgotten.

An object brought from Italy was hanging on the wall of the small antechamber, a Florentine mirror in a tortoise-shell frame, formed from a combination of some twenty little convex mirrors hexagonal in shape, like the cells of a beehive, and each mirror enclosed, in its turn, by a narrow border which had once been the shell of a living creature. Zeno looked at himself there in the gray light of a Parisian dawn. What he saw was twenty figures compressed and reduced by the laws of optics, twenty images of a man in a fur bonnet, of haggard and sallow complexion, with gleaming eyes which were themselves mirrors. This man in flight, enclosed within a world of his own, separated from others like himself who were also in flight in worlds parallel to his, recalled to him the hypothesis of the Greek Democritus, about an infinite series of identical universes in each of which lives and dies imprisoned a series of philosophers.

The fantasy evoked a bitter smile. The twenty little figures of the mirror smiled, too, each alone in his frame. He then saw them turn their heads half away and direct themselves toward the door.

PART TWO

IMMOBILITY

Obscurum per obscurius
Ignotum per ignotius

       –Ancient rule of the alchemists

Proceed toward the obscure and unknown
through the still more obscure and unknown.

RETURN TO
BRUGES

AT SENLIS Zeno found accommodation in the coach which the Prior of the Cordeliers of Bruges had taken for return from a chapter meeting of his order in Paris. This Prior proved to be more learned than his habit might have indicated, and was not without some knowledge of the world and its ways, nor devoid of interest in men and things round about him; the two travelers fell to talking freely by the time they reached Picardy, where the horses strained against the sharp winds of the plains. Zeno withheld little more from his companion than his true name, and the fact that legal proceedings had been instituted against his book. He reflected, however, that the perception and tact of the Prior were such that he might have divined more about Dr. Sebastian Theus than he would have judged it courteous to reveal.

In passing through Tournai, their progress was slowed by the press of people in the streets. On inquiry they learned that all these folk were making for the marketplace, to witness there the hanging of a certain tailor Adrian, who had been convicted of having Calvinist leanings. His wife had been found equally guilty, but since decency forbade that a creature of her sex should hang overhead, her skirts billowing in midair, they had resorted for her to the older custom of burial alive. Such stupid brutality appalled Zeno, though his disgust was concealed by a masque of complete impassivity, for he had made it a rule to express no feelings in any dispute between the Breviary and the Bible. The Prior, on his part, while abhorring heresy, as befitted his calling, deemed the punishment somewhat harsh; his comment, however guarded, evoked in Zeno that almost excessive sympathy which is stirred by the slightest sign of moderation coming from a man whose position in life, or whose garb, does not suggest that one might expect so much. Even when the carriage had regained open country, and the Prior had begun to speak of other things, Zeno still felt as if he himself were suffocating under spadeful upon spadeful of earth. Then suddenly he realized that a full quarter hour had elapsed, and that the poor soul whose death agonies he was sharing had already ceased to feel them herself.

At Dranoutre they passed alongside the Ligre estate; the tall iron fences and the balustrades looked neglected; the Prior mentioned Philibert Ligre, who, according to him, was calling the tunes in Brussels in the Council of the new Regent, or Governess, who ruled over the Low Countries. The opulent Ligre family had long since ceased to reside in Bruges. Philibert and his wife now lived almost continually in Pradelles, their estate in Brabant; there they could more readily dance attendance upon the foreign masters. Such patriotic expressions of scorn for the Spanish authorities and their lackeys was not lost upon Zeno. A short way farther on, the travelers were accosted by Walloon Guards, steel-helmeted and leather-breeched, and were arrogantly ordered to show their letters of passport. With icy disdain the Prior complied, and had the papers passed out to them. Decidedly, things had changed in Flanders.

Upon arriving in Bruges, the two men finally separated at

the marketplace, after mutual expressions of courtesy and offers of service in the future. The Prior continued in his hired coach to his monastery, and Zeno set off on foot, carrying his boxes and his bundles. He was surprised to find his way so easily again in the streets of this city, which he had not revisited for more than thirty years.

He had sent word in advance to Jan Myers of his arrival. This friend, first his master and then his colleague, had more than once proposed that Zeno return to share with him his comfortable house on Woodmarket Wharf. Myers's servant, a large, sullen woman, received the visitor at the door, holding a lantern but yielding so little way on the threshold that he brushed heavily against her as he hastily stepped inside.

Jan Myers was seated in his armchair, his gout-ridden limbs extended at a safe distance from the heat of the fire. The master of the house and the visitor each repressed, with some adroitness, a start of surprise: the spare, brisk Jan Myers of yore had changed into a fat little old man, whose lively eyes and sly smile were now almost buried in folds of rosy flesh; the handsome Zeno of former days had become a gaunt man with gray hair.

Forty years of practice had enabled the physician of Bruges to amass what he needed to live in comfort; his table and his wine cellar were good, even too good for a gout victim's diet. His servant Catherine, with whom he had had some dalliance in the past, was extremely ignorant, but was diligent and faithful, and did not gossip, nor did she install lovers in her kitchen to consume choice morsels and vintage wine. When the two men sat down to supper, Jan Myers cracked some of his favorite jokes about the clergy and their dogma. Though Zeno remembered that he used to find such pleasantries amusing, they seemed rather flat to him now; nevertheless, thinking once more of the tailor Adrian at Tournai and of Dolet at Lyons, then of Servetus at Geneva, he said to himself that at a time when religion was leading to savagery, the rudimentary skepticism of this good fellow certainly had its value. For himself, however, being more advanced in methods of negating assumptions, at first, in order to see if thereafter something positive can be reaffirmed, and of breaking down a whole in order to watch the parts recompose themselves on another plane or in some other fashion, he no longer felt able to laugh at those easy jests.

The Pyrrhonism typical of a barber-surgeon was strangely coupled, in Jan Myers's case, with certain superstitions which he still retained. He prided himself on his interest in the occult, though his efforts in that respect were naïve; Zeno had the utmost difficulty not to let himself be drawn into explanations of the three sublime substances, or of lunar Mercury, all of which seemed to him rather too long for the very evening of his arrival. In matters of medicine old Jan had a strong inclination toward novelties, even though out of caution he had practiced strictly according to the methods taught him; he was therefore hoping for a specific for his gout from Zeno. As to the writings of his visitor which were under suspicion, the old man did not fear that the turmoil made about them would rouse much disturbance in Bruges if the true identity of Dr. Sebastian Theus should chance to be discovered. In this city, so preoccupied with petty local quarrels, and suffering from its silted harbor like a sick man from his gravel, no one had taken the trouble to look at those books.

Zeno lay down on the bed which had been made for him in the upper room. The October night was cold. Catherine came in with a brick which she had heated on the hearth and swaddled in woolen cloths. Kneeling down beside the bed, in the alcove, she inserted the hot bundle under the covers and then touched the traveler's feet and ankles, massaging them for some time. Suddenly, without a word, she began to kiss the nude body all over, avidly. In the light of the candle stub which she had set down on a chest, this woman's face was ageless, and not very different from that of the servant who, nearly forty years before, had taught him how to make love. He did not restrain her from lying down beside him, heavily, under the covers. This big creature was comparable to the bread and ale of which one partakes with indifference, feeling neither distaste nor delight. When he awoke she was already belowstairs, at her work as a servant again. Throughout the whole day she did not raise her eyes to him, but she served him abundantly at mealtime, with a kind of coarse solicitude. When night came he bolted his door, and could hear the servant's heavy footsteps going away after she had silently tried the latch. The next day she conducted herself no differently toward him than she had done the day before; it seemed that she had installed him once and for all among the objects which peopled her existence, like the furniture and the utensils of the doctor's house. But by oversight, more than a week later on, he forgot to bolt his door: she entered with a foolish smile, gathering her skirts up high to exhibit her heavy limbs. The temptation was so grotesque as to prevail upon his senses. Never had he felt thus the brute power of sheer flesh independently of the person, the face, the body's features, and even of his own preferences in matters of love. This woman who panted beside him on his pillow was a Lemure, a Lamia, one of those nightmarish female forms that one sees on the capitals of church columns, a being hardly capable, it seemed, of human speech. At the height of her pleasure, however, a string of obscenities in Flemish, which he had had no occasion to hear or to use since his schoolboy days, escaped from those thick lips like so many bubbles; thereupon he stopped her mouth with the back of his hand. But the following morning repulsion took over: he was angry with himself for having had anything to do with this creature, just as one is provoked with oneself for having consented to sleep in a doubtful bed of some inn. From this time on he did not forget to close himself in each night.

He had planned to stay with Jan Myers only long enough to allow for subsiding of the storm which the seizure and destruction of his book had caused. But it sometimes seemed to him that he would remain in Bruges to the end of his days, whether because this city was a trap dug for him at the end of his travels, or because a kind of inertia was keeping him from departing. Jan Myers, scarcely able to walk, turned over to him the few patients that he still treated; this slender practice was not of a nature to awaken the envy of other physicians of the city, as had been the case in Basel, where Zeno had capped off the general irritation of his compeers against him as a foreign doctor by publicly teaching his art before a chosen circle of students. In Bruges his contacts with his colleagues were limited to a very few consultations, during which the Sieur Theus deferred politely to the opinion of the oldest or the best known among them; or he confined himself to brief exchanges about the weather, or about some local incident.

Conversations with the patients turned, of course, on the subject of the patients themselves. Many of these had never heard anything about a Zeno; for others he was only a vague item of hearsay among the varied echoes of their past. The philosopher who had once devoted a short work to the substance and properties of Time could now observe that its sands were quickly engulfing all memory of men. Those thirty-five years could have been half a century. Rules and practices which were new and much debated when he was studying in Louvain were thought today to have existed always. Events which had shaken the world at that time were no longer mentioned. People who had died only twenty years ago were confused already with those of an earlier generation.

Some few recalled the opulence of old Justus Ligre, but they disagreed as to whether he had had one, or two, sons. There had also been a nephew, they thought, or a bastard of Henry Justus, who had turned out badly. The banker's father was said to have been High Treasurer of Flanders, like his son, or Secretary General in the Regent's Council, like Philibert Ligre today. The Ligre house in Bruges, long unoccupied, had its ground floor rented currently to artisans. Zeno revisited the factory which was once Colas Gheel's domain; it was now a cordage factory. Not a soul among the workers remembered that man who, though early besotted by beer, had been in his way a leader and a prince before the time of the mutinies at Oudenove and the hanging of his minion. Canon Bartholomew Campanus was still living, but he seldom went out, overwhelmed as he was by infirmities which come with age, and luckily Jan Myers had never been summoned to treat him. Nevertheless, Zeno took the precaution of avoiding the church of Saint Donatian, where his old master still attended offices, seated in his place in one of the choir stalls.

As a precaution, also, the physician had taken his diploma from Montpellier, which bore his real name, and locked it in a casket of Jan Myers's, keeping with him only a parchment which he had formerly purchased for use in case of need from the widow of an obscure German doctor named Gott. The better to cover his tracks, he had given that name the Greco-Latin form of *Theus*. With Myers's help, he had invented for himself around this unknown personage one of those confused but very ordinary biographies which have the merit of resembling dwellings with more than one means by which to enter or to leave. For more semblance of authenticity he added a few incidents from his own life, carefully chosen so as not to interest or surprise anyone, and the investigation of which, if it should take place, would not lead very far.

Thus, Dr. Sebastian Theus was born at Zutphen in the bishopric of Utrecht, the natural son of a woman of the region and of a physician from Bourg-en-Bresse who was employed in the household of Madame Marguerite of Austria. Educated in Cleves at the expense of a protector who chose to remain anonymous, he had first thought of entering an Augustinian monastery in that city, but his leaning toward his father's profession had prevailed; he had studied at the University of Ingolstadt, and then at Strasbourg, and had practiced for some time in the latter city. An ambassador from

Savoy had brought him in his suite to Paris and to Lyons, so as a result he had seen something of France and the Court. On returning to Imperial territory, he had intended to go back to settle in Zutphen, where his good mother was still living, but, although he said nothing about it, he had doubtless suffered at the hands of folk of the so-called Reformed religion who now abounded there. It is then that he had accepted, as a means of livelihood, this post of substitute which Jan Myers had offered him (Myers had previously known his father in Mechlin). He went as far, also, as to admit to having been a surgeon in the army of the Catholic King of Poland, but he antedated that engagement by a good ten years. And last, he was a widower, having married the daughter of a doctor in Strasbourg.

These fictions, to which in any case he would resort only if indiscreet questions were posed, highly amused old Jan. But the philosopher sometimes felt that the insignificant mask of Dr. Theus was becoming fixed to his face; that imaginary life could well have been his own. Someone asked him one day if he had not met a certain Zeno in the course of his travels. It was almost without lying that he answered "No."

Little by little, from the gray background of these monotonous days, certain elements began to stand out in relief, and some landmarks could be defined. Each evening at supper Jan Myers would go into detail about the history of the households which Zeno had visited that morning, narrating a comic or tragic anecdote, commonplace enough in itself, but revealing as many cabals in this slumbering city as there were in the Grand Seraglio, and as much debauchery as in a brothel of Venice. Different temperaments and characters would emerge from these dully uniform lives of stockholders or church-wardens; groups would become established, formed as they were everywhere by the same appetite for money or for intrigue, the same devotion to the same Saint, the same ills or the same vices. The suspicions of the fathers, the pranks of the children, the harsh words between aged man and wife were no different from what he had seen in the Vasa family or in princely palaces in Italy; but the small size of the stakes here in Bruges gave enormous proportions, by contrast, to the passions involved. These lives, so bound and limited, made the philosopher realize the value of an unattached existence. The opinions, like the temperaments, fell rapidly into pre-established categories. One could surmise which people would attribute all the evils of the time to the libertines or to adherents of the Reformation, and would find that Madame the Governess was always right. Zeno could have finished their discourses for them, or could have invented in their place their lies about the Italian disease contracted in their youth, and the evasion, or the slight, offended start when he would ask on behalf of Jan Myers for payment of forgotten fees. He could wager, to a certainty, what would come from each familiar mold.

The only place in town where it seemed to him that a free mind shed its light was, paradoxically, the cell of the Prior of the Cordeliers. Zeno had continued to frequent this man as a friend, and next, rather soon, as his physician. These visits were rare, neither one of them having much time to spare. Zeno chose the Prior as his confessor when it seemed to him needful to have one; the monk was little given to pious homilies, and his exquisite French was restful to the ear after the sound of the thick Flemish speech. Their conversation touched on everything, save for matters of belief; but public affairs, above all, were what interested this man of prayer. He was close to a few of the noblemen who were trying to struggle against foreign tyranny, approving their stand though at the same time fearing a bloodbath for the Belgian nation. When Zeno reported these forebodings to Jan Myers, the old man merely shrugged his shoulders, saying that the humble had always been shorn while the mighty made off with the wool. But still it was vexatious, he added, for the Spaniard to speak of placing a further tax upon foodstuffs, and a poll tax of one percent on revenue.

§

Sebastian Theus usually returned late to the house on Wood-market Wharf, for he preferred the damp air of the streets and long walks outside the city walls, along the grayed fields, to the overheated parlor. One particular evening, coming back in the season when night fell early, he noticed as he crossed the antechamber that Catherine was busily examining sheets in the cupboard placed under the stairs. She did not stop to light his way, as she would ordinarily do, managing furtively each time, at the same turn in the corridor, to brush the fold of his cloak. In the kitchen the fire on the hearth had died out. Zeno had to feel his way there in order to light a candle. On the table of the adjoining room the body of old Jan Myers, still warm, was neatly extended. Catherine entered with the sheet which she had chosen for a shroud.

"Master died of a stroke," she said.

She looked like one of those women, veiled in black, who come to wash the dead in the homes of Constantinople, and whom he had seen at their work during the time that he served the Sultan. The death of the old physician was not wholly a surprise to him. Jan himself had expected his gout to mount to his heart. A few weeks before, he had made a will in the presence of the parish notary, couching it in the usual pious formulas and leaving his property to Sebastian Theus, with a room for Catherine high under the eaves which she might have to the end of her days. The philosopher looked more closely at the convulsed and swollen face of the dead man; an unusual odor, and a brown stain at the corner of the lips, aroused his suspicions. He went up to his own room and delved into his chest, to find that a thin glass phial there had lost a finger's breadth of its contents. Zeno recalled that one evening he had shown the old man this mixture of animal and vegetable poisons procured in a laboratory in Venice. A faint sound made him turn around: Catherine was watching him, standing on the doorstep, as she had doubtless spied upon him through the slot of her kitchen door when he had let her master see those few objects brought back from his journeys. He seized her by the arm and she fell to her knees, pouring forth a confused torrent of words and tears.

"*Voor u heb ik het gedaan!* I did it for you," she repeated between sobs.

He pushed her away roughly, and went down again to keep watch over the dead man. In his way, old Jan Myers had known how to enjoy life; his ailments were not so painful but that he could have indulged in his padded existence for a few months more, a year, perhaps, or two years, to put it at the best. This inane crime was depriving him, unreasonably, of his modest pleasure in belonging still to this world. The old man had never been other than kind to him; Zeno was seized with a bitter pity for the victim of this atrocity, and with rage, though in vain, against the poisoner, a rage which doubtless the dead man himself would not have felt to such a degree. Jan Myers had always employed his not inconsiderable wit and ingenuity to mock the world's follies; this wanton of a servant rushing to enrich a man who had no interest in her would have provided him matter for a good tale, had he lived. As he now was, lying peacefully on that table, he seemed a hundred leagues distant from his own mishap; in any case, the former barber-surgeon had always ridiculed those who suppose that thinking or suffering continues when the power to walk or to digest is gone.

§

The old man was buried in the church of his parish, Saint Jacobus. On returning from the obsequies Zeno noticed that Catherine had moved his clothes and his doctor's chest into the master's chamber; she had made the fire there, and had carefully prepared the large bed. Without a word he carried his possessions back into the small room which he had occupied from the time of his arrival. As soon as he entered into possession of his inheritance, he surrendered it, by an act before a notary, in favor of the old hospice of Saint Cosmus, on Long Street, which adjoined the monastery of the Cordeliers. Such pious donations were becoming rare in this city, where the great fortunes of earlier days no longer abounded, so Dr. Theus's generosity was admired, as he had surmised that it would be. Jan Myers's home would become from that time on an asylum for the aged and enfeebled; Catherine would live there as servant to the house. The uninvested money that was left over would be used to repair a part of the buildings of Saint Cosmus; the ancient hospice was a dependency of the order of the Cordeliers, and the Prior entrusted Zeno with the establishment, in such rooms as were still habitable, of a dispensary for the poor of the quarter, and for the peasants who came in great numbers to the city on market days. Two monks were delegated to help in the small pharmacy. This new post, like his substitute practice for Jan, was too modest to attract the jealousy of his colleagues; for the moment the niche which he had chosen was secure. Jan Myers's old mule was moved into the stable at Saint Cosmus, where the gardener of the monastery saw to his care. A bed was made up for Zeno in an upper room of the hospice, and he also transported there some of the books of the old barber-surgeon; his meals were brought in to him from the refectory.

The winter was passed in these repairs and rearrangements; Zeno persuaded the Prior to let him install a steam bath in German style, and submitted to him some notes on the treatment by hot vapor of rheumatic patients and pox victims. His knowledge of mechanics helped him in laying the heat pipes, and in planning the construction of an economical stove. On Woolmarket Street a blacksmith had set up shop in the former stables of the Ligre household; Zeno would go there each evening to file, hammer, rivet, or solder in perpetual consultation with the master ferrier and his helpers.

The youths of the quarter who gathered there to pass the time marveled at the skill of his thin hands. It was during this uneventful period that he was recognized for the first time. He was alone in the dispensary, as always at evening, after the two monks finished their work; it was a market day, and the usual procession of poor folk had continued all afternoon from the hour of nones. Someone more knocked at the door: it was an old woman who came each Saturday to sell her butter in town, and who wanted a remedy for her sciatica. Zeno looked on the shelf for a stone jar which was filled with a strong revulsive. He came close to her to explain how to use it. Suddenly he saw in her pale-blue eyes an expression of joyous astonishment which made him, in his turn, recognize her. This woman had worked in the kitchens of the Ligre household at a time when he was still a child. Greete (her name came back to him now) was married to the valet who had brought him home after he first ran away. He remembered that she had been kind to him when he had wandered around among her kettles and porringers; she had let him take pieces from the hot bread on the table, and from the unbaked pastry ready for the oven. She was about to exclaim aloud when he placed a finger on his lips. The old woman seemed to understand; she had a son who was a carter, and who, on occasion, had done some smuggling into France and back; her poor old husband, now practically paralyzed, had had trouble with the lord of the manor over a few sacks of apples stolen from the orchard adjacent to their farm. She knew that it was sometimes wise to be in hiding, even when one is rich and a nobleman (social categories in which she still placed Zeno). She kept silent, but in departing she kissed his hand.

The incident should have disturbed him in proving to him that he daily risked being recognized in the same way; but, on the contrary, he experienced a feeling of pleasure from it which was new to him and wholly unaccountable. To be sure, he reasoned that he now knew of a small farm near the city walls, in the direction of the village of Saint Peter of the Dyke, where he could pass a night in case of danger, and a carter whose horse and wagon could be of use; but these observations were only pretexts which he made to account for that feeling. That child to whom he no longer gave a thought, that immature being whom it was rational, and yet in a sense absurd, to identify with himself, was remembered enough by someone else to have been recognized in Zeno the man, and the concept of his own existence was thereby fortified, as it were. Between himself and a human creature a link had been formed, however slight, which was not of the intellect, as in his relations with the Prior, nor, as in the case of the few sensuous connections which he still allowed himself, of the flesh. Greete returned almost every week to have the ailments of her aged body attended to, but she rarely missed the chance of bringing a present, perhaps some butter wrapped in a cabbage leaf, a piece of shortbread which she had made, or a handful of chestnuts. She would watch him while he ate, her old eyes merry with enjoyment. The two of them shared the intimacy of a carefully guarded secret.

THE ABYSS

LITTLE BY little, certain almost imperceptible changes began to take place in Zeno, the result of new habits which he had acquired, much as a man who daily partakes of one certain food is finally changed by it in his substance and even in his form, growing stout or thin and drawing strength from these viands, or else, in absorbing them, contracting ills unknown to him before. But as soon as he paused to examine the difference between his present and his past life, the contrast appeared negligible, for he was practicing medicine, as he had always done, and it hardly mattered that his patients now were paupers rather than princes. He had chosen the name of Sebastian Theus somewhat arbitrarily, but even his right to the name of Zeno was not wholly clear. *Non habet nomen proprium:* he was one of those men who are perpetually surprised at being in possession of a name, just as one marvels, in passing before a mirror, at possessing a face, and that it should be precisely the face that it is.

His existence was clandestine, and was subject to certain other constraints, but it had always been so. He never spoke of the thoughts which counted most for him, for he had long known that he who reveals himself by mere talk is only a fool; it is simpler to let others make use of their mouths to emit sounds. His rare bursts of discourse had never been more than the occasional dissipation of a nature essentially chaste. He lived almost immured in his hospice at Saint Cosmus, the prisoner of a city, and of a quarter within that city, and, within that quarter, of a half dozen rooms overlooking, on one side, the kitchen garden and outbuildings of a monastery; on the other, a blank wall. His country walks (now fewer than before) in search of botanical specimens always led him past the same plowed fields and the same towpaths, along the same strips of woodland and the edge of the same dunes; he would smile somewhat bitterly at this round, the passing and repassing of an insect circling incomprehensibly over one spot of earth. But he reflected that such a contraction of one's surroundings, and an almost mechanical repetition of the same motions, occurs each time that one harnesses one's faculties to accomplish any single specific and worthwhile task.

His sedentary life weighed on him like a sentence of imprisonment which, as a precaution, he might have imposed upon himself. But the sentence was revocable: many times already, and under other skies, he had installed himself thus temporarily or, as he thought, for good, like a man who has rights of citizenship both everywhere and nowhere; there was nothing to prove that he would not resume tomorrow the wandering life which had been his previous lot, and his choice. And nevertheless, his destiny moved on: though he did not know it, a gradual change was at work within him. Like a man swimming against the current, and in the dark of night, he had no landmark whereby to calculate exactly how far or in what direction he was being carried.

Yet at first, on finding his way again in the network of alleys in Bruges, he had supposed that this halt, so removed from the highroads of knowledge and ambition, might afford him some repose after thirty-five years of turmoil. He had expected to feel something of that timid security which an animal has in the lair where it has chosen to live, reassured by the very narrowness and obscurity. But he was mistaken. This immobile existence was seething, as it were, in place; a sense of almost terrifying activity thundered within him like a subterranean river. The anguish which oppressed him was other than that of a philosopher persecuted for his books. Similarly, time, which he had imagined would hang heavy as lead upon his hands, sped and subdivided, like particles of mercury. The hours, the days, the months all had ceased to accord with the indications of the clocks, or even with the movements of the stars. It seemed to him sometimes that he had remained throughout his whole life in Bruges, but at other times that he had arrived there only the day before.

Places, too, seemed to move, and distances faded as did the days. This butcher, that hawking peddler could as well have been in Avignon, or Vadstena; that horse they were whipping he had seen fall in Adrianople, and that drunken fellow had begun his flood of oaths and vomit at Montpellier. The infant mewling there in his nurse's arms was surely born in Bologna twenty-five years earlier; as for the Sunday Mass, which he never failed to attend, he had heard its introit in a church of Cracow five winters ago.

He seldom thought of the incidents of his past life; they had already vanished, like dreams. Sometimes, for no apparent reason, he would call to mind that pregnant woman, in a town of Languedoc, for whom he had consented to perform an abortion, in spite of his Hippocratic oath, in order to spare her an ignominious death when her jealous husband should return. Or again, he might recall the grimace of His Swedish Majesty as he swallowed a potion, or would suddenly remember his servant Aleï helping their mule to ford a river, between Ulm and Constance; or he would wonder about his cousin Henry Maximilian, who perhaps was dead by this time.

A lane closely bordered with overhanging trees, where the puddles never dried, would remind him that a certain Perrotin had lain in wait for him, in the rain, at the edge of a lonely road the day after a quarrel. The cause of dispute was no longer clear, but he could reconstruct the scene of two bodies gripped together in the mud, a bright blade falling to the ground, and Perrotin, stabbed by his own knife, letting go, having become himself mud and earth. This old affair had ceased to matter, nor would it have been of more consequence had the soft, warm corpse been that of a clerk twenty years of age.

This Zeno who walked so rapidly on the wet, slippery paving stones of Bruges could feel passing through him (like the wind from the sea passing through his worn clothes), the stream of those thousands of beings who had already lived on this point of the sphere, or would be here in days to come, up to the time of that catastrophe that we call the end of the world; wholly without seeing it, these phantoms passed through the body of this man who had not yet existed during their lifetime, or would no longer exist when they should come into being. To this legion of larvae were endlessly added the nameless folk whom he had encountered in the street perhaps only a moment before, perceived there at a glance, and then straightway discarded into that formless mass of what is past. Time, place, and substance were losing those attributes which for us are their boundaries: form had ceased to be more than the torn bark of substance; substance dripped away into a void which was not its true counterpart; time and eternity were but one and the same, like dark water entering a vast expanse of dark water. Zeno sank into these visions much as a Christian does in his meditation upon God.

Ideas, too, seemed to drift and merge. The act of thinking interested him now more than did the doubtful products of thought itself. He tried to observe himself while engaged in thinking, just as with his finger on his wrist he might have counted the pulsations of his radial artery, or, beneath his ribs, the coming and going of his breath. All his life long he had been amazed at the way ideas have of agglomerating, divorced from feeling, like crystals in strange, meaningless formations; and of growing like tumors, devouring the flesh that conceives them; or of assuming certain human lineaments, but in monstrous wise, like those inert masses to which some women give birth, and which are, after all, only the incoherent dreams of matter. He found that a goodly number of the mind's productions are no more than such deformed mooncalves. Other conceptions, less impure and more precise, forged as if by a master workman, make for illusion when viewed from afar; though commanding our admiration for their parallels and their angles, like intricate iron grills, they are nevertheless only bars behind which the understanding imprisons itself, abstract fetters already eaten into by the rust of false premises.

There were moments when he trembled, as if on the verge of a transmutation: some particle of gold appeared to be born within the crucible of the human brain; yet the result was but an equivalence, as in those fraudulent experiments wherein Court alchemists try to prove to their royal clients that they have found something, although the gold at the base of the alembic proves to be only that of an ordinary ducat, long passed from hand to hand, and put there by the charlatan before the heating began. He knew now that ideas die, like men; in the course of half a century he had witnessed the decline of several generations of notions, all falling into dust.

Another, more fluid metaphor for the world of thought gradually suggested itself to him, derived from his former voyages at sea. A philosopher who was trying to consider human understanding in all its aspects would behold beneath him a mass molded in calculable curves, streaked by currents which could be charted, and deeply furrowed by the pressure of winds and the heavy, inert weight of water. It seemed to him that the shapes which the mind assumes are like those great forms, born of undifferentiated water, which assail or replace each other on the surface of the deep; each concept collapses, eventually, to merge with its very opposite, like two waves breaking against each other only to subside into the same single line of white foam. Zeno watched this disordered flood go by, sweeping with it, like so much wreckage, the few palpable verities of which we had felt assured.

At times it seemed to him that under that confused flow he caught sight of some unmoving substance, one that might stand in relation to ideas as ideas do to the words with which they are expressed. But what was there to prove that this substratum is the final layer, or that its apparent fixity does not conceal motion too rapid for human comprehension? Since he had ceased to speak his thoughts aloud, or to consign them to booksellers' stalls, such deprivation had induced a deeper descent than ever inside himself in search of pure concepts. Now, for the sake of a more profound study, he temporarily relinquished even the concepts, ceasing to think (just as for a moment one holds one's breath), the better to hear the noise of wheels revolving so fast that we do not perceive that they turn.

§

From the realm of the mind he came back to that denser world of substance which is contained within the limits of form. Enclosed in his room, he no longer spent his waking hours trying to acquire a more just view of relations between things, but instead in meditation, wholly unformulated, on the nature of things. Thus he rectified that error of our intellect which is to apprehend objects only in order to make use of them, or, conversely, to reject them without sufficiently penetrating into the specific substance of which they are made. Water, for example, had meant to him something to quench thirst, and a liquid for washing; it was one constituent part of a universe created by that Christian Demiurge of whom Canon Campanus used to discourse to him, speaking of the Spirit floating on the waters; it was likewise the essential element for Archimedes in hydraulics and for Thales in physics; for the ancient alchemists it symbolized a downward-moving force. As engineer he had calculated its displacements, and as physician had measured it out in his doses; as alchemist he had waited until its drops should form again in the tube of the alembic.

Now, renouncing for a time all methods of observation which distinguish and particularize from without, and pursuing the internal vision of the hermetic philosophers, he allowed the all-prevailing water to invade the room like a flood tide. The chest and stool were set floating; the walls caved in under its pressure. He yielded to this flow which fits into all forms but refuses to be compressed within them; he passed through those changes in condition by which a sheet of water becomes mist and rain turns to snow; he took on the temporary immobility of ice, and after that the trickle of the transparent droplet inexplicably aslant on the windowpane, fluid challenge to all calculation of its course. He forwent the sensations of warmth and cold inherent to the body, and the water bore him along, a corpse, as indifferently as it would have swept with it a mass of seaweed.

Restored to his flesh, he contemplated the aqueous element present there, too: urine in the bladder, saliva within the lips, and water in the liquid of the blood. Then coming back to the element of which he had always felt himself a part, he turned his meditation toward fire to feel that blessed and tempered heat which we share with the four-footed beasts and birds of the sky. He thought of the devouring fire of fevers which he had tried, often in vain, to extinguish. He noted the avid leap upward of newborn flame, and then the red joy of a burning heap, and finally its end in black ashes.

Daring to go still further in his experiment, he united himself wholly with that implacable ardor, destroyer of all that it touches; he recalled fires of executions, such as he had seen on the occasion of an Act of Faith (so called) in a small town of Leon where four Jews had perished, accused of having pretended to embrace the Christian religion while continuing, even so, to perform the rites handed down to them from their forefathers; there was also a heretic burned with them, a man who denied the efficacy of the sacraments. Zeno reproduced for himself the experience of that pain too piercing for human language to describe; he became that very man whose nostrils were filled with the odor of his own flesh burning, and coughed in the surrounding smoke (which was not to be dissipated during his lifetime). He saw a blackened leg rise up straight, its joints licked by the flames, like a branch twisting on a mighty hearth fire; but at the same time he tried to reflect that the fire and the wood, themselves, were innocent. He remembered the day following an Act of Faith celebrated at Astorga, when he had walked with the old monk Don Blas de Vela, the alchemist, over that calcined ground which had reminded him of the charcoal burners; the learned Jacobin had bent down to collect with care from among the dead coals certain small, light bones, whitened by the fire; he was searching among these for the *luz* of Hebraic tradition, that particular bone which withstands flame, and serves as seed for resurrection of the flesh. In former times Zeno had smiled at those cabalic superstitions, but did so no longer. In a sweat of anguish, he would raise his head and, if the night were sufficiently clear, would look through the window's small panes to consider, with affectionate detachment, that inaccessible fire of the stars.

§

Whatever he did, his meditation brought him back to the body, his principal subject of study. He knew that his equipment as a physician was composed equally of manual skill and empirical remedies, the latter supplemented by findings which also grew out of experimentation and which led, in their turn, to theoretical, and always tentative, conclusions; an ounce of reasoned observation, he had learned, was worth more in these matters than a ton of vague hypotheses. And still, after so many years spent in anatomizing the human machine, he was provoked with himself for having failed to venture more boldly, exploring that realm bounded by our skin in which we consider ourselves kings, but where we are only prisoners.

Years ago, in Istanbul, the dervish Darazi, with whom he had made friends, had passed on to him his methods for such exploration. Darazi had acquired these disciplines in Persia, in a monastery of a dissident sect (for Mohammed, like Christ, has his heretics); that kind of research which Zeno had begun in a garden court of Eyoub, where a spring bubbled forth, was resumed now by him in his garret in Bruges. It took him farther into the inner world of the body than had any of his experiments *in anima vili*, as the phrase would have it. Lying on his back and contracting his abdominal muscles, he would dilate the cage of the thorax where paces that creature, so quickly frightened, that we call a heart; attentively he would fill his lungs, employing his full knowledge to make of himself a mere sack of air, counterbalancing the weight of the heavens. Darazi had advised him to breathe in this way, to the very roots of his being. Together with the dervish, Zeno had also made the opposite experiment, that of the initial effects of slow strangulation.

He lifted his arm, and was astonished to find that the command was given, and received; he did not know what master, better served than he himself was, had countersigned the order; for truly some thousand times he had verified the fact that simply to will an act, even with all his mental power concentrated within him, could not make him so much as blink or frown, no more than a child's insistent order can make stones move. To accomplish such a motion, he would require the tacit acquiescence of some part of the self which is already in closer relation to the body's mysterious depths. Thus, meticulously, as one separates the fibers of a stem, he separated one from another these different forms of will.

As best he could, he controlled the complicated movements of his brain at its work, but did so only as a craftsman might cautiously touch a mechanism not of his own assembling (and any failure of which he would be unable to repair): Colas

Gheel knew more about how his looms operated than he himself did about the delicate movements, under his skull, of his mechanism for observing and weighing matters. His pulse, which he had so diligently studied, was wholly unaware of orders emanating from his intellectual faculty, but it would increase or falter when affected by fears or suffering which his mind would not stoop to acknowledge. The tool of sex would respond to the incitement of his hands, but this act deliberately undertaken would throw him momentarily into a state where his will was no longer in control. In the same way, once or twice in his life, he had scandalously, and in spite of himself, burst into a flood of tears. His bowels, far greater alchemist than he had ever been, regularly performed the transmutation of corpses, those of beasts and of plants, into living matter, separating the useful from the dross without help from him. *Ignis inferioris Naturae:* those spirals of brown mud, precisely coiled and still steaming from the decocting process which they have undergone in their mold, this ammoniac and nitric fluid passed into a clay pot, were the visible and fetid proof of work completed in laboratories where we do not intervene. It seemed to Zeno that the disgust of fastidious persons at this refuse, and the obscene laughter of the ignorant, were due less to the fact that these objects offend our senses than to our horror in the presence of the mysterious and ineluctable routines of our bodies.

Probing more deeply into this total night within us, he turned his scrutiny upon the fixed armature of bones hidden under the flesh, which would endure longer than he, and would remain as the only witnesses, after a few centuries, to attest to the fact that he had ever lived. He withdrew into them, allowing himself to be reabsorbed into their mineral substance, where human passions and emotions could not enter. Then drawing the transitory flesh back over himself again like a curtain, he tried to consider himself as a reunited whole, extended upon the bed's coarse sheet: sometimes he would voluntarily distend the picture which he was constructing for himself of this island of life, his domain, this continent hardly explored as yet, of which his feet represented the antipole; sometimes, on the contrary, the process was one of reducing himself to a mere point in a vast universe. Employing certain prescriptions of Darazi, he would try to make his consciousness pass from his brain to other regions of his body, somewhat as a capital of a realm may be transposed to a distant province. In all this he was attempting to cast a few gleams of light here and there into these dark internal galleries.

Formerly, together with Jan Myers, he had made sport of the pious folk who regarded the human machine as patent proof of a Creator-God; but now the atheists' respect for this chance masterpiece which man's nature is, in their eyes, seemed to him equally a butt for derision. For this body, so rich in powers still obscure to us, is defective, too; he had even dreamed, in his more audacious moments, of contriving an automaton which might be less rudimentary than we men are. Turning over and over, in his mind's eye, the pentagon of our five senses, Zeno had ventured to postulate other, more complex constructions, in which the universe would be more perfectly reflected. The list of those nine doors of perception opening into the body's dark wall, which Darazi used to recite to him (bending down one after the other the end joints of his tawny fingers), had at first appeared to him a clumsy attempt at classification by a semibarbarous anatomist; but it had served to draw his attention to the precariousness of the channels on which we depend for apprehending everything we know, and for existing. Our limitations are such that it would suffice merely to stop up two of these narrow openings to close off the world of sounds, and two other entrances to establish total darkness. If a gag is pressed against three of these openings, three so near each other that the palm of a hand can readily cover them, then everything is over with for this creature whose life depends upon his power to breathe. This cumbersome envelope of flesh which he had to wash, feed, and water, heat at the fireplace or beneath the pelt of some slaughtered beast, and put to sleep at night like a child or like a helpless old man, was hostage to the whole of nature, and even more hostage to his fellow men. It was by this flesh and this skin that he would possibly be exposed to the anguish of torture; the weakening of this mechanism one day would keep him from concluding correctly the idea which he might have begun to sketch.

If at times he mistrusted the workings of his mind (which for convenience he isolated from the rest of his substance), it was chiefly because that weakling was dependent upon the body for service. He was tired of this compound of unstable fire and heavy clay. *Exitus rationalis:* a temptation as compelling as carnal desire lay before him; disgust, or even vanity, perhaps, urged him toward the performance of that act which would end all. But he shook his head gravely in negation, as if in the presence of a patient who asks too soon for a certain remedy or for food. There would always be time either to perish along with this heavy, corporeal framework, or to continue without it in some insubstantial and unforeseeable form of life, though not necessarily in a state more advantageous than this life that we lead in the flesh.

§

Rigorously, and almost against his will, this voyager at the end of a stage of more than fifty years' duration now for the first time obliged himself to retrace, in his mind, the roads which he had traveled, distinguishing what had been fortuitous from what was deliberate or necessary, and likewise trying to sort out the little that seemed to come from himself, and the part which he shared in common with all men. Nothing was exactly like (or exactly opposite to) what he had at first wished, or had imagined in advance. His errors in calculation arose sometimes from the effect of an element which he had not even guessed was present, and sometimes from a mistake in his estimate of time; for that entity revealed itself as both more retractile and more extensible than the clocks would indicate.

At the age of twenty he had thought himself freed of those routines and prejudices which paralyze our actions and put blinders on our understanding; but his life had been passed thereafter in acquiring bit by bit that very liberty of which he had supposed himself promptly possessed in its entirety. For no one is free so long as he has desires, wants, or fears, or even, perhaps, so long as he lives. As physician, alchemist, engineer, astrologer, he had worn the livery of his time, whether willing or no, and in so doing had allowed the world in which he moved to incline his faculty of judgment in certain directions. Thus, because of his hatred of lies, but also because of an element of acridity in his disposition, he had launched upon quarrels over matters of opinion where some inane assertion is answered by an equally fatuous negation. In spite of being on his guard in his evaluations, he had caught himself judging the crimes of republics and princes more odious than he otherwise would have done, and their superstitions more absurd, if they posed a threat to his life or if they burned his books; and conversely, he had sometimes been guilty of crediting a dunce with too great merit (whether he were mitered, crowned, or wearing the tiara), if the favor of such a one would have permitted him to test his ideas in practice. The desire to arrange, or to modify and regulate, at least one segment of the nature of things had drawn him into the retinues of men of power, but he had ended only by building here and there what proved to be castles of sand, or by pursuing a mirage.

He took count of his past illusions. In the Sultan's palace, his friendship with the powerful but ill-fated Ibrahim, Grand Vizier to His Highness, had led him to hope that he might carry out his plan for draining and cleaning the marshes surrounding Adrianople; he had set his heart upon a rational reform of the hospital for the Janizaries; through his efforts, precious manuscripts of Greek physicians and astronomers collected long ago by Arab scholars were being bought up whenever possible, some of them containing, midst much worthless stuff, a truth to be recaptured. And in particular there had been a certain text of Dioscorides that he burned to procure, containing fragments of more ancient writings, from Crateüas; it happened to belong to the Jew Hamon, the physician who was his colleague in the service of the Sultan . . . But Ibrahim's tragic fall had swept all those projects away with him, and the disgust which this reversal inspired in Zeno, after so many other vicissitudes, obliterated even the memory of those abortive endeavors.

In Basel he had merely shrugged when the cowardly burghers there had finally refused him a chair at the University; they were frightened by rumors that reported him to be a sodomite and a sorcerer. (He had been each of these things at one time or another, but names bear no relation to facts; they stand only for what the herd imagines.) Nevertheless, for a long time thereafter he felt his gall rising at the very mention of those robed fools.

He had bitterly regretted arriving too late in Augsburg to obtain from the Fuggers that post of physician in the mines which would have enabled him to observe the maladies of laborers underground, submitted as they are to the potent metallic influences of Mercury and of Saturn; for he had envisaged possibilities of chemical combinations and cures as yet unknown. Of course, he could clearly see that all these ambitious projects had been useful in transporting his mind, so to speak, from one place to another; it is better not to draw near too soon to the immobility of things eternal. Viewed from a distance, however, this agitated existence seemed no more than a storm of sand.

It was the same for the complicated domain of sensual pleasures. Those which he had preferred were the most secret and most dangerous, in Christian lands, at least, and at the time when he happened to have been born. Possibly he had sought them out only because they were prohibited, and thus had necessarily to be concealed, making for violent sundering of custom, and a plunge into that seething realm which lies beneath the visible and licit world. Or perhaps this inclination was attributable to tastes as simple but as inexplicable as those which we have for one fruit rather than for another: it mattered little to him what the reason was. The essential was that his excesses, like his ambitions, had, in sum, been rare and brief, as if it had been his nature to exhaust rapidly whatever the passions could teach or give.

This strange magma which preachers define by the not ill-chosen name of lust (since it would seem to be a matter of the luxuriance of the flesh expending its force) defies examination because of the variety of substances which compose it, and which in their turn break down into other components, themselves complex. Love is one part of the mixture, though less often, perhaps, than is admitted; but the concept of love is itself far from simple. This so-called lower world connects with what is most subtle in human nature. Just as even the most vulgar ambition is still an effort of the mind striving to bring order to things or to improve them, the flesh in its audacity takes upon itself the mind's capacity for curiosity, and indulges in fantasies, as the mind likes to do; the wine of lust derives its strength from the soul's sap, as well as from that of the flesh.

As for desire for a young body, he had only too often associated it with the unattainable project of shaping for himself the perfect disciple. Other feelings were also mixed therein, such as all men avowedly experience. Fray Juan at Leon and François Rondelet at Montpellier had been brothers whom he had lost while they were still young; for his servant Aleï, and later for Gerhart at Lübeck, he had felt the solicitude of a father for his sons. Such consuming passions had seemed to him then an inalienable part of his liberty as a man, but now it was wholly without them that he felt himself free.

The same reflections applied to the few women with whom

he had had physical intimacy. He had little interest in seeking past reasons for those brief attachments, though they were possibly of more significance than the others because he had formed them less spontaneously. Was it a matter of sudden desire in presence of particular lineaments in a body; or was it need for that profound repose which the female of creatures sometimes dispenses? Or was it by some base conformity to custom? . . . Was it even because of something more secret than an affection or a vice, a vague effort to try out the effect of hermetic teachings about that perfect pair who together constitute the hermaphrodite of ancient times? . . . Why not say instead that, at the time, chance simply came in the form of a woman?

Thirty years back, in Algiers, out of compassion for her youth and desolation, he had purchased a girl of good Spanish stock who had been abducted by pirates from a shore near Valencia; he intended to send her back to Spain as soon as he could do so. But in his small house on the Barbary coast an intimacy was established between them which strongly resembled that of marriage. It was the only time that he had had to do with a virgin, and he retained less the memory of a conquest in their first intercourse than that of a creature whom he had to tend and reassure. For several weeks this moody beauty was the companion of his bed and board, and she rendered him gratitude such as is offered only to a protecting Saint. It was without regret that he confided her to a French priest who was about to embark for Port-Vendres with a small group of captives of both sexes; all were being returned to their families in their own land. The modest sum of money with which he had provided her would doubtless have permitted her to regain her native Gandía . . .

Later on, outside the walls of Buda, during the siege, he had been allotted as his share of booty a hardy young Hungarian girl. He had accepted her rather than singularize himself further in an army camp where his name and appearance already set him apart, and where he had to endure the inferiority of being a Christian (whatever he might think to himself of the Church's dogma); but he would not have dreamed of abusing the right of war with respect to her had she not been so avid to play her part as prey. Never, it seemed to him, had he tasted more fully of the fruits of Eve . . . Then, the morning that the city was taken, he had entered into it as one of the suites of dignitaries sent in by the Sultan. Shortly after his return to camp, he learned that an order had come, during his absence, to dispose of the slaves and portable possessions with which the army had become encumbered; corpses and bundles of stuffs were still floating on the surface of the vast river . . . For a long time thereafter, the thought of that ardent body, so fast grown cold, served to deter him from any carnal alliance. But finally he had gone back to those burning plains peopled with statues of salt, and visited by angels with long, curling locks.

§

In the North, the Lady of Froso had graciously received him as he was coming back from his long travel to the very rim of the polar regions. She was a woman whose every aspect had beauty: her tall stature, her fair complexion, her hands so skillful in binding wounds and in wiping away the sweat of fever; likewise the ease with which she walked on the forest's soft floor, calmly raising her rough woolen robe above her bare legs as she forded the streams. Versed in the art of Lapland's magic healers, she had taken him into their nomad huts at the edge of the marshes, where they treated their patients by fumigations and steam baths, to the accompaniment of chanting . . . On returning at evening to the small manor house in Froso, she had offered him rye bread and salt, berries and dried meat, all set forth upon a table spread with a white linen cloth; then she had joined him, with the tranquil familiarity of a spouse, in the great bed of the upper chamber. She was a widow, and she was expecting, when Saint Martin's Day should come, to choose for husband some freehold farmer of the district in order to keep the domain from reverting to the guardianship of her older brothers. Zeno could well have chosen to remain there, practicing his art in that province large as a kingdom, writing his treatises beside the stove, and mounting to the small tower at night to observe the stars . . . Nevertheless, after a week or ten days of the Northern summer (in truth, only one long day without dark), he was again on his way to Uppsala, to which the Court had removed at that time of year. He was hoping to keep his place in the monarch's favor, and to make of young Erik that royal disciple who is ever the last and loftiest dream of the sage.

§

But even the effort to evoke the memory of these persons tended to overstress their importance, and made too much of the carnal adventure. Aleï's visage did not recur to him oftener than did those of the wounded soldiers whom he had had to leave freezing on the roads of Poland, in the campaign there, and whom, for lack of means and time, he had not been able to try to save. The adulterous wife of the burgher of Pont-Saint-Esprit had been repugnant to him, with her rounded belly hidden under gathers of heavy lace, her hair tightly frizzed around drawn, sallow features, and her pitiable, crude lies. The coquettish glances which she darted at him, even in the depth of her anguish, had angered him; she knew no other way to subjugate a man. And nevertheless, he had risked for her sake his good name as a physician: his haste to act before the return of the jealous husband, the miserable remnant of human conjunction which had had to be buried under an olive tree in the garden, the payment in gold for silence on the part of the servants who had nursed Madame, and had washed the bloodstained sheets—the whole affair had created between him and that unfortunate woman an intimacy born of complicity; he had known her better than a lover knows a casual mistress.

The Lady of Froso had been for him benevolence itself, but

not more so than that baker's wife with the pitted face who had sustained him one evening in Salzburg when he had taken shelter under the arch of the doorway of her shop. It was after his flight from Innsbruck; he was exhausted and numb with cold, having pushed on without pause through a blizzard, and over mountain roads. Through the slot of the shutter of her shop window she had scrutinized this man sitting huddled outside on her small stone bench; doubtless taking him for a beggar, she had handed him out a loaf still warm from the oven. Then, cautiously, she had replaced the shutter hook. He was well aware that this mistrustful benefactress was equally capable, had circumstances suggested it, of throwing a brick at him, or a shovel; but, for all that, she stood for him as one evidence of human benignity.

In the final reckoning, friendship and aversion alike counted for as little as did carnal blandishments. Certain beings who had accompanied him, or had merely crossed his path, were fused now in the anonymity of distance, though without losing anything of their distinct particularities, like forest trees which, seen from afar, seem to merge one into another. In such perspective Canon Campanus was becoming one with Riemer the alchemist (whose doctrines, however, the Canon would have abhorred), and even one with the deceased Jan Myers, who, were he still alive, would also have been eighty years of age. Good Cousin Henry in his leathern jacket and Ibrahim in his long caftan, Prince Erik and Lorenzo the Tyrannicide, with whom he had formerly passed some memorable evenings in Lyons, were now only different faces of a same solid, which was man. The attributes of sex in these memories counted for less than might have been supposed, given the wisdom or follies of desire: the Lady of Froso could have been a male companion; Gerhart, on the other hand, had had the delicacy of a girl.

For those fellow creatures approached, and then quitted, in the course of existence, it was much as for the ghostly figures seen at night beneath our eyelids just before sleep comes, with its dreams; they never come back twice, but appear to us in almost terrifying specificity and intensity; sometimes they pass, and then flee with the speed of a meteor, but often they contract and disappear, as if folding in upon themselves under our scrutiny. Mathematical laws more complex and even less known than those of the mind, or of the senses, seemed to preside over the flitting of these phantoms.

But the contrary was also true. Events proved to be fixed points, even though he had left those of the past behind him, and a turn in the road ahead concealed events yet to be; it was the same for the people he had known. Memory was only a way of gazing from time to time on beings who now reside within us but who do not depend upon our power of recollection for their continued existence. In Leon, where Don Blas de Vela had bid him wear, for the time, the habit of a Jacobin novice (in order the more easily to make of him his assistant in alchemical research), a young monk of Zeno's same age, Fray Juan, had been his bedfellow in the crowded monastery; newcomers shared by twos and threes the bundles of hay and thin covers. Zeno had arrived worn down with a rasping cough, to live within walls where wind and snow came through. Fray Juan nursed his comrade as well as he could, stealing hot soup from the Brother who was cook. An *amor perfectissimus* endured for some time between these two youths; Zeno's blasphemies and negations had no effect upon that tender heart, filled as it was with the special devotion paid to the Beloved Apostle John. When Don Blas was driven off by his monks, who saw him as a dangerous cabalist and sorcerer, and was forced to descend the steep road of the monastery, howling maledictions the while, it was Fray Juan who, though neither his intimate nor his disciple, chose to accompany the old man in his downfall.

For Zeno, on the contrary, this monkish conspiracy provided the chance to break for good with a profession distasteful to him, and to leave Leon, therefore, going in secular attire to study elsewhere such sciences as are less imbedded in the stuff of dreams. Whether or not his master had kept to Judaic rites was of no concern to the young clerk, for whom, in accordance with the bold formula subversively handed down from generation to generation of young clerics, Christian, Jewish, and Mohammedan Law were together no other than the Three Impostures.

Don Blas must surely have died on the road, or in the prisons of some Inquisitorial court; it had taken thirty-five years for this former pupil of his to recognize the wisdom, inexplicable though it was, which lay hidden beneath the old man's madness. As for Fray Juan, if he was still alive somewhere on this earth, he would soon be sixty . . . The picture of the two wanderers had been deliberately obliterated from Zeno's mind, along with that of those few months passed in robe and cowl. And nevertheless, Fray Juan and Don Blas were still laboring their way down that stony path in the harsh winds of April, nor did he have to evoke the memory of them in order for them to be there. His fellow student, François Rondelet, walking over the heath and discussing with him projects for the future, coexisted with the François lying nude on the marble table of the demonstration room, at the university; and Dr. Rondelet, explaining the articulation of the arm, seemed to be addressing the dead youth himself, rather than the students, and to be discoursing across the years with a Zeno now grown older.

Unus ego et multi in me. These statues did not change; fixed in their posts, they had their places forever on some even plane which was, perhaps, eternity itself; time was no more than a connecting trail between them. But there was a relationship between these figures of the past: services which he had failed to render to one he had later rendered to another; thus, he had failed to succor Don Blas, but he had supported Joseph Ha-Cohen in Genoa, who had nonetheless continued to regard him as a dog of a Christian. Nothing came to an end: the masters or colleagues who had passed on to him an idea, or thanks to whom he had formed quite an opposite notion, continued to pursue, half heard by him, their irreconcilable controversy, each one from within his own conception of the world, like a magician within his circle. Darazi, who was seeking a god more personal and closer to him than was his jugular vein, would never cease to debate with Don Blas, for whom God was the One Unmanifest; and Jan Myers would laugh his silent laughter at the very sound of the word God.

§

For nearly half a century Zeno had used his mind, wedge-like, to enlarge, as best he could, the breaks in the wall which on all sides confines us. The cracks were widening, or rather, it seemed that the wall was slowly losing its solidity, though it still remained opaque, as if it were a wall of smoke and not of stone. Objects no longer played their part merely as useful accessories; like a mattress from which the hair stuffing protrudes, they were beginning to reveal their substance. A forest was filling the room: the stool, its height measured by the distance that separates a seated man's rump from the ground, this table which serves for eating or writing, the door connecting one cube of air, surrounded by partitions, with another, neighboring cube of air, all were losing those reasons for existing which an artisan had given them, to be again only trunks or branches stripped of their bark, like the Saint Bartholomews, stripped of their skin, in church paintings; here and there the carpenter's plane had left lumps where the sap had bled. These corpses of trees were laden with ghostly leaves and invisible birds, and still creaked from tempests long since gone by. This blanket and those old clothes hanging on a nail smelled of animal fat, of milk, of blood. These shoes gaping open beside the bed had once moved in rhythm with the breathing of an ox at rest on the grass; and a pig, bled to death, was still squealing in that lard with which the cobbler had greased them.

On all sides there was violent death, as in a slaughterhouse, or in a field of execution. The terrified cackling of a goose could be heard in the quill pen scratching its way, over old rags, to record ideas deemed worthy of lasting forever. Everything was actually something else: this shirt that the Bernardine sisters laundered for him was, in reality, a field of flax, far more blue than the sky; but it was, at the same time, a mass of fibers put to soften in the bed of a canal. The florins in his pocket, stamped with the head of the late Emperor Charles, had been exchanged or given away, stolen, weighed, or shaved off a thousand times before he had thought them, for one brief moment, his own; but all such turnover and back and forth between hands avaricious or prodigal was of short span as compared with the inert duration of the metal itself, which had lain infused in earth's veins before Adam had ever lived. The brick walls around him were resolving into mud from which they came, and which they would again become one day.

This annex to the monastery of the Cordeliers where he lived, reasonably warm and protected, was ceasing to be a dwelling, a place geometrically marked off for man, a solid shelter for mind and spirit even more than for body. At most, it was only a hut in the forest, a tent along the edge of a road, a shred of cloth stretched between him and infinity; mist was penetrating in through the tiles, as were the incomprehensible stars. The dead, by hundreds, were occupying this house, and living beings, too, all as lost as the dead: for dozens of hands had laid this paving, molded these bricks, sawed the timbers, nailed, sewed, or stuck together its parts; but it would have been as hard to find, say, the artisan who had woven that length of rough wool, even were he still alive, as to evoke a dead man. People had dwelt herein as a worm lives in its cocoon, and would dwell here after his time. He reflected that a rat, well hidden or wholly invisible behind a partition, or an insect, boring from within through a weakening joist, would both view with a perspective different from his own these spaces and solids which he called his bedchamber . . .

He looked above him. In the ceiling, a reused beam bore the date 1491. At the time that those figures had been carved (to record something no longer of importance to anyone), he did not yet exist, nor did the woman who bore him. He tried turning them around, as in a game: the year 1941 after the Incarnation of Christ. He strove to imagine such a year, wholly unrelated to his own existence, and of which but one thing was known, the certainty that it would come. Thus he was walking, as it were, over his own dust.

But like the grain of the oaken beam overhead, time did not feel those dates cut by man's hand. The earth was revolving in its orbit around the sun, unaware of the Julian calendar, or of the Christian era, continuing to form its circle, like a smooth ring, without beginning and without end. Zeno reminded himself that for the Turks this was the year 973 of the Hegira, but the heretic Darazi had secretly reckoned in accordance with the era of Khosroes. Passing in his reflection from the year to the day, he reckoned that at this moment the sun farther east was rising above the rooftops of Pera. The chamber began to lurch and roll; the bed ropes creaked like cordage; the bed was sliding from west to east in inverse direction to the apparent movement in the sky. Any notion that he was lying securely on a stable spot of Belgian earth was a final error; an hour from now, the point of space where he was reposing would contain the sea and its waves, and later still, the Americas and the continent of Asia. Those regions to which he would never go were daily superposing themselves, in the abyss of space, over this hospice of Saint Cosmos. Zeno himself was being dispersed like ashes in the wind.

§

SOLVE ET COAGULA . . . He knew well what that formula signified, the rupture of established notions, a great crack in the heart of things. As a young clerk he had read in Nicolas Flamel the full description of the *opus nigrum*, of that attempt at dissolution and calcination of forms which is the first but most difficult part of the Great Work. The operation would come of itself, regardless of one's desire, so Don Blas de Vela had often solemnly assured him, once the necessary conditions had been fulfilled. The student had seized upon these precepts, which seemed to him to have come from some illuminating, if sinister, book of magic, and had pondered them hard. In those early days he had mistaken this whole alchemical process of separation and reduction (so dangerous that hermetic philosophers spoke of it only in veiled terms, and so arduous that whole lifetimes were consumed, most of them in vain, to accomplish it) for what was mere easy rebellion. Later on, rejecting the trumpery in all those teachings, vague dreams as ancient as human illusion itself, and retaining from his alchemist masters only certain practical recipes, he had chosen to dissolve and coagulate matter in the strict sense of experimentation with the body of things. Now the two branches of the curve, the metaphysical and the pragmatic, were meeting; the *mors philosophica* had been accomplished: the operator, burned by the acids of his own research, had become both subject and object, both the fragile alembic and the black precipitate at its base; the experiment that he had thought to confine within the limits of the laboratory had extended itself to every human experience.

Did it follow, then, that the subsequent phases of the alchemical quest might prove to be other than dream, and that one day he would come to know also the ascetic purity of the White Phase of the Great Work, and finally the joint triumph of mind and senses which characterizes the Red Phase, the glorious conclusion? From the depth of the fissure an alluring Chimaera was rising. Zeno's answer was now an audacious "Yes," just as once he had boldly said "No."

Suddenly he stopped short, reining himself in against such hopes: the first phase of the Work had taken him his whole life. Time and strength would fail him to go further, even supposing that there were a route, and that by such a route a human being could pass. Either this putrefaction of ideas, this death of instincts and shattering of forms, processes all almost insupportable to human nature, would rapidly give way to veritable death (and it would be curious to see just how death would come), or else the mind, after its return from vertiginous realms, would resume its habitual routines, its faculties somewhat liberated, however, and, as it were, cleansed. It would be well worthwhile to witness the effects.

§

He was beginning to see effects. The tasks of the dispensary left him unfatigued. His hand and his eye had never been more sure. The ragged souls who patiently awaited the opening of the clinic each morning were tended with as much care and skill as he had formerly employed to treat the great of this world. His complete freedom from ambition and from fear in his profession allowed him to apply his methods without impediment, and almost always with good results; such total application left little room even for pity.

His spare, sinewy body and naturally strong constitution seemed to be fortified by the approach of age: he suffered less from cold, and apparently was little affected by freezing winters or humid summers; he was no longer tormented by the rheumatism which had begun to afflict him in Poland, or the after-effects of tertian fever contracted long ago in the East. He ate with indifference whatever was brought in to him from the refectory by one of the Brothers whom the Prior had assigned to the hospice, or else he would choose from among the modestly priced dishes at the inn. At this period of his existence, meat and blood, entrails, and all that had ever lived and breathed disgusted him as food, for an animal dies in pain just as man does, and it repelled him to be digesting death's agony. From the days when he had himself slaughtered a pig at a butcher's in Montpellier (in order to verify whether or not the arteries' pulsation coincided with the contraction of the heart), he had ceased to see any use in distinguishing between terms for a slaughtered beast and a slain or dying man.

His preferences in food went to bread, beer, and porridge, all of which retain something of the heavy savor of earth; and likewise to the succulent greens and refreshing fruits, or the sapid root vegetables. Both the Brother cook and the innkeeper admired his abstinence, assuming that his intention was pious. Sometimes, however, he set himself thoughtfully to the task of eating a morsel of tripe or a bit of liver, cooked rare, in order to prove to himself that his refusals were decisions of the mind rather than some peculiarity of his sense of taste.

His attire had never been of importance to him, and now from lack of attention, or from disdain, he no longer renewed it. In matters of love he was still the physician who had formerly recommended the benefits of love-making to his patients, just as at other times one might recommend wine. For he continued to consider love's burning mysteries as the only means of access for many of us to that fiery realm of which we are perhaps the infinitesimal sparks. But the sublime ascent of such experience is of brief duration, and he wondered whether an act so subject to material routines, and so dependent upon the instruments of physical generation, is not a thing for the philosopher to try, but then to renounce thereafter. Chastity, which he had once viewed as a superstition to be fought, now appeared to him as one aspect of his serenity: that detached understanding which one has of others when one no longer desires them was greatly to his liking. Once, however, when a new acquaintance had charmed him, he pursued such sports anew, and was surprised at his own powers. In opposite vein, he fell into a rage one day at a monk; the rascal was going about town selling unguents which he had stolen from the dispensary. Zeno's anger in this case was less instinctive than the result of deliberate intent. He even allowed himself a momentary feeling of vanity after some operation well performed, somewhat as one lets a dog roll freely on the grass.

§

One morning, during one of his outings in search of herbs, an insignificant, almost grotesque incident became subject for meditation, affecting him much as a revelation clarifies some holy mystery for a man of piety. He had left the city at daybreak to reach the edge of the dunes, taking with him a magnifying glass which he had had ground according to his specifications by a spectacle-maker of Bruges, and which permitted him to examine more closely the rootlets and seeds of the plants as he collected them. Toward noon he lay down for a nap, face down in a sandy hollow, his head upon an arm and his glass fallen from that hand to lie under him on a tuft of dry grass. On awaking, he thought that he saw an extraordinarily mobile creature next to his face, an insect or mollusk which stirred in the shadow of his head. It was spherical in form, and its central part, of a brilliant, humid black, was encircled by a zone of dull, or slightly roseate, white, around the periphery of which grew a fringe of hairs; these issued from a kind of soft, brownish outer shell streaked with crevices between slight swellings. An almost terrifying power of life dwelt within that fragile thing. In less than an instant, and even before his vision could be formulated in thought, Zeno realized that what he was seeing was only his own eye reflected and enlarged by the glass, behind which the grass and sand formed a backing like that of a mirror.

He rose, deep in reflection. He had caught himself in the act of seeing: quite outside the usual limits of perspective, he had gazed at close range on that small but vast organ, so near and yet so alien, quick to move but vulnerable, endued with incomplete and yet prodigious power, the instrument upon which he depended for beholding the universe. No theory could be derived from this vision, although it had strangely increased his knowledge of himself, and had likewise expanded his concept of the multiple objects of which he was composed. Like the eye of God depicted in popular woodcuts, this human eye was becoming a symbol. What imported was to gather in the little that it would filter from the world before night should come, then to assess its evidence, and, if possible, to rectify its errors. In a sense this organ served to counterbalance chaos.

§

He was beginning to emerge from the dark defile. In truth, he had already come through it more than once, and would come out of it again. Treatises devoted to the soul's ordeal were mistaken in assigning successive phases to that adventure: on the contrary, all its phases were intermingled; everything was subject to infinite restatement and repetition. The soul turned about in a circle in its quest. Long ago, in Basel, and in many other places, he had passed through this same long night. The same verities had been learned and relearned several times. But the experience was cumulative: the pace gradually became surer; the eye could see farther through certain shadows; the mind was at least becoming aware of certain laws. Like a man who is climbing, or perhaps descending, a mountainside, he was rising or ascending in place; at best, at each turning the same abyss would open below him, sometimes on the right, sometimes at his left. The gain in actual ascent was measurable only as the air became more rarefied, and as new peaks appeared behind those which had seemed to bar the horizon.

But the notion of ascension or descent was wrong, for stars burn below as on high; he was neither at the bottom of the gulf nor at its center. The abyss was both beyond the celestial sphere and within the human skull. Everything seemed to be taking place within an infinite series of curves closing in on themselves.

§

He had gone back to his writing, but without planning to

make his productions public. Among the ancient treatises on medicine he had always admired Hippocrates' third book of the *Epidemics* for its exact description of clinical cases and their symptoms, their progress from day to day, and their outcome. Zeno was keeping a similar record in respect to the patients treated at the hospice of Saint Cosmus. Perhaps some physician living after him would be able to extract certain benefits from this journal, kept by a doctor practicing in Flanders in the time of His Catholic Majesty Philip II.

A more daring project occupied him for some time, that of a *Liber Singularis* where he intended to set down, in minute detail, all that he knew about one man, who was himself: his temperament, his comportment, his acts avowed or hidden, fortuitous or intentional, his thoughts, and also his dreams. Reducing this plan as far too vast, he limited himself to a single year lived by this man, and then to a single day; but still the immensity of the material was beyond him, and he soon perceived that of all pastimes this particular one was the most dangerous, so he dropped it.

Now and then, by way of diversion, he would set down in writing what purported to be prophecies. In reality, these brief compositions satirized the errors and monstrosities of his times, but he cast them in the unfamiliar aspect of some novelty or prodigy. On occasion, and just to amuse him, he would communicate a few of these strange enigmas to the organist of Saint Donatian, with whom he had made friends after operating upon the man's good wife for a benign tumor. The organist and his spouse would puzzle their heads, trying to divine the meanings as if the writings were mere riddles; then they would laugh, not seeing the double intent.

§

One thing that engaged his attention during those years was a tomato plant, a botanical rarity grown from a cutting which he had obtained, only with great difficulty, from a unique specimen brought back from the New World. This precious vine, which he kept in his laboratory, inspired him to take up his earlier studies again on the movement of sap: by using a cover to prevent evaporation of the water fed to the earth in the pot, and by careful weighing of the whole each morning, he succeeded in measuring how many liquid ounces the plant absorbed each day by its powers of imbibition. After that experiment he tried to make an algebraic calculation as to what height that same faculty could raise the fluids inside a stem or a tree trunk.

He corresponded on this subject with the learned mathematician who had received him in his home, some six years before, in Louvain. The two of them exchanged formulas, and Zeno eagerly awaited his friend's replies. Furthermore, he was beginning to think again of new journeys.

THE PRIOR'S
ILLNESS

O N A Monday in May, on the day of commemora-
tion of the Holy Blood, Zeno was sitting alone in his
accustomed dark corner at the Great Hart Inn, dispatching
his meal as usual. But the tables and benches near the windows
giving on the street were particularly crowded, for the procession could be seen from them as it passed. One of these tables
was occupied by the mistress of a notorious brothel in Bruges,
dubbed "Pumpkin" because of her girth; she had with her a
small, pasty-faced man who passed for her son, and two fair
damsels of her establishment. Zeno knew this "Pumpkin"
through repeated complaints of one of her girls, a consumptive
who came to him from time to time to get something for her
cough. The poor creature poured forth endless tales of her
employer's mean tricks, of how she cheated and stole the girl's
best linens.

On conclusion of the Mass, the Walloon Guards broke
ranks at the entrance of the church, and a small group from
among them came into the inn to be served. Their officer
found the "Pumpkin's" table to his liking, so he promptly

ordered its four occupants to take themselves off. The son and the two whores needed no second bidding, but the "Pumpkin," a woman of spirit, refused to budge. As a Guard tugged at her to make her get up, she clung to the table, overturning the dishes; a slap from the officer left a livid streak across her fat, yellowed face. Squealing, biting, and clutching to benches and doorjamb, she had to be dragged or pushed outside by the Guards; one of them, just to make folks laugh, poked her hind end with the point of his sword. Meanwhile, the officer installed himself in the conquered seat and addressed his further haughty orders to the servant who had begun to wipe up the floor.

Not a soul made a move to rise. One or two of the onlookers snickered in servile accord, but most of those present averted their eyes, or cursed silently into their plates. Zeno watched the scene with disgust mounting to the point of nausea; even if the soldiers' brutality could be effectively challenged, the occasion was poor indeed: the "Pumpkin" was despised by all, and whoever might choose to defend her would only become a butt for coarse jokes. It was learned later that the fat procuress had been whipped for breach of peace, and then sent home. Hardly a week passed, however, before she was doing the honors of her house as usual, and showing her battle scars to all who cared to see.

When Zeno went to pay his respects to the Prior, he found that he had retired to rest after the fatigue of the procession, but was already apprised of the incident. Zeno recounted what he himself had witnessed, and the monk sighed. Setting down his steaming cup of tisane, he said:

"This woman is the very scum of her sex, and I do not blame you in the least for having sat still. But would we have protested such an indignity, intimidated as we are, even if the woman had had the virtues of a Saint? This 'Pumpkin,' low as she is, nevertheless today had right on her side, which is to say that she had both God and His angels."

"God and His angels, however, did not come to her aid," the physician ventured to observe.

The religious answered with some heat: "Far be it from me to question the holy miracles of Scripture, but in our lifetime, my friend (and I am more than sixty), I have never yet seen that God intervenes directly in our earthly affairs. He delegates Himself, acting only through us poor human creatures." He went to a cabinet drawer to look for two sheets of paper, closely overwritten, and handed them to Dr. Theus, saying, "Read this. My godson, Monsieur de Withem, one of the Patriots, keeps me informed of atrocities of which, otherwise, we should learn only too late, when the shock about them has already died down; or, if we do hear of them at once, the report is sugared over with lies. Men have little imagination, my doctor friend; we are disturbed, and rightly so, over maltreatment of a procuress, but that is because the cruelties are perpetrated here before our eyes. Infamies committed some ten leagues hence do not deter me from consuming this infusion of mallow."

"Your Reverence's imagination, in any case, is strong enough to make your hands tremble, and spill what is left of this tisane," the doctor interposed kindly.

But the Prior only sponged at his gray woolen robe with a handkerchief, and his voice sank to a murmur, as if he spoke against his will. "Nearly three hundred men and women have been executed at Armentières, declared rebels against God and their King. Go on reading, my friend."

Zeno finished the letter and gave it back to the Prior, saying quietly: "The poor folk whom I treat already know the consequences of the rioting at Armentières. As to the other abuses with which these pages are filled, they are now the common talk of the marketplace and the taverns. News like this flies low to the ground. The burghers and the officials, snug inside their comfortable homes, catch only vague rumors, at the most."

"Alas, no," rejoined the Prior, sadly vexed. "Yesterday, after Mass, speaking with my fellow priests outside Notre Dame, I ventured to touch upon public events. Not one of these pious folk but approved the aim, if not the means, of the Inquisitorial Court; at least, there was no more than mild protest against its bloody excesses. And I count apart the Rector of Saint Giles, who declares that we can burn our own heretics without foreigners coming in to teach us how."

"He keeps to the old traditions," Sebastian Theus remarked with a smile; but the Prior, now fully in ire, burst out:

"Am I any less fervent a Christian or pious Catholic than they? One does not sail on a splendid ship his whole life long without detesting the rats that gnaw at its planks. But these executions by fire and the sword, and these burials alive, only serve to harden the hearts of the men who inflict them, and of all who rush to behold the spectacle, as well as to harden the sufferers themselves in their error. The obdurate are thus set up as martyrs. We are being made fools of, my friend. The Tyrant is managing to slaughter our Patriots while claiming to avenge God."

"Would Your Reverence approve these executions if you judged them efficacious for restoring unity in the Church?" Sebastian dared to broach the question, and the Prior answered in distress.

"Do not tempt me, my good friend. I know only that our father Francis, who was trying to resolve civil discords when he died, would surely have approved of our Flemish gentlemen for working toward a compromise."

The physician, however, expressed a doubt. "These same lords may have been rash in asking the King to tear down the placards on which he chose to publish the solemn anathema pronounced upon heretics by the Council of Trent."

"And why should they not demand it!" exclaimed the Prior. "Those placards, guarded by the King's sentries, are an insult to the freedom of our cities. Every malcontent is now labeled a Protestant. May God forgive me if I say that they would even have accused this procuress of Evangelical leanings . . . As for the Council, you know as I do how heavily, if discreetly, our Rulers' wills weighed upon its deliberations: Emperor Charles was concerned for the unity of the Empire, above all, and that is natural; King Philip aims at supremacy for Spain. Had I not discovered early in life, alas, that at Court everything is intrigue and counterintrigue, distortion of words and abuse of power, perhaps I should never have mustered sufficient piety to give up worldly things and to enter the service of our Lord."

"Your Reverence must doubtless have suffered great reverses," Dr. Theus commented, in a tone of deferential inquiry.

"No, quite the contrary," said the Prior. "I have been a courtier who stood in the late Emperor's good graces, and my negotiations on his behalf were more fortunate than my feeble talents deserved; furthermore, I was blessed with a good and devout wife. I shall have been one of the privileged in this world of pain and sorrow."

His brow was moist with sweat, a symptom of fragile health, it seemed to the physician. But the priest, preoccupied, turned to him to ask, "Did you not say that the humble folk who come to you for care look with sympathy upon the movements of the so-called Reformation?"

"No, I said nothing like that, nor noticed anything of the kind," Sebastian cautiously replied; then he added, with a touch of irony, "Your Reverence is well aware of the fact that those who hold dangerous views usually know how to keep quiet." He continued, thoughtfully, "It is true that the thrift and simplicity of the Evangelical sects have their attractions for some of the poor. But most of them are good Catholics, if only from habit."

"From habit," the monk repeated sadly.

"For my part," Dr. Theus resumed, deliberately choosing to speak at some length in order to give the Prior's emotions time to cool, "what I see chiefly in all this is the eternal confusion in human affairs. The Tyrant is detested by all right-thinking folk; yet no one denies that His Majesty is the legitimate ruler of the Low Countries, by inheritance from an ancestress who was the very idol of Flanders. (I do not go into the question of whether or not it is just to bequeath a country as one would bequeath a carved sideboard; such are our laws.)

"The gentlemen who, for demagogic reasons, take the name of 'Beggars' are like Janus, traitors to the King whose vassals they are, but heroes and patriots for the crowd. On the other hand, the quarrels between the lords and the dissension in our cities are such that many prudent persons prefer even the exactions of the Foreigner to the disorder which would follow if he were overthrown. Our Spanish overlords are savagely persecuting the so-called Reformists, but the majority of our Patriots are good Catholics, and even so they are subject to the same pursuit. These Reformists pride themselves on the austerity of their ways, but their leader in Flanders, Monsieur de Brederode, is a dissolute rascal. Our Governess, anxious to retain her post, promises to suppress the Courts of Inquisition, but in the same breath she announces the establishment of other judicial bodies to send all heretics to be burned at the stake. The Church in its charity insists that those who finally make confession in their dying moments be subjected only to hanging or beheading, without longer torment; but it thereby incites some wretches to perjury, and to misuse of the sacraments. The Lutherans, on their side, slaughter the miserable remnants of the Anabaptists whenever they can.

"The ecclesiastical State of Liége, which by definition stands on the side of the Holy Church, is profiting from the sale of arms, openly, to the royal troops, and surreptitiously to the Patriot 'Beggars.' Although everyone loathes the mercenaries hired by the Foreigner (and the more so that, their pay being scant, they recoup at the citizens' expense), the burghers demand the protection of these same halberdiers because of the bands of brigands overrunning the countryside in these times of troubles. Furthermore, the burghers, jealously guarding their civil privileges, look askance, in principle, at the nobility and the monarchy; but the heretics come, for the most part, from the lowly, and all bourgeois hate the poor. In this din of voices and clash of arms, and sometimes, too, amid the goodly clink of coins, what we hear least of all are the screams of victims broken on the wheel or torn with tongs. So goes the world, my lord Prior."

In profound melancholy the Superior took up Sebastian's discourse. "During High Mass," he said, "I prayed, as is the custom, for the welfare of our Governess and of His Majesty. As to the Governess, let be; Madame is not a bad woman, she is trying, however, to make concessions both to the ax and to the chopping block. But must I pray for a Herod? And must one ask God to grant prosperity to the Cardinal de Granvelle in his so-called retirement, from which he continues to harass us, since he still advises the King? Our religion obliges us to respect established authority, and I do not gainsay that. But authority is delegated, too, and the lower it descends in rank, the coarser and viler the faces it assumes; the traces of our own cowardice and apathy are reflected, almost grotesquely, upon them . . . Must I go even so far as to pray for the welfare of the Walloon Guards?"

"Your Reverence can always ask God to enlighten those who rule over us," the doctor proposed.

"My first need is that He should enlighten me, myself." The Cordelier spoke with true compunction.

Since this discussion of public affairs was agitating the religious too much, Zeno directed the conversation to the needs and expenditures of the hospice. As he took his leave, however, the Prior detained him, signaling to him to reclose the door of the cell, out of precaution, and saying:

"I hardly need to recommend to you the utmost circum-

spection. You can see that no one is too high in place, or too
low, to avoid suspicion and affront. Let none know what we
have said."

"No one, were it not my own shadow," Dr. Theus assured
him.

"Your relations with this monastery are now close," the
monk reminded him. "Keep well in mind that there are many
persons in this town, and even within these walls, who would
gladly charge the Prior of the Cordeliers with rebellion or
with heresy."

§

Such talks were resumed rather often; the Prior seemed to
hunger for them. This man, though so highly esteemed, appeared to Zeno to be as lonely as himself, and even more in
danger. At each visit the physician could detect more clearly
on his friend's face the signs of an illness, as yet indefinable,
which was sapping his strength. The Prior's pity and anguish
over the wretchedness of the times could have been the sole
cause of this inexplicable decline; or, on the contrary, they
could have been its effect, and could have indicated that his
constitution was too greatly undermined to support the
world's ills with that robust indifference which most men betray. Zeno finally persuaded His Reverence to take some tonic
each day, mixed with wine; to please the physician His Reverence consented.

Zeno, too, had taken a liking to these exchanges of view,
which, though courteous, were almost free from dissembling.
Nevertheless, he left them each time with a vague feeling of
imposture. Once more, just as one is obliged to speak Latin at
the Sorbonne, he had had to adopt a foreign language in order
to be understood, thus somewhat distorting his thought even
though he knew perfectly the turns of phrase and the inflec-
tions. In this case the language was that of the respectful, if
not devout, Christian and of the loyal subject, a subject, how-

ever, alarmed by the state of the world. Once more, and out of deference to the Prior's views even more than from precaution, he was consenting to start from premises on which, for himself alone, he would have refused to build; laying aside his own concerns, he constrained himself to expose only one facet of his thought, and that always the same, the side which best reflected the preoccupations of his ailing friend.

Such falsification, though inherent in human relations, and already second nature to him, was disturbing in this otherwise free commerce between two honest, disinterested men. The Prior would have been surprised to learn how little the subjects debated at great length between them in his cell ever figured in the solitary cogitations of Dr. Theus. Not that the troubles of the Low Countries left Zeno unmoved; but he had lived too much in a world devastated by war to feel the same spasm of pain as the Prior of the Cordeliers did in presence of these new proofs of man's barbarity.

As to his own danger, it seemed to him reduced for the moment rather than increased by the public turmoil. No one was thinking about the insignificant Sebastian Theus. By force of circumstances he was more than ever enveloped in that secrecy which all practitioners of magic vow to keep for the sake of their art; he had become truly invisible.

§

On an evening of that same summer, at the hour for curfew, he mounted to his garret after locking the door as usual. Ordinarily the hospice closed with the ringing of the Angelus; only once, when an epidemic had filled Saint John's Hospital to overflowing, had the physician taken it upon himself to keep patients in the ground-floor room, installing pallets of straw there for the fever-ridden victims. On this evening Brother Luke, whose duty it was to wash the tiled floor, had just departed with his mop rags and pails. Suddenly Zeno heard the sharp sound of gravel tossed against his window; it recalled to him the long-past times when he used to join Colas Gheel after the workmen's evening bell. He dressed again and went down.

It was Josse Cassel, the son of the blacksmith on Wool-market Street. Josse explained to him that a cousin from Saint-Pierre-lez-Bruges had broken a leg; a horse which he was leading to his uncle to be shod had kicked him, and he lay now in a very bad state in a small room back of the forge. Zeno gathered what was needed and followed Josse through the streets. At a crossing they encountered the night watch, but were allowed to proceed after Josse explained that he had gone for a doctor for his father, who had just crushed two fingers with a blow from his hammer. This lie gave the physician cause to ponder as they continued on their way.

The wounded youth lay on an improvised bed. He was a rustic of about eighteen, called Han, a kind of blond wolf with his shaggy hair plastered to his cheeks by sweat, and half fainting from pain and loss of blood. Zeno administered a restorative and examined the leg: the bone protruded from the flesh at two points, and the flesh itself hung in shreds. Nothing in this accident resembled effects from a horse's kick; no hoof or shoe marks were visible anywhere. In such a case amputation was the wiser course, but the sufferer, seeing the doctor pass the blade of his saw through the fire, revived enough to howl; the blacksmith and his son were hardly less alarmed, fearing, if the operation should turn out badly, to have a dead body on their hands. Changing his plan, Zeno decided to try first to reduce the fracture.

The poor boy was hardly the better for this procedure: the attempt to stretch the limb in order to join the pieces of the bone drew screams from him like those of men put to torture; the surgeon had to widen the wound with cuts from a razor and feel inside to remove any splinters. Then he washed the surface with a strong wine, of which, by good fortune, the blacksmith possessed a jar. Father and son worked meanwhile to prepare bandages and splints. The small room was suffocating for them all, since the two men had carefully padded all openings lest the cries be heard.

When Zeno left Woolmarket Street, at last, he was wholly uncertain as to the outcome. The boy was at the lowest ebb, and only his youthful vigor gave him something of a chance. The physician went back daily thereafter, sometimes in the early morning and sometimes after the closing of the hospice, to wash the flesh with a vinegar which would clean it of any seepage. Later on he used rosewater on the edges of the wound to keep them from drying out or growing inflamed. As far as possible he avoided the night hours, when his coming and going would be noticed by the watch. Although both father and son held to their story of a horse's kick, it was tacitly understood that the affair was best kept silent.

Toward the tenth day an abscess formed; the flesh became spongy, and the fever, which never had completely abated, rose like fire. Zeno kept the patient on a drastic diet; the boy called for food in his delirium. One night the leg muscles contracted with such violence as to break the splints. The doctor admitted to himself that weakly, out of pity, he had not sufficiently tightened the clamps; now the stretching and reduction had to be done all over again. This time the pain was worse than in the initial ordeal, but Han supported it better because Zeno had surrounded him with opium smoke.

After seven days the drains inserted in the abscess had emptied it, and the fever terminated in heavy sweats. Zeno left the forge light of heart, for once, and with the feeling of having had on his side the goddess Fortune, lacking whom all skill is in vain. It seemed to him that throughout the past three weeks, along with and during his other work and preoccupations, he had been continuously exerting all his powers to effect this healing. Such perpetual concentration surely was very close to what the Prior would have called the state of mental prayer.

§

But certain avowals had escaped the injured lad in his delirium. Josse and the blacksmith finally, of their own accord, confirmed and completed the story so compromising to them all. Han came from a poor hamlet very near Zevecote, three leagues from Bruges, where some gruesome events had recently taken place; everyone knew about them. It had all begun with an itinerant Calvinist preacher whose sermons had inflamed the village; these yokels, already at odds with the local curate (who gave no quarter in collecting tithes), stormed the church, hammers in hand, smashing the altar statues and the Virgin carried in all the processions, and stealing the embroidered skirts, the cloak, and Our Lady's gilt halo, making off with all the humble treasures of the sacristy. A squadron led by a certain Captain Julian Vargaz came at once to suppress the disorders. Han's mother, in whose house they found a length of satin embroidered with seed pearls, was beaten to death, after the usual violences, although for the latter object she was no longer quite of the age desired. The other women and children were driven out, left to scatter as best they could through the fields. Some of the men of the hamlet were hanged on the common green; while Captain Vargaz was directing these executions, he was struck on the forehead by a bullet from a harquebus, and fell dead from his horse. The shot had been fired from the loft of a barn; the soldiers rushed to beat and stab through the mounds of hay, but found no one, so finally set the place on fire. Certain that they had burned the assassin, they withdrew, taking with them their Captain's corpse slung across his saddle, and also led off a few head of confiscated cattle.

But Han had jumped from the haymow, breaking his leg in the fall. Clenching his teeth not to cry out in pain, he had crawled to the edge of the pond and had hidden there under a heap of refuse and straw until the soldiers left, trembling the while lest the fire spread to his wretched cover. Toward evening, when he could no longer hold back his groans, he was discovered by the peasants of a neighboring farm who had come to see what was left to pillage in the deserted hamlet. The marauders were goodhearted souls; they decided between them to hide Han inside a covered cart and send him in town to his uncle. He arrived there in a dead swoon. Pieter and his son felt sure that no one had seen the light van enter their courtyard from Woolmarket Street.

The report that Han had died in the burning barn served to shield him from pursuit, but his security depended upon the silence of the peasants, who at any moment might speak out, of their own accord, or surely would do so under torture. Pieter and Josse were risking their lives in harboring a rebel and an image-breaker; the danger for the physician was equally grave. After six weeks the convalescent could hop about, using a crutch, but adhesions at the scar still made him suffer cruelly. Both father and son implored the doctor to rid them of this youth, who, in any case, was hardly one to inspire affection: his long confinement had left him whimpering and snarling; it was tiresome to hear him forever relating his one act of prowess, and the blacksmith, who already begrudged him the loss of the costly wine and the beer that he had swilled, flew into a rage upon learning that this good-for-nothing had asked Josse to bring him a wench.

Zeno considered that Han would be better hidden in the larger city of Antwerp, where perhaps, once wholly healed, he could join the small band of rebels under Captain Hendrick Thomaszoon, or under Captain Sonnoy, on the other bank of the Scheldt. These partisans were doing their utmost to harass the royal troops from boats ambushed here and there along the coasts of Zeeland.

The physician bethought him of old Greete's son, who, as a carter, had to make the trip to Antwerp weekly with his bags and bundles. When the matter was partly confided to this man, he was willing to take the young fellow along and deliver him into safe hands; still, some money would be needed to make this escape. Pieter Cassel, in spite of his haste to see his nephew packed off, declared that he had not another penny to spend on Han's behalf. As for Zeno, he had nothing. After some hesitation, the doctor went directly to the Prior.

§

The holy man was saying his Mass in the chapel adjoining his cell, and was nearly at the end. After the *Ite, Missa est* was pronounced, and the priest had offered his silent prayers of thanksgiving, Zeno asked for a word with him, and straightway related the whole episode.

"You have run great risks in all this," said the Prior gravely.

"In this sadly confused world," the philosopher replied, "a few prescripts are fairly clear. The care of the sick is my calling."

The Prior nodded agreement. "No one will lament Vargaz," he continued. "You remember, do you not, monsieur, the insolent soldiers who encumbered all our streets at the time that you first reached Flanders? Under various pretexts the King was still imposing that army upon us two full years after the war with France had ended. Think of it, two years! This Vargaz had re-enlisted here in order to continue practicing upon us the same brutalities which had made him so odious to the French. We can hardly exalt the young David of Scripture without praising the lad whom you have saved."

"It must be acknowledged that he is a good shot," the physician concurred, waiting to see what the priest would say further.

"I should like to believe that God guided his hand," the monk affirmed with vigor. "But a sacrilege is a sacrilege. Does this boy Han admit to taking part in the destruction of the statues?"

"Yes, he even vaunts himself on it. But what I see chiefly in boasting like this is the indirect expression of remorse," Sebastian said, and continued guardedly: "In the same vein I interpret certain things uttered in his delirium. A few preachings from dissenters have not sufficed to make the boy lose all memory of his former Ave Marias."

"Do you yourself find no grounds for such remorse?" the priest was quick to ask.

"Does Your Reverence take me for a Lutheran?" countered the philosopher, with a suggestion of a smile.

"No, my friend. I fear that you have too little faith to be a heretic."

The physician took the precaution to shift the discussion promptly to a subject other than that of the orthodoxy of Sebastian Theus, saying, "Everyone suspects the authorities of implanting these preachers, true or feigned though they be, in the villages. Thus our overlords provoke excesses in order to repress us as they please thereafter."

"Indeed, I know only too well the tricks of the Council of Spain," the religious interposed, with some impatience. "But I should not need to explain my scruples to you. I am the last to desire that some poor wretch should be burned alive for the sake of certain theological niceties quite beyond his grasp. In these attacks upon Our Lady, however, there is a kind of violence which smells of Hell itself. If it were, say, a matter of one of those Saint Georges or Catherines whose legends do no harm, while charming the piety of the people, but whose actual existence is questioned by our scholars . . . Am I more shocked, possibly, because we Franciscans pay special devotion to Our Lady ('that high goddess,' as a poet whom I read in my youth called her), and we assert that she is immune from Adam's sin; or am I more touched than a religious should be by the memory of my dear wife, who bore with grace and humility that same beautiful name of Mary . . . No crime committed against our faith arouses my indignation so much as an offense against that Mary in whom was carried the Hope of the world, against Her who was appointed at the dawn of time to be our Advocate in Heaven . . ."

"Yes, I think that I understand," Sebastian said, seeing tears in the Prior's eyes. "You are grieved because some ruffian has dared to strike down what you believe to be the purest form ever assumed by Divine Kindness. Certain Jews (I have been much among physicians of this people) have spoken similarly to me of their Shekinah, who stands for God's tender benevolence . . . It is true that she has no visible form for them . . . But insofar as we give human guise to the Ineffable, I see no reason why it should not be endued with certain female traits, for without them we reduce the nature of things by half. If the beasts of the forest have some sense of sacred mysteries (and who knows what does go on in the mind of wild creatures?), they doubtless envisage a holy and perfect doe alongside the Divine Stag. Does a notion like this offend the Prior?"

"Not at all," the priest replied, "no more than does the symbol of the Lamb without spot. And Mary, too, is she not the pure and perfect Dove?"

Sebastian, meditating, continued: "Nevertheless, such symbols have their dangers. My fellow alchemists employ figures like 'the Milk of the Virgin,' 'the Black Raven,' 'the Universal Green Lion,' and 'the Copulation of Metals' to designate the various operations of their art wherever the subtlety, or the virulence, of these phases exceeds the power of words which men commonly use. The result of this mode of expression is, however, that the more obtuse minds see little beyond the material image, while the more judicious tend to disdain a form of knowledge which, although it could carry them far, seems to them to be imbedded in a morass of dreams . . . But I need not go on with the comparison."

"The difficulty is insoluble, my friend," the Prior acknowledged. "If I say to poor ignorant folk that the golden veil and blue robe of Our Lady are but feeble representations of

Heaven's splendors, and that Heaven, in its turn, is but a poor portrayal of Supreme Good, itself invisible, they will conclude from my words that I believe neither in Our Lady nor in Heaven. Would I not then be offering them a still greater lie than in urging reverence for such emblems? For verily, the symbol is one with the thing signified."

"Let us come back to the lad whom I have been tending," said the physician with new insistence. "Surely Your Reverence does not suppose that this Han thought to assault the Advocate appointed by Divine Mercy for all time? On the contrary, what he did was to cleave asunder a block of wood attired in a velvet robe, which some preacher tells him is an idol; and I venture to say that this impiety, which rightly incenses the Prior, will have seemed to him in conformity with the heavy common sense which Heaven has granted him. This rustic has no more intended to insult the Instrument of the World's Salvation than he thought of avenging his Belgian fatherland when he killed Captain Vargaz."

"He has nevertheless done both of these things," the Prior rejoined.

"I wonder," the philosopher said, musing. "It is you and I who are seeking to give meanings to the violent action of a simple young peasant."

Suddenly, almost brusquely, the Prior asked, "Does it mean so much to you, Doctor Theus, to have this boy escape?"

"Yes, it does; for apart from the fact that my own safety is involved, I prefer not to see my masterpiece thrown to the fire." The reply was made in a jesting tone, but then Sebastian added, with more frankness, "Contrary, though, to what the Prior may be thinking, there is no other reason."

"So much the better," the religious observed. "You can wait for the outcome with greater calm. Nor do I myself wish to ruin your handiwork, friend Sebastian. Take the sum you need. You will find it in that coffer."

Zeno looked as directed and drew forth a purse hidden under some linen; sparingly, he selected from it a few pieces of silver. As he restored the pouch to its place, he somehow caught and partly pulled out a piece of harsh cloth, which he did his best to disengage. It proved to be a hair shirt; dark spots of blood were still drying on it here and there. The Prior averted his face, as if embarrassed.

"Your Reverence's health is not sufficiently good to permit of such rigorous practices," the physician warned him gravely.

"Indeed, I would wish to increase them," the religious protested, "in atonement for the sinful state of our world. Your occupations, Sebastian, may have left you no time to reflect upon the general disaster. What is bruited about everywhere is unhappily only too true. The King has just assembled an army in Piedmont with the Duke of Alva in command, he who was victor at Mühlberg and in Italy is said to be a man as hard as iron. These twenty thousand men with their beasts of burden and their baggage are crossing the Alps at this very moment to swoop down upon our wretched provinces . . . We may soon be regretting even a Captain Vargaz."

"They have good reason for haste, before the passes are blocked for the winter." The surmise was that of the man who had once fled from Innsbruck over icy mountain roads.

"My son is a staff officer to the King, and I greatly fear, therefore, that he accompanies the Duke." The Prior spoke as if forcing himself to make a painful avowal. "We all have our share in evil."

At this point he was seized with a coughing spell such as had already troubled him several times during the course of the conversation. Sebastian, resuming his function of physician, took his friend's pulse, speaking only after a pause.

"Anxiety and concern may explain why the Prior looks so unwell. But this cough which has persisted for several days, and this continued loss of weight, have causes which it is my duty to seek out. Would Your Reverence allow me to examine your throat tomorrow, employing an instrument of my own construction?"

"Whatever you please to do, my friend," the Prior consented. "The rainy summer has doubtless made for this sore throat. And you can see for yourself that I have no fever."

§

Han departed that very evening with the carter. He was to pass as groom for the horses; some slight limp which remained would not hinder him in this capacity. His conductor set him down in Antwerp at the house of an agent of the Fuggers who was secretly inclined toward the Patriots. This man lived at the port, so he put Han to work on the endless opening and renailing of the boxes of spice. Word reached Bruges toward Christmas that the young fellow, now strong and firm again on the mended leg, had hired on as ship's carpenter aboard a slaver fitting out for Guinea. There was always need on craft like that for hands skilled not only in repairing damage to the vessel but also in building or shifting the pens, or in fashioning irons and fetters; the ability to use firearms was important, as well, in case of mutiny. The wages were good, so Han had chosen this employment in preference to the uncertain pay he would have had under Captain Thomaszoon with his Sea Beggars.

§

Winter came on. The Prior, of his own accord, had given up preaching the Advent sermons because of his chronic hoarseness. Dr. Theus managed to persuade his patient to pass an hour abed after dinner, in order to conserve his strength; or at least to rest in the armchair which he had recently consented to have placed in his cell. Since the rule of the Order forbade the use of either fireplace or stove, Sebastian convinced the monk, not without some difficulty, to allow himself the comfort of a brazier.

One afternoon the doctor found him with his spectacles on, busily checking over the accounts. The bursar of the monastery, Pierre de Hamaere, stood before his Superior, listening to his observations. Although Zeno had not addressed this Brother ten times in his life, he felt a hostility toward him which, he sensed, was reciprocal. Pierre departed after having kissed His Reverence's hand with his usual genuflection, both servile and haughty. The news of the day was particularly somber: Count Egmont and his fellow Patriot, the Count of Hoorne, incarcerated in Ghent for nearly three months now on the charge of high treason, had just been refused their right of judgment by their peers, a privilege which, if exercised, probably would have spared them their lives. The town was seething over such a denial of justice.

Zeno avoided being the first to speak of this inequity, not knowing if the Prior had been informed about it yet. He recounted, instead, the absurd conclusion of Han's story. On hearing it, the religious sighed wearily, saying, "The great Pius II condemned the traffic of slave ships long ago, but who takes heed of that now? It is true that we have even more pressing injustices here among us . . . What do they say in town about this new indignity to the Count?"

"They pity him more than ever for having trusted in the King's promises."

"Lamoral is great-hearted, but he has small judgment," the Prior remarked, with more calm than Zeno had expected. "A good negotiator is less sanguine."

Docilely he took the drops of the astringent measured out for him by his physician, who watched him closely, concealing the sadness he felt. For he had no faith in the virtues of this far too simple remedy, and was vainly seeking a more powerful specific with which to treat the Prior's throat. The absence of fever had led him to abandon his hypothesis, that of phthisic. If there were a polyp in the throat, it would perhaps explain this continued hoarseness and cough, and this increasing trouble in breathing and swallowing.

The Prior handed back the empty glass, saying, "Thank you." Then he requested, "Do not leave me today too soon, Sebastian, my friend."

At first they spoke at random. Zeno had seated himself close to the monk in order to spare him the effort of forcing his voice. The ailing man suddenly reverted to the subject of his principal concern.

"A shocking injustice like the one to which Lamoral has now been subjected brings in its train a whole series of other wrongs, equally wicked, but they pass unnoticed," he said, speaking low to save his breath. "The Count's steward was arrested soon after his master; they broke him on the wheel with an iron crowbar in the hope of obtaining from him some avowals. Not a vein or a bone in his body was left whole . . . I said my Mass this morning on behalf of the two Counts, and doubtless every household in Flanders is praying for their salvation in this world or in the next. But who thinks to pray for the soul of this miserable fellow, who had nothing to divulge, anyhow, since he had no part in his Lord's secret endeavors."

"I believe that I see what you are suggesting," Sebastian Theus commented. "Your Reverence is paying tribute to the fidelity of a humble man."

"Not exactly that," the Prior demurred. "This steward was dishonest, enriching himself, they say, at his Lord's expense. It seems, too, that among Egmont's possessions he kept back a painting which the Duke of Alva had been ordered to acquire for His Majesty, one of our Flemish grotesques where ludicrous demons are seen torturing the damned. (Our King, you know, has a taste for paintings . . .) Whether or not this lowborn man might have turned informer is of no importance anyhow, since the Count's case already stands as if judged. But I tell myself that this nobleman will die as befits his rank, with a stroke of the ax, on a scaffold draped in black, consoled by the grief of a populace which looks up to him, rightly, as a true lover of his Belgian fatherland. The executioner who strikes the blow will have asked his forgiveness, and he will be accompanied by his chaplain's prayers, speeding him on to Heaven . . ."

"This time I follow you," said Zeno. "Your Reverence is concluding that, in spite of all the platitudes of the philosophers, rank and title do procure for their possessors certain substantial advantages. It is useful, after all, to be a grandee of Spain."

"I express myself poorly," the Prior said feebly. "It is because this man has no station, and is insignificant and doubtless ignoble, endowed only with a body vulnerable to pain and a soul for which God himself has shed His blood, that I pause to contemplate his dying moments. They have told me that he was heard screaming in his agony for more than three hours."

"Take care, my lord Prior," Sebastian cautioned, pressing the hand of the religious in his own. "This poor fellow has suffered for three hours, but for how many days and nights will Your Reverence continue to relive that agony? You are putting yourself through greater torment than the executioners meted out to this victim."

"Do not say that," the Prior exclaimed, shaking his head in denial. "This steward's anguish and his persecutors' fury pervade the whole world and overflow the bounds of time. This suffering and this rage have existed for one moment in the eternal gaze of God, and nothing can now prevent them from being a part of that eternity. Every ill and every sorrow is infinite in its substance, my friend, and they are also infinite in number."

"What Your Reverence says of grief could also be said of joy."

"Yes, I know . . . I have had my share of joys . . . Every innocent joy is something still left to us from Eden . . . But happiness has no need of aid from us, Sebastian. Only grief and pain call for our charity. When the day comes, at last, that makes us aware of the suffering endured by all living creatures, then joy, too, becomes impossible for us, just as it would be impossible for the Good Samaritan to loiter, drinking with tavern girls, while his charge lies bleeding beside him. Even how Saints can be serene on earth, or in beatitude in Heaven, I no longer comprehend."

"If I understand anything of the language of devotion," Zeno said, trying to temper his friend's anguished admission, "the Prior is passing through his 'dark night' of the soul." But the monk rejected this suggestion, pleading, "I beg of you, my friend, do not reduce this deep distress of mine to some pious trial on the road to perfection . . . Besides, I do not claim to be on that road . . . Let us look instead at the darkness in which man is dwelling. Alas, one fears to err in questioning the order of things, but still, Sebastian, how do we dare send back to their Maker these souls whose sins we augment with the sins of blasphemy and despair because of the torture to which we subject their bodies? Why have we allowed bigotry, insolence, and rancor to enter into debates on doctrine? Such discussions should take place only in the clear heavens. Sanzio was right to place the Disputation on the Blessed Sacrament there when he painted it in the Holy Father's apartments . . .

"For after all, if the King had deigned last year to hear the protest of our noblemen . . . If earlier, in the time of our childhood, Pope Leo had kindly received an uncouth Augustinian monk, who was asking only for what all our institutions always need, I mean to say, reforms . . . This German rustic was scandalized by abuses which shocked me myself when I visited the court of Julius III; nor was he wrong in reproaching our Orders for an opulence that encumbers us, and is not wholly put to the service of God . . ."

"The Prior can hardly be said to dazzle us with his luxury," the physician interrupted, smiling.

"I have every comfort," the religious insisted, extending his hand toward the graying coals.

After some reflection the philosopher returned to the regrets just expressed by the Prior. "Your Reverence should not, out of generosity, exaggerate the adversary's worth. *Odi hominem unius libri:* Luther has propagated a worship of 'the Book' that is idolatrous, far worse than many of those practices which he terms superstitious; and his doctrine of salvation by faith alone, without works, lowers man's dignity."

"I grant you that," the Prior agreed, surprised that his friend should feel so strongly on these issues. "But after all, like him, we all revere the Scriptures, and like him we lay humbly at the Saviour's feet whatever merit we gain from our works."

"Yes, to be sure, Your Reverence, and that is perhaps what would make these bitter debates altogether incomprehensible to an atheist."

"Pray do not insinuate a thing which I do not wish to hear," murmured the Prior.

"I say no more," the philosopher promised, "but shall remark only that the Reformed lords of Germany, playing bowls with the heads of rebellious peasants, are no better than the mercenaries of the Duke; and that Luther courts the great of this world just as does the Cardinal de Granvelle."

"Luther has chosen the side of order, as we all do," the religious concluded, with infinite fatigue.

It was snowing outside in gusts. As the doctor rose to go back to his dispensary, the Superior reminded him that few of the ailing would venture forth in such rude weather, and that the Brother whose duty it was to assist him would suffice for those who might come. Then, with great effort, he took up the discussion again, saying:

"Let me tell you what I would not avow to a churchman, just as you might impart to me, rather than to a colleague, some daring conjecture in anatomy. I can bear it no longer, the state of things, my friend . . . Think of it, Sebastian, sixteen hundred years will soon have passed since the Incarnation of our Lord, and we lie sleeping over the cross as we would on a pillow . . . One might almost assume that, since the Redemption has taken place once and for all, the only thing that we have to do is to adjust ourselves to the way the world goes, or, at most, to procure our salvation, each for himself. We exalt Faith, it is true; we parade it in the streets, and if need be, we sacrifice to it thousands of lives, including our own. We also pay great observance to Hope as a theological virtue; yet only too often we have sold it to the pious at a price in gold. But who is concerned about Charity, except for a few Saints, and even so I tremble to think of the narrow limits within which they practice it . . .

"Even at my age, and in this garb, my compassion has often seemed to me too tender, a flaw in my nature which I should strive against . . . But then I ask myself, what if one of us should embrace martyrdom, not for the sake of Faith, which has witnesses enough already, but for Charity alone? If one of us were to climb upon the gallows or mount the faggot heap in place of, or at least alongside, the meanest of victims, we should perhaps find ourselves on a new earth, and under a new sky . . . Surely the worst scoundrel or the most pernicious heretic will never be more beneath me than I myself am beneath Jesus Christ."

"What the Prior envisages greatly resembles what we alchemists call 'the arid way,' or 'the swift way,'" said Sebastian Theus gravely. "It is, in sum, an attempt to transform everything in a single stroke, and by our own feeble forces . . . But that path is the most dangerous of all, my lord Prior."

"Never fear," the invalid reassured him, with a rather guilty smile. "I am only a weak, uncertain man, and must govern my sixty monks the best that I can . . . Would I deliberately induce them into some hazardous endeavor? Heaven's door is not to be opened by a sacrifice which is merely an act of will. The oblation, if it is made, must be offered otherwise."

"It takes place of itself when the victim is ready." Zeno was meditating aloud, recalling the secret admonitions of hermetic philosophers to their followers.

At these words the Prior regarded him in astonishment. "The Victim, the Host . . ." he repeated reverently, savoring the beauty of that word. "We are often told that you alchemists consider Jesus Christ to be the true Philosophers' Stone, and that your *Opus Magnum* is equivalent to the sacrifice of the Mass."

"Yes, some say so," replied Zeno laconically, replacing a coverlet which had slipped from the Prior's knees. "But what can we conclude from such equations other than that the human mind has a certain bent?"

"We are both prey to doubt," the Prior said, his voice suddenly trembling. "We have known doubt, you and I . . . How many nights have I struggled against the thought that God is only a tyrant over us, or else an impotent monarch, and that all of us, except for the atheist, who denies His very existence, utter blasphemies when we define Him . . . But illness opens certain things to our eyes: a glimmer of light has come to me. What if we are mistaken in postulating that God is all-powerful, and in supposing our woes to be the result of His will? What if it is for us to establish His Kingdom on earth? I have said to you before that God delegates himself; now I go beyond that, Sebastian. Possibly He is only a small flame in our hands, and we alone are the ones to feed and keep this flame alight; perhaps we are the farthest point to which He can advance . . . How many sufferers who are incensed when we speak of an almighty God would rush from the depth of their own distress to succor Him in His frailty if we asked them to do so?"

"Such a notion ill accords with the dogmas of the Holy Church."

"No, no, my friend; for I abjure in advance anything I have said which might further tear that Robe without Seam. God reigns omnipotent, I grant you that, in the world of the spirit, but we dwell here in the world of flesh. And on this earth, where He has walked, in what guise have we seen Him except as a babe on the straw, just like the innocents left lying on the snow when our moorland villages are devastated by the King's troops? Or as a vagabond, with no stone whereon to lay His head? Or as a man condemned and hanged at a cross-

roads, asking, in His turn, why God has abandoned Him? We
are indeed weak, each one of us, but there is some consolation
in the thought that He may be even weaker than we, and
more discouraged still, and that it is our task to beget Him and
save Him in all living beings . . ."

Stopping himself, he leaned his massive head, as if it were
suddenly exhausted of thought, against the back of his armchair and said, coughing, "Please excuse me. I have given you
the sermon which I can no longer preach from the pulpit."

Sebastian bent over him in friendly fashion while drawing
on and hooking his long outer gown, saying: "I shall reflect
upon the thoughts which the Prior has been so gracious as to
share with me. But before taking my leave, may I offer him a
hypothesis in exchange? The philosophers of our day, most of
them, postulate the existence of an *Anima Mundi*, a Soul of
the World, which is sentient and more or less conscious, and
with which all things are informed; I have myself conjectured
as to the silent cogitations of stones . . . And nevertheless,
the only facts that we know seem to indicate that pain, and
consequently joy, and therefore good and what we call evil,
justice and what for us is injustice, and finally the faculty of
understanding (under one form or another) through which
we distinguish these opposites, all exist only in the world of
flesh and blood, or perhaps also (who knows?) in the world
of sap and vegetation. Feelings cross through our flesh along
nets of nerves, like a pattern of lightning flashes; the stem
grows toward the light, its Sovereign Good, but suffers when
it lacks water and when it retracts in the cold, or has to resist
as best it can the encroachments of other plants. All the rest, I
mean the mineral kingdom and the world of spirits, if such a
world exists, is perhaps insentient and calm, well beyond our
joys and our pain, or as yet incapable of them. Our tribula-
tions, my lord Prior, are possibly only an infinitesimal exception in the fabric of this universe, and thus we could explain
the indifference of that immutable substance which we de-
voutly call God."

The Prior repressed a shudder. "What you suggest is terrifying," he answered. "But, if it be so, then we belong more than ever to the world of the Lamb who bleeds, and of the grain which is crushed for the sacrament. Go now in peace, Sebastian."

§

Zeno recrossed the arcade which connected the monastery with the hospice of Saint Cosmus. The snow, swept by the wind, was piling in great white drifts. Regaining his own quarters, he went straight to the small room where he had arranged the books inherited from Jan Myers. The old man had acquired a treatise published twenty years before by Andreas Vesalius, who had fought, like Zeno himself, against blind adherence to Galen in favor of a more complete knowledge of the human body. Zeno had encountered the celebrated physician only once, before the period of his brilliant career at Court; then he had died of the plague, as he was returning from a journey to the East. Having confined himself within the strict limits of his medical profession, Vesalius had had no cause to fear persecution other than that of pedants, but he had met with his share of annoyance from them. He, too, had stolen corpses, and he had informed himself as to man's internal structure by assembling bones from beneath the gallows and from among the ashes at the stake; or more indecently still, by secretly obtaining from the embalmed bodies of personages of rank such parts as a kidney, or the content of a testicle (substituting a wad of lint in its place), since nothing thereafter would indicate that these specimens came from Their Highnesses.

Placing the folio volume under the lamp, Zeno searched for the plate which shows a cross section of the esophagus and the larynx, with the tracheal artery. The drawing seemed to him one of the least correct of the sketches made by the great anatomist, but he was aware that Vesalius, like himself, had often been obliged to work too rapidly, and on bodies already in a state of putrefaction. He put a finger on the spot where he suspected that a polyp was growing in the Prior's throat, and would sooner or later shut off the patient's breath. Once in Germany he had had the chance to dissect the corpse of a vagabond who had died of this same thing; the memory of that experience, together with the recent examination using the *speculum oris*, led him now to diagnose some malign action going on beneath the obscure symptoms of the Prior's illness: a particle of flesh was slowly devouring the neighboring organs. One might almost have said that ambition and violence, so alien to the nature of this religious, were enclosed in that recess of his body, from which they were working finally to destroy this man of peace and good will. If the physician were not mistaken, Jean Louis de Berlaimont, Prior of the Cordeliers of Bruges, former High Forester to the Queen Dowager, Mary of Hungary, plenipotentiary of the Emperor at the Treaty of Crespy, would die a few months hence, strangled by the lump at the base of his throat—unless, meanwhile, the polyp in its progress should break a vein, and thus drown the sufferer in his own blood. Apart from the possibility (never inconsiderable) of an accidental death which might, so to speak, overtake the illness itself, the fate of this holy man was as firmly sealed as if his life were already over.

The growth was too internal to be reached either with a cauterizing iron or a scalpel. The only chance of prolonging this dear friend's life lay in sustaining his strength by prudent diet: it would require some study to procure semi-liquid foods which would be both nourishing and light, and which the patient could swallow without too much difficulty when the further narrowing of the throat should have rendered the daily fare of the monastery too hard for his consumption. It would be well, also, to see to it that he be spared the purges and bleedings of the usual practitioners, which in three fourths of the cases do no more than barbarously deplete the human substance. When the time should come to allay excessive pain, opiates would prove helpful; it would be wise from now on to divert the patient with harmless medicaments, if only to preclude for him the anguish of feeling himself abandoned to his malady. For the moment medical science could go no further.

He blew out the lamp. It had stopped snowing, but the white glare and the mortal cold pervaded the small bedchamber; the steep, icy roofs of the monastery gleamed like glass. A single, yellowish planet shone dully in the south, in the constellation of Taurus, not far from radiant Aldebaran and the rainy Pleiades. Zeno had long since ceased to draw horoscopes, considering that our relations with distant spheres are too confused to serve as a basis for exact calculation, even if from time to time some strange results have to be admitted. Nevertheless, as he leaned on the deep window ledge he gave way to somber speculation. He was well aware that, according to their respective nativities, both he and the Prior had the worst to fear from this position of Saturn.

DISORDERS OF THE
FLESH

FOR SOME months now Zeno had had as his assistant a young monk of eighteen, a welcome replacement for the drunken Brother who stole salves to sell, and who had finally been expelled from the monastery. Brother Cyprian was a country boy who had entered the Order at the age of fifteen; he knew barely enough Latin to make the responses at Mass, and he spoke only Flemish, in the thick accent of his own village. One often came upon him humming a refrain learned, probably, in the days when he had driven oxen before the plow. He still had some boyish failings, such as his habit of dipping his hand, on the quiet, into the sugar jar reserved for the making of juleps. But this lazy lad had no equal in laying on a poultice or in rolling a bandage; sores and abscesses neither frightened nor disgusted him. Children who had to be treated at the clinic were disarmed by his smile, and patients too weak to go home alone through the city were entrusted by Zeno to his guidance. Happily gaping his way along the streets, enjoying the noise and bustle, Cyprian trotted from the dispensary to Saint John's Hospital, lending or borrowing medicaments, and perhaps finding a bed for some beggar who could not be left to die on the ground, or, at best, persuading some pious woman of the quarter to take the tattered creature in. Early in the spring, before the monastery garden was in flower, he got into a scrape by stealing some hawthorn branches to adorn the Blessed Virgin of the arcade. His simple head was stuffed with superstitions inherited from old wives' tales in his village: he had to be kept from sticking the penny pictures of some saintly healer over the patients' sores. He believed in the werewolf who howls in lonely streets, and he was apt to see witches and sorcerers all around him. Holy Mass, according to him, could not be completed without one of these votaries of Satan hidden somewhere in attendance. When he happened to be the only acolyte at Mass in the otherwise empty chapel, he suspected the celebrant of being a sorcerer, or else he imagined that some invisible magician was lurking in the shadows. He claimed that on certain days of the year the priest had to make a supply of sorcerers, a work which was accomplished by reciting the baptismal prayers backward; for proof of this assertion he explained that in his own infancy his godmother had hastily retreated with him from the font on seeing that Mynheer the Curate was holding his breviary upside down. To protect oneself from sorcery one avoided touching the person suspected, or at least placed one's hand higher on that person than he did on you. One day when by chance Zeno had touched him on the shoulder, Cyprian managed to brush the physician's cheek a moment after.

The two of them were together in the back room of the dispensary on a morning following Low Sunday. Sebastian Theus was bringing his record book up to date. Cyprian was languidly crushing cardamom seeds with a pestle. From time to time he stopped to yawn.

"You are asleep on your feet," said the doctor sharply. "Am I to suppose that you passed the night in prayer?"

The boy smiled with a knowing air. "The Angels meet at night," he said, after a glance in the direction of the door.

"The wine cruet goes from hand to hand and the tub is ready for the Angels' bath. They kneel down before the Fair One, who embraces and kisses each one; her maidservant unbinds her long tresses, and the two of them stand naked, as they would be in Paradise. The Angels take off their woolen robes and marvel at each other clothed only in the skin God gave them; the candles glow and then go out, and each one does as his heart desires."

"Fine tales you tell!" the physician exclaimed with disdain. But a dull disquietude came over him. He recognized these angelic appellations and these mildly lascivious descriptions: they had been part of the trappings of certain sects now forgotten which were thought to have been destroyed in Flanders, by fire and sword, more than half a century ago. He remembered that as a child, sitting with the servants by the kitchen fireside in the house on Woolmarket Street, he had heard these assemblies spoken of in low tones: the followers were said to know each other in the flesh. "Where have you picked up this dangerous rubbish?" he asked severely. "Get better stuff for your dreams."

"These aren't just stories," the boy answered, with an offended air. "When Mynheer wants to come, Cyprian will take him by the hand to lead him, and he will see and touch the Angels for himself."

"Surely you jest," said Dr. Theus, rather more firmly than his suspicions justified him in doing.

Cyprian went back to his work on the cardamom seeds. Once in a while he would hold one of the dark grains to his nose the better to smell the good, spicy odor. It would have been prudent to disregard the boy's words, but curiosity got the better of Zeno. He asked, with some irritation, "And when and where do you hold these nocturnal gatherings that you say you have? It is not so easy to leave the monastery at night. Some monks, I know, jump the wall . . ."

"They are fools," Cyprian said, with contempt. "Brother

Florian has found a passageway through which the Angels can come and go. Florian loves Cyprian well."

"Keep your secrets to yourself," the physician bade him with vehemence. "How do you know that I am not going to betray you?"

The youth gently shook his head in dissent. "Mynheer would not wish to harm the Angels," he replied, in the insinuating and impudent tone of an accomplice.

The sound of the door knocker interrupted them. Zeno started as he had not done since the precarious days of Innsbruck, and went to open the door. It was only a young girl suffering from a lupus, who always came wearing a black veil, not because of shame for her appearance, but because Zeno had noticed and had warned her that light increased the spread of the malady. It was a relief at the moment to receive and treat this unfortunate. Other poor patients followed. No further compromising conversation was exchanged between the doctor and his helper for several days. But Zeno watched the young monk from this time on with quite another eye. A disturbing and provocative body and soul dwelt under that monastic frock. At the same time it seemed to him that a crack had opened in the ground beneath this, his refuge. Without admitting it to himself, he sought an opportunity to learn more about the situation.

His chance came on the following Saturday. He and Cyprian were seated at a table cleaning his instruments after the hospice had closed. Cyprian's hands moved diligently in and out among the sharp pincers and the surgical knives. Suddenly, planting his two elbows in the midst of this cutlery to rest his chin in his upraised hands, he began to chant under his breath, to the tune of some ancient and intricate air:

> *"I call and I am called,*
> *I drink and yet they drink me,*
> *I eat and yet am eaten,*

I dance, and everyone sings,
I sing, and everyone dances . . ."

"Pray now, what refrain is this?" the physician asked
brusquely. Actually, he had recognized the verses as coming
from an apocryphal gospel condemned by the Church; he had
heard them recited several times by hermetic practitioners
who credited them with occult power.

"It's the canticle of Saint John," the boy answered inno-
cently. And leaning across the table, he continued in a tender
and confidential tone: "Spring has come, and the dove sighs;
the Angels' bath is all warm. They take each other by the
hand and sing softly, for fear of being heard by the wicked.
Yesterday Brother Florian brought a lute, and he played, very
low, such sweet music that it brought tears to the eyes."

In spite of himself, Sebastian Theus asked a question
further: "Are there many of you in this venture?"

The boy counted on his fingers. "There is Quirin, my
friend, and the novice François de Bure, who is fair of face,
and has a fine, clear voice. Matthew Aerts comes from time to
time," he continued, and he added two more names that the
doctor did not know. "Brother Florian rarely misses the
Angels' assemblies. Pierre de Hamaere never comes, but he
loves the Angels."

Zeno was not expecting mention of this monk, a man supposedly austere. There had been hostility between him and
the doctor from the beginning; the accountant had opposed
the renovation of some parts of Saint Cosmus, and had several
times tried to cut down on the money allotted to the hospice.
For a moment it seemed to him that the strange avowals of
Cyprian were only a snare set by Pierre to trap the physician.
But the boy went on:

"The Fair One does not always come either, only when her
wicked guardians do not frighten her. Her black maid brings
the blessed breads of the Bernardines, wrapped in snow-white
linen. The Angels have no shame or jealousy, and no law

forbidding the sweet use of the body. The Fair One gives the consolation of her kisses to all who seek them, but she loves only Cyprian."

"What is her name?" the doctor asked, for the first time suspecting an actual person behind what had seemed to him, until then, the mere amorous fabrications of a youth deprived of girls, deprived of them, at least, from the time that he had been obliged to forgo dallying with milkmaids under the willows.

"We call her Eve," said Cyprian softly.

A handful of coals was burning in a brazier on the window shelf, where it served to melt gum for applying eye salves. Zeno seized the boy by the hand and dragged him toward the tiny flame, then held captive a finger for a second or two over the incandescent mass. Cyprian paled to his very lips, which he bit in order to keep from crying out in pain. Zeno was hardly less pale himself. He freed the hand immediately thereafter.

"How will you endure flame like that burning over your whole body?" he demanded, speaking in a low voice. "Find something less dangerous for pleasure than your assemblies of Angels."

While Zeno was speaking, Cyprian, with his left hand, had reached for a bottle on a shelf that contained oil of lilies, and was using it to anoint the burned member. Zeno helped him, but in silence, to bandage the finger.

§

At this moment Brother Luke entered with a tray prepared for the Prior, to whom a soothing potion was sent each evening. Zeno took charge of the tray, and proceeded alone up to the monk's cell. The next day the whole alarming incident seemed to have been no more than a bad dream, but he saw Cyprian in the hall, busy washing the foot of an injured child, and still wearing his bandage. Thereafter, and always with the same dread and unbearable anguish, Zeno would shift his glance away from the scar of the burned finger, but Cyprian seemed to manage to put it almost coyly before the doctor's eyes.

§

Now, instead of the alchemical speculations that had gone on in the small room at Saint Cosmus, there began the anxious pacing back and forth of a man who sees danger and seeks a way out. Slowly, like objects emerging from mist, the facts underlying Cyprian's divagations were becoming apparent. The Angels' bath and their wanton gatherings were not hard to explain. Beneath the city of Bruges lay a network of subterranean passages branching from warehouse to warehouse and from cellar to cellar. Only an abandoned dwelling stood between the outbuildings of the monastery of the Cordeliers and the Bernardine convent; Brother Florian, who was something of a mason as well as a painter, while at work on repairs to the chapel and the cloisters, could have found some remains of ancient steam baths or laundry rooms which had now become a secret chamber and amorous refuge for these mad young folk. Florian was a scamp of some twenty-four years of age who had passed his early youth in wandering over the land, making portraits of noblemen in their châteaux and of burghers in their town houses, receiving from them in exchange his food, and a pallet of straw for his bed. In Antwerp he had made a sudden decision to become a monk, entering a Franciscan monastery there, but that house had been evacuated at the time of the riots, so a place had been found for him, since the past autumn, with the Cordeliers of Bruges. Dashing, merry, inventive, he was always surrounded by a band of apprentices performing their acrobatics on his ladders. This featherbrain could have met with some remnant of those heretical Beghards, or of those Brothers of the Holy Spirit exterminated as a sect at the beginning of the century, and could have picked up from them, like a contagion, that flowery language and those seraphic appellations which he later transmitted, probably, to Cyprian. Unless, on the other hand, the young rustic had himself gathered up all such incriminating jargon among the superstitions of his village, like the germs of some forgotten pestilence which continued to breed in secret in the back of a cupboard.

§

Zeno had noticed a tendency to irregularity and disorder in the monastery from the time that the Prior had fallen ill: the offices of the night hours, he heard, were but laxly attended now by some of the Brothers. A whole group were mutely resisting reforms which the Prior had established in conformity with the recommendations of the Council; the most dissipated among the monks hated Jean Louis de Berlaimont for setting an example of austerity; the strictest, on the contrary, distrusted him for his benignity, which they judged extreme. Factions were already forming in anticipation of electing the next Superior. The audacities of the Angels had doubtless been facilitated by this atmosphere of interregnum. What was most extraordinary was that a man so cautious as Pierre de Hamaere should let these lads run the mortal risk of nocturnal meetings, and then commit the still greater folly of involving two girls there; but doubtless Pierre was in no position to refuse anything to Florian and Cyprian.

At first Zeno had supposed that these feminine appellations were only ingenious nicknames used among these boys, or that the two girls were simply dreams. Then he recalled that there was much talk in the quarter about a young maiden of rank who had come around Christmastime to lodge with the Bernardine Sisters during the absence of her father; as a magistrate in the Council of Flanders, he had gone to submit his accounts to the Court at Valladolid. The beauty of this girl, and her costly apparel, not to mention the dark skin and great earrings of her little maidservant, all served as subject for comment in the shops and in the street. The Damsel de Loos went about with her little Moorish maid to attend service at various churches, or to make purchases from the trimmings merchant or from the pastry shop. There was no reason to think that Cyprian had not exchanged, first glances, and then words, with these beauties during the course of some errand, or that Florian, while repairing the frescoes of the choir, had not found means to win the maidens over either for himself or for his friend. Two daring girls could very well manage to steal at night through a labyrinth of corridors to the midnight meetings of the Angels, thus providing those boyish imaginations, fed with imagery from the Scriptures, with a Shulamite and an Eve.

§

One morning, shortly after Cyprian's revelations, Zeno went to the pastry shop of Long Street to buy wine of hippocras, which made up a third of the potion given to the Prior. Idelette de Loos was selecting some delicate wafers and some crullers at the counter. She was a girl of not more than fifteen, slender as a reed, with long hair so blond as to be almost white, and with eyes as limpid as spring water. The flaxen hair and pale-blue eyes reminded Zeno of the youth who had been his inseparable companion at Lübeck. That was at the time when, together with the boy's father, the learned Aegidius Friedhof, a rich jeweler of Broad Street, he was making special studies into the amount of alloy which can be added to the nobler metals and into techniques for soldering them. The thoughtful young Gerhart had been both a source of delight and a studious disciple . . . He had taken such a liking to the alchemist that he wished to accompany him on his travels toward France, and the father had consented, since the son could thus begin his tour of Germany, preliminary to becoming a master jeweler; but Zeno had feared that a boy so gently reared would suffer from the harshness of life on the road, along with its other dangers. Those tender associations of Lübeck, like a kind of Saint Martin's summer in the period of his travels, came back to him now, no longer reduced to some dry specimen stored away in his memory, like those carnal experiences which he had formerly evoked in meditating upon himself, but heady as a wine, the intoxicating effects of which should at all costs be avoided. Such recollections and feelings brought him closer to this passion-ridden troupe of Angels, whether he wished it or not.

But other memories came surging around the dainty visage of Idelette de Loos: something audacious and headstrong about her brought Jeannette Fauconnier back to him from oblivion, that darling of the students at Louvain who had been his first conquest in love; Cyprian's visible pride seemed less childish to him now, and less vain. He strove to go even further back in memory, but the thread broke: the little Moor was laughing as she crunched sugared almonds, and Idelette, in departing, tossed to this stranger with graying locks one of those smiles which she darted at every passer-by. Her ample gown filled the narrow entranceway, and the baker, who was one to run after women, called his customer's attention to the damsel's manner of gathering her skirts in one hand, thus exposing her ankles and drawing the handsome silks tightly over her thighs.

"Girls who show their forms let everyone know that they want something besides buns," said he, leering, to the physician.

The pleasantry was one of those which men feel obliged to exchange between themselves, so Zeno dutifully laughed at it in his turn.

§

The pacing of the floor by night continued: eight steps from the coffer to the bed, and twelve from the window to the door; he was wearing down the flooring with what was already the walk of a prisoner. He had always known that certain of his passions, considered by the Church as heresy on the part of the flesh, could bring down upon him the fate reserved for heretics, that is to say, burning at the stake. We grow accustomed to the ferocity of the laws of our century, just as we do to the wars which human imbecility provokes, or to inequality in social conditions, and to lack of protection on the highway or filth in cities. It was accepted by all that one could be burned alive for having loved Gerhart, just as one could be burned for reading the Bible in the vernacular. These laws, which were rendered inoperable by the very nature of what they claimed to punish, affected neither the rich nor the great of this world: the Nuncio at Innsbruck had boasted about obscene verses which would have caused some poor monk, had he written them, to be thrown into the fire; no lord had ever been seen dying in flames for having seduced his young page; but to more obscure, unimportant individuals such laws brought woe. Nevertheless, obscurity itself was a refuge, for in spite of the hooks, the nets, and the luring torches everywhere, most fish pursue their trackless path through the dark depths of ocean with hardly a concern for those of their bloodied companions who flop and flounder on the deck of a fishing bark.

But he knew, too, that an enemy bent on revenge, or one moment of rage and madness in a crowd, or simply the inept inflexibility of a judge, was sufficient to bring death upon the so-called guilty, who perhaps, after all, were innocent. Indifference was likely to turn into fury, and semicomplicity into execration. All his life long he had known this fear, mingled with many others. But one endures less readily for others what one accepts with some composure for oneself.

These troubled times encouraged secret denunciations on many matters. The rabble, at heart delighted with the image breakers and their activities, threw themselves avidly upon any slander which could lower the prestige of the powerful monastic Orders, whom they begrudged their riches and their authority. At Ghent, a few months back, nine Augustinian monks suspected, rightly or wrongly, of sodomy had been burned in public after atrocious torture in order to satisfy the excited cravings of idlers who were stirred up against the Church. The fear of seeming to silence a scandalous affair had kept the ecclesiastical authorities from inflicting mere disciplinary punishment within the Order itself upon the culprits, as would have been the wiser course. The situation of the Angels was even more dangerous than that in which the monks of Ghent had found themselves. Amorous relations with the two girls, which ordinarily might have mitigated (in the view of the average man) what was considered evil in the whole adventure, served only to expose these unfortunates still further. For the Damsel de Loos would become the object of attention on which the malevolent curiosity of the people would center, and the secrecy of the meetings by night would depend henceforth upon whether or not the girls would yield to the feminine tendency to babble, and whether or not an untimely pregnancy should occur. The greatest danger of all lay in those angelic appellations, in those candles and childish rites of wine and blessed bread, in those recitations of apocryphal verses, which no one, not even their authors, had ever in the least understood, and finally in the nakedness, which nevertheless hardly differed from that of boys playing around a pond. Irregularities which certainly deserved a sound slap would lead in this case to death for such mad hearts and weak heads. Not a soul would have the common sense to find it natural that ignorant children, marveling in their newly discovered joys of the flesh, should make use of the sacred phrases and imagery which had been instilled in them from their earliest breath. Just as the date and nature of the Prior's death was virtually determined in advance by his illness, so the end for Cyprian and his comrades was as definitely fixed, it seemed to Zeno, as if they had already shrieked their last in the devouring flames.

Seated at his table, scribbling vague numbers or symbols on the margins of a register there, he told himself that his own position was highly vulnerable. Cyprian had insisted on making a confidant of him, if not an actual accomplice. A detailed interrogation would almost inevitably reveal Zeno's true name and person, and it was no more a consolation to be arrested for atheism than for sodomy. Nor was he unmindful of the ever-present danger to himself for the care which he had lavished upon Han, and the precautions taken to keep him out of the grasp of the law; that whole affair could cause him to be dealt with any day as a rebel, that is to say, simply, hanged. It would have been prudent to leave, and at once. But to abandon the Prior at this moment was unthinkable.

§

Jean Louis de Berlaimont was dying, slowly, and in conformity with what was known of the usual course of his malady. He had grown so thin as to be almost emaciated, a change which was the more noticeable in this man, formerly of robust constitution. Since the difficulty of swallowing had increased, Sebastian Theus had ordered some light nourishment prepared by old Greete, certain purées and syrups which she made, following old recipes once in great favor in the kitchen of the Ligre household. Although the sick man tried to get some enjoyment from them, he could hardly partake of them, and Zeno suspected that he suffered continuously from hunger. His voice was almost totally gone; he reserved the few words he had strength to utter for only the most urgent communications with his subordinates and with his physician. The rest of the time he wrote his wishes or his orders on scraps of paper which were placed for him on his bed; but, as he managed to observe once to Sebastian, there was no longer very much of anything to write or to say.

The physician had requested that as few reports as possible of events outside the monastery should be transmitted to the patient, hoping to spare him the recital of atrocities committed by the special Tribunal for the Tumults, which was meting out its punishments from Brussels and had come to be known as the "Council of Blood." But news seemed to filter through to him, somehow. Toward mid-June the novice who took charge of the Prior's bodily needs was discussing with Dr. Theus what day it was that they had last given him his bath of bran water, which refreshed his skin and seemed to restore to him a measure of well-being for a time. The Prior turned his haggard face toward them and murmured, with effort: "It was Monday, the sixth, the day the two Counts were executed."

A few tears ran silently down his hollow cheeks. Zeno learned, shortly thereafter, that Jean Louis de Berlaimont was related to Lamoral by his late wife. A few days passed before the patient was able to write and to confide to his doctor a word of consolation for the Count's widow, Sabina of Bavaria; she was but a step from the tomb herself, they said, worn down as she was by anxiety and grief. Sebastian Theus took the note to give it to a messenger, but Pierre de Hamaere, who was prowling about in the corridor, interposed, fearing for the monastery some imprudence on the part of his Superior.

Zeno handed the brief letter over to him with disdain. The accountant gave it back after having read the contents: there was nothing incriminating in such condolences offered to the illustrious widow, and in the promises to pray for the departed, for the Countess Sabina was treated with deference even by the officers of the King.

§

After much thought about the secret affair which so weighed upon him, Zeno persuaded himself that, in order to ward off the worst results, it would suffice to send Brother Florian away to restore other chapels elsewhere. Left to themselves, Cyprian and the novices would not dare to go on with their nocturnal sessions; nor was it impossible, for the other part of the situation, to suggest to the Bernardine Sisters that they should keep better watch over their two young boarders. Since the transfer of Florian depended wholly upon the Prior, the physician decided to tell the sick man the little that he needed to know in order to determine him to act without delay. He waited for a day when the patient might feel less ill. This was the case on a certain afternoon in early July, when the Bishop had come in person to ask for news of the Prior. His Lordship had just left; Jean Louis de Berlaimont, dressed in his habit, was lying on his bed, and the effort he had made to receive his guest with his usual courtesy seemed to have given him back, momentarily, some of his animation and strength. Sebastian noticed a tray, with its food almost untouched, on the table.

"Kindly thank that good woman for me," said the religious, in a voice less feeble than of late. "I have eaten very little, it is true," he added, almost gaily, "but it is not bad for a monk to be forced to fast."

"The Bishop has surely accorded the Prior a dispensation to relieve him from such obligations," the physician replied, taking the same light tone.

The monk smiled, and then commented: "His Lordship is a highly cultivated gentleman, and I believe him to be a good man, although I am one of those who opposed his nomination by the King (who was disregarding our ancient customs). It was a pleasure to recommend my physician to the Bishop."

"I am not seeking another position," Sebastian rejoined easily.

The Prior's face already showed his fatigue. "I do not wish to complain, Sebastian," he said patiently, embarrassed, as always, when he spoke of his own ills. "My suffering is indeed bearable . . . But there are troublesome consequences. For example, I am uncertain about receiving Holy Communion . . . A cough or a spell of hiccups must not . . . If some medicine could only slightly relieve this sore throat . . ."

"Sore throat is curable, my lord Prior," the physician prevaricated. "We are counting very much on this fine summer weather . . ."

"To be sure," the Prior answered abstractedly. "To be sure . . ."

He offered his thin wrist, and the doctor took his pulse. The Brother assigned to nursing duty was temporarily out of sight, so Sebastian took the opportunity to remark casually that he had just seen Brother Florian. "Yes," said the Prior, desiring perhaps to show that he still remembered names. "They will put him to work on restoring the frescoes in the choir. There is not enough money to pay for new paintings . . ." He seemed to think that the monk with the brushes and paint jars had only just arrived. Contrary to the rumors which circulated through the monastery corridors, Zeno considered Jean Louis de Berlaimont to be in full possession of his faculties, but his thinking was now directed inward, so to speak. Suddenly the sick man made a sign to the doctor to bend over him, as if there were a secret to be whispered; but the subject of the Brother painter was already far from his mind.

"The oblation of which we talked one day, friend Sebastian, you remember . . . But there is nothing to sacrifice . . . It hardly matters whether a man of my age lives or dies . . ."

"It is important to me that the Prior should live" was the physician's firm response. But he had given up the idea of asking the priest for help on the matter of Florian. Any appeal might become the equivalent of a denunciation. Such confidences given to a man so ill might, by inadvertence, escape from his weary lips; it was even possible that this patient, now wholly exhausted, might evince a severity which was not natural to him. And finally, the incident of the note of condolence proved that the Prior was no longer master in his own house.

§

Zeno made still another attempt to frighten Cyprian. He spoke to him of the disaster of the Augustinians at Ghent, which the young monk must have known something about, anyhow. The result was not at all what he had expected.

"The Augustinians are a stupid lot," the Cordelier answered, without more to say on the subject.

But three days later he came, obviously greatly disturbed, to the doctor. "Brother Florian has lost a talisman that he got from a gypsy," he said, in agitation. "It seems that something very bad could happen if it is not found. Now if Mynheer, with all the powers that he has . . ."

"Indeed, no. I am no merchant, selling amulets," retorted Sebastian Theus, turning away.

§

A day passed. That night, on a Friday or Saturday, the philosopher was at work upstairs among his books when some light object was tossed through the open window. It was a switch of hazelwood. He went to look out. A shadowy gray figure, of which he could discern only vaguely the face, hands, and bare feet, stood below, beckoning. It was Cyprian. After a moment he departed, disappearing under the arcade.

Zeno returned to the table and sat down, trembling. He was seized with a violent desire, but knew in advance that he would not yield to it, just as in other cases one knows in advance that one will give in, in spite of still stronger resistance. There was no question of following the reckless youth toward some vague debauch or some nocturnal magic ritual. But in this life without respite, and in presence of the slow destruction which was going on in the Prior's flesh, and perhaps in his soul, as well, he was tempted to forget those overwhelming forces of cold, darkness, and perdition in the embrace of a warm young body. Should he, perhaps, read into Cyprian's persistence an effort to win a man deemed to be useful, and believed, in addition, to be endowed with occult powers? Or was this all just one more example of the eternal attempt at seduction made by an Alcibiades upon a Socrates?

A still wilder idea crossed the alchemist's mind. Could it be that his own desires, curbed for the sake of investigations even more subtle than those which the flesh attempts, would have taken this childish but dangerous form, wholly external to his own being? *Extinctis luminibus:* he blew out the lamp. In vain did he try, as an anatomist and not as a lover, to picture with disdain the games in which these voluptuous children were indulging. He told himself that the mouth, where kisses are distilled, is only the hollow cavern for mastication, and that the mark of lips on a glass's rim is disgusting, even if those lips have just been pressed in passion. Vainly did he evoke such images as that of white worms hugged together, or of poor, entrapped flies stuck in honey. Vainly because, whatever one might say, Idelette and Cyprian, François de Bure and Matthew Aerts had beauty. The abandoned underground room was truly a magic chamber; the great flame of carnal desire had power to transmute everything, as did the fire of the alchemist's furnace; it was worth the risk of burning at the stake; naked white bodies had the gleam of those phosphorescences which attest to the hidden virtues of stones.

But by the next morning revulsion had set in. The worst dissipation in some low tavern was better than these mummeries of the Angels. Downstairs, in the drab receiving room and in the presence of an old woman who came every Saturday to be treated for sores from varicose veins, the doctor reprimanded Cyprian harshly for having dropped the box of dressings. Nothing unusual could be read on the young monk's face, though the eyelids were slightly puffy. That nocturnal solicitation could have been but a dream.

§

The messages coming from the small group, however, were now redolent of hostility and irony. One morning on entering the back workroom of the clinic, the philosopher found on the table, clearly in evidence, a design much too skillfully drawn to have come from Cyprian, who could barely guide a pen to sign his name. It was surely the fantastical mind of Florian which had been at work to produce this conglomeration of figures, one of those gardens of delights encountered from time to time among painters, in which simple folk see a satire of sin, while others, more clever than they, see quite the contrary, a mad carnival of sensual exploits: thus, a fair damsel enters a fountain's basin to bathe, accompanied by her lovers; two other lovers, revealed only by the position of their bare feet, are embracing behind a curtain. A youth tenderly parts the knees of a beloved object who resembles him like a brother. From the mouth and private orifice of a boy, prostrate on hands and knees, branch delicate flowers, growing up toward the heavens. A Moorish maiden carries a gigantic red raspberry on a tray. Pleasure allegorized in this fashion became a sorcerer's game, a dangerous kind of jest. Pensively, the philosopher tore up the obscene page.

Two or three days later another lascivious jest awaited him: someone had removed from a closet several pairs of old shoes, used by the monks for crossing the garden in time of rain or snow; these shoes were placed conspicuously in view on the floor in wanton disorder, riding each other. Zeno dispersed them with a vigorous kick; the pleasantry was gross. More disturbing was an object which he found one night in his bedchamber, a pebble on which a face and feminine or hermaphrodite attributes had been clumsily drawn with crayons; the small stone was bound round with a lock of blond hair. The philosopher burned the ringlet and threw the magic doll contemptuously into a drawer. Finally the persecutions came to an end; he never demeaned himself by so much as speaking to Cyprian about them. He began to think that the Angels' follies would terminate by themselves, for the simple reason that everything comes to an end.

§

The public woes brought business, so to speak, to the hospice of Saint Cosmus. With the regular patients there were now mingled visitors who were rarely seen twice: country folk dragging with them a jumble of belongings thrown together on the eve of a flight, or snatched from a house on fire: scorched bedding, featherbeds with their contents protruding, cauldrons and chipped pots. Women carried their children inside their bundles of soiled linen. Almost all these refugees, driven from their rebel hamlets by the King's troops, were suffering from wounds or bruises, but their principal misery was simply hunger. Some of them crossed the city like herds changing pasture, not knowing what the next stop would be; others were coming to relatives who had settled in this less harassed area, and therefore still had roofs overhead and a few farm animals. With the help of Brother Luke, Zeno managed to have some bread to distribute to the most destitute among them. Less plaintive and bewildered, but actually more anxious and fearful, were the men recognizable as members of a profession or a trade, traveling usually alone or in small groups of twos and threes, and coming from cities of the interior where they were doubtless wanted by the Court of Blood. Fugitives of this class wore good town clothing, but their ragged shoes and swollen feet, covered with blisters, betrayed miles of walking such as these folk of sedentary lives had never known. They kept silent as to their destinations, but Zeno knew through old Greete that these Patriots were taken by fishing boats, which left almost daily from isolated points on the coast, to England or to Zeeland, according to what the passengers' means and the state of the wind permitted. He saw to it that they were given care, without having to answer questions.

Dr. Theus hardly left the Prior now, but he could repose some confidence in the two monks of the clinic who had by this time learned at least the rudiments of the art of healing. Brother Luke was a sensible man, mindful of his duties, whose thinking did not go beyond the immediate work in hand. Cyprian had the merit of a certain gentleness and kindness in dealing with the patients.

§

Opiates could no longer be used to ease the Prior's pain. He had refused one evening to take his soothing potion. "Understand me, Sebastian," he pleaded anxiously, no doubt fearing resistance on the physician's part. "One would not wish to be sleeping at the moment when . . . *Et invenit dormientes* . . ."

The philosopher made a sign of acquiescence. His role at the dying man's side from this time on consisted of making him swallow a few spoonfuls of broth, or, with the help of a Brother nurse, of lifting this tall, wasted body which already smelled of the tomb. Returning late to Saint Cosmus, he would lie down to sleep fully clad, always expecting that the Superior might have the choking spell from which he would not recover.

§

One night he thought that he heard rapid footsteps approaching his room along the stone corridor. He rose in great haste and opened the door. There was nothing, no one. Nevertheless, he rushed directly to the Prior.

Jean Louis de Berlaimont was sitting up in his bed, supported by the bolster and pillows. His eyes, wide open, turned toward the physician with what seemed to the latter a boundless solicitude. "Flee, Zeno!" he managed to say distinctly. "After my death . . ."

A fit of coughing interrupted him. Zeno, stunned, had instinctively turned around to see if the night nurse, seated on his stool, could have heard. But the old monk was half asleep, his head a-nod. The Prior, exhausted, had fallen back aslant on his cushions, in a kind of feverish torpor. Zeno bent over him, his own heart beating, tempted to rouse him in order to obtain one word or one glance more. For he doubted the testimony of his own senses, and even of his reason. When a moment or two had passed, he sat down beside the bed. After all, it was not impossible that the Prior had known his name from the beginning.

The invalid stirred, his body quivering feebly. Zeno rubbed his feet and legs for some time, as the Lady of Froso had formerly taught him to do. This treatment was worth more than any opiate. He ended by falling asleep himself at the bedside, his head in his hands.

In the morning he went down to the refectory to have a bowl of warm soup. Pierre de Hamaere was there. All the alchemist's fears had been awakened, almost superstitiously, by the Prior's warning cry. Zeno took Pierre de Hamaere aside and said to him point-blank: "I hope that you have dealt firmly with the follies of your friends." He was going on to speak of the safety and honor of the monastery, but the accountant saved him from this absurdity by his vehement response.

"I know nothing whatsoever of this whole affair," he said, and made off, with a great clacking of sandals.

§

The Prior received extreme unction that same evening, and for the third time. The small cell and adjoining chapel were crowded with monks, each holding a taper. Some were weeping; others were only decorously present at the ceremony. The sufferer, semiconscious and trying, it seemed, to breathe with as little effort as possible, gazed on the small yellow flames as if without fully seeing them. When the prayers for the dying had ended, the attendants filed out, leaving behind them only two monks with their rosaries. Zeno had stood apart, but now he resumed his usual place.

The time for verbal communication, even the briefest, had passed; the Prior limited himself to requests by signs for a little water, or for the urinal hung on a corner of the bed. It seemed to Zeno that within this world in ruins, like a treasure beneath a heap of rubble, a spirit subsisted still, with which it was perhaps possible to remain in contact above and beyond the use of words. He continued to hold the invalid's wrist, and even so feeble a connection appeared to suffice for passing on some slight strength to him, and for receiving in return some degree of serenity. From time to time, thinking of the tradition that would have it that the soul of a man who is dying floats over him like a flame wrapped round in mist, the physician peered into the surrounding shadow, but what he saw was probably only the reflection, in the windowpane, of a lighted candle. Toward the small hours of the morning Zeno withdrew his hand; the moment had come to let the Prior advance alone toward those last gates; or perhaps, on the contrary, he was now accompanied by those invisible figures whom he must have summoned to him in his death agony. Shortly thereafter the sick man appeared to hover on the brink of an awakening; the fingers of his left hand seemed to search vaguely for something on his chest, at the place where formerly, doubtless, Jean Louis de Berlaimont had worn his insignia of the Golden Fleece. On the pillow Zeno could see a linen scapular, the cord of which had come untied. The doctor replaced it on the patient's chest; the dying man pressed his fingers upon the pious object as if he were now content. His lips moved noiselessly. By listening closely, however, Zeno managed to hear the end of a prayer, repeated probably for the thousandth time:

". . . *nunc et in hora mortis nostrae.*"

A half hour went by; the physician then asked the two monks to see to the final care to be given to the body.

§

He attended the funeral services of the Prior, standing in one of the side aisles of the church. The ceremony had called forth a good many people. Zeno recognized the Bishop, sitting in the front row of the choir, and nearby, leaning on his cane, an old man too crippled to rise but still visibly strong, who was none other than Canon Bartholomew Campanus, having now acquired the prestige and assurance that comes with great age. The monks, half hidden under their hoods, looked all alike. François de Bure was swinging the incense pot; he had, indeed, the face of a young angel. From the newly repainted frescoes of the choir gleamed the gold halo of a Saint, or the spot of color which was his cloak.

The new Superior was a person of no special interest, but he was known for his piety, and was said to be an able administrator. Rumor had it that, on the advice of Pierre de Hamaere, who had worked toward his election, he would probably have the hospice of Saint Cosmus closed very soon, for it was judged too costly. Perhaps, too, there had been some tales to the authorities about services rendered to fugitives from the Tribunal of the Tumults. Still, no such comment had been made to the physician. Little did he care: he had decided to depart, to disappear immediately after the last rites for the Prior.

This time he would take nothing with him. He would leave his books behind; anyhow, he no longer consulted them very much. His manuscripts were neither so valuable nor so compromising that he needed to keep them with him, instead of leaving them to end one day or another in the refectory stove. Since it was the summer season, he decided to abandon his long coat and his winter clothing; a simple jacket over his best garments would suffice. He would put his instruments, wrapped in a little linen, into a sack, together with some rare and costly medicines. At the last minute he added also his two old horse pistols. Each detail of this reduction to bare essentials had been the object of long deliberation. He did not lack for money: apart from the small sum that he had saved for this journey from the slender emoluments allotted to him by the monastery, he had received, a few days before the Prior's death, a packet delivered by the old monk who served as night nurse; it contained the purse from which he had previously drawn money for Han. The Prior seemed not to have used it since that time.

His first intention had been to hire the cart of Greete's son to get as far as Antwerp, and from there to slip into Zeeland or Gueldre, both of which had openly revolted against royal authority. But if, after his departure, some suspicion should fall upon him, it would be better if this old woman and her carter son were in no way compromised. He made the decision to go on foot to the coast, and there procure a boat.

§

The evening before his departure he exchanged some words for the last time with Cyprian, whom he found singing in the back workroom. The boy had an air of quiet contentment which exasperated the physician.

"I should like to think that you have forgone your diversions during this period of mourning," he said curtly, without preamble.

"Cyprian hardly cares any longer about those midnight meetings," the young monk answered, with the childish habit he had of speaking of himself as if it pertained to someone else. "He meets the Fair One all alone, and in broad daylight."

He needed little prodding to explain that along the canal he had found an abandoned garden where he had broken open the gate, and where Idelette sometimes joined him. The Moorish maid kept watch for them, hiding behind a wall.

"Have you thought of taking precautions for your Fair One? Your life can depend upon whether or not the girl would talk if you get her with child."

"Angels conceive not; neither do they bring forth children," Cyprian replied in the falsely assured tone of those who recite set formulas.

"Bah! Leave off this fool's talk," Zeno exclaimed in disgust.

§

That last evening in the city he supped, as he often did, with the organist and his wife. After the meal the musician took his guest along, as usual, to Saint Donatian, to hear what would be played on the great organ there the following Sunday. The air enclosed in the sonorous pipes rushed forth, filling the empty nave with sound more harmonious and more powerful than that of any human voice. One motet of Roland de Lassus, in particular, came back to the physician all night long, weaving in and out of his projects for the future as he lay (for the last time, he reflected) on his bed in the cell of Saint Cosmus. No use to set off too soon; the city gates opened only at sunrise. He wrote a note to leave behind, explaining that a friend in a neighboring town had fallen ill, and had sent for him to come at once, but that he would doubtless be back in less than a week's time. (Always best to keep some opening for a possible return.) When he did slip cautiously from the hospice that morning, the street was already bathed in the dim gray light of a summer dawn. The pastry cook, opening the shutter of his shop, was the only one, he noted, to see him depart.

A WALK ON THE

DUNES

HE REACHED the Damme Gate just as they were raising the portcullis and lowering the drawbridge. The guards nodded to him courteously; they were familiar with these morning excursions of the herbalist, and his pack was no cause for special concern.

He strode at a rapid pace along the canal. It was the hour when the market gardeners were entering the city to sell their produce; many of these folk knew him, and wished him Godspeed. One man, who had planned to come to the hospice that very day to be treated for rupture, was distressed to learn that Dr. Theus was going away. The physician assured him that he would be back toward the end of the week, but this was a lie hard to tell.

§

It was one of those fine mornings when the sun slowly pierces the mist. The walker was filled with a sense of well-being so strong as to be almost joy. To cast off the care and anguish which had darkened these recent weeks it seemed that no more was needed than to make his way resolutely to some point on the coast where he could find a ship. Daylight was burying the dead, and the open air was dispelling past fear and horror. Bruges, though only a league behind him, could as well have been in another century, or in another sphere. He marveled to think that by his own choice he had imprisoned himself for nearly six years in the hospice of Saint Cosmus, sinking into a monastic routine (worse than those ecclesiastical patterns which he had rejected in disgust at the age of twenty), and attaching so much importance to petty intrigues and to the small scandals inevitable within closed walls. It seemed to him now that he had almost insulted the infinite possibilities of existence by withdrawing for so long a time from the vast outer world. Assuredly, the mind's effort to penetrate the inner meaning of things leads to awesome depths, but it nullifies the very process which living is. For a time, far too long, he had forsworn the delight of advancing straight ahead in the actuality of the moment, leaving his lot again to chance, not knowing where he would sleep the night, or how after some days had passed he would earn his daily bread. Change was rebirth for him, and almost a metempsychosis: the mere alternate motion of his limbs, as he walked, was satisfying to his soul. He used his eyes only to guide his steps, though all the while feasting on the rich green of the grass. It was good to hear the whinny of a colt galloping alongside a hedge, or the grinding sound of cart wheels which portend no danger. Departure spelled total liberty.

He was nearing the town of Damme, the old port for Bruges, where formerly, before this coast was silted over, great vessels had put in from foreign shores. Those bustling days had gone by; cows grazed now where wool sacks used to be unloaded. Zeno recalled having heard Blondeel, the engineer, implore Henry Justus to advance some part of the funds needed to fight the sands' encroachment; but the man of skill, who would have saved the city, had been spurned by the shortsighted banker. These avaricious men of affairs are all of a kind; they never behave otherwise!

The traveler stopped in the square to buy a loaf of bread. The doors of the burghers' houses were beginning to open. At one of them a pink-cheeked matron in a crisp linen wimple loosed a poodle to let it run gaily about; it sniffed the grass before stopping suddenly to settle into that contrite pose all dogs assume when relieving themselves, then bounded off again to its play. A troop of children passed, chattering on their way to school, chubby and merry as robins in their bright attire. (But subjects of the Spanish King they were, nevertheless, Zeno reflected, and would all be marching off one day to crack the skulls of those scoundrelly French.) A cat stole by, returning home with his prey, the limp claws of a bird protruding from his mouth. From the cook shop came the savory odor of pies and roast meat, mingling with the stale smell from the butcher shop nearby; the butcher's wife stood rinsing her bloodstained threshold with great buckets of water. Outside the town was the customary gallows, raised on a grassy knoll, but the body hanging there had been exposed so long to sun, wind, and rain as to have almost acquired the gentle aspect of old abandoned things; a friendly breeze played through its faded rags. A company of crossbowmen were setting forth to shoot wood thrush, hearty burghers all, who clapped each other on the back as they exchanged jocosities; each of them had a pouch slung over his shoulder that would soon contain those small, warm parcels of life which an instant before had been singing in the open sky. Zeno hastened his step.

For a while he was alone on a road which wound through pasturelands, where the whole world seemed composed of pale sky and lush green grass a-sway on the ground, rippling incessantly like water. For a moment he called to mind the alchemical concept of *viriditas*, of the innocent piercing-through of Being from within the nature of things, a blade of life in its purest form; but then he ceased to pursue all such thoughts in order to give himself over entirely to the purity of the morning.

After some quarter of an hour he caught up with a peddler who was walking ahead of him, carrying his pack. They exchanged greetings; the man complained that trade was poor since so many of the inland villages had been pillaged by the King's mercenaries, but he added that here, at least, things were quiet; nothing much was taking place. Zeno went on, faster, and was soon alone again. Toward midday he sat down to eat his bread upon a hillock from which he could already catch the gleam, in the distance, of the long gray line of the sea.

A traveler with a long staff came to sit beside him, a blindman who, like Zeno, drew something from his beggar's bag to break his fast. The physician admired the dexterity with which the blank-eyed fellow disburdened himself of the bagpipes on his back, unbuckling the strap and placing the instrument carefully on the grass. He was pleased that the day was fine, for he earned his livelihood by playing for young folk dancing at the inns, or in the courtyards of the farms. He would sleep this night at Heyst, where he was to play on Sunday; from there he would go on in the direction of Sluys. Thank Heaven, there were always boys and girls enough for him to make his profit everywhere, and sometimes to take his own pleasure. Would Mynheer believe it? From time to time there are women who take a fancy to blindmen. The misfortune of losing one's eyes is less bad than one might think!

Like many a person so afflicted, this sightless traveler both used and abused the verb *see:* he "saw" that Zeno was a man in full vigor of age, one who, in addition, was educated; he "saw" that the sun was still high in the sky; he "saw" that the person passing on the path behind them was a woman slightly lame, wearing a yoke from which hung two pails. Not everything, however, was false in this assurance: it was he who first perceived a snake gliding through the grass. He even tried to kill "the dratted beast" with his staff. Zeno parted from him, after giving him a farthing for alms, and consequently was followed with shrill cries of benediction as he went on his way.

The road circled around a rather large farm, the only one left in that region where the grit of sand could already be felt underfoot. The domain had a fair aspect, with its soil held down here and there by clusters of hazelnut trees, its wall bordering the canal, and its courtyard shaded by a linden; the woman with the yoke who had recently passed him was resting on a bench in the yard, freed now of her harness, but with her two pails beside her. Zeno hesitated, then passed on. This place, called Oudebrugge, he remembered, had belonged to the Ligre family; perhaps it was still in their possession. Fifty years ago his mother had come here with Simon Adriansen, shortly before her marriage to him, to collect the rent for Henry Justus from this farm. They had made a pleasure outing of the visit; his mother had sat down on the canal bank and removed her shoes and stockings to dangle her feet in the water; seen through it they seemed even whiter than before. Simon kept dropping crumbs on his gray beard as he ate. The young woman had deftly opened a hard-boiled egg for the child to give him the precious shell for his game. The sport was to run with the wind on the nearby dunes while holding this very light object on his open palm. The shell escaped, of course, to flutter on ahead and then to alight for an instant, like a bird, so that one had perpetually to try to snatch it up again in a race complicated by irregular curves and sharp angles. It sometimes seemed to Zeno that he had kept on playing this game his whole life through.

He was already advancing less rapidly as the sand increased in the soil. The road, marked only by wheel ruts, mounted and descended as it crossed the dunes. He met with two soldiers coming from the opposite direction; they were doubtless garrisoned at Sluys; he was glad to be armed, for any soldier encountered in a lonely place may turn readily into a bandit. These two, however, merely mumbled a greeting in German, and appeared to be delighted when he answered them in the same tongue. At last, at the top of a rise, he could make out the village of Heyst and its jetty of wooden piling, in the shelter of which were four or five fishing boats. More boats were riding at anchor farther out. This hamlet on the edge of the vasty deep had, on a very small scale, all the essential commodities of a city: a covered market, which probably served for auctioning off fish, a church and a mill, an esplanade with, of course, a gallows; its low-roofed houses were tucked in between lofty barns. The Pretty Dove, the inn which Josse had indicated to him as a rallying point for the fugitives, was a mere hovel near the dune, with a broom stuck in its dovecote to stand for a sign, thus announcing that this poor hostelry was also a rustic brothel. In such a place one would have to watch over one's luggage, and the money on one's person.

In the small garden, among the hopvines, a customer who had drunk more than his fill was disgorging his beer. A woman shouted something to this sot from a dormer window, then withdrew her frowsy head, doubtless to return to a good snooze all by herself. Josse had given Zeno the password, which he, in turn, had learned from a friend, so the philosopher entered and greeted the company assembled in the common room. It was smoky inside, and dark as a cave; the hostess, squatting on the hearth, was making an omelet, and a young lad was helping, working the bellows. Zeno sat down at a table, embarrassed at having to recite the required phrase; he spoke like an actor on the boards at a Fair: "Where there's a will . . ."

". . . there's a way," said the woman, completing the old saw as she turned around. "Where do you come from?"

"Josse has sent me," he answered.

"He sends us people a-plenty," said the hostess, with a broad wink.

"Don't mistake yourself about me," the traveler replied, displeased to discern in the shadows, draining a tankard, a sergeant in a plumed bonnet. "I have all my papers."

"Then what are you coming here for?" protested the hostess. "Don't worry about Milo," she continued, designating the soldier with her thumb. "He's my sister's friend. He's one of us. You'll have something to eat, of course?"

The question being almost an order, Zeno agreed to have something. The omelet, she said, was for the sergeant; she brought Zeno some stew in a wooden bowl and it was passable, after all; the beer was good. It turned out that the officer was Albanian, and that he had crossed the Alps in the rearguard of Alva's troops. The hostess seemed to follow his Flemish without too much trouble, although it was garbled with Italian. He complained of having shivered with cold all winter here; nor were the gains what he had been told in Piedmont they would be: for Lutherans who could be pillaged or held for ransom were far less numerous than was claimed back there, a trick for luring troops across the mountains.

"That's so," the hostess joined in, in a consoling tone. "We never make so much as folk think we do." Then she called, "Mariken!"

Mariken came downstairs, her hair covered now with a shawl, and sat down beside the sergeant. The two of them ate with their hands, and from the same plate, Mariken fishing out the best bits of bacon from the omelet and stuffing them into the beloved's mouth. The boy at the bellows had meanwhile disappeared.

Zeno pushed his bowl aside and asked to pay.

"Why in such a hurry?" the hostess responded casually. "My man and Niclas Bambeke will come to supper soon. Poor souls, they have only cold fare on the water."

"I'd rather see the boat at once," Zeno urged, again requesting his bill.

"Well, the meat now," she explained politely, "that's twenty farthing, and five for the beer, and five ducats for the sergeant's permit. Then the bed is extra. They won't set sail, you know, before tomorrow morning."

"I have my passport already," the traveler demurred at her mention of a fee.

"No passport counts unless Milo says so," the proprietress declared in firm tones. "He is King Philip here."

"It's not yet said that I'll take ship, after all," Zeno countered.

"No bargaining," the Albanian scolded from the back of the room, raising his voice. "I'm not wearing myself out night and day on the wharf to watch who's leaving or who's staying."

Zeno paid what was asked, from a purse which he had taken the precaution to fill with just the amount of silver needed for travel, so that it would not be assumed that he had more hidden on him somewhere. "What is the name of the boat?" he inquired.

"The same as here," she answered, "*The Pretty Dove*. Better not mistake it, eh, Mariken?"

"For sure, no!" the wench exclaimed. "With *The Four Winds* they'd get lost in the mist and run straight on Vilvoorde!"

This jest seemed cause for high mirth on the part of the two women, and even the Albanian understood it enough to burst out laughing. Vilvoorde was a fortress some thirty miles inland.

"You can leave your bundles here," the hostess remarked to Zeno, good-naturedly; but he replied, "As well stow them aboard at once."

As he left, Mariken snorted, "There's a trustful fellow for you!"

On the threshold he barely missed colliding with the blind-man, who was coming to play that evening for the young dancers. The musician recognized Zeno and saluted him obsequiously. On his way to the harbor, he encountered a few soldiers headed for the inn, one of whom asked Zeno if he were coming from the Pretty Dove. Since his answer was affirmative, they let him pass. It was indeed clear that Milo was master here.

The seagoing *Pretty Dove* was a rather large sailing vessel with a rounded hull resting on the sand at low tide, so Zeno could get close to it, hardly wetting his feet. Two men were at work on the rigging, and had with them the lad who only a short time before had been plying the bellows at the tavern fire. A dog ran in and out among the heaps of cordage, and farther on, in a puddle, lay a gory mass of herring heads and tails, showing that the fruits of the catch had been taken elsewhere. On seeing the traveler approach, one of the men jumped ashore and presented himself.

"Jans Bruynie, that's me. Josse is sending you here to cross to England? But first let's know what you want to pay."

Zeno now realized that the boy had been hastily dispatched from the inn to report the new arrival, and that there must have been speculation as to his degree of wealth. "Josse spoke to me of some sixteen ducats in all," he answered cautiously.

"That's when there is a party, sir. The other day I had eleven people. Can't take more than eleven. Sixteen ducats per Lutheran, that makes a hundred and seventy-six. I don't say that for one man alone . . ."

"I do not belong to the reformed religion," the philosopher interrupted. "I have a sister in London married to a merchant . . ."

"We have a lot of those sisters," Bruynie broke in facetiously. "It's fine to see folk risking seasickness all of a sudden to go kissing and hugging their relatives."

"Tell me your price," Zeno insisted, but he received more bargaining in reply.

"Well, sir, I'm not against your taking a trip to England, but this voyage, I don't like it. Considering that we're practically at war . . ."

"Not yet," the physician interjected as he stroked the dog, which had followed its master to the shore.

"It's six of one and half dozen of the other," the man continued. "The voyage is permitted because it's not yet forbidden, but it's not exactly permitted, even so. In the time of Queen Mary, Philip's wife, things went well: if I may say so, with due respect to you, they burned the heretics there just as we do. Now, everything goes awry: the Queen is bastard, and has bastards of her own. She claims to be a virgin, but that's only to try to look like Our Lady. In that country, priests are drawn and quartered, and the sacred vessels are used for shit. That's bad. I'd rather stay here and fish along the coast."

"But you can fish in open sea, too," Zeno reminded him.

"When we go fishing we come home as we wish; if I go to England, it's a voyage that can be long . . . The wind, you know, or a calm . . . And if anyone should come to pry into my cargo, a queer merchandise going over, and on the return . . . Once," he added, lowering his voice, "I even brought back powder for My Lord of Nassau's muskets. Not a good time to be sailing in my little shell that day!"

"There are other boats," the philosopher observed, with assumed indifference.

"Maybe, sir, maybe not. The *Saint Barbara* works along with us, ordinarily; she's damaged; nothing doing with her. The *Saint Boniface* has run into trouble . . . There are some vessels still at sea, of course, but devil knows when they'll return. If you're not too pressed for time, you could go to Blankenberghe, or to Wenduyne, but you'll find the same prices as here."

"And that one, there?" Zeno asked, indicating a slighter craft aboard which a small man on the poop deck was placidly cooking his meal.

"*The Four Winds?* Go ahead, if you want to chance it," Jans Bruynie answered in an ominous tone.

Zeno sat down on an empty cask, considering what to do. The dog came to rest his muzzle on the traveler's knee. "In any case, you will be leaving at dawn?" he inquired.

"Yes, but to fish, my good sir, only to fish. To be sure, if you had, say, fifty ducats . . ."

"I have forty," said the physician, firmly.

"Call it forty-five, then, and done; I don't want to fleece a customer. But if you have nothing more urgent to do than

going to see your sister in London, why not stay a few days at
the Pretty Dove . . . ? These runaways with their tails between their legs, they keep coming all the time . . . You
would then pay only your share."

"I prefer to take off without waiting."

"I thought so . . . And it's more prudent, because suppose
the wind changes . . . Have you squared with the bird those
two have at the inn?"

"If you are speaking of the five ducats they extorted from
me . . ."

"That's not our deal," Bruynie interrupted disdainfully.
"The women fix things with him so that there's no trouble on
land. Hi, Niclas," he called to his comrade, "here's the
passenger!"

A red-haired man of enormous bulk mounted halfway up
through a hatch. "This is Niclas Bambeke," the shipmaster
announced. "There's Michiel Sottens, too, but he's gone for
supper at home. You'll eat with us at the Dove, won't you?
Just leave your gear here."

"I'll need it for the night," said the physician, holding on to
his satchel, which Jans Bruynie wanted to take over. "I'm a
surgeon, and I have my instruments with me," he added, in
order to explain the bag's weight, which might otherwise have
raised some conjectures.

"Mynheer the Surgeon has also provided himself with firearms," said the skipper sarcastically, observing from the
corner of his eye the metal butts of the pistols which the
doctor now wore in his pockets, thus forcing the latter
slightly agape.

But Niclas Bambeke said approvingly, as he jumped from
the vessel, "That's only wise of a man, I tell you. One meets
with ugly folk, even at sea."

Zeno followed close behind them to mount again to the inn,
but when he came to the corner of the market building he
turned off at an angle, letting them think that it was only to
make water. The other two walked on ahead, discussing

something or other animatedly, escorted by the boy and the dog, who were darting in and out about them. Meanwhile, Zeno continued on around the building, and soon after regained the shore.

§

By this time night was falling. Some two hundred steps farther on was a chapel, half in ruins and sinking into the sand. Zeno looked inside. The last high tide had left a pool of water in the nave, and the statues were salt-eaten. In such a place, he reflected, the Prior would doubtless have composed himself to pray; Zeno settled down in the entrance, facing the shore and resting his head on his bag. On the right, the dark hulls of the boats were still visible; on the poop of *The Four Winds* a lantern was a-light.

The traveler mused upon what he would do in England. The thing of first importance would be to avoid being taken for a Papist spy in the guise of a refugee. He could see himself roaming the London streets, seeking a post as a naval surgeon, or a place at some physician's like that he had held at Jan Myers's. He did not speak English, but a language is quickly acquired, and in any case Latin would serve him well. With a little luck he could find employ with some great lord interested in aphrodisiacs or in remedies for his gout. He was accustomed to promises of ample salaries not always paid; to a seat high at the table and sometimes low, according to the humor of milord or of His Highness that day; and to disputes with ignorant local medics hostile to a foreign practitioner, whom they promptly dubbed a charlatan. He had already seen all that at Innsbruck, and elsewhere. He would have to remember, also, never to speak of the Pope otherwise than in execration, as they spoke of Calvin here, and to deem King Philip ridiculous, just as England's Queen was mocked everywhere in Flanders.

The lantern of *The Four Winds* moved and came toward him, swinging from the extended arm of a man who was approaching, and who came to a stop in front of Zeno. It was the small, bald skipper. Zeno rose up halfway and the man addressed him: "I saw Mynheer come to lie down here. My house is nearby; if His Lordship fears the damp of night . . ."

"I am well where I am," Zeno replied curtly.

"Could I ask His Lordship, without wishing to seem too curious, how much they charge for England?"

"You must surely know their prices," Zeno said, disdaining further discourse.

"It's not that I blame them, Your Lordship. The season is short: Mynheer must realize that after All Saints' Day it is not always easy to set sail. But at least they should be honest . . . You don't imagine that for that price they will take you as far as Yarmouth? They will turn you over, in mid-sea, to fishermen from that country, and you will begin again to pay for new charges."

"It's one way of doing things, I suppose," the traveler commented, with indifference.

"Has Mynheer not said to himself that it is risky for a man who is no longer young to set off alone with three such strapping fellows? A blow from an oar comes quick. They would sell your clothes to the English, and then—they're safely rid of you."

"Have you come to propose taking me to England on *The Four Winds*?" Zeno questioned, ignoring the warning.

"No, not that, Mynheer; my boat is not large enough. And even Friesland is very far, too. But if it is only a matter of a change of air, Mynheer must know that Zeeland is slipping through the King's hands. The Beggars are swarming there now, ever since the Prince of Nassau himself commissioned Captain Sonnoy . . . I know the farms where the Messieurs Sonnoy and de Dolhain take on their provisions . . . May I ask the profession of His Lordship?"

"I take care of my fellow men," the physician answered.

"On the frigates of these gentlemen Mynheer will have

occasion to nurse some fine blows and wounds. And one can get there in a few hours when one knows how to trim sail. One can even leave before midnight; *The Four Winds* doesn't draw much water."

"How would you avoid the patrol at Sluys?"

"I know people there, Mynheer. I have friends. But His Lordship would have to take off his good clothes and dress like a poor sailor . . . If by chance anyone came aboard . . ."

"You have not indicated your price."

"Would fifteen ducats be too much for His Lordship?"

"The price is not high, but are you certain, in the dark, of not sailing to Vilvoorde?"

At this unexpected question from Zeno the small man scowled in fury, and burst out: "You dirty Calvinist, you! Scorner of the Holy Virgin! It's *The Pretty Dove* who tried to make you believe that?"

"I say only what people have told me," Zeno rejoined laconically.

The man departed, cursing; but after some ten steps he turned back, causing his lantern to spin around; the angry visage had become servile again, and he resumed his unctuous tone as he spoke.

"I see that Mynheer knows the news, but he must not let folk tell mere tales. His Lordship will excuse me for having been a trifle sharp, but I had no hand, me, in the arrest of the Prince of Battenbourg. It wasn't even a pilot from these parts . . . And then there's no comparison for gain: My Lord of Battenbourg is a big fish to catch. Mynheer can be sure that he will be as safe on my boat as if he were in the house of his saintly mother . . ."

"That's enough." Zeno closed him off. "You say that your bark can set sail at midnight, that I can change my clothes in your house near here, and that your price is fifteen ducats. Now leave me in peace."

But the fellow was not of the kind to be easily discouraged. He did not obey the order until after having assured His

Lordship that, in case he felt too fatigued, he could restore himself at very little cost by staying in his humble house, and need not depart before the following night. Captain Milo would close his eyes to the matter, for, after all, he wasn't bound to Jans Bruynie. When Zeno was finally left alone, he asked himself why, in Heaven's name, he would tend upon such rascals devotedly if they were ill, since he would gladly kill them in their present state of good health! When the lantern had resumed its place on the poop of *The Four Winds*, he arose. The dark night concealed his movements. Slowly he covered a quarter of a league in the direction of Wenduyne, his bundle under his arm. Doubtless it would be the same thing everywhere, he told himself. It was impossible to decide which of these two clowns was lying, or if, by chance, both were speaking truth. It could also be that both were lying, and that all this was only rivalry between two poor wretches. Whosoever wished could decide.

Although he was not yet far from Heyst, its lights were hidden from him by a dune. He selected a hollow, sheltered from the breeze and well above the line of high tide, as could be guessed, even in the dark, from where the damp sand began. The summer night was warm; there would still be time to make his decision at daybreak; he spread his cloak over him. Mist veiled the stars, except for Vega, near the zenith; the sea was making its eternal sound; thus beside it he fell into a dreamless sleep.

He was awakened before dawn by the cold; a pale light invaded both sky and dune, and the mounting tide was almost lapping his shoes. He was shivering, but the cold bore already within it the promise of a fine summer day. His legs were stiffened after lying motionless all night, and as he gently rubbed them, he watched the formless sea give birth to its waves, each so soon to vanish. The mighty sound which had endured from the world's beginning rolled on. He let a handful of sand trickle through his fingers. *Calculus:* with this flow of atoms began and ended all cogitation on the science of numbers. To crumble our rocks in such wise, it had taken more centuries than all the days enumerated in the Bible's stories. The meditations of ancient philosophers had taught him, from his earliest youth, to look with disdain upon these poor six thousand years which are all that Jews and Christians care to know of our world's venerable antiquity, measuring it by the short span of what man himself can remember. Once, in the peat bogs of Dranoutre, the peasants had shown him some immense tree trunks which they supposed had been brought there by the tides of the Great Deluge; but there have been floods other than that to which is appended the story of a patriarch who loved wine, just as there has been destruction by fire other than the absurd catastrophe of Sodom. He recalled how Darazi had spoken of myriads of centuries which add up to no more than a single respiration of Infinite Being. Zeno reckoned that on the coming twenty-fourth of February, if he should still be alive, he would be fifty-nine. But the contemplation of these nearly threescore years evoked the same train of thought as did this handful of sand: a vertiginous prospect of countless numbers emanated from them. For more than one and a half billion seconds he had lived here and there on the earth while Vega was turning close to the zenith, and the sea was resounding on all the shores of the world. Fifty-eight times he had seen the new grass of spring, followed by summer's abundance. It mattered little if a man of his age were to live on or to die.

The sun was already warm when, from the height of the dune, he saw *The Pretty Dove* hoist sail and put out to sea. This weather would have been good for his voyage. The heavy vessel receded from sight faster than one might have supposed. Zeno settled down again in his lair of sand, letting the friendly warmth eliminate all trace of cramp from the night; in the sunlight his blood glowed red through his closed eyelids. He weighed his chances as if they were those of someone else. Armed as he was, he could force the scoundrel at the rudder of *The Four Winds* to land him on some shore frequented only by Sea Beggars; or he could, on the contrary, put a bullet through the fellow's head if he started to turn the prow toward some galley of the King's. He had used this same pair of pistols without compunction to dispatch a brigand who had assailed him long ago, in the great Bulgarian forest; just as he had felt after thwarting Perrotin in his ambush, he came out of that encounter feeling himself more a man. But now the notion of having to blow out the brains of this knave seemed to him merely revolting. The advice to join the crews of the Messieurs Sonnoy or de Dolhain, in his capacity of surgeon was good; it was in their direction that he had sent Han at the time when these pirate Patriots had not yet acquired the authority and resources so recently gained, thanks to the new uprisings. A post with Prince Louis of Nas-. sau was not impossible; this gentleman surely lacked trained physicians in his service. The life of a Partisan, or Sea Rover, differed little from the one he had lived in the Polish armies, or with the Turkish fleet. If worse came to worst, one could even wield a cauterizing iron or a scalpel for some time among the troops of the Duke. And the day that revulsion from war should overcome him, there remained the hope of going on foot to some corner of the world where, for the moment, this most atrocious of human stupidities was not raging. Any of these alternatives was feasible. But he had to remind himself, too, that perhaps, after all, he might never be disturbed in Bruges.

He stretched and yawned. These alternatives no longer interested him. He removed his shoes, now heavy with the same sand on which he lay, and contentedly thrust his feet through the warm, fluid surface to seek and find the fresh dampness below. He took off his clothes, weighting them carefully down with his luggage and his shoes, and advanced toward the sea. The tide was already receding: he waded across gleaming pools of water less than knee-high to encounter the surf beyond them.

Naked and alone, he let past events and their circumstances

slip from him much as his garments had done. He became anew that Adam Kadmon of hermetic tradition, primordial man who dwells at the center of things, he who defines and names what is inherent but undefined everywhere else in the universe. Without him, nothing in this vastness had a name: accordingly, he abstained from thinking that the bird which fished, as it balanced on the crest of a wave, was a seagull, or that the strange creature in a pool, moving members so different from those of man, was a starfish. Meanwhile, the tide was still going out, leaving behind it shells with spirals as perfect as those of Archimedes; the sun was mounting almost imperceptibly, and in its rise was shortening the human shadow on the sand. Filled with a reverent notion (for which he would have been put to death on any of the public squares of Christendom or the lands of Mohammed), he reflected that the most adequate symbols of a conjectural Supreme Good are those very ones which are held, absurdly, to be the most idolatrous: the fiery globe above is the only God visible for us creatures, who would perish without it. Likewise, the most real of angels was this seagull, which possessed what Seraphim and Thrones did not have, the clear evidence of existing.

In this world unburdened by concepts, even ferocity was pure: the fish wriggling beneath the wave would soon be only a choice morsel, bleeding under the beak of the bird fishing here, but the bird was giving no false pretext for its hunger. Both fox and hare (trickery and fear) inhabited the dune where he slept, but the killer did not evoke laws promulgated long ago by some wise fox, or handed down by a fox-god. The victim did not suppose itself punished for its crimes or, when dying, protest to the end that it had remained loyal to its prince.

The violence of the seething waters was without anger. Death, which is always unclean among men, was undefiled in this solitude. One step more on this frontier between fluid substance and sheer liquid, between the sand and the sea, and the power of some wave stronger than others would make him lose his footing; an agony so brief and without witness would be slightly less a death. He might one day regret that he had not made an ending like that. But such a possibility was much like the projects for England or for Zeeland, born of yesterday's fears, or of dangers to come, neither of which were present in this moment without shadow, for they were plans formed by the mind, and not immediate necessities forcing themselves upon the whole being. The hour of passage had not yet sounded.

He turned back again toward his clothes, which he had some difficulty in finding, covered as they were already with a light layer of sand. The ebb tide had altered the distances in this short time. His footprints on the wet shore had been promptly absorbed by the oozing flood, while on the dry sand the wind was effacing every mark. His body, so freshly bathed, had forgotten its fatigue. Another morning at the seaside came back to him, adding itself to this one without break, as if that brief interlude of sand and water had lasted ten years: during his stay in Lübeck he had gone to the mouth of the Trave with the jeweler's son to gather Baltic amber. The horses, too, had bathed with them in the sea: relieved of their saddles and housings, and wet with spray, they became again creatures existing in their own right instead of being only habitual, docile mounts. One fragment of amber, Zeno recalled, contained an insect trapped in the resin; he had gazed, as though through a small window, at the tiny beast imprisoned within an age of this earth to which he had no access. He shook his head, as one does to drive off a persistent bee: too often now he relived distant moments of his own past, not out of regret or nostalgia, but because the walls of time seemed to have burst. That day at Travemünde was fixed in his memory like some almost imperishable matter, vestige of a period when it had been good to exist. If he should live ten years more, it would then perhaps be the same for this day today.

He resumed his human carapace, but without satisfaction. A remainder of yesterday's bread, and his gourd half filled with cistern water, reminded him that his route, to the end, would be among his fellow men. He would have to be on his guard against them, but also to continue to receive their services and to render the same to them in return. He balanced his bag evenly over his shoulder and suspended his shoes by their laces to his belt in order to give himself the pleasure of walking barefoot for a longer time. Avoiding Heyst, which seemed to him now like an ulcer on the fair surface of the sands, he kept to the dunes. From the top of the nearest height he turned back to look at the sea. *The Four Winds* was still anchored at the jetty and other craft had come into port. Another sail, on the horizon, had the clean curve of a bird's wing; it was, perhaps, the boat of Jans Bruynie.

§

He walked for nearly an hour, avoiding the trodden paths. In a dell between two hummocks sown with spear grass he saw a group of six persons coming toward him, an old man with a woman beside him, two men of middle age, and two fellows armed with clubs. The woman and the old man were making their way with difficulty through the shifting sand. All of them wore the dress of city dwellers. They seemed to prefer to pass by without attracting attention, but they responded when Zeno addressed them, quickly reassured by the interest which this courteous traveler showed, and by the fact that he spoke to them in French. The two young men had come from Brussels; they were Catholic Patriots who were trying to join the troops of the Prince of Orange. The other group was Calvinist; the old man was a schoolmaster from Tournai who was escaping to England along with his two sons; the woman, who kept wiping his brow with her handkerchief, was his daughter-in-law. The long road on foot was more than the poor man could endure; he sat down for a moment on the sand to catch his breath, and the others formed a circle around him.

This family had joined with the two young burghers from

Brussels at Eecloo: the mutual danger and mutual flight made companions of these folk who in other times would have been enemies. The Patriots spoke admiringly of Lord de La Mark, who had sworn to let his beard grow until the two Counts were avenged; he had taken to the woods with his partisans, and there he hanged without pity whatever Spaniards fell into his hands: it was men like him who were needed in the Low Countries. From these fugitives from Brussels Zeno also learned details of the capture of the Prince of Battenbourg with eighteen gentlemen of his suite, betrayed by the pilot who was transporting them to Friesland: these nineteen persons had been incarcerated in the fortress of Vilvoorde, and beheaded. The schoolmaster's sons turned pale at this account, fearful as to what awaited them when they should reach the shore. Zeno calmed them in saying that Heyst seemed fairly secure provided that one paid one's fee to the captain of the port; ordinary fugitives ran little risk of being betrayed as a prince would be. He asked if the men from Tournai were armed; they were, and even the woman had a knife. He advised them not to separate; if together, they need hardly fear being robbed during the crossing; it would nevertheless be wise to sleep with one eye open both at the inn and on the deck of the ship. As to the man of *The Four Winds*, he was not to be trusted, but the two solid fellows from Brussels would doubtless know how to keep him in hand, and once in Zeeland, the chance of meeting with groups of insurgents seemed good.

The schoolmaster rose painfully to his feet. Zeno, interrogated in his turn, explained that he was a physician of the region, and that he, too, had thought of going across the sea. The questions did not go further than that; his affairs did not interest them. In separating from them he gave the schoolmaster a phial containing a medicine, drops which would improve his breathing for a while. They thanked him heartily as he took his leave.

He watched them continue toward Heyst, and suddenly

decided to follow them. With several people, the voyage was less hazardous; during the first days on another shore they could even be of help to each other. He took some hundred steps, keeping behind them, then slowed his pace, letting the distance between himself and the small band increase. The thought of having to face Milo or Jans Bruynie again filled him, in advance, with a feeling of insupportable weariness. He stopped short and turned in a direction away from the sea. He thought again of the old man's blue lips and shortness of breath. This teacher abandoning his humble profession, braving sword, fire, and sea in order to attest openly to his faith in the predestination of most of mankind to Hell, seemed to Zeno a goodly specimen of the universal dementia. But beyond such follies of dogma, he reflected, there doubtless exist among all restless human creatures certain repulsions and hatreds rising from the depths of their natures, feelings which, if a time ever comes when it will no longer be the fashion to exterminate each other for the sake of religion, will manifest themselves otherwise. The two Patriots from Brussels seemed more reasonable, but these young men who were risking their hides for the cause of liberty nevertheless prided themselves on being loyal subjects of King Philip; all would go well, according to them, as soon as the country was rid of the Duke. But unhappily the maladies of this world are far more inveterate than that.

He was again passing through Oudebrugge, and this time entered the farm courtyard. The same woman was there: seated on the ground, she was plucking grass for some young rabbits caged inside a large basket. A child still in skirts kept turning around her. Zeno asked for a little milk and something to eat. She got up with a grimace of pain and asked him to draw the jar of milk from the well himself, as her rheumatic hands made it hard to turn the winch. While he worked the pulley she went into the house and brought out some white cheese and a piece of tart. She excused herself for the quality of the milk, which was thin and bluish. "The old cow has

almost gone dry," she explained. "It's as if she was tired of
giving. When they take her to the bull she does not want him
any more. We'll soon have to kill her for meat."

Zeno asked if the farm belonged to the Ligre family. She
looked at him with sudden mistrust, and inquired, "You
wouldn't be the agent, by chance? We don't owe anything
before Michaelmas."

He reassured her, explaining that he was gathering herbs
for pastime, and was on his way back to Bruges. The farm did
belong, as he had thought, to Philibert Ligre, lord of Dranoutre and Oudenove, a big bonnet in the Council of Flanders. As the good woman explained, rich folk have a whole
string of names.

"I know," said he, "I come of that family."

She looked as if she scarcely believed him. This traveler on
foot had nothing about him which was exactly magnificent.
He mentioned having come once to the farm a very long time
ago. Everything was much as he remembered it, but smaller.

"If you came, I was here," said the woman. "It's fifty years
since I've budged from the place."

It seemed to him as he recalled that outing of long ago that
they had given their leavings to the tenants, but he no longer
recalled the faces. She came to sit down by him on the bench;
he had put her on memory's trail. "The masters came here
sometimes in those days," she continued. "I am the old
farmer's daughter; there were eleven cows. In autumn we
always sent a cart loaded with pots of salted butter to the
masters in Bruges. Now it's not the same; they let everything
go . . . And then, with my hands, it's hard to work in cold
water."

She rested her hands on her lap, interlacing her deformed
fingers. Zeno advised her to plunge them every day in warm
sand. "Sand, that's what we don't lack for here," she said.

The child continued to spin around in the courtyard, like a
top, making incomprehensible sounds meanwhile. He was
very likely feeble-minded. She called to him, and a marvelous

tenderness lighted her sharp face as soon as she saw him trot toward her. Carefully she wiped away the slaver at the corners of his mouth. "There's my little Jesus," she said gently. "His mother works in the fields with the two that she's nursing."

Zeno asked about the father. He was the skipper of the *Saint Boniface*. "The *Saint Boniface* has had some trouble," he remarked, with the air of someone in the know.

"It's taken care of now," the woman replied, "he's going to work for Milo. He has to earn for us: of all my lads only two are left to me. For I've had two husbands, I have, sir," she continued, "and ten children to the three of us. Eight of them lie in the cemetery. All that work and pain for nothing . . . The younger one helps for a few hours at the miller's on the days when there's wind, so we always have bread to eat. And he has the right, too, to the sweepings. The soil here is poor for grain."

Zeno looked at the dilapidated barn. Over the door, according to the custom, someone had once fastened an owl, which had doubtless been struck down with a stone and nailed up alive; its feathers (what was left of them) were stirring in the breeze. "Why have you tortured that creature which was only beneficial to you?" he asked, pointing with his finger to the great bird of prey crucified above him. "These owls eat the mice which devour the grain."

"I don't know, sir," the woman answered, "but it's the custom. And then, their cry warns of a death."

Zeno made no reply to this explanation. She evidently wished to ask him something.

"These fugitives, sir, that they carry on the *Saint Boniface* . . . Of course, it's profit for us all around here. Even today I sold something to eat to six of them. And then there are some that make you ache to see . . . But one asks oneself just the same, if it's an honest traffic, that one. People who run away, they don't make off for nothing . . . The Duke and the King must surely know what they're doing."

"You are not obliged to know anything about these people," said the traveler.

"There now, that's very true," she said, nodding.

From her heap of grass Zeno had taken a few stalks and poked them into the sides of the basket for the rabbits to nibble. "If these little beasts please you, sir, they're yours," she continued, in an obliging tone. "Nice and plump, tender, just ready . . . They would have been killed and dressed on Sunday, anyhow. Only fivepence apiece."

"Me?" he exclaimed, surprised. "What, then, will you eat on Sunday for dinner?"

"Sir," she said, with pleading eyes, "it's not just food . . . With this money and threepence for the bite of cheese and the milk, I'll send my daughter-in-law to get a drop at the Pretty Dove. The heart, it has to be warmed from time to time, too. We'll drink to your health."

She lacked change for his florin, she said. He had suspected as much; never mind, it was not important. Satisfaction had made her younger: after all, it was perhaps she, that girl of fifteen, who had curtsied when Simon Adriansen gave her a few pennies. He took his bag and headed for the gate with the usual exchanges of leave-taking.

"Don't forget them, sir," she said, holding the basket out to him. "It will please your lady: none so good as this in the city. And since you're more or less in the family, you'll tell them, please, to make repairs for us before winter. It rains in all year round."

§

He set out again, with the basket under his arm, like a peasant going to market. The road soon entered a grove, and then opened into fallow fields. Sitting down on the edge of the drainage ditch, he put his hand cautiously into the basket. Slowly, and almost voluptuously, he stroked the little animals soft of fur and supple of spine; under their tender flanks their hearts beat strongly; they continued to eat, without a sign of fear. He wondered what vision of the world, and of himself, was reflected in their large, ever-moving eyes. Lifting the lid, he let the conies take to the fields. Rejoicing in their liberty, he watched them escape into the brush, lascivious, voracious creatures, architects of subterranean labyrinths, timid, yet playing with danger, helpless except for the strength and agility of their loins, and indestructible only by reason of their inexhaustible fertility. If they should manage to avoid the snares and clubs, the falcons and martens, they could still continue their playful leaps and bounds for a time; their fur would whiten in winter along with the snow, and in spring they would begin anew to feed on the fresh green grass. So reflecting, their liberator pushed the basket with his foot into the ditch.

The remainder of the way was made without incident. He slept that next night under a clump of trees, and arrived rather early in the morning at the gates of Bruges, where he was greeted as usual with respect by the guards.

As soon as he re-entered the city, the anguish which had been momentarily submerged came again to the surface; in spite of himself he found himself listening to the remarks of the passers-by, but heard nothing unusual about certain young monks, or anything having to do with the love affairs of a beautiful young girl of noble family. No one was speaking, either, of a physician who had cared for rebels, and who went under an assumed name. He arrived at the hospice in time to succor Brother Luke and Brother Cyprian, who were trying to cope with a crowd of sick people. The note which he had left before his departure was still lying open on the table; he crumpled it between his fingers; yes, his friend at Ostend was improving. That evening at the inn he allowed himself a choicer and more leisurely supper than he ordinarily did.

THE MOUSE TRAP

MORE THAN a month passed without trouble. It was understood that the hospice would close its doors shortly before Christmas; but this time Dr. Sebastian Theus would leave openly, and for Germany, where he had previously lived and practiced. Zeno proposed to himself, privately, to go north toward Lübeck, though he never mentioned in public those regions which had gone over to Lutheranism. It would be good to see Aegidius Friedhof again, his wise friend, and to find Gerhart arrived to manhood. Perhaps it would be possible to obtain that post of regent, at the Hospital of the Holy Ghost, of which the opulent jeweler had virtually assured him in the past.

From Ratisbon his fellow alchemist Riemer, to whom Zeno had finally sent word of himself, now wrote him some unexpected good news. A copy of his *Protheories* which had escaped the Paris bonfire had somehow made its way to Germany; a scholar at Wittenberg had translated the book into Latin, and its publication had reawakened echoes of glory around the philosopher's name. The Holy Office at Rome took umbrage at the work, as had the Sorbonne earlier, but the learned man of Wittenberg and his colleagues found, on the contrary, that these texts (which Catholics considered stained with heresy) exemplified the right to free examination of the Bible. Likewise, Zeno's aphorisms, explaining miracles as the result of fervor in the person favored with miraculous experience, seemed to these theologians to combat Papist superstitions, and at the same time to support their own doctrine of salvation by faith. Thus, in their hands the *Protheories* became a slightly distorted instrument, but such bias has to be expected as long as a book exists and works upon men's minds.

There was even some thought of proposing to Zeno (if they could find trace of him) a chair of natural philosophy at that Saxon University. The honor, he knew, was not without risk, and it would be prudent to decline it in favor of other and freer endeavors; but the chance for direct contact with scholars tempted him after this long withdrawal into himself. And to see a work long considered dead begin again to stir filled him in every fiber of his being with the joy of a resurrection. About the same time, his *Treatise on the Physical World* (never reprinted since the execution of Dolet) had reappeared at a publisher's in Basel, where it seemed that everyone had forgotten the bitter quarrels over him, and the suspicions of earlier days. His bodily presence scarcely mattered any more: his ideas had spread and taken root without him.

Since his return from Heyst, he had heard no more talk of the little group of Angels. He was careful to avoid any private encounter with Cyprian, so the boy's flow of confidences was shut off. Certain measures which Sebastian Theus had hoped that the former Prior of the Cordeliers might take, in order to avoid general disaster, had recently been accomplished of themselves in one way or another. Brother Florian was leaving soon for Antwerp, where his monastery, one of those burned down in the past by the iconoclasts, was being rebuilt; he was to paint the frescoes in the cloister arches.

Pierre de Hamaere was visiting different affiliates in the provinces, to go over their accounts. The new administration in the monastery in Bruges had ordered some work done in the cellars, and had condemned certain parts of them which were falling in ruin; thus the Angels had lost their secret retreat. The nocturnal meetings must certainly have ceased, therefore, and the shocking imprudences had doubtless given way by this time to such furtive sins as are commonly committed in cloisters. As for the meetings of Cyprian and the Fair One in the abandoned garden, the season now was hardly favorable for them, and perhaps anyhow Idelette had procured a gallant of greater prestige than that of a young monk.

For such reasons as these, possibly, Cyprian's countenance had darkened; he no longer sang his peasant refrains, and he went about his tasks with a dreary air. Sebastian Theus had at first supposed that the young aide had been downcast, like Brother Luke, because of the imminent closing of the hospice. One morning, however, he noticed that the boy's face was streaked with traces of tears.

Zeno bid him come into the back workroom and closed the door; they were alone there again as they had been on the day following Low Sunday, at the time of Cyprian's dangerous avowals. Zeno was first to speak. "Has something happened to the Fair One?" he asked brusquely.

"I do not see her any more," the boy replied in a choking voice. "She has shut herself in with her Moor, and says that she is ill in order to hide her burden." He went on to explain that the only news he received came through a lay sister whom he had won over partly by small gifts and partly because she was genuinely moved by the state of the Fair One, whom she was assigned to attend. But it was difficult to communicate through this woman, for she was simple to the point of stupidity. The secret passages once in use between the monastery and the convent no longer existed, and in any case the two girls, now frightened by the merest shadow, would no longer have dared attempt to go out at night. It is true that Brother

Florian had access, as a painter, to the oratory of the Bernardine Sisters, but he was now washing his hands of the whole affair.

"He and I have quarreled," said Cyprian, somberly.

The women expected Idelette to be delivered at the time of the festival of Saint Agatha. The physician calculated that they would therefore have nearly three months, still, to wait. By then he would already have been for some time in Lübeck. "Do not despair," he said, trying to cope with the young monk's dejection. "Women are very courageous and clever in these matters. If the Bernardines do discover this misadventure, they will have no advantage in making it known. A newborn child is easily deposited at an orphanage door and entrusted to public charity."

Cyprian stood unheeding, gazing at the shelves. "These jars and bottles are full of roots and powders," he said, in agitation. "She will die of fear unless someone comes to help her. If Mynheer were willing . . ."

"Do you not see that it is too late, and that I have no means of coming near her? Let us not add to all these disorders some gruesome accident."

"The parson at Ursel has cast off his robe and has fled to Germany with his beloved," Cyprian said suddenly. "Could we not . . ."

"With a girl of this rank, and in this condition, you would be recognized before you could get beyond the Freehold of Bruges, so think no further of that. But no one would be surprised to see a young Cordelier begging his bread along the roads. Leave without her. I can furnish you with a few ducats for the journey."

The boy only sobbed in response, "No, I cannot," and collapsed on the table, his head in his hands. Zeno looked down on him with infinite compassion; flesh was a trap in which these two children had been caught. He stroked the tonsured head of the young monk affectionately, then left the room.

§

The thunder fell sooner than might have been supposed. Toward Saint Lucy's Day he happened to be at the inn and heard his neighbors discussing some news in those excited whispers which never signify anything good, for they nearly always pertain to someone's misfortune. A girl of noble birth, who boarded with the Bernardines, had strangled a child born prematurely, but alive, of which she had just been delivered. The crime had been discovered only because of the little Moorish servant of the young lady, who had fled in terror from her mistress's room and had roamed like one mad in the streets. Some kind folk (not unmoved in part by curiosity) had taken the Moor in; though her gibberish was hard to follow, she had ended by explaining the whole affair. After that, it had been impossible for the Sisters to keep the watch from seizing their boarder. Some gross pleasantries about the hot blood of young noblewomen and the little secrets of nuns were mingled with indignant exclamations everywhere. In the dull life of this small city, where even the great events of the day barely made a stir, this scandal was of more interest than some twice-told tale of a church-burning, or of hangings of Protestants.

When Zeno left the inn, he caught sight of Idelette passing in Long Street, inside the watch's wagon. She was extremely pale, with the pallor of a woman who has just given birth, but her cheeks and her eyes were burning with fever. A few people gazed on her with pity, but most of the onlookers hooted at her, among them the pastry-shop cook and his wife. These lesser folk of the quarter were thus purging feelings of envy for the splendid attire and mad expenditures of this pretty doll. Two girls of the "Pumpkin's" establishment, who happened to be there, were the most rabid, as if the young lady had ruined their calling!

Zeno went home, his heart wrung as if he had just seen a hind abandoned to hounds. He searched for Cyprian at the hospice, but the young monk was not there, and Zeno did not dare inquire for him at the monastery for fear of causing him to be remarked.

He still hoped that when Idelette was questioned by the chief of the watch, or by the court clerks, she would have the presence of mind to invent for herself some imaginary lover. But this child, who had bitten her hands the night long to keep from shrieking in pain, lest such cries should give the alarm, had come to the end of her endurance. She spoke and wept freely, concealing neither the meetings with Cyprian at the water's edge, nor the games and laughter in the assembly of Angels. What was most horrifying to the scribes who recorded these avowals (and later on to the public who avidly received the echoes) was the consumption of the blessèd bread and wine stolen from the altar, and eaten and drunk in the light of holy candle butts; for the abominations of the flesh seemed to be accompanied by every kind of sacrilege. Cyprian was arrested the next day; the turn of François de Bure, of Florian, of Brother Quirin and two other novices implicated came next. Matthew Aerts was arrested, too, but was immediately set free on a verdict of "error as to the person." (One of his uncles was an alderman in the Freehold of Bruges.)

§

For several days the hospice of Saint Cosmus, already half closed (its physician supposedly leaving for Germany the following week), was thronged with sensation seekers. Brother Luke maintained a stony face; he refused to believe in any part of the whole affair. Zeno treated the patients, but disdained to answer any of their questions. A visit from Greete, however, moved him almost to tears, for the old woman only nodded her head and repeated that it was indeed sad.

He kept her by him the rest of the day, asking her to wash and repair his linen. In irritation, he had ordered the door of the hospice closed early by Brother Luke, but the old woman sewing and ironing near a window calmed him, sometimes by her friendly silence and sometimes by her talk, which had a kind of tranquil wisdom. She told him details of the life of Henry Justus which he had not known, of low miserliness, or of familiarities taken with maidservants (with or without their consent). He was, however, a rather good man, she added; on his best days he would readily crack a joke and might even give you a penny or two. She remembered the names and faces of numerous relatives of Zeno of whom he knew nothing: it was thus that she could recite a whole list of brothers and sisters who died young, strung along between Henry Justus and Hilzonda. He meditated for a moment on what might have been the destinies of those shoots from a same tree, all so soon cut off. For the first time in his life he listened attentively to a long account concerning his father, whose name and story he knew, but to whom only bitter allusion had been made in his presence during his childhood. A prelate as a matter of form, and to satisfy his own and his family's ambitions, that young Italian nobleman had given great parties, had walked arrogantly about in Bruges with his red velvet cape and golden spurs, and had trifled with a girl as young but less unfortunate, on the whole, than Idelette today. What came of it was these works, these vicissitudes and meditations, and these projects which had gone on for fifty-eight years. Everything in this world (the only one to which we have access) is indeed stranger than habit would lead us to believe. At last, while Zeno thought on these things, Greete put her scissors back in her pocket with her thread and needle case, and announced that his linen was now ready for his travel.

After she had left him, he heated the stove for the steam bath which he had installed in a corner of the hospice, built on the model of his bath in Constantinople; but he had rarely used this one in Bruges for his patients; they were often resistant to such attention. He prolonged his ablutions, trimming his nails, and shaving meticulously. In the past he had several times let his beard grow, as a matter of necessity in the armies or on the highway, and elsewhere the better to disguise himself, or, at the least, not to seem singular in contravening fashion; but he preferred the cleanness of a naked visage. The water and steam reminded him of the bath ceremoniously taken on his arrival in Froso, after his expedition to Lapland. Sign Ulfsdatter had waited upon him herself, according to the practice of the ladies of her country, and had maintained the dignity of a queen while performing those duties of a servant. He recalled the great tub there with the copper rim, and the design embroidered on the towels.

He was arrested on the following day. Cyprian, to escape torture, had avowed whatever they asked of him, and a great deal more. The result was a summons for Pierre de Hamaere, who was just then at Oudenaarde. As for Zeno, the testimony of the young monk was of a kind to bring him to disaster: the physician, to believe the boy, had been the confidant and the accomplice of the Angels from the beginning. It was he who had provided Florian with the philters needed to seduce Idelette for Cyprian's benefit, and who later proposed some evil potions to make her pass the fruit of her womb. The accused also invented an intimacy of unlawful nature between himself and the physician. Later on, Zeno had the chance to reflect upon these allegations, which were the exact reverse of the facts: the simplest hypothesis he could construct was that the terrified boy was seeking to prove himself innocent by laying charges upon someone else; or perhaps, having wished to obtain favors and caresses from Sebastian Theus, he had ended by believing that he had actually received them. One always falls into some kind of trap, so it might as well be that one.

In any case, Zeno was ready. He yielded without resistance. On arriving at the prison he astonished everyone by giving his true name.

PART THREE

PRISON

None è viltà, ne da viltà procede
S'alcun, per evitar più crudel sorte,
Odia la propria vita e cerca morte . . .

Meglio è morir all'anima gentile
Che supportar inevitabil danno
Che lo farria cambiar animo e stile.
Quanti ha la morte già tratti d'affanno!
Ma molti ch'hanno il chiamar morte a vile
Quanto talor sia dolce ancor non sanno.

–Giuliano de' Medici

It is no villainy, nor from villainy proceeding,
If to avoid a crueler fate someone
Hates his own life and seeks for death . . .

Better to die, for one of noble soul,
Than to support the inevitable ill
That makes him change both heart and bearing.
How many has death already saved from anguish!
But those who hold the call to death as vile
Do not yet know how sweet sometimes it is.

THE INDICTMENT

THE PHYSICIAN passed only one night in the common jail. The very next morning he was transferred, and not without a certain deference, to a room overlooking the court in the old Hall of Records. Though solidly locked and barred, this chamber afforded almost every commodity that a prisoner of note might consider his due; an alderman accused of embezzlement had once been held here, and longer ago a nobleman, whom the French faction had bribed; there could scarcely be a more decent place of detention. But the night in jail had sufficed to cover Zeno with vermin, and it took him several days to get rid of this host.

To his surprise, he was allowed to send for his linen, and soon even his writing case was restored. Books, however, were refused him. Before long, he was granted permission to walk daily in the courtyard, where the ground was now alternately frozen or muddy, and where he was accompanied by the rascal assigned to him as jailer.

Nevertheless, one fear was ever present, that of torture. That men should be paid to torment their fellow men systematically was a hideous fact that never ceased to appall this man, whose calling it was to heal. Long since, he had steeled himself, less against the pain of torture (which in itself is hardly worse than what a wounded man feels when operated upon by a surgeon) than against the horror that such pain should be deliberately inflicted. Gradually, however, he had accustomed himself to the idea that he was, in spite of himself, afraid. If, in any case, he should one day finally break down under bodily torture, and shriek or groan, or bear false witness, as Cyprian had done, the blame would lie with those who could succeed in shattering all manly spirit in their victim. But the ordeal so greatly dreaded never came. Certain potent influences were evidently beginning to intervene. Still, these protective powers could not keep his terror of the rack from persisting somewhere within him, to the last; he had to repress a shudder each time anyone opened the door.

Eight years ago, on returning to Bruges, he had supposed that he would find all recollection of him faded into oblivion, or lost in the general ignorance of things past. He had based his slender security on this assumption. But some specter of him must have survived, crouching deep in a few folks' memories; in the light of this scandal it emerged, a figure more real to everyone now than the man with whom they had casually rubbed elbows for so long. Bits of vague hearsay would suddenly coagulate, amalgamated as they were with common notions about magicians, renegades, buggers, or foreign spies, such as are ever and everywhere afloat in the popular imagination. Not a soul had recognized Zeno in the person of Sebastian Theus, but in retrospect everyone had known him all along! Nor had anyone in Bruges read his books before this time; they were doubtless little more read today, but the knowledge that they had been condemned in Paris and questioned in Rome gave one and all their chance to pronounce upon these scribblings as dangerous.

Surely a few inquisitive minds, with some shade of perspicacity, must have suspected his identity very early; Greete was not the only one with memory, and eyes to see. But those persons had kept quiet, seeming thus to count as friends rather than enemies; or perhaps they were enemies who were simply biding their time. Zeno had also wondered if anyone had warned the Prior of the Cordeliers about him, or if, on the contrary, that dignitary had surmised, on welcoming an unknown traveler into his coach at Senlis, that he had to do with the philosopher whose much disputed book was being burned, at the moment, in a public square of Paris. Zeno inclined to the second of these alternatives, choosing to feel the utmost obligation to this man of great, good heart.

However all that might be, the aspect of his disaster had changed. He had ceased to be an obscure figure in a debauch implicating a handful of novices and two or three evil monks; instead, he was once more becoming the protagonist of his own play. The charges against him were increasing, but at least he would not be the insignificant personage that Sebastian Theus probably would have been, summarily disposed of by some hasty judgment. His trial threatened to drag on because of certain questions of jurisdiction. Crimes in common law were judged in the last instance by the civil magistrates, but in so complex a case, involving as it did both atheism and heresy, the Bishop of Bruges wanted to have the final word. Such a demand was deemed offensive on the part of a churchman only recently established here by the King, and in a city which had hitherto been content not to be a bishopric; many folk thought that this prelate was an agent of the Inquisition, thus slyly implanted in Bruges. He himself saw the trial as a chance to justify the powers of his office in the public eye by conducting matters with strict impartiality.

Canon Campanus, in spite of his advanced age, put all his energy into the case. He proposed the admission, as auditors to the trial, of two theologians from the University of Louvain, from which the accused man held his degree of canon law. The Canon won his point, but whether this arrangement was made in accord with the Bishop, or in opposition to him, no one knew.

Certain fanatical spirits held the extreme view that so impious a sinner, whose doctrines must be confuted at all costs, should be judged directly by the tribunal of the Holy Office in Rome, and that therefore it would be wise to send him (well guarded, of course) to do his reflecting in some jail cell of the Dominicans, in their monastery of Saint Mary-above-Minerva. But more reasonable folk, on the contrary, preferred to see this miscreant judged here in Bruges, where he was born and to which he had returned under an assumed name, and where his presence in the heart of a devout community had encouraged disorders. This man Zeno had passed two years at the court of His Swedish Majesty; he was perhaps a spy of the Northern powers. It should not be forgotten, either, that formerly he had dwelt among infidel Turks; it was important to know if he had abandoned the Christian religion, as rumor would have it. The affair was settling into one of those cases with multiple charges which threaten to last for years, and which serve to drain all the sickly humours of a town.

In this general hubbub the allegations which had led to the arrest of Sebastian Theus fell back into second place. The Bishop, who was opposed in principle to the charges of magic, disdained the story of the love potions, which he considered nonsense; but some of the civil magistrates believed it firmly, and for the lesser folk the crux of the matter was there.

Gradually, as in all trials which temporarily excite the mob, two strangely dissimilar cases seemed to be evolving on two different levels: the cause as it appeared to men of law and to churchmen, both of whom commonly sit as judges, and the cause as fabricated by the rabble, who thirst for monsters or victims. The local prosecutor for criminal cases had promptly eliminated the charges of familiarity on the part of the accused with the small Adamite group, the Angels, since Cyprian's imputations were contradicted by the six other prisoners: they knew the physician only from having seen him in the arcades of the monastery, or in Long Street; Florian took all

the credit for having drawn Idelette into the group by promises of kisses and sweet music, and dances in which they took
hold of hands to make a round; he had no need of mandrake
root, said he; as to an abortive draught, Idelette's crime itself
belied the story, and the young damsel solemnly swore that
she had never asked for, or had to refuse, anything of the
kind; finally, and better evidence still, Zeno seemed to Florian
a fellow already old, who dabbled in sorcery, true enough,
but who was ill-disposed toward the Angels' games, out of
malice, and wanted to draw Cyprian away from them. From
these sundry, incoherent avowals the most that could be
concluded was that the so-called Sebastian Theus had learned
from his attendant something of the debaucheries of the bath
without accordingly fulfilling his duty, which was to denounce the culprits to the authorities.

The plausibility of an odious intimacy between him and
Cyprian remained, but the whole quarter sang the praises of
the physician for his fine virtues and good conduct; there was
even something rather dubious in such an unblemished reputation. An investigation was made, however, on this matter of
sodomy which had aroused the curiosity of the judges: after
some searching they thought that they had found a suspect,
the son of a patient of Jan Myers with whom the defendant
had formed a friendship early in his stay in Bruges. But they
stopped there, out of respect for a good family; and besides,
this young nobleman, who was well known for his handsome
appearance, had been long in Paris, where he was finishing his
studies. (Such a discovery would have made Zeno smile: the
liaison had been limited to a few exchanges of books.) Less
elevated acquaintances, if there were any, had left no trace.
But in his writings the philosopher had often advocated experimentation with the senses, utilizing the body's capabilities
to the full; indulgence in the most sinister pleasures could be
deduced from such a precept. So the presumption remained,
but for lack of evidence on the point the tribunal fell back on
the charge of subversive beliefs.

Other accusations were more immediately threatening to the defendant, if such a distinction could be made. The Cordeliers themselves charged the physician with having turned the hospice into a relay station for fugitives from justice. Brother Luke proved to be extremely helpful on this subject, as on a great many others; his opinion was firm and clear: everything in the whole story was false, he stated. The dissipations of the Angels' bath had been much exaggerated; Cyprian was naught but a young fool who had let himself be taken in by a pretty girl; the physician was irreproachable. As to rebels in flight, or Calvinists, if some few of them did cross the threshold of the hospice, well, they wore no placards around their necks, and a body had more to do than go worming things out of them. Having thus delivered the longest discourse of his life, he withdrew.

But he rendered still another notable service to Zeno. While putting the deserted hospice in order, he happened upon the flat pebble, traced over with a human face, which the philosopher had thrown away in some corner. The monk simply tossed the object into the canal, since it was not a thing to leave lying around.

The organist, on the contrary, proved to be prejudicial to the accused man; not that he and his spouse had anything but good to say of him, but it had been a shock to them, it had, to learn that Sebastian Theus was not Sebastian Theus. The most harmful thing this witness did was to mention the *Comic Prophecies*. These two good souls had laughed over them so much. The manuscript was soon found at Saint Cosmus, in a cupboard of the room where Zeno kept his books; and his enemies knew well how to make use of it.

§

While scribes were copying, with their varied fine and full strokes, the twenty-four charges brought against Zeno, the misfortunes of Idelette and the Angels were coming to a close. The crime of the Damsel de Loos was patent, and the penalty for it was death; not even the presence of her father would have saved her. Along with other Spanish notables, he was held as a hostage in Spain, and got word of her catastrophe only much later on.

Idelette made a good and pious ending. The execution had been advanced a few days so as not to fall within the festival of the Nativity. Public opinion was now completely reversed: touched as they all were by the repentant countenance and tearful eyes of the Fair One, everyone pitied this girl of fifteen. Rightly, by law, Idelette should have been burned alive for infanticide, but her noble birth allowed her the privilege of being decapitated instead. Unhappily, the executioner lacked surety of hand, intimidated as he was by so delicate a neck on the block; he had to strike three times. Justice done, he ran away, wildly hooted at by the crowd, and pelted with wooden shoes and showers of cabbages snatched from their baskets on the market square.

The Angels' trial lasted for a longer time: an effort was made to obtain admissions from them which would have revealed secret ramifications, going back, perhaps, to that sect of the Brothers of the Holy Ghost which had been exterminated early in the century; supposedly the two groups had believed in and practiced the same errors. But Florian, that madcap, remained intrepid; vainglorious even under torture; he declared that he owed nothing to the heretical teachings of a certain Adamite Grand Master, Jacob van Almagian (a Jew, to boot), who had died some fifty years ago. It was wholly on his own, and without the aid of theology, that he had discovered the pure paradise of bodily delights. All the red-hot pincers in the world would not make him say otherwise.

The only one who escaped the death sentence was Brother Quirin, who had had the fortitude to play mad the whole time, even in the midst of torture, and who was consequently sequestered as such. The five others condemned made a pious end, like Idelette. Through the medium of his jailer, who was well versed in this kind of negotiation, Zeno had bribed the executioners so that these young persons should be strangled before the fire might touch them. (This slight accommodation was widely in use, and served most opportunely to round out the meager salaries of the hangmen.) The stratagem worked for Cyprian, François de Bure, and one of the novices; it saved them from the worst torment, but did not, of course, spare them the terror which they had to suffer beforehand. On the contrary, the arrangement failed for Florian and the other novice, whom the executioner could not discreetly reach in time to help; they could be heard screaming in the flames for nearly half an hour.

The accountant, too, was at the scene, but he was already dead. For as soon as he had been brought back from Oudenaarde, and put behind bars in Bruges, he had had some poison brought to him by friends of his in town. In conformity with custom he was burned, although dead, at the stake, since he could not be burned alive. The philosopher cared little for this crafty contriver, but it had to be admitted that Pierre de Hamaere had proved capable of taking his fate in hand and of dying like a man.

Zeno learned all these details from his jailer, whose tongue was loose at both ends. The rascal apologized for the mistiming that had occurred in relation to two of the condemned men; he even proposed to return part of the money, although the accident, he repeated, was no one's fault. The physician merely shrugged his shoulders at this. He had clad himself now in mortal indifference: the important thing was to conserve his strength to the last. That night, however, was passed without sleep. Racking his brain for some antidote to the horror, he reflected that Cyprian or Florian would assuredly have thrown themselves into the fire, if it were to rescue someone: the atrocity lay less in the cruelty of those deaths than in the sum of human stupidities leading to them.

Suddenly something flashed in his memory: early in his travels he had sold his recipe for liquid fire to the Emir Noureddin, who had used it in a naval battle in Algiers; perhaps they had gone on employing it from that time. In offering it thus, he had done nothing out of the ordinary; any other artificer would have done the same, and this invention (which had burned alive hundreds of men) had even appeared to be an advance in the art of war! Given the barbarity in both cases, violent combat in which each man has a fighting chance is certainly less of an abomination than torture and death judicially prescribed in the name of a beneficent God; nevertheless, he, too, by that device had himself been the author and accomplice of outrages inflicted upon the miserable flesh of mankind, and it had taken him thirty years to feel remorse. This feeling, he knew, would doubtless have been merely a subject for amusement to admirals and princes. As well get out of this hell on earth, soon.

§

No one could complain that the theologians assigned to list officious and heretical (or frankly impious) propositions in the writings of the defendant had not duly performed their task. They had procured the translation of the *Protheories* in Germany, and the other works were in Jan Myers's library, long since transferred to Saint Cosmus. To Zeno's great amazement, the Prior had owned the *Prognostications of Things to Come*.

The prisoner was specifically accused of adhering to errors of philosophers long since condemned by the Church, or to theories considered liable to censure. In going over the list, Zeno took a certain pleasure in grouping those propositions, or rather, the objections made to them, so as to form a kind of chart of man's opinions in this year of grace 1569, at least for what concerned the abstruse realms where his own mind had ventured. It was clear, for example, that, although Copernicus' system was not proscribed by the Church, the best informed among those gentlemen in clerical collars and mortarboards were already dubiously shaking their heads, saying that it could not fail to be so, soon; his assertion that the sun and not the earth is the world's center, though tolerated if presented as a timid hypothesis, was not the less an affront to both Aristotle and the Bible; furthermore, it offended man in his need to see his own dwelling place as the middle of the Whole. Zeno found it understandable that a view so opposed to the evidence of our senses should prove displeasing to ordinary minds, for he knew from his own experience, without going further afield, how greatly the concept of an earth in motion disrupts habits of thought which we all acquire as part of our equipment in life. For himself, he had found it inebriating to belong to a world which was no longer limited to this poor hovel of man, but the mere notion of any such expansion made most people sick and dizzy.

Still worse than the audacity of putting the sun in earth's place at the center of things was the error of Democritus, namely, the belief in an infinite number of worlds. This theory, which would deprive the sun itself of its privileged place, and deny the existence of a center, seemed to the majority of minds a heinous impiety. Far from launching joyously, as the philosopher had done, up through the sphere of the fixed stars into those cold or burning spaces, men felt lost in that immensity; the bold spirit who might venture to demonstrate the existence of such regions became a renegade.

The same prejudices obtained in the still more dangerous domain of pure concept. Averroës was held in error for his hypothesis of an impersonal God everywhere present within the world, a world itself eternal. This conception seemed to deprive the worshipper of his chief resource, a God made in his own image, who reserves his bounty and his wrath alike for man alone. Origen's error, the idea that the soul is eternal, without beginning or end, aroused strong indignation because it reduced our present life to a thing of slight import. Men were willing to have immortality open out before them, whether in Heaven or in Hell, according to their deserts, but no one welcomed the thought of an eternity extending both forward and back, and in which one exists, but not in one's own person.

Pythagoras' error, attributing to animals souls like ours in essence and in kind, was even more shocking to the featherless biped who claims to be the only living creature to endure forever. The proposition drawn from Epicurus, that death is an end of being (although an hypothesis wholly consistent with what we observe in corpses and in cemeteries), wounded to the quick not only man's avidity for staying alive but also his pride, which foolishly assures him that he deserves to live on.

All these opinions were supposedly offensive to God; the real objection to them, however, was that they undermined the importance of man. It was to be expected, therefore, that they would lead their proponents to prison, or worse still.

Coming down from the sphere of pure concept to the tortuosities of human conduct, it was clear that fear, even more than pride, was the main motive of the execrations. A philosopher who dared to recommend free play of the senses, and to treat of carnal pleasure without disdain, was enraging to the rabble, for in this domain they were governed greatly by superstition, and even more by hypocrisy. It mattered little whether he who risked offering such advice were or were not more austere, and in some cases even more chaste, than his relentless detractors; they agreed that no death by fire or torture could expiate such atrocious license, and precisely because the crime of audacity of mind seemed to render more odious the crimes of the body alone. Similarly, the indifference of a sage to his native land and religion (since any country is a homeland for him, and any religion valuable in its way) was exasperating to the throng, prisoners all. If this renegade philosopher (who, nevertheless, denied none of his true beliefs) was becoming a scapegoat for his enemies, it was because each of them, at some time, had wished secretly, or perhaps without even knowing it, to escape from the circle wherein he was enclosed, and where he would eventually die. A rebel who rose against his king provoked something of the same envy and anger among those who stood for order above all; his "No" was a rebuke to their perpetual "Yes." But in the popular judgment the worst of these Sons of Darkness, who thought so strangely, and for themselves, were those who were known for some virtue, for they were much more to be feared when they could not be wholly despised.

§

De Occulta Philosophia: in order to conserve his strength the captive was hardly dwelling any longer on the issues in question, but the insistence of some of the judges on magic practices to which he was said to have been given recently, or in the more distant past, disposed him to meditate on that thorny subject, which had occupied him, though secondarily so, all his life. In that realm, especially, the views of learned men were the reverse of those of the crowd. For the common herd, a magician was someone both revered and hated for his powers, which they supposed to be immense: there again, envy was raising its ugly head. But when Zeno's lodgings were searched, it was disappointing to find only the work of Agrippa of Nettesheim, which both Canon Campanus and the Bishop possessed, too, and a more recent work, that of Giambattista della Porta, which Monseigneur had also on his desk. Since the questioners obstinately persisted on these matters, however, the Bishop, in order to be fair, chose to make some interrogation himself of the defendant.

Although fools fear magic as the science of supernatural power, the system disquieted the prelate, he acknowledged, because on the contrary, as its practitioners explained it, it left no place for Christian miracle. In discussing the subject with him, Zeno was almost wholly sincere. The universe as seen by the magician, he agreed, is constituted of attractions and repulsions governed by laws still mysterious to us, but not necessarily impenetrable to human understanding. Among the substances we know, lodestone and amber are apparently the only ones to reveal, even in part, those secrets which no one has explored, as yet, and which someday, perhaps, will elucidate the whole. The great virtue of magic, and of alchemy, her daughter, is to postulate the unity of matter, with the result that certain philosophers of the alembic and the crucible have even conjectured that matter could be of the same nature as light and thunderbolts. That postulate carries us perilously far, but no adept of the science worthy of his name would fail to recognize the dangers.

The sciences of mechanics, in which, Zeno explained, he had been much engaged, are akin to these same magical pursuits in that they try to transform knowledge about things into power over these things, and indirectly into power over man. In a sense, everything is magic: magic, for example, is the science of herbs and metals, which allows the physician to influence both malady and patient; magical, too, is illness itself, which imposes itself upon a body like a demoniacal possession of which sometimes the body is unwilling to be healed. The power of sounds, high or low, is magic, disturbing the soul, or possibly soothing it. Magic, above all, is the virulent force of words, which are almost always stronger than the things for which they stand; their power justifies what is said about them in the *Sepher Yetsira*, not to mention between us the Gospel According to Saint John. Magical is the prestige which surrounds a monarch, and which emanates from the ceremonies of the Church; and magical in their effect, likewise, are the scaffolds draped in black and the lugubrious roll of drums at executions; all such trappings transfix and terrify the gaping onlookers even more than they awe the victims. And finally, love is magic, as is hatred, too, imprinting as they do upon the brain the image of a being whom we allow to haunt us.

His Lordship nodded thoughtfully, but then remarked that a universe so organized left nothing to the personal will of God, and Zeno agreed, though fully aware of the risk he thus ran. The two scholars exchanged some views on what is meant by the personal will of God, through what intermediaries it works, and if it is requisite for the operation of miracles. For instance, the Bishop found nothing wrong in Zeno's interpretation of the stigmata of Saint Francis in his *Treatise on the Physical World*, explaining them as an extreme effect of overpowering love, which always molds the lover in the likeness of the beloved. The philosopher was indiscreet, though, in offering this explanation as the only one possible. Zeno denied, however, that his interpretation had been exclusive.

Inclining toward the side of the adversary, for the moment, by a kind of civility obtaining between dialecticians, Monseigneur recalled that of yore the blessed Cardinal Nicholas of Cusa had advised against display of fervor around miraculous statues and Hosts that bleed in the monstrance. Venerable scholar that he was (he, too, had postulated an infinite universe), he seemed almost to have accepted in advance the doctrine of Pomponazzi, who held that miracles were produced wholly by the imaginative faculty, as Paracelsus and Zeno would have it for magical apparitions. But scoffers and heretics are more numerous today than in the holy Cardinal's time, and if he were alive, in order not to seem to countenance them, he would probably keep his more daring views to himself. After all, he had controlled the Hussite error as best he could.

Zeno could acquiesce, indeed, in this view: there was certainly less freedom of opinion in the air than ever. He even added, by way of returning dialectical courtesies to His Lordship, that to speak of an apparition as wholly in the imagination does not mean that it is only imaginary, in the vulgar sense of the term, for the gods and the demons who dwell within us are decidedly real. On hearing the first of these two plurals, the Bishop frowned; but he was a cultivated man and knew that some allowance must be made for those who have read their Greek and Latin authors. Meanwhile, the physician was continuing; he described the close attention he had always paid to any hallucinations of his patients: in this condition the true nature of the person comes to light, and with it sometimes an authentic heaven or a veritable hell.

But to return to the subject of magic, and to other doctrines analogous to it, Zeno observed that it was not only superstition that had to be fought but also the gross skepticism which boldly denies whatever is invisible and unexplained. On this point the two men were in accord without reserve. In conclusion they touched upon the chimaeras of Copernicus: this wholly hypothetical terrain was not dangerous for the accused man. At the most he could be charged with presumption for having presented as highly plausible an obscure theory which contradicted Scripture. The Bishop, without going so far (as did Calvin and Luther) as to denounce a system which makes mockery of Joshua's command to the sun, nevertheless judged the theory less acceptable for good Christians than that of Ptolemy; he also made a very rational objection to it, mathematically, based on a computation of parallaxes. Zeno agreed that many points still awaited proof.

§

On returning home, that is to say, to prison, and knowing well that the outcome of this malady of incarceration would be fatal, Zeno tried to devise ways to keep from reflecting. He was weary of hair-splitting argument. Better to provide his mind with mechanical occupations: they would prevent falling into terror, or rage; he himself was the patient now who had to be supported, and not allowed to despair. Here his knowledge of other tongues came to his aid; he had known the three or four erudite languages that are learned in school, and during his life and travels had familiarized himself more or less well with the vernacular of a good half dozen other countries. Often he had regretted dragging about this encumbrance of words which he no longer used: there was something grotesque in knowing the exact sounds or signs in ten or twelve different languages for the notion of truth or the notion of justice. But now the whole worthless clutter served him for pastime: he established lists, formed groups, compared alphabets and rules of grammar. For several days he toyed with the project of a logical form of speech, which would be as exact as is musical notation, and capable of expressing all possible conditions and relationships. He invented some coded language, as if he had someone to whom to address secret messages. Mathematics, too, were useful as diversion: he reckoned the stars' progression above the prison roof, and painstakingly reworked his calculations of the quantity of water absorbed and evaporated each day by the plant which was doubtless drying up by this time in his laboratory.

He fell to thinking again at some length of flying and diving machines, and of mechanical devices for recording sounds, thus imitating human memory. He and Riemer had once designed apparatus for all these things, and he sometimes still sketched them in his notebooks. But he had grown distrustful of such artificial extensions to man's feeble body: even if a diver can descend into the sea inside a bell made of leather and iron, he will suffocate in the water when left to his own resources; and what is the use of ascending the skies with the help of pedals and machines so long as human flesh remains a heavy mass which falls like a stone? Above all, of what importance is it to find a means of recording human discourse; the world is already too full of that babble of lies.

Certain things came to mind abruptly, out of oblivion, such as fragments of alchemical tables that he had learned by heart at Leon. Then there were other exercises: sometimes testing his memory and sometimes his judgment, he would force himself to retrace step by step certain of his surgical operations: that transfusion of blood, for example, which he had twice tried. The first attempt had succeeded beyond his expectation, but the second had brought sudden death, not to the one who had given of his blood, but to him who had received it, as if between two red liquids running from two different individuals there were actually sympathies and aversions of which we know nothing. Doubtless similar accords and repulsions could explain for us the cause of sterility and fecundity among couples. The word *fecundity* brought him back, in spite of himself, to Idelette, and the sight of her carried away by the watch. Breaches were opening in his defenses, however carefully prepared: one evening, seated at his table and vaguely studying the candle's flame, the thought of the young monks thrown on the burning pyre flashed upon him; horror, pity, and anguish, and then anger, which soon gave way to hate, all together brought a flood of tears, to his shame. He was no longer sure about what or whom he was weeping in this way. It was clear that prison was sapping his strength.

Formerly, at the bedsides of his patients, he had often heard dreams recounted. He, too, had dreamed dreams. Folk are usually content to draw from such visions portents which sometimes prove true, since they reveal the sleeper's secrets; but he surmised that these games the mind plays when left to itself can indicate to us chiefly the way in which the soul perceives things. Accordingly, he sought to enumerate the qualities of substance as seen in dream: lightness, impalpability, incoherence, total liberty with regard to time; then, the mobility of forms which allows each person in this state to be several people, and the several to reduce themselves to one; last, the sense of something akin to Platonic reminiscence, but also the almost insupportable feeling of necessity. Such phantom categories strongly resemble what Hermetists claim to know of existence beyond the grave, as if the world of death were only continuing for the soul the awesome world of night.

Life, itself, however, as regarded by a man who was about to leave it, was also acquiring the strange instability of dreams, with their peculiar sequence of events. Zeno seemed to pass from one state to the other, much as he did from the

Hall of Records, where he was interrogated, to his firmly
locked cell, and from his cell to the walled courtyard below,
now covered with snow. He beheld himself at the door of a
slender turret where His Swedish Majesty used to lodge him
at Vadstena. A great elk which Prince Erik had pursued into
the forest a day previous was standing before him, motionless
and patient like an animal waiting for help. The dreamer
divined that it lay with him to hide and save the wild creature,
but he did not know how to make it cross the threshold of
that human dwelling. The elk was black, or seemed so, all wet
and gleaming, as if it had crossed over to him through a river.
Another time he was in a boat, and was leaving a river mouth
for open sea. The day was fine and sunny, with a wind. Hundreds of fish darted round the prow, carried by the current or
swimming ahead of it in their turn, passing from fresh to salt
water; and this migration and departure was full of joy.

But there was no longer need to dream. Things were, of
themselves, taking on the colors which they have only in
dreams, recalling the pure green, red, and white of alchemical
nomenclature: thus, an orange which arrived one day to
adorn his table, luxuriously, shone there for long like a ball of
gold; its perfume and its savor bespoke likewise the same perfection. Several times he thought that he heard solemn music,
like that of an organ, if the music of organs could pour forth
in silence; the mind, rather than the faculty of hearing, was
receiving those sounds. If he brushed even ever so slightly the
rough surface of a brick covered with lichen, he felt that he
was exploring whole worlds. One morning, while making his
round in the courtyard with his guard, he noticed a layer of
ice on the worn pavement; beneath the transparent surface
ran a vein of water, trembling as it searched its way; finally
the tiny flow found its downward path.

One time, at least, he was host to a daylight apparition. A
comely but melancholy child of some ten years of age had
installed himself in the room. Clad all in black, he looked like
a young prince from one of those castles that we visit only in

dreams, but Zeno would have thought him real had he not suddenly appeared there, without having had to enter and advance into the room. The child resembled him, but still was not the boy who had grown up in Woolmarket Street. Zeno searched for some clue in his past, which contained but few women: with Casilda Pérez he had been prudent, little caring to send that poor girl back to Spain pregnant by him; the Hungarian captive at Buda's walls had met her death soon after he had possessed her (his one reason for recalling her at all); the others had hardly been more than low wenches thrown in his way by the hazards of travel, bundles of flesh and petticoats for which he had felt small relish.

But the Lady of Froso had proved to be different: she had loved him enough to hope to offer him permanent shelter, and had wanted a child by him; he would never know if that wish, which lies deeper than mere bodily desire, had ever been fulfilled. Could it be that a spurt of semen, traversing the night of the womb, had ended by bringing this young creature into being, who was and yet was not himself, thus prolonging and perhaps multiplying his substance? A feeling of infinite fatigue swept over him, but in spite of himself he felt a certain pride. If that phantom was his child, then he, philosopher though he was, was caught up in the game (as he already was, anyhow, by his writings and by the various acts of his life); he would not get out of this labyrinth until the end of time.

The child of Sign Ulfsdatter, born of the long white nights (a possibility among all things possible), was contemplating the exhausted man with grave astonishment, as if to ask him questions for which Zeno had no replies. It would have been hard to say which of the two regarded the other with more pity. All at once the vision ended, as suddenly as it had formed. The child, who was perhaps imaginary, disappeared. Zeno forced himself not to think of him again; it was doubtless only a prisoner's hallucination.

The night guard, one Hermann Mohr, was a tall, heavy, taciturn fellow who slept, with an eye always open, at the end of the corridor; he seemed to have only one passion, that of oiling and polishing the locks and bolts. But Gilles Rombaut was an engaging rogue. He had seen something of the world, having been both soldier and peddler; his endless prattle kept Zeno informed as to what was said or done in town. It was he who disposed of the sixty sous allotted to the captive per day, the sum granted to all prisoners of honorable, though not noble, rank. He brought food in surfeit, knowing full well that his pensioner would hardly touch it, and that these same meat pies and sausages would finally come to the table of the Rombaut couple and their four offspring. Since the philosopher had seen for himself the inferno of the common jail, he found little charm in such gross abundance of victuals and clean linen (rather well laundered by the wife Rombaut); but a kind of comradeship had been formed between him and the jolly fellow, as seldom fails to happen when one brings food to another, takes him for his walk, shaves him, and empties his closestool. The rascal's reflections were agreeable antidotes to theological and judicial jargon: Gilles was not very sure that there is a Good Lord, given the ugly state of this world of ours. Idelette's misfortunes had cost him a tear or two: too bad that they had not allowed such a pretty young thing to live. He thought the Angels' doings ridiculous, though at the same time he declared that folk take their pleasure as they can, and that there is no accounting for tastes. For his part, he liked wenching, a pastime less dangerous, but costly, and sometimes it led to trouble for him at home. As for public affairs, he did not give a fig.

He and Zeno played cards together; Gilles always won. The prisoner-doctor prescribed for the family Rombaut. A goodly portion of Kings' Day cake which Greete had left for Zeno at the Hall of Records proved too tempting for the scoundrel, so he confiscated it for the benefit of his own household; nor was it at all a misdeed, he reasoned, since in any case the prisoner had too much to eat. Zeno never knew that Greete had offered him this timid token of her fidelity.

§

When the time came, the philosopher defended himself rather well. Some of the charges which had finally been retained were absurd: he had certainly not embraced the faith of Mohammed while he was in the East; he had not even been circumcised. It was less easy to exonerate himself for his service to the barbarous Turk in a period when that Infidel's fleets and armies were fighting against the Emperor. Zeno explained that he was the son of a Florentine but was established in a practice in Languedoc at that time, and considered himself a subject of the Very Christian King Francis, who always maintained good relations with the Sublime Porte. This argument was hardly solid, but certain legends quite propitious for the defendant were being spread about the town on the subject of this visit to the Levant: Zeno was reported to have been one of the secret agents of the Emperor in heathen lands, and probably it was only discretion that kept him from revealing the fact. The philosopher did not contradict this notion, or others equally romantic, not wishing to discourage friends unknown to him, who evidently had set the rumors running.

The two years passed with the King of Sweden were still more incriminating because more recent, and because no mist of legend could embellish them. The question here was to know if he had lived as a Catholic in that country gone over to the so-called Reform. Zeno denied that he had ever abjured the Faith, but he did not add that he had attended Protestant preaching (though as seldom as was possible). The charge of espionage for a foreign power came up again, whereupon the defendant antagonized everyone by arguing that if he had been responsible for learning and transmitting anything to anybody he would have installed himself in a city less far removed from the current of affairs than was Bruges.

But just so, this long residence in his native town under an assumed name made the judges skeptical: they saw sinister depths in such concealment. It was admissible that a miscreant condemned by the Sorbonne should have hidden himself for a few months in the house of one of his friends, a barber-surgeon little noted for his Christian piety, but that a clever man, who had had kings for patients, should have adopted the impecunious existence of a doctor to the poor, over a very long period of time, was altogether too strange to be innocent. On this point the defendant was short of a reply: he no longer knew, himself, why he had lingered so many years in Bruges. By a kind of delicacy he refrained from alluding to the affection which had bound him more and more closely to the late Prior; besides, that reason would have seemed valid only to him. As to detestable relations with Cyprian, the accused man denied them outright, but everyone noticed that his language lacked the virtuous indignation which would have been fitting on his part. They did not renew the charge against him for having treated and fed fugitives at Saint Cosmus, because the new Prior of the Cordeliers, judging wisely that his monastery had already suffered too much from the whole affair, insisted that those rumors of disloyalty should not be revived around the doctor of its hospice.

The prisoner had conducted himself very well up to this time, but he burst out in fury when the Prosecutor for Flanders, Pierre Le Cocq, bringing up the old subject of magic and undue influences, pointed out that the infatuation of Jean Louis de Berlaimont for the physician could be explained as the work of a spell. In spite of having explained to the Bishop that in a sense everything is magic, Zeno was enraged that the exchange between two free minds should be thus degraded. The Most Reverend Bishop did not comment on the apparent contradiction.

When interrogated on matters of doctrine, the defendant was as agile as is possible for a man bound up in the subtleties of a powerful spider web. The question of whether or not worlds are infinite in number particularly preoccupied the two theologians called in as auditors: there was lengthy argu-

ment as to whether *infinite* means the same thing as *unlimited.*
Longer still was the verbal fencing over Zeno's heretical im-
plication that the soul is eternal, or perhaps survives only in
part, or only for a time; for Christians these latter alternatives
amounted to an assumption of outright mortality for the soul.
Zeno ironically reminded the judges of Aristotle's definition
of the several parts of the soul, and of the ingenious elabora-
tion of that definition later on by Arabic scholars. Were we,
he asked, postulating the immortality of the vegetative soul or
of the animal soul, of the rational soul or of the intellectual
soul, or finally of the prophetic soul; or were we speaking of
the immortality of an entity underlying all those parts? At a
given moment in the discussion, the philosopher made the
point that, after all, some of his own hypotheses were not
unlike the hylomorphic theory of Saint Bonaventura, which
implies a certain corporeality of souls. The judges denied the
validity of the comparison, but Canon Campanus, who was
present at this debate, felt a glow of pride at his pupil's skill in
argumentation, remembering how, long ago, he had taught
him these scholastic niceties.

It was in the course of this session that were read aloud
(somewhat too lengthily, to the judges' taste, who considered
that they already knew quite enough to render a verdict) the
notebooks in which forty years previous Zeno had copied
quotations from pagans or from notorious atheists, and from
those Church Fathers who contradicted each other. Unfortunately, Jan Myers had carefully conserved this youthful arsenal of skepticism: its trite arguments were at this date even
more annoying to the defendant than to His Lordship, but the
non-theologians were shocked by them, far more than by
the audacities of the *Protheories,* which were too abstruse to
be easily comprehended.

Finally, and in a lugubrious silence, were read those *Comic
Prophecies* with which Zeno had formerly regaled the organist and his wife, as if with simple riddles. The grotesque
world depicted therein, such as is seen in pictures by certain

painters, seemed suddenly terrifying to the auditors. The judges listened, ill at ease, as if in the presence of madness, to the story of the bee robbed of its wax in order to honor certain of the dead, though these dead men have no eyes to see the holy candles vainly consumed before them; nor have they ears to hear supplications, nor hands to bestow blessings. Bartholomew Campanus himself paled at the mention of princes of Europe and their subjects weeping and groaning at each spring equinox over a rebel tried and condemned long ago in the East; and at references to impostors or fools who make promises or threats in the name of a mute and invisible Lord whose stewards they say they are, without proof for their assertions. Nor did anyone laugh at the portrayal of the Holy Innocents slaughtered and put on spits by the thousands each day, in spite of their pitiful bleating; nor at the image of men sleeping on birds' feathers and transported to the heaven of dreams; neither at the mention of small bones of the dead determining the fortune of the living when tumbled on a board stained with blood of the vine; even less was anyone amused at descriptions of sacks pierced at both ends and raised on stilts, spreading over the world a foul wind of words, and swallowing the whole earth to digest it in their gizzards. Beyond the blasphemous intention visible in more than one place with regard to Christian institutions, a still more drastic disdain of mankind could be felt in these lucubrations, and it left a vaguely sickening taste in the mouth.

For the philosopher himself this reading had likewise the effect of a bitter regurgitation, and his deepest melancholy came from the fact that his auditors were incensed by the bold man who was trying to show our wretched human condition in its full absurdity, but were not outraged by that condition itself, which nevertheless they had, to some small degree, the power to change. The Bishop proposed that these idle jests be dropped, but immediately thereafter the doctor in theology Hieronymus van Palmaert, who evidently detested the defendant, came back to the quotations collected by Zeno and asseverated that the trick of drawing upon ancient authors for impious and destructive opinions was even more wicked than to assert such views directly. His Lordship found such censure excessive. Upon this, the apoplectic countenance of the doctor took fire; he asked in a very loud voice why they had troubled *him* to give his opinion on matters of erroneous doctrine and comportment which would not have cost a village judge a moment's hesitation.

Two things highly prejudicial to the defendant occurred during this session. A tall, coarse-featured woman presented herself in a state of great agitation. She was Jan Myers's former servant, Catherine. She had left the house on Timber Wharf, having soon had her fill of caring for the aged cripples whom Zeno had established there, and was now washing dishes at the "Pumpkin's" brothel. She accused the physician of having poisoned Jan Myers with his nostrums brought from foreign lands; inculpating herself in order to bring destruction upon the prisoner, she declared that she had helped him in the task. The vile fellow had inflamed her senses beforehand by means of nefarious potions until she had become his slave, body and soul. She poured forth a flood of prodigious detail about her carnal intercourse with the physician; one could conclude that her familiarity with the whores and patrons at the "Pumpkin's" had afforded her much instruction in the intervening years.

Zeno firmly denied having poisoned old Jan, but admitted to having known this woman twice in the flesh. The flagging attention of the judges was, of course, quickly revived by Catherine's testimony, bawled forth with violent gesticulation; and the effect upon the public, pushing into the courtroom door, was enormous: all the sinister rumors concerning this sorcerer, they exclaimed, were but the better confirmed. The foul slut, launched now at full speed, kept on; she was ordered to stop and had to be thrown from the hall, shouting curses on the judges the while; finally they sent her to the madhouse, there to rave to her heart's content. The magistrates, however, remained perplexed: since Zeno had not accepted the inheritance willed to him by the barber-surgeon, his disinterestedness seemed clear, and left no motive for crime; on the other hand, his refusal of the legacy might have been inspired by remorse.

While they were deliberating on this matter, an accusation even more serious for him, in the current state of public affairs, claimed the attention of the judges: they received an anonymous letter, evidently coming from neighbors of the old blacksmith Cassel. Its message was that for two whole months the doctor had come each day to the forge to treat a wounded man who was none other than the assassin of the late Captain Vargaz, and this same doctor had cleverly arranged for the murderer to escape. Happily for Zeno, Josse Cassel, who could have spoken on many a thing, was at the time in Gueldre in the service of the King, having just joined the regiment of the Sire of Landas. Old Pieter, now alone, had abandoned the forge and gone back to the village where he had some land, no one knew exactly where. Zeno made the proper denial, and found an unexpected ally in the magistrate who had formerly inscribed the death of Vargaz's assassin on his register; having stated there that the murderer had died in a burning hayloft, he did not care to be accused of having negligently investigated this already distant affair. The author of the letter was not discovered, and Josse's neighbors, when questioned, made ambiguous replies: no one in his right mind would have admitted having waited two years before exposing such a crime. But the accusation was grave, and added weight to the charge of having sheltered fugitives in the hospice.

For Zeno the trial was hardly more than the equivalent of one of those games of cards with Gilles, which, out of distraction or indifference, he was always losing. Just like those pieces of bright-colored cardboard which enrich or ruin the players, each part of the legal game had an arbitrary value; exactly as in blanque or in omber, it was understood that one should shuffle and reshuffle the cards, pass, hold on to one's trumps, keep one's cards out of sight, or bluff. In any case, the truth, had one spoken it, would have upset everybody. It was hardly distinguishable from lies: When he was telling the truth, this very truth included falsehood: for example, he had forsworn neither the Christian religion nor the Catholic faith, but, had it been needful, he would have done so calmly, with good conscience, and would perhaps have become Lutheran had he returned (as he had hoped to do) to Germany. He was right in denying any carnal relation with Cyprian, but there had been one evening when he had desired that body, now turned to ash; in a sense, the allegations of the unfortunate boy were less false than Cyprian himself had perhaps believed in making them. No one was accusing the physician now of having proposed an abortive potion to Idelette, and he had been honest in denying having done so, but with the mental reservation that he would have helped her had she implored him for aid in time, and that he regetted his inability thus to spare her her lamentable death.

On the other hand, when his denials had been literally no more than outright lies, as in the episode of the care given to Han, unadulterated truth would have been no less a lie. Services rendered to the rebels did not prove, as the Prosecutor thought with indignation, and the Patriots with admiration, that he had embraced the cause of the latter: not a soul among these opposed fanatics would have understood his cool detachment and devotion to his calling.

The skirmishes with the theologians had had their charm, but he knew very well that no lasting accord exists between those who seek, ponder, and dissect, and pride themselves on being capable of thinking tomorrow otherwise than they do today, and those who accept the Faith, or declare that they do, and oblige their fellow men to do the same, on pain of death. Unreality reigned, tediously, in those colloquies where questions and replies failed to match. Zeno even fell asleep during one of the last sessions; a nudge from Gilles, who kept always at his side, recalled him to order. Indeed, one of the judges was sleeping also. This magistrate awoke thinking that the death sentence had already been passed, and that made everyone laugh, including the defendant.

§

Not only in the tribunal, but in town as well, opinions had been aligned, from the beginning, according to complicated patterns. The Bishop's position was not clear, but it evidently incarnated moderation, if not actual indulgence. Since His Lordship, by virtue of his office, was one of the pillars of the monarchy in Flanders, a goodly number of those in the government imitated his attitude; Zeno was becoming almost the protégé of the party of order. But certain charges against the prisoner were so grave that moderation with regard to him had its dangers. The relatives and friends whom Philibert Ligre still had in Bruges were hesitating: the accused man was, after all, a member of the family, but they doubted if that were reason either to crush or to defend him. Others, on the contrary, who had had to suffer from the ruthless manipulations of the Ligre bankers encompassed Zeno within their rancor: the very name put the bit between their teeth. The Patriots, who were numerous among the burghers and who predominated among the common people, ought to have supported this man in misfortune, since he was said to have succored their like. Some few of them did, in fact, take his part, but most of these Partisans inclined toward Evangelical doctrines, and detested, above all, anything that smacked of atheism or debauch; besides, they loathed monasteries, and this man Zeno seemed to them to have made common cause with monks in Bruges. Only a few persons, friends unknown to the philosopher, and attached to him by sympathies arising, in each case, from different causes, were trying discreetly to serve him without drawing upon themselves the attention of Justice (which nearly all of them had reason to mistrust). This group let no occasion go by to cloud the issues, counting upon such confusion to obtain some gain for the prisoner, or at least to subject his persecutors to ridicule.

Canon Campanus was probably never to forget that early in February, shortly before the fatal session where Catherine had burst in, the Honorable Judges had remained for a moment on the threshold of the Record Hall, exchanging points of view after the Bishop had departed. Pierre Le Cocq, who was the Duke of Alva's man of all work in Flanders, called attention to the fact that they had lost nearly six weeks over paltry details, when it would have been so simple to apply the penalties provided by law. Nonetheless, he declared himself pleased that this trial so devoid of real importance, since it related to none of the great concerns of the day, was offering the public a useful diversion by reason of its very insignificance: the populace in Bruges were less disturbed by what was happening in Brussels at the Tribunal for the Tumults when they were preoccupied here at home with Master Zeno. And besides, it was not bad, at a time when everyone was reproaching the courts for their supposed arbitrariness, to show that in Flanders all form in legal matters was still strictly observed. Lowering his voice, he added that the Most Reverend Bishop had wisely employed the authority which some persons thought was not rightly his, though they were certainly mistaken; but it was mete, perhaps, to distinguish between the function and the man: His Lordship had certain scruples which he should discard if he wished to continue to busy himself with the duties of a judge. The populace greatly desired to see this individual burned at the stake, and everyone knows that it is dangerous to take from a mastiff the bone that has been dangled before his eyes.

Bartholomew Campanus happened to know that the powerful Prosecutor was deeply indebted to what was still called, in Bruges, the Ligre Bank. The next morning he dispatched a courier to his nephew Philibert and the Lady Martha, his wife, asking them to dispose Pierre Le Cocq to find some angle favorable to the prisoner.

A NOBLE ABODE

THE SUMPTUOUS mansion of Forestel had been rather recently constructed by Philibert and his wife. It was done in the Italian style then in fashion, and everyone admired its long series of connecting rooms with gleaming parquetry floors and high windows giving on the park (where rain and snow were falling on this February morning). Painters who had studied in Rome or in Venice had covered the ceilings of the reception halls with inspiring scenes from secular history, and from Greek myth: the generosity of Alexander, for example, and the clemency of Titus; Danaë deluged by the shower of gold, and Ganymede transported to the heavens. A Florentine cabinet encrusted with jasper, ebony, and ivory (contributions from the three realms) was further adorned with small twisted columns and feminine nudes, each multiplied in turn by mirrors inset; it had also some secret drawers, opened by springs. But Philibert was too clever to entrust his papers of State to such complicated traps like the interior of a conscience; as for hiding love letters therein, he had never written or received any. His passions (very moderate, in any case) went to the kind of pretty girl to whom one does not write.

The chimney above the hearth was decorated with medallions representing the Cardinal Virtues; below them, a fire burned between two cold and polished pilasters; the massive stumps hauled in from the neighboring forest were the only natural objects in all this splendor which had not been planed, waxed, or varnished by workmen's hands. Arranged in rows on a credence were a few books showing their backs of vellum, or of leather stamped with gold, works of devotion which no one ever read; long ago Martha had sacrificed Calvin's *Institutes of the Christian Religion,* since this heretical book, as Philibert had politely pointed out to her, was far too compromising to have around. Philibert himself possessed a collection of genealogical treatises, and a handsome volume of Aretino (put away in a drawer), which from time to time he showed to guests while the ladies were talking of jewels, or of flowers in the set-beds.

Perfect order reigned in these rooms that had just been put to rights after a reception on the preceding evening. The Duke of Alva and his aide-de-camp, Lancelot de Berlaimont, had consented to sup and pass the night on their return from a military inspection in Mons and its surrounding region. The Duke was too weary to mount the great staircase without undue fatigue, so they had prepared his bed in one of the ground-floor rooms, under a tent of tapestries to protect him from drafts; these rich hangings were supported by pikes and trophies of silver. Already every trace of that heroic couch had disappeared. Regrettably, the distinguished visitor had slept badly there.

The conversation at supper had been both substantial and prudent: they had spoken of public affairs in the tone of those who participate in them and know what to believe; as a matter of good taste, they had not dwelt long on any one point. The Duke displayed full confidence in the way things

were being handled in Lower Germany and in Flanders: the
uprisings had been put down; the Spanish monarchy had no
need to fear that Middelburg or Amsterdam would ever be
wrested from it, no more than would Lille or Brussels. He
could pronounce his *Nunc dimittis*, and was already beseech-
ing the King to replace him. The Duke was no longer young,
and his complexion attested to a liver disorder; his lack of
appetite, in fact, obliged his hosts to restrain their own
hunger. Lancelot de Berlaimont, however, ate on undisturbed,
all the while giving details of life in the armies. The Prince of
Orange had been defeated, the young officer assured the company; only it was annoying, for discipline's sake, that the
troops were so irregularly paid. The Duke frowned at this
added comment, and began to speak of other things; it seemed
to him hardly strategic at the moment to lay bare the pecuni-
ary afflictions of the royal cause. Philibert, who knew exactly
to what figure the deficit mounted, preferred likewise not to
discuss money matters at table.

As soon as their guests had departed, in the gray dawn,
Philibert, displeased with having had to proffer compliments
so early in the morning, went back upstairs to bed, where he
liked best to work because of his gouty leg. For his wife, on
the contrary, it was not at all unusual to be about at this hour.
She rose every day with the first rays of light, and was now
walking with her firm tread through the empty rooms, here
and there righting a gold or silver bauble which a servant had
slightly misplaced on a dresser, or scratching, with her fingernail, an almost imperceptible trickle of wax on a console table.
While she was thus occupied, a secretary from upstairs
brought her the letter of Canon Campanus, already opened.
Accompanying it was a brief, ironical note from Philibert,
indicating that she would find in it news of their cousin, her
brother.

Seated before the fireplace and protected from too great
heat by an embroidered screen, Martha began to read the long
missive. The pages, covered with diminutive writing in black

ink, rustled between her thin hands framed in their starched lace cuffs. But soon she paused in her reading, to reflect. Bartholomew Campanus had informed her of the existence of this half-brother, her mother's son, on her arrival in Flanders as a bride; the Canon had even urged her to pray for the impious man, not knowing that Martha had ceased to pray. For her, the story of that illegitimate son had been just one more stain on a mother already sullied. She had readily identified the philosopher-physician, celebrated for his care of plague victims in Germany, with the man clad in red whom she had received at Benedicta's bedside and who had questioned her so strangely on their parents, long gone. Many a time she had thought of that fearsome visitor, and had encountered him, too, in dreams. He had seen her in her nudity quite as much as he had seen Benedicta bare on her deathbed, and he had sensed the fatal vice of cowardice that she bore within her, though it remained invisible to all who mistook her for a righteous woman. The very thought of Zeno's existence was a thorn in her flesh: he had been the rebel that she had not dared to be; while he was wandering over the roadways of the world, her path had led her only from Cologne to Brussels. Now he had fallen into that dark prison which she had once abjectly feared for herself; the punishment which hung over him seemed to her just, for he had lived after his own fashion, and the risks that he ran in so doing were of his own choosing.

She turned her head, disturbed by a draft of cold air: the fire at her feet could heat only the smallest part of the great hall. Such icy cold was what one feels, they say, when a ghost passes by: that man now so near his death had always been a ghost for her. There was nothing behind Martha, however, but the vast hall, magnificent and empty. The same, sumptuous emptiness had reigned throughout her life. Her only memories which were at all tender were those related to Benedicta, whom God had taken from her (supposing that there was a God), and whom she had not even been capable of nursing to the end. The Evangelical faith which had enflamed her in her youth she had stifled under a bushel: nothing was left of it now but ashes. For more than twenty years the certainty of her damnation had never left her; it was all that she had retained from a doctrine which she dared not confess in public.

But this consciousness of her own hell had finally taken on a somewhat settled and phlegmatic aspect: she considered herself damned much as she thought of herself as wife to a rich man to whose fortune she had joined her own, and as mother to a brainless roisterer who was chiefly good for drinking and dueling, in company with other young gentlemen; or again, as she knew that Martha Ligre would one day die. She had been virtuous without effort, having never had lovers to turn away; the feeble ardors of Philibert had no longer been addressed to her after the birth of their only son, so she had not even the chance for licit pleasure. She alone was aware of the desires which had sometimes passed through her body, but she had not so much quelled them as treated them with disdain, as one disdainfully treats a passing indisposition. She had been a just and fair mother for her son, but without overcoming his ingrained insolence or winning his love; she was said to be hard, even to the point of cruelty, to her valets and her maidservants but, of course, one has to make oneself respected by that rabble. Her attitude in church was edifying for everyone, but deep within her she despised these mummeries. If this brother, whom she had seen only once, had passed six years under a false name, hiding his vices and practicing his feigned virtues, as his enemies claimed, it was nothing compared to the lie she had lived all her life. She picked up the Canon's letter and mounted the stairs to see Philibert.

As always when she entered her husband's room she pursed her lips in contemptuous disapproval of his errors of comportment and diet. Philibert lay sunk in soft pillows, which were bad for his gout, and his comfit box, at hand's reach, was equally bad for him. He had time to stuff under his covers the

Rabelais which he kept by him to amuse himself between dictations. Holding herself very erect, Martha sat down on a chair placed rather far from the bed. Husband and wife exchanged a few remarks on the visit of the preceding evening; Philibert praised Martha for the excellent planning and serving of their repast, which unfortunately the Duke had scarcely touched. Together they commiserated over his ailing aspect. For the benefit of the secretary, who was assembling and arranging his papers before going to copy them in the next room, the portly Philibert observed, reverently, that although people talked a great deal about the courage of the rebels executed by the Duke's order (and anyhow they were doubling the number involved), not enough was said of the fortitude of this statesman and warrior, who was dying in harness for his master. Martha indicated her agreement.

Once the door was closed behind the secretary, Philibert added more dryly: "Public affairs seem to me less secure than the Duke believes, or wishes to have it believed. Everything will depend upon the toughness of his successor."

Instead of replying, Martha asked if he found it wholly necessary to lie under such heaps of eiderdowns, sweating.

"I need my wife's good advice on something more important than my pillows," he reproved her in the tone of mild derision which he often employed. "Have you read our uncle's letter?"

"The whole business is rather dirty," Martha answered, with some hesitation.

"All business is dirty where the Law sticks its nose, or the Law makes it so if it is not so already," the Councilor rejoined. "The Canon, who takes the matter strongly to heart, perhaps finds that two public executions in one family are too much."

"Everyone knows that my mother died at Münster as a victim of the Tumults," Martha snapped back, her eyes darkening with anger.

"To be sure, that is all that anyone needs to know, and it is what I myself advised you to have carved on a wall of the church," Philibert replied, with gentle irony. "But for the moment I am speaking to you of the son of that irreproachable mother . . . It is true that the Prosecutor for Flanders is inscribed on our books, that is to say, on the books of Tucher's heirs, as owing a great sum, and that he could find it very commodious to have certain debts canceled . . . But money does not arrange everything, at least not so easily as people who, like the Canon, have little of it may think. The case seems to me already too far advanced, and Le Cocq perhaps has reasons of his own to ignore such persuasion. Are you very greatly moved by all this?"

"Remember that I do not know this man," Martha said coldly, although, on the contrary, she perfectly well recalled the moment in the dark vestibule of the Fugger mansion when that stranger had lifted his mask, his obligatory protection as a doctor treating the plague. But it was true that he knew more about her than she did about him, and in any case, this remote part of her past was something that concerned her alone, and Philibert had no right of access to it.

"Note that I have nothing against my cousin, your brother, whom I would greatly desire to have here for curing my gout," the Councilor resumed, bracing himself more squarely against his cushions. "But what notion seized him to go bury himself in Bruges like a hare hiding among hounds, and worse still, under a false name that would dupe none but fools . . . The world asks of us only some slight discretion, and some prudence. What is the good of publishing views which offend the Sorbonne and the Holy Father?"

"Silence is a heavy burden to bear," exclaimed Martha suddenly, as if in spite of herself.

The Councilor looked at her with mock incredulity, then said, "Very well, let us help this fellow get out of trouble. But remark that if Pierre Le Cocq consents to desist, I become obligated to him instead of him to me; and if by chance he does not consent, I shall have to swallow a refusal. It is possible that Monsieur de Berlaimont would be grateful to me for saving from an ignominious death a man whom his father was protecting; but either I am much mistaken or this young Lancelot cares little for what goes on in Bruges. What does my dear wife propose?"

"Nothing that you could reproach me with afterward," she answered impassively.

"Good, then," the Councilor concluded, with the satisfaction of a man who sees the chance of a quarrel receding. "Since my gouty hands keep me from holding a pen, you will perhaps be so obliging as to write for me to our uncle, recommending us to his holy prayers . . ."

"Without mentioning the principal point?" Martha put in knowingly.

"Our uncle is subtle enough to understand an omission," he answered, nodding his approval. "It is important that the courier should not depart empty-handed. You surely have some tasty provisions to send for Lent (some fish patties would do), and a length of some fine material for his church."

Husband and wife exchanged glances. Martha admired Philibert for his circumspection as other wives would admire their men for their courage or virility. Everything was going so well that he had the imprudence to add: "The whole trouble comes from my father, who had this bastard nephew reared like a son. Had he been put out to an obscure family, and not sent to school . . ."

"You speak about bastards as a man of experience," she interrupted, with ponderous sarcasm.

He could smile at this jibe unrestrainedly, for she had already turned her back upon him and was on her way to the door. That natural child he had had by a chambermaid (and which anyhow was perhaps not his) had facilitated their conjugal relations more than it had disturbed them. She always came back to this one grievance, letting others pass, which were more considerable, without saying a word, and possibly (who knows?) without even remarking them.

He called her back to say: "I have kept a surprise for you. This morning I received something better than a courier from our uncle. Here are letters confirming the elevation of our domain of Steenberg to the status of a viscount's seat. You will recall that I had Steenberg substituted for the estate of Lombardy, fearing that the latter title would be joked about for the son and grandson of bankers."

"Ligre and Foulcre sound like good enough names to my ears," she coolly but proudly protested, using the French form of Fugger, as was the custom.

"No, they suggest a little too much the labels on money-bags," the Councilor objected. "We live in a time when a fine name is indispensable for advancing oneself in Court. One has to run with the wolves, my dear wife, and strut with the peacocks."

When she had gone he reached for the comfit box and took a mouthful. He was not fooled by her pretense of disdain for titles: all women love tinsel. But there was something that slightly spoiled the taste of the sugar-coated almonds for him: it was too bad that nothing could be done for that poor beggar without compromising oneself.

Martha descended the great stairway again. In spite of herself, this wholly new title rang agreeably in her ears; in any case, their son would be grateful to them for it one day. By comparison, the Canon's letter was diminishing in importance. But the reply, still to be made, was a disagreeable task; she fell to thinking once more, bitterly, that Philibert, after all, always did as he pleased, and that she, all her life, would have been no more than the wealthy housekeeper of a wealthy man. By a strange contradiction, this brother that she was abandoning to his fate was nearer to her at this moment than her husband or her only son: together with her mother and Benedicta, he composed part of a secret world wherein she remained enclosed. In a sense, she was condemning herself in condemning him. She sent for her head steward to give him the order for assembling the gifts to go back with the courier, who was stuffing himself in the kitchens while waiting.

The head steward had a little business which he would have liked to speak about to Madame: there was a wonderful opportunity. As Madame well knew, the property of Monsieur de Battenbourg had been confiscated after his execution, and everything was still sequestered, pending payment of debts to individuals before the State could sell off the possessions. One could not complain that the Spanish did not conduct matters according to the regulations. But thanks to a former concierge of the dead man, the steward had had wind of the existence of one lot of tapestries which was not included on the inventory, and which could be disposed of separately. These were all fine Aubussons representing episodes from Sacred History: *The Worship of the Golden Calf, Saint Peter's Denial, The Burning of Sodom, The Scapegoat, The Jews Thrown into the Fiery Furnace.* The meticulous steward put his list back into his vest pocket. Madame had lately mentioned that she would like to replace the hangings in the Hall of Ganymede. And in any case, those pieces would increase in value with time.

Martha reflected a moment, then made a sign of assent. These were not profane subjects, like those to which Philibert was rather too much given. And she thought that she had formerly seen these tapestries in the mansion of Monsieur de Battenbourg, where they produced a truly noble effect. It was, indeed, an occasion not to be missed.

THE CANON'S VISIT

THE JUDGMENT was finally pronounced on the morning preceding Mardi Gras. Soon after the hour of the midday meal, Zeno was informed that Canon Bartholomew Campanus awaited him below in the parlor of the Records Hall. The prisoner descended, accompanied by Gilles Rombaut. The Canon requested that the jailer leave them alone together, and Rombaut complied, but as a precaution, he turned the key in the lock as he went out.

The old man had sat heavily down in a high-backed armchair drawn up beside a table, his two canes near him on the floor. In his honor a good fire had been built on the hearth, and its flame served to supplement the cold, grudging light of that February afternoon. The Canon's broad face, lined with countless fine wrinkles, seemed almost rosy in firelight, but Zeno noted the tear-reddened eyelids, and the repressed trembling of the lips. The two men hesitated as to the manner of greeting each other: the Canon made a vague movement in an effort to rise, but his age and his infirmities precluded such an act of courtesy, nor was he sure that such homage offered to a man condemned to death would have been wholly correct;

Zeno remained standing a few feet away, but was the first to speak.

"*Optime pater*," he began, going back to the appellation he had used for the Canon in the time of his school days, "thank you for your good offices, great and small, during my captivity. I could guess the source of these attentions soon enough. Your visit now is a further favor, and one for which I did not hope."

"If only you had disclosed yourself earlier!" the old man exclaimed in affectionate reproach. "You have always had less confidence in me than in that barber-surgeon . . ."

"Are you surprised at my mistrust?" Zeno demurred. He began to rub his fingers methodically, stiffened as they were by the damp of his room, insidious in this winter season, even though he was lodged on an upper storey. Taking a seat near the fire, he stretched out his palms to the blaze.

"*Ignis noster*," he said gently, employing an alchemical formula which Campanus himself had been the first to teach him.

The words made the Canon shudder, and he strove to steady his voice in order to explain. "My part in these services that friends have tried to render you amounts to very little. You will remember, perhaps, that formerly my lord Bishop and the late Prior of the Cordeliers were gravely opposed. But these two holy men finally came to value each other. On his deathbed the Prior recommended you to the Most Reverend Bishop, and accordingly My Lord has insisted that you be equitably judged."

"For that I thank him," the condemned man replied.

The Canon perceived a touch of irony in that response, so he warned: "Remember that My Lord was not the only one to hand down the verdict. He urged indulgence, however, to the very last."

"Is that not the customary procedure?" Zeno queried, somewhat sharply. "*Ecclesia abhorret a sanguine*."

Wounded, the Canon protested: "This time the recommendation was sincere. Unfortunately, the crimes of atheism and impiety are patent in your case, and you have wanted them to be so. Still, in common law, nothing has been proved against you, thanks be to God; but you know, as I do, that for the populace, and even for most of the judges, some ten presumptions mount up to the equivalent of conviction. To begin with, the accusations of that deplorable boy, whose name even I prefer not to recall, have done you great harm . . ."

"Still, you did not imagine me sharing the pleasures of the bath, and in the light of stolen altar candles, to boot?"

"No one believed that," the Canon replied gravely. "But do not forget that there are other forms of complicity."

Musing a moment, Zeno remarked, "It is strange that for Christians the supreme evil is constituted of so-called errors of the flesh. No one chastises savagery and brutality, barbarity and injustice with the same fury and disgust. No one will judge those good folk obscene who will come to watch me tomorrow, writhing in the flames."

At this the Canon raised a hand to cover his face, as if to ward off a blow. Zeno, observing the gesture, said coolly, "Forgive me, Father. *Non decet.* I will cease to commit the indecency of trying to show things for what they are."

When the old man regained his voice it had sunk almost to a whisper. "May I say that what confounds me in this whole turn of events, of which you are victim, is the extraordinary linking of evil with evil: impurity in every form, childish pranks possibly intended as sacrilegious, violence committed against a newborn innocent, and finally, worst of all, violence committed against oneself, perpetrated by Pierre de Hamaere. I admit that at first the whole sinister affair seemed to me grossly inflated by the Church's enemies, if not actually invented by them. But a Christian and monk who deals himself death is a bad Christian and a bad monk, and this crime is surely not his first . . . It pains me to find your great learning implicated in all this."

"The violence committed by that poor girl against her

child strongly resembles that of an animal gnawing off one of its limbs in order to tear itself free from the trap where men's cruelty has left it to die." The philosopher's tone was bitter. "As to Pierre de Hamaere . . ."

But here prudence bade him break off; he reflected that the one thing he might have found to praise in that man was, precisely, his suicide. In his own total destitution, as a man sentenced to die, one chance was left to him still, to be carefully conserved, and one secret to guard.

He began anew. "Surely you have not come here to discuss the trial of a few unfortunate souls. Let us put these precious moments to better use."

The Canon, however, with the obstinacy of old age, continued his sad enumeration. "Jan Myers's housekeeper also did you great wrong. No one respected that wicked man Myers, and I supposed him to be entirely forgotten, anyhow. But the suspicion of poisoning revived his name on every tongue. I have scruples about counseling a lie, but it would have been better to have denied any carnal intercourse with that shameless domestic."

The admonition met with derision. "Indeed, I marvel that two nights abed with a servant will prove to have been one of the most dangerous actions of my life!"

Campanus sighed, discouraged that this man whom he dearly loved seemed barricaded against him. He ventured another approach. "You will never know how heavily your disaster weighs upon my conscience. I am not referring to what you have done, for I know little of that, and wish to believe it innocent, even though experience in the confessional has taught me that worse actions can be allied to virtues like yours. I am speaking of that fatal revolt of the intellect which would transform perfection itself into vice, and the seeds of which I have perhaps unintentionally implanted in you. Alas, how the world has changed, and how beneficent the sciences and ancient learning seemed in the days when I was studying letters and the arts . . . When I think that I was the first to teach you those Scriptures which you hold in contempt, I wonder if a firmer master, or one more learned than I . . ."

"Do not grieve, *optime pater*," Zeno consoled him. "The revolt which troubles you was within me, or perhaps was of the times."

"Your designs for flying bombs and for chariots propelled by wind, which made the judges laugh, made me think, instead, of Simon Magus," said the Canon, looking anxiously on his pupil of yore. "But I have also recalled those fantastical machines of your youth, which produced only tumult and disturbance. Alas, it was on that very day that I obtained the Regent's assurance of a post for you which would have led to fortune and honors . . ."

"It might also have brought me to this same point by other ways. We know less about the routes and the aim of a man's life than a bird does about its migrations."

But Bartholomew Campanus, lost in reverie, was looking back on a young clerk again at twenty. It was he whom the Canon wished to save, if not in body, then at least in soul.

"Do not attribute more worth than I do to those mechanical feats," Zeno said disdainfully, returning to the subject again. "In themselves they are neither good nor bad. They are like certain discoveries of the alchemist who lusts only for gold, findings which distract him from pure science, but which sometimes serve to advance or to enrich our thinking. *Non cogitat qui non experitur.* Even in the physician's art, wherein I have chiefly engaged, metallurgical and alchemical invention plays its role. But mankind being what it is, and what it doubtless will remain to the end of time, I admit that it is bad to empower fools to upset the natural order of things, and to let madmen climb the skies. As for me, in the condition in which the court has put me," he added dryly, with a laugh which horrified the Canon, "I have come to the point of blaming Prometheus for his gift of fire to men."

"I have lived these eighty years without suspecting how far judges may go in their malice," the old man burst out in indignation. "Hieronymus van Palmaert declares himself glad that you are dispatched to explore for yourself your infinite worlds; and Le Cocq, that vile man, mocks you in proposing to send you on one of your own celestial bombers to fight Maurice of Nassau."

"He is wrong to laugh. These chimaeras, unhappily, will take form and substance the day that our reckless breed strives as hard to realize them as it has to build its Louvres and its cathedral churches. 'He will come down from the sky, the King of Terrors, with his swarms of locusts and his games of slaughter . . . O cruel beast that man is! Nothing will be left on earth, or under the earth, or in the water, which will not be persecuted, despoiled, or destroyed . . . Open, thou Gulf Eternal, and swallow this unbridled race while yet there is time . . .' "

"What are you saying?" the Canon asked in alarm.

"Nothing," the philosopher answered distractedly. "I was merely reciting one of my *Grotesque Prophecies.*"

Campanus sighed again, this time fearing that the prolonged anguish had been too great for even this strong brain, and that the approach of death had driven Zeno delirious. "You have, indeed, lost your faith in the excellence and sublimity of man," he said, sadly shaking his head. "One begins by doubts about God, and then . . ."

"Man is as yet an enterprise, beset by time and necessity, by chance, and by the stupid and ever-increasing primacy of sheer numbers." Zeno was speaking more soberly now. "It is men who will kill off man."

He fell silent for a time, apparently overwhelmed. His dejection seemed a good sign to the Canon, whose chief dread was a soul too sure of itself, intrepid and girded against fear and repentance alike; so, proceeding with care, he resumed the discourse. "Am I to believe, then, as you have said to the Bishop, that the Great Work had no other aim, for you, than the perfecting of the human soul? If that is the case," he continued, somewhat disappointed in spite of himself, "you would be closer to us than My Lord and I had dared hope, and those secrets of magic art which I myself have contemplated only from afar are no more than what the Holy Church teaches daily to its adherents."

"Yes," said Zeno grimly, "daily for sixteen hundred years."

The Canon hesitated as to whether or not this rejoinder contained a note of sarcasm. But moments were too precious to spare, so he let it pass and went on. "My dear Son, do you think that I have come for a debate with you which is no longer in season? I have better reasons to be here. Monseigneur has pointed out to me that with you it is not a matter of heresy, properly speaking, as it is for those detestable sectarians of our time who are warring upon the Church. Yours are subtler impieties, the danger of which, on the whole, is evident only to scholars. The Most Reverend Bishop assures me that although your *Protheories* were justly condemned for degrading our holy dogmas to the level of vulgar notions shared in common with even the most ignorant pagans, the work could quite as well serve for a new *Apologetic;* the same propositions need only show that our great Christian verities are the supreme statement of intuitions already infused in the natural man. You know as I do that what matters is the way things are put . . ."

"I believe that I understand the direction this discourse is taking," Zeno commented. "If tomorrow's ceremony were to be replaced by one of retractation . . ."

"Do not hope for too much," the Canon cautioned him, assuming Zeno's accord. "It is not liberty that we offer. But my lord Bishop guarantees that he can arrange for your detention in a monastery of his choosing, *in loco carceris;* your comfort in the future will depend upon the services you will be able to render to our good cause. As you know, perpetual imprisonment is something from which one can almost always manage to get free."

"Your attempt at rescue comes very late, *optime pater,*"

Zeno said, as if half to himself. "It would have been better to muzzle my accusers in the beginning."

"We did not flatter ourselves that we could win the Prosecutor of Flanders to our side," said the Canon, swallowing down the bitterness aroused by his vain effort with the wealthy Ligres. "That kind of man rushes to gain a conviction like a dog seizing upon prey. We were obliged to let the procedure go on, awaiting our chance thereafter to use what powers remain to us. The minor orders formerly conferred upon you leave you subject to the Church's censure, but they also assure you protections which coarse secular justice does not afford. It is true that I trembled to the very end of the trial lest, out of defiance, you should make some irreparable avowal . . ."

"But you would have been forced to admire me had I done so out of contrition," Zeno interposed wryly.

"I beg you not to confound the Court of Bruges with the institution of the confessional," said the Canon in irritation. "What counts in court is that the deplorable Brother Cyprian and his accomplices contradicted each other, that we have rid ourselves of the infamies of the charwoman by shutting her up in the madhouse, and that the ill-disposed persons who accused you of healing Captain Vargaz's assassin have faded from view . . . Happily, crimes which relate only to God are under our jurisdiction."

"Do you consider the care of a wounded man a crime?"

"My opinion would be irrelevant here," the Canon answered evasively. "If you wish to know it, I hold that any service rendered to another must be judged meritorious, but the element of rebellion mingled with such service in your case is never good. The late Prior, whose sympathies sometimes inclined to the rebels, would doubtless have approved only too much of that seditious charity. Let us at least felicitate ourselves on the fact that no proof of the action could be produced."

"They would have done so, easily enough, had they put me to torture, from which your good offices saved me," said the prisoner, with a deprecatory shrug. "I have already thanked you for that."

"We took refuge in the rule, *Clericus regulariter torqueri non protest per laycum*," said the Canon with the air of a man who is registering a triumph. "But remember that on certain points, like that of morals, you will continue to be strongly suspect, and might have to appear before a tribunal, *novis survenientibus inditiis*. It is the same for matters of rebellion. Think what you like of the governing powers in this world, but reflect that the interests of the Church will continue to be linked with those of order as long as the rebels against the State make common cause with heresy."

"I understand all that," said the condemned man, nodding in assent. "My safety, precarious at best, would depend entirely upon the good will of the Bishop, whose power could decline or whose point of view could change. There is no way to prove that in six months' time I may not again be just as close to the flames as I am at this moment."

"But that fear is one which you must have had all your life?" the Canon inquired.

By way of reply, the prisoner explained: "Once, at the time when you were teaching me the rudiments of science and letters, some person convicted of a crime, whether rightly or wrongly, was burned alive in Bruges; one of our household servants reported the execution to me in detail. To add to the interest of the spectacle, they had fastened the prisoner to the stake with a long chain, enabling him to run all aflame until he fell, on the ground, or, to speak more exactly, on the burning coals. I have often reflected that that horror could serve as allegory for the plight of a man who is left *almost* free."

"Do you imagine that we are not in the same position, all of us?" the priest admonished him. "My existence has been peaceful and, if I dare call it so, innocent, but one does not

live eighty years without knowing the meaning of con-
straint."

"Peaceful, yes," the philosopher agreed. "Innocent, no."
Thus, repeatedly, in spite of themselves, the talk between
the two men was resuming the disputative tone of their old
debates between master and pupil. The Canon, resolved to
bear with anything, prayed silently that words might be given
him to convince his auditor.

"*Iterum peccavi*," Zeno said at last, in a more even voice.
"But do not be dismayed, Father, that your kind intentions
can appear to me like a trap. My few encounters with the
Most Reverend Bishop have not shown him to be a man of
great compassion."

"It is true that the Bishop cares no more for you as a person
than does Le Cocq," the Canon admitted, choking back his
tears. "I alone . . ." Then, more calmly, he continued: "But
apart from the fact that you are a pawn in the game played
between them, My Lord is not without human vanity, and
takes pride in leading an impious man back to God, especially
one so capable of influencing others of his kind. Tomorrow's
ceremony will be a far more significant victory for the Church
than your death would have been."

"The Bishop must be aware that in me the Christian verities
would have an apologist who is highly compromised."

"There you are mistaken," the old man promptly replied.
"A man's reasons for making a retractation are quickly forgotten, but his writings endure. Already some of your friends
are interpreting your years at Saint Cosmus, so suspect to
your accusers, as the humble penitence of a Christian who
regrets his bad life and changes his name in order to devote
himself, in obscurity, to good works. God forgive me," he
added with a feeble smile, "if I have not myself cited the
example of Saint Alexis coming back to live, disguised as a
beggar, in the palace where he was born."

"But Saint Alexis was in constant danger of being recognized by his pious wife," said the philosopher lightly. "My fortitude would not have gone so far."

Campanus frowned, shocked once more by such casual unconcern. The pain on his aged face moved Zeno to pity, and to speak more gently again. "It seemed certain that death was at hand, and that nothing was left for me but to pass my last few hours *in summa serenitate* . . . That is, if I were capable of so doing," he said, as if aside, and with a friendly nod of his head, which seemed mad to the Canon but which was actually addressed to a stroller reading Petronius in a street of Innsbruck. "But you tempt me, Father; I see myself explaining in all sincerity to my readers that the sneering yokel who boasted of having countless Jesus Christs in his field of grain is a good subject for droll stories, but that such a clown would surely understand nothing of alchemy and its transmutation; or again, I might assert that the rites and sacraments of the Church have as much virtue as my medicines do, and sometimes more.

"Not that I speak as one who believes," he added, forestalling any joyous response on the Canon's part. "I am only trying to make clear that the simple 'No' no longer appears to me a sufficient answer, though it does not follow that I am ready to pronounce a simple 'Yes.' It still seems to me a blasphemy to enclose the inaccessible principle of all being inside a Person, who is cut on a human pattern; and nevertheless, in spite of myself, I feel some kind of god present in this flesh of mine, this body which tomorrow will turn to smoke. Would I dare to say that it is this god who obliges me to answer 'No' to your offer?

"But then," he argued against himself, "since all systems of thought are built upon arbitrary foundations, why not Christian dogma, too? Furthermore, every doctrine which gains general adherence makes some concession to human stupidity; it would be the same if by chance one day Socrates were to be worshipped instead of Mohammed or Christ.

"But if this is true," he concluded, brushing a hand across

his brow in sudden fatigue, "why renounce bodily salvation, and the satisfactions of mutual accord? It seems to me that already, for hundreds of years now, I have weighed and re-weighed all these things . . ."

"Let me guide you," the Canon proposed, almost tenderly. "God alone will be judge of whatever degree of hypocrisy your retractation tomorrow may contain. You yourself are no judge; what you take for a lie is possibly an authentic profession of faith now forming within you, though you do not know it. Truth has its own secret ways to penetrate a soul which has ceased to resist it."

"Admit the same, then, for lies and imposture," the philosopher calmly rejoined. "They, too, can enter an unguarded soul. No, good Father. Though I have lied, at times, in order to stay alive, I begin to lose my aptitude for lying. Between you and us, between the views of Hieronymus van Palmaert and that of the Bishop and your own, on the one hand, and mine on the other, one sees a likeness here and there, and often a compromise, but never a sustained accord. These views may be traced like curved lines extending from a common surface, that of the human intellect; they diverge at once, but then meet again only to separate once more, sometimes intersecting in their trajectories, or, on the contrary, often merging on a segment of the latter. No one knows whether or not these curves come together at a point beyond our horizon. To call them parallel is false."

"You are saying *we*," murmured the Canon, almost in fright. "And still you are alone."

"Truly so," Zeno affirmed. "Happily, I have no lists of names to furnish to anyone whomsoever. Each of us alchemist philosophers is his own master, and his sole disciple. Each starts the Great Experiment anew, *ex nihilo*."

"The late Prior of the Cordeliers could not have known the abyss of revolt in which you were choosing to live," said the Canon, turning acrimonious. "He was a good Christian, and an exemplary monk, even though too indulgent for others in matters of belief. You doubtless lied to him a great deal, and often."

The prisoner cast a glance that was almost hostile at this man who had come to save him. "No," he said, "you are mistaken. We met on ground far beyond any differences." He rose as if it were his right to dismiss the visitor.

With this the old priest's dismay gave way to anger. "You are making your pride of opinion into an impious faith, and consider yourself a martyr to it," he exclaimed in indignation. "You seem to want to force the Bishop to wash his hands of your case . . ."

"The expression is unfortunate," quipped the philosopher.

The old man stooped to pick up the two canes which served him as crutches, dragging forward his heavy chair, but Zeno bent down and handed the canes to him. With effort the Canon got to his feet. The jailer now on duty, Hermann Mohr, was keeping close watch in the corridor; alerted by this sound of footsteps and moving chairs, he unlocked the door, supposing the conversation ended. But Campanus, raising his voice, called to him to wait a moment. The half-opened door closed again.

"I have poorly fulfilled my mission," said the old priest, suddenly grown humble. "Your very steadfastness appalls me because it means a total insensibility with regard to your soul. Whether you know it or not, only false pride makes you prefer death to the public remonstrance which precedes retractation . . ."

"With lighted taper and response in Latin to the Latin discourse of Monseigneur," the prisoner broke in sarcastically. "I acknowledge that that would have been a bad moment or two to pass . . ."

"Death, also, will be a bad moment," said the Canon, grief-stricken.

Zeno tried, then, to explain his thought. "Perhaps I might tell you that, judging from a certain degree of madness, or on the contrary, of wisdom, it seems hardly important whether it be I or some other person that they burn, or whether this execution takes place tomorrow or two centuries from now. Not that I flatter myself that such noble sentiments will hold up before the trappings of execution: we shall see shortly if I have truly within me that *anima stans et non cadens* which our philosophers define. But possibly too high a value is placed upon a man's fortitude at the moment of death."

"My presence here only hardens you further," the old man said sorrowfully. "I desire, however, before leaving you, to point out a legal advantage which we took care to leave you, and which, perhaps, you have not noticed. We are not unaware that in the past you fled from Innsbruck after having been secretly warned of a warrant for your arrest, sent out by the local Inquisitor. We are keeping this point to ourselves, for if it were known it would place you in the disastrous position of *fugitivus*, and would render your reconciliation with the Church very difficult, if not impossible. You will therefore not have to fear that certain acts of submission might be made in vain . . . You have still a whole night ahead of you to reflect . . ."

But the philosopher's only reply was the melancholy observation "Ha! You prove to me that all my life long I have been spied upon even more closely than I had supposed."

They had moved gradually toward the door, which the jailer had opened again. The Canon bent his head near that of the condemned man to whisper, "In what concerns bodily pain I can promise you that in any case you have nothing to fear. Monseigneur and I have made all the necessary arrangements."

"I thank you both for it," said Zeno, recalling bitterly that he had done the same, but to no avail, for Florian and one of the novices.

By this time the old man was weighed down with fatigue. The notion of making the prisoner escape crossed his mind, but it was absurd, and not to be thought of. He would have liked to give Zeno his blessing, but feared that it would be ill received, and for the same reason dared not kiss him. Zeno, on his part, started to kiss the hand of his former master, but refrained, fearing that the gesture might smack of servility. What the old priest had tried to do for him had not managed to make Zeno love him.

§

In order to come to the Records Hall in such bad weather the Canon had employed a litter; the bearers were waiting outside, chilled through with cold. Hermann Mohr wanted the prisoner to go up again to his cell before the visitor was conducted to the main entrance, so the old master watched his former pupil mount the stairs, accompanied by the jailer. Then the concierge of the prison opened and closed a series of doors, one after another, to lead the way outside and helped the departing churchman into his litter, drawing the leather curtain around him, to close him in. Bracing his head against a cushion, Bartholomew Campanus began, with ardor, to recite the prayers for the dying, but the effort proved to be only mechanical; though the words rolled from his lips, he could not follow them in thought.

The route to his home passed through the market, where the execution would take place on the morrow if meanwhile the night brought the prisoner to no better state of mind; and the Canon doubted that it would, knowing well that Luciferian pride. He remembered that in the preceding month the so-called Angels had been executed outside the city, at the entrance to Holy Cross Gate, since carnal crime was considered such an abomination that even punishment of the offenders must be kept almost clandestine. But the death of a man convicted of atheism and impiety was, on the contrary, a spectacle altogether edifying for the people. For the first time in his life these long-standing arrangements, established by ancestral wisdom, appeared to the old man open to question.

It was the eve of Mardi Gras; revelers were already abroad in the streets, saying and doing the customary impertinences. The Canon was fully aware that the announcement of an execution at such a time added to the excitement of the rabble. Twice some rowdies stopped the litter and opened the curtain to look inside, doubtless disappointed not to find some fine lady to scare. One of these fools wore a drunkard's mask, and regaled the priest with indecent burblings through the bloated lips; the second thrust a livid ghost-face in between the curtains, without saying a word. Behind him came a masquerader with a pig's snout, proffering a tune on a flute.

On reaching his own doorstep the old man was welcomed by Vivine, who was waiting for him, as she always did, in the low-vaulted entry of their well-warmed house, peering through a Judas window to see if her uncle would be coming soon for supper. The Canon had adopted her as his niece, and taken her as housekeeper, after the Curate Cleenwerck had died. Like her Aunt Godelieve before her, she had grown fat and foolish, not without having had her share of hopes and mishaps in this world. For they had betrothed her, rather tardily, to one of her own cousins, one Nicolas Cleenwerck, a squire of the countryside around Caestro, where he owned some good farm land; he also held the very lucrative post of Lieutenant General for the bailiwick of Flanders. Unfortunately, shortly before the date set for the marriage, this very desirable intended had drowned in crossing the pond of Dickebusch, when the ice had begun to melt. Vivine's poor head was never quite the same after that blow, but she continued to be a good manager and clever cook, just as her aunt had been; there was no one like her for making cordials and preserves. In these recent months the Canon had tried, without success, to get her to pray for Zeno, whom she no longer even remembered; but he did persuade her from time to time to fit out a basket for a poor prisoner.

He refused the supper of roast beef which she had prepared for him, and went at once upstairs to bed. He was trembling with cold, so Vivine set about to fill a warming pan with good hot embers and passed it between the sheets, under the embroidered down comforter. It took him a very long time, nevertheless, to fall asleep.

ZENO'S ENDING

WHEN THE door of Zeno's cell had closed on him again, with a great clank of the key and grating of iron bolts, he drew up his stool to the table and sat down, pensive. It was still full daylight: the "dark prison" of alchemical allegory was, in his case, decidedly light; through the grillwork protecting the window a leaden white was reflected from the snow-covered courtyard below. Gilles Rombaut, before ceding his place to the night guardian, had left the prisoner's supper on a tray, as he always did; on this evening it was even more copious than usual. But Zeno pushed it aside: it seemed absurd and almost obscene to transform those aliments into blood and lymph which he would no longer employ. Distractedly, however, he poured a few mouthfuls of beer into a pewter goblet and drank the bitter liquor down.

His conversation with the Canon had put an end to what had been for him, since the morning's verdict, the solemnity of death. Now his fate, supposedly sealed, hung again in the balance. The offer which he had rejected remained good for some hours more: a Zeno capable of acquiescing was perhaps hiding in a corner of his consciousness, and the night that was still to come might give this coward the advantage over the philosopher. Because that one chance in a thousand remained, the future, so short and for him so deadly, was acquiring, in spite of the sentence passed, an element of incertitude which was that of life itself; and, by a strange dispensation which he had observed also in his patients, death was thus preserving a kind of deceptive unreality. Everything was fluctuating; it would continue to do so to his very last breath. And nevertheless his decision had been taken: he recognized it less in indications of lofty courage and sacrifice than in some indefinable, blind refusal which seemed to close him off like a block from outside influences, and almost from sensation itself. Thus installed in his own ending he was already Zeno *in aeternum*.

On the other hand, and placed, so to speak, in reserve behind the resolution to die, there was another, more secret resolve which he had carefully concealed from the Canon, that of dying by his own hand. But there, too, a vast and harassing liberty of choice was left to him still: he could hold to this decision or renounce it, as he wished; he could perform the act that terminates all or, on the contrary, could accept that *mors ignea* adjudged to him, hardly different from the death of an alchemist who sets his long robe afire, by chance, in the coals of his slow-burning stove.

This choice between execution and suicide, suspended to the very last in some fibril of his thinking substance, did not oscillate between death and a semblance of life, as that of refusing or agreeing to retract had done, but concerned only the means, the place, and the exact moment. It was for him to decide if he would end in the market amid insults and jeers, or finish tranquilly within these gray walls. Next, it was up to him to retard or hasten by some few hours that final act, to choose, if he wished, to see the sun rise on a certain eighteenth of February 1569, or to die today, before the fall of night. Resting his head in his hands, elbows propped on his knees, he sat still and almost at peace, gazing off into the void. As when a dangerous calm occurs in the midst of a hurricane, neither his mind nor time itself was moving. The great bell of Notre Dame sounded the hour: he counted the strokes. All of a sudden came complete reversal: the calm ceased, swept away by a rush of anguish like a wind driving dangerously in circles. Shreds of bitter remembrance twirled and twisted in this tempest, some of them torn from memories of the auto-da-fé at Astorga thirty-seven years earlier, others from details of Florian's recent execution, and some from chance encounters with the hideous residue of judgments executed on public squares of cities he had crossed through. One would have said that the news of what was to happen had only just reached his body, providing each of his senses with its quota of horror: he saw, felt, smelled, and heard what would be the incidents of his death tomorrow on the marketplace. The vegetative soul, carefully kept in ignorance of the deliberations of the reasoning soul, was apprised suddenly, and from within, of what Zeno had hidden from it. Something inside him broke like a cord; his mouth became wholly dry; the hair stood up on his wrists and the backs of his hands, and his teeth chattered. Such disorder, unlike anything he had ever experienced, terrified him more than all the rest of his disaster: pressing his hands hard against his jaws to control them, and breathing deep to slow his racing heart, he managed to put down this veritable riot in his flesh. But that was enough: he must bring things to their conclusion before a collapse of his body or his will should leave him unable to cope with his own ills. His mind, fully lucid again, reckoned with countless dangers, hitherto unforeseen, each of which threatened to prevent his rational exit.

He surveyed the situation with the eye of a surgeon taking stock of his instruments and calculating his chances: it was four o'clock and his meal had been served; they had been even so obliging as to leave him a candle, as usual. The jailer who had locked him in on his return from the prison parlor would reappear only after curfew, and after that would not come back again until dawn. It seemed, therefore, that he had the choice of either of two long intervals during which to accomplish his task. But this night was not like others: some importune message could come from the Bishop or the Canon, requiring that the door be opened again; an intruder in frock and cowl, or a member of some Confraternity for the Good Death, moved by a pity more cruel than kind, would sometimes elect to sit beside a man condemned, trying to save his soul by persuading him to pray. It was possible, too, that his intention might be forestalled: perhaps at any moment now they might come to bind his hands. He listened for the sound of footsteps or the grinding of prison doors below; everything was quiet, but the moments were more precious than they had ever been in his previous forced departures.

With a hand that trembled still, he raised the lid of his writing case, which was placed upon the table. Between two thin slats, ostensibly joined, the treasure that he had concealed was safely there, a slender, supple blade less than two inches long. At first he had carried it in the lining of his doublet, but had transferred it to this hiding place after his judges had duly inspected and returned the case to him. Some twenty times each day he had assured himself of the presence of this object, which once he would not have deigned to salvage from a gutter. He was glad that prudence had already led him to abandon the resource of poisons; these priceless but encumbering wares, so fragile and unstable, were almost impossible to keep on one's person, or to secrete for long in a bare cell; furthermore, they would inevitably have exposed his project. For as soon as he had been apprehended in the laboratory of Saint Cosmus, and twice later on (after the death of Pierre de Hamaere, and after Catherine's testimony had brought the question of poisoning to the fore), he had been searched for suspect tablets or phials. Without their help, however, he was losing the privilege of one of those instantaneous deaths which are the only merciful endings. But this razor-tip, so painstakingly filed, would at least spare him the need of tearing his body linen to make a noose (not always efficacious, that), or of struggling with a potsherd to open a vein, perhaps without result.

Fear in its passage had gripped his bowels. He went over to the jar placed in a corner of the room and voided. For a moment the odor of matter cooked and rejected by human digestion filled his nostrils, once more reminding him of the connections between life and corruption. His hand was steady now as he fastened his aglets. The jug on the shelf was full of icy water with which he wet his face, retaining a drop on his tongue. *Aqua permanens:* for him, however, this water would be his last. Four steps brought him back to the bed on which he had slept, or lain wakeful, for sixty nights: among the thoughts whirling through his mind was this—that the spiral of his travels had brought him back to Bruges, that Bruges for him had been reduced to the area of a prison, and that his destiny was ending on this narrow rectangle. There came a murmur from the ruins of one part of his past more disdained and forgotten than others: in a cloister at eventide the soft, throaty voice of Fray Juan was speaking Latin with a Castilian accent: "*Eamus ad dormiendum, cor meum.*" But this was no time for sleeping.

Never had he felt more alert, both body and soul: the rapidity and economy of his movements were those of his great moments as a surgeon. He unfolded the coarse woolen blanket, thick as felt, and shaped it into a kind of trough on the floor, beside the bed, to hold and absorb at least a part of the liquid to be shed. For further security he took the shirt that he had worn the day before and twisted it into a long roll before the door; it was important that no trickle on the paving, which slanted slightly, should reach the corridor too soon, allowing Hermann Mohr, if he should raise his head above his workbench, to notice a dark spot forming upon the tiles. Next he noiselessly removed his shoes. This last precaution was hardly needed, but silence seemed a safeguard.

He lay down on the bed, placing his head squarely on the hard pillow. In so doing, he gave a thought to Canon Campanus, who would be horrified by this ending, but who nevertheless had been the first to have him read the writers of antiquity, whose heroes perished in this way; but this irony merely flickered on the surface of his mind without distracting him from his sole aim. He raised himself enough to bend forward, slightly drawing up his knees; swiftly, with that barber-surgeon's dexterity on which he had always prided himself among the more prized but less certain talents of the physician, he slashed the tibial vein on the external side of his left foot, at one of the habitual points for administering a bleeding. Then quickly lying back on his pillow, hurrying to prevent the fainting which could always occur, he sought and cut the radial artery on his wrist, hardly feeling the brief and superficial pain caused by severing the skin.

Fountains of blood leaped forth; the red liquid spurted, as it always does, eager, one would say, to escape from the dark labyrinths where it circulates enclosed. He let the left arm hang down to facilitate the flow. The victory was not yet complete; it could be that someone might enter by chance, and that he would be dragged tomorrow, bloody and bandaged, to the stake. But each minute that passed was a triumph. He threw a glance at the blanket already black with blood. Now he could understand the popular notion that this fluid is the soul itself, since soul and blood were escaping together. Those ancient errors contained some simple truths. He noted, with something like a smile, that this was a fine occasion to verify his old experiments on the systole and the diastole of the heart. But acquired knowledge did not count from this time on, any more than did the memory of events or of people he had met; he was still attached for some moments more to the slight thread of this person, but the person, once lightened of ballast, was no longer distinguishable from the being. With effort he raised himself slightly, not because it was important for him to do so, but in order to prove to himself that this movement was still possible. For it had often happened to him in the past to reopen a door simply in order to confirm the fact that he had not closed it behind him forever; or to turn back to some passer-by, just quitted, thus denying the finality of a departure. Such actions had been a way of demonstrating to himself his liberty as a man, limited though it was. This time the act was irreversible.

His heart was beating wildly: a violent, disordered activity reigned in his body, as in a kingdom already overthrown, but where the combatants had not all surrendered as yet. He felt a kind of pity for this body which had served him well and which could have lived, all things considered, some twenty years more; he was destroying it now in this way, without being able to explain to it that he was only sparing it worse indignities. He was thirsty, but there was no way to quench this thirst. Just as the three quarters of an hour, more or less, passed since his return to this room had been crowded by innumerable thoughts, sensations, and motions succeeding each other with lightning speed, so the distance of a few feet from the bed to the table had extended to equal the space between two celestial spheres: the pewter goblet was afloat in another world. But this thirst would end soon. He was dying the death of the wounded calling for water on the edge of a battlefield, and was including them in the same detached compassion that he felt for himself.

The blood of the tibial vein was no longer running steadily; with great effort, as one lifts an enormous weight, he succeeded in moving his foot so as to let it hang down from the bed. His right hand, still grasping the blade, had been slightly cut by its edge, but he did not feel the cut. His fingers were twitching on his breast, seeking vaguely to unbutton the collar of his doublet; he strove vainly to suppress this useless agitation, but he recognized these contractions and this bodily anguish as good signs. An icy shudder went through him, as when nausea sets in; this, too, was as it should be.

Through the clangor of bells, the noise of thunder, and the

shrill cries of birds coming back to their nests, all of which beat inside his ears, he could hear from without the distinct sound of something dripping: the blanket, saturated, could no longer hold the blood, which was spilling over upon the tile floor. He tried to calculate the time it would take for the red pool to reach the other side of the threshold, beyond the frail barrier of linen. But no matter: he was saved. Even if by ill luck Hermann Mohr should soon open that door, the bolts were slow to draw, and astonishment and fear would send him running down the stairways to seek help; all this would leave time for the final escape. What they would burn tomorrow would be no more than a corpse.

The vast roar of life in flight was continuing: a fountain at Eyoub, the rush of a spring coming out of the ground at Vaucluse, in Provence, a torrent between Froso and Östersund, all these raced through him without need on his part to recall their names. Then, in the midst of this tumult, he heard a death *râle*. He was breathing hard in loud but shallow aspirations which no longer filled his chest; someone who was not exactly he, but who seemed to be placed slightly behind him, on his left, was viewing these last convulsions with indifference. So breathes an exhausted runner once he has reached his goal.

Night had fallen, but without his knowing whether it was only within him or in the room: to him everything now was night. And night was also in motion: darkness gave way to more darkness, abyss to abyss, somber densities to somber densities. But this darkness, different from what the eyes see, quivered with colors issuing, as it were, from the very absence of color: black turned to livid green, and then to pure white; that pure, pale white was transmuted into a red gold, although the original blackness remained, just as the fires of the stars and the northern lights pulsate in what is, notwithstanding, total night. For an instant which seemed to him eternal, a globe of scarlet palpitated within him, or perhaps outside him, bleeding on the sea. Like the summer sun in polar regions, that burning sphere seemed to hesitate, ready to descend one degree toward the nadir; but then, with an almost imperceptible bound upward, it began to ascend toward the zenith, to be finally absorbed in a blinding daylight which was, at the same time, night.

He could no longer see, but external sounds reached him still. As once before at Saint Cosmus, hurried footsteps echoed along the corridor: it was the turnkey who had just caught sight of the dark pool on the floor. A moment earlier, the dying man would have been seized by terror at the thought of being retaken, and forced to live and to die for some hours more. But the anguish was over for him: he was free; this person who was coming to him could be only a friend. He made, or thought that he made, an effort to rise, without knowing clearly whether someone was coming to help him, or if, on the contrary, he was going to give help. The rasping of keys turning and bolts shoved back was now for him only the triumphant sound of an opening door.

And this is as far as one can go in the death of Zeno.

ALS ICH KAN

AUTHOR'S NOTE

The Abyss represents the final development of an isolated fragment, some forty pages originally intended as the first chapter of a vast novel, conceived and in part feverishly composed between 1921 and 1925, when I was between eighteen and twenty-two. This chapter was simply called "Zeno" at the time, and was to form one section of a broad fresco extending over several centuries and portraying several groups of persons related either by blood, or by temperament and way of thinking. For some years that far too ambitious novel was carried on along with the first drafts of another work (which was later to become *Memoirs of Hadrian*), but both projects were provisionally set aside about the year 1926. Still later on, some ten pages were added to the "Zeno" (these proving eventually to be a nucleus for the long chapter in *The Abyss* on the meeting of the two cousins at Innsbruck). The fragment, thus increased, was published in 1934 under the title "D'après Dürer" in the volume *La Mort conduit l'Attelage*, along with two other fragments from the first project, "D'après Greco" and "D'après Rembrandt." Those three corresponding titles were an afterthought, chosen to

give a certain unity to three stories of similar historical background, while heightening the contrasts between them; but
the choice was misleading in that it suggested a systematic
imitation of the work of three painters, which was not at all
the case.

La Mort conduit l'Attelage received very generous praise at
the time of its appearance; on rereading some of those articles,
I am still touched and grateful. But the author of a book has
his own reasons for being more severe than his judges: he sees
the flaws at closer range; he alone knows what he wished to
do, or should have done. In 1955, a few years after completing Memoirs of Hadrian, I turned to those three stories again,
intending merely to correct them in preparation for reprint-
ing. But the physician-philosopher-alchemist took hold on me
anew, and the first result of that renewed contact was the
chapter "A Conversation in Innsbruck," dating from 1956.
The rest of the book was completed in its final form only
between 1962 and 1965. At the most, some dozen pages of
Zeno's fifty-page story, as first published, now remain, modified and scattered throughout the long novel as it appears
today; but the main structure of the narrative, tracing Zeno
from his illegitimate birth in Bruges to his death in a jail of
that same city, is still unchanged. The first part of the present
work, "The Wanderings," follows rather closely the plan of
"Zeno–D'après Dürer" of 1921–34; the second and third
parts, "Immobility" and "Prison," are wholly developed from
the last six pages of that text of more than forty years ago.*

Indications of this nature, I realize, can be tiresome coming

* The title "D'après Dürer" had been chosen for the episode of Zeno because
of the well-known engraving Melancholia, in which a somber, winged figure
who doubtless symbolizes genius in man, sits in bitter meditation among his
various implements and tools. One literal-minded reader objected to the title
because Zeno's story was "more Flemish than German." The remark is
better suited to the novel as now completed, since the second and third
parts, nonexistent in 1934, are set wholly in Flanders, and since themes of
horror and disorder in the world as portrayed by Bosch and Brueghel pervade the present work, but did not appear in the early sketch.

from the author herself, and during her lifetime. I have decided to give them, nevertheless, for the few readers who may be interested in the genesis of a book. What I should like chiefly to stress here is that *The Abyss,* just like *Memoirs of Hadrian,* is one of those works undertaken in early youth, then abandoned and resumed in turn, according to the circumstances, but with which the author has lived all his life. The only difference between the histories of these two compositions is purely accidental, namely, that a sketch of what was to become *The Abyss* appeared in print thirty-one years before completion of the final text, whereas the first versions of the *Hadrian* did not have that chance, or that mischance. In all other respects the two novels were constructed over the years in the same way, in successive layers, as it were, until finally in both cases the last version was composed and completed in a single impulsion. I have said elsewhere what I consider to be the advantages, at least insofar as I am concerned, of such long-enduring relations between an author and a character who, though chosen in our early youth, does not fully reveal his secrets to us until we have reached maturity. In any case, this method is followed rarely enough to justify inclusion of the few details just given, even if only to avoid possible confusion in matters of bibliography.

* * *

The creation of a fictitious "historical" character, like Zeno, would seem to require bibliographical evidence even less than does a free reconstruction of a real person who has left his traces in history, like the Emperor Hadrian. The two proceedings, however, are alike in many respects. In the latter case, the novelist, trying to portray his personage fully and in the round, as he was in life, can never study too closely or with too ardent attention all available materials about his hero as they have been handed down by history and tradition. In the case of a fictitious character, in order to give him that specific reality conditioned by time and place, without which a "historical novel" is merely a more or less successful costume ball, the author can draw only upon facts and dates of man's past, that is to say, also upon history. Zeno, supposedly born in 1510, would have been nine years old at the time that the ageing Leonardo da Vinci was dying in his self-imposed exile at Amboise; thirty-one at the death of Paracelsus, whom I portray my alchemist-physician as emulating, though sometimes opposing, too; thirty-three when Copernicus died, very shortly after the publication of his great work (his theories, however, having long circulated in manuscript form among certain advanced groups, a fact which explains why the young student at Louvain could have been informed about them). At the time of the execution of the printer Etienne Dolet, to whom I refer as the first publisher of my imagined character, Zeno would have been thirty-six, and forty-three when Michael Servetus was executed, that Spanish theologian and physician who, like Zeno, sought to trace the circulation of the blood. Represented as almost an exact contemporary of the anatomist Vesalius, the surgeon Ambroise Paré, the botanist Cesalpino, and the philosopher and mathematician Jerome Cardan, Zeno of Bruges is to die five years after Galileo's birth, and a year after that of the radical, long-persecuted philosopher Campanella. Giordano Bruno, destined to be burned alive by order of the Inquisition just thirty-one years after Zeno is condemned for holding some of the same views, would have been about twenty at the time of Zeno's suicide.

Although there is no question here of constructing, mechanically, a synthetic character, a thing which no conscientious novelist would consent to do, the philosopher imagined in this story has much in common with those actual personages just named, living within the span of his same century, and also with certain other figures who had dwelt in the same places as he, had run similar risks, or had pursued the same goals. A few such parallels may be indicated, some of them deliberately sought out and utilized as a starting point for the imagination, others, on the contrary, noted down as a kind of verification as I proceeded, or even after the book was published.

Thus, the illegitimate birth of Zeno and his education for an ecclesiastical career recall some elements in the life of Erasmus, son of a cleric by a townswoman of Rotterdam, and beginning his adult years as an Augustinian monk. The uproar caused by young Zeno's installation of an improved loom for the local artisans is based on occurrences of the kind toward the middle of the century (as early as 1529 in Danzig, where the inventor of a similar machine was said to have been put to death; in 1533 in Bruges, where the magistrates forbade use of a new process for dyeing yarns; somewhat later on in Lyons, where more fully mechanized printing presses evoked riots). Certain violent aspects in the character of Zeno in his youth could remind us of Etienne Dolet (the murder of Perrotin, for example, recalling, though remotely so, Dolet's murder of his comrade Compaing). The young clerk's periods of study, first under the Mitered Abbot of Saint Bavon, in Ghent, who is supposed here to be versed in alchemy, and next with the Jacobin monk Don Blas de Vela, a Cabalist of Jewish origin, resemble, on the one hand, Paracelsus' instruction received from the Bishop of Settgach and the Abbot of Spanheim, and, on the other, Campanella's studies in the cabala under the Jew Abraham. Likewise, Zeno's long journeys, his threefold career as alchemist, physician, philosopher, and even the molestation he suffers in Basel, all follow closely upon what is known or reported about Paracelsus; the episode of his sojourn in the East, without which no hermetist's biography would be complete, is suggested also by the peregrinations, whether real or legendary, of that great German-Swiss chemist. The story of the girl captive in the Kingdom of Algiers is a typical, even trite, incident of Spanish romances of the time; the portrait of Sign Ulfsdatter, the Lady of Froso, takes into account the high repute of Scandinavian women of the period as healers and herbalists. Zeno's life at the Swedish Court is based partly on the life of the astronomer Tycho Brahe at the Court of Denmark, and partly on what is reported of a certain Dr. Theophilus Homodei, physician to John III of Sweden a generation later. The account of the surgical operation performed upon the peasant Han is derived from the record of an operation of the same kind in the *Memoirs* of Ambroise Paré.

In the domain of more private matters, it may be worth noting that the suspicion of sodomy (and sometimes the practice, concealed as much as possible, and denied when there was need) played its part in the lives of Leonardo da Vinci and of Dolet, of Paracelsus and of Campanella, much as I present it here in the life of Zeno. Likewise, the precautions taken by the alchemist-philosopher in seeking protectors, sometimes among the Protestants and sometimes within the established Church, are typical of those of many atheists and deists of the period who were more or less persecuted. Notwithstanding these compromises dictated by necessity, in the debate between the Church and the Reformation, Zeno remains closer to the Catholic side, as do so many other free minds of the same century; as does Bruno, for example, who will nevertheless die condemned by the Holy Office, and as does Campanella, in spite of his thirty-one years of imprisonment under the Inquisition.*

On a purely intellectual level, the Zeno of this novel, still marked by scholasticism, though reacting against it, stands halfway between the subversive dynamism of the alchemists and the mechanistic philosophy which is to prevail in the immediate future, between hermetic beliefs which postulate a

---

* It is not for me to discuss here the reasons for this attitude on the part of many philosophers of the sixteenth century. It has been admirably analyzed by Léon Blanchet, *Campanella* (Paris, 1920). J. Huizinga's book on Erasmus, starting from different premises, shows the same results in Erasmus' case. We need only observe that the Prior of the Cordeliers was not mistaken in detecting in Zeno's criticism of Luther an indirect attack upon Christianity itself.

God immanent in all things and an atheism barely avowed, between the somewhat visionary imagination of the student of cabalists and the materialistic empiricism of the physician. Such a position is not unique in his century. His scientific research has been conceived of, in great part, in accordance with the *Notebooks* of Leonardo da Vinci, particularly for what they contain about the functioning of the cardiac muscles; his anatomical experiments thus anticipate the work of Harvey. His study of how sap rises in plants, and of their powers of "imbibition," well in advance of the work of Hales, is suggested to me by a remark of Leonardo, and is intended to represent an effort on Zeno's part to verify a theory actually formulated in his time by Andrea Cesalpino.* The hypotheses on changes in the earth's crust come also from Leonardo's *Notebooks,* but it should be pointed out, of course, that meditations of the sort, inspired by classical philosophers and poets, are fairly commonplace in Renaissance poetry. Zeno's opinions on the origin and nature of fossils are close to those expressed not only by Leonardo but also by the physician Hieronymus Fracastor, as early as 1517, and by the naturalist Bernard Palissy, some forty years later. Our philosopher's hydraulic projects and his "mechanical utopias" (especially his designs for flying machines), and finally his invention of a formula for liquid fire, for use in naval battles, are modeled on analogous inventions of Leonardo and a few other experimenters of the sixteenth century. Such activities exemplify the preoccupations of a type of mind not uncommon to the age, but which may be said to have crossed the Renaissance almost subterraneously, remaining closer both to the Middle

---

* For the medical and surgical experiments of Zeno, see E. Belt, *Les Dissections anatomiques de Léonard de Vinci,* and F. S. Bodenheimer, *Léonard de Vinci, biologiste* in *Léonard de Vinci et l'expérience scientifique au XVIe siècle* (Paris, 1953). For the statement of Cesalpino's theory, and for the research of Renaissance botanists in general, consult among other sources the first part of the work of Emile Guyénot, *Les Sciences de la vie aux XVIIe et XVIIIe siècles* (Paris, 1941).

Ages and to our own times, already alerted, as it were, to our triumphs and our dangers.* Presentiments of these dangers can be read in alchemical treatises, which abound in warnings against misuse of technical inventions by the human race. Their admonitions now seem to us prophetic. Similar warnings are to be found also, though in a very different context, in the writings of Leonardo and Cardan.

In a few cases the very statement of a thought or feeling has been borrowed from one of Zeno's historic contemporaries, the better to confirm that such views are authentic for the period. One reflection on the folly of war is taken from Erasmus, another from Leonardo. The text of Zeno's *Grotesque Prophecies* is borrowed from Leonardo's *Profezie*, except for two lines which come from a quatrain of Nostradamus. The sentence about the identity of matter, light, and thunderbolts summarizes two striking passages of Paracelsus.†

The discussion of magic between Zeno and the Bishop draws upon authors of the time, such as Agrippa of Nettesheim and Giambattista della Porta, who, moreover, are named in the text at this point.

Nearly all the alchemical formulas quoted in Latin come from three great modern works on alchemy, Marcelin Berthelot, *La Chimie au Moyen Age*, 1893; Carl Jung, *Psychology and Alchemy*, 1953;‡ Julius Evola, *La Tradizione Ermetica*, 1948. Written from different points of view, these three studies together form a useful approach to the ever

---

* "Liquid fire" was long the secret weapon of Byzantium, and eventually contributed to the Mongol conquest. Its use was forbidden by the second Lateran Council (1139), and the interdiction was respected, partly because the indispensable primary material, naphtha, was practically unobtainable by Western military engineers. The invention of gunpowder relegated this fire to the domain of forgotten "progress" until our time. Zeno's invention would have consisted of taking the old Byzantine formula and combining with it new ballistic methods. On this subject see R. J. Forbes, *Studies in Ancient Technology* Vol. I (Leyden, 1964).

† Paracelsus, *Das Buch Meteororum* (Cologne, 1566), quoted by B. de Telepnef, *Paracelsus* (St. Gallen, Switzerland, 1945).

‡ From the German revised edition of 1952.

enigmatic realm of alchemic thought. In alchemical treatises, the formula *L'Oeuvre au Noir*, given as the French title to this book, designates what is said to be the most difficult phase of the alchemist's process, the separation and dissolution of substance. It is still not clear whether the term applied to daring experiments on matter itself, or whether it was understood to symbolize trials of the mind in discarding all forms of routine and prejudice. Doubtless it signified one or the other meaning alternately, or perhaps both at the same time.

A certain number of events which still concern us occurred during the sixty years which encompass Zeno's lifetime. First, close to 1510, the scission of what remained of ancient medieval Christianity into two parties, theologically and politically opposed. On one side, the failure of the Reformation, turning into Protestantism, and crushing what could be called its own left wing; on the other, the corresponding failure of Catholicism, encasing itself for four centuries to come in the iron corselet of Counter Reformation; the great explorations turning more and more into sheer exploitation of the known world; the sudden advance of capitalist economy concomitant with the beginning of the monarchic era. Such movements, far too vast to be wholly apparent to the people living through them, have indirect bearing upon Zeno's life, and a more direct effect, perhaps, upon the lives and conduct of the secondary characters, who are more deeply entrenched than he in the routine habits of their century. Thus Bartholomew Campanus was drawn on the model, already outmoded, of an ecclesiastic of the preceding century, for whom humanistic learning presented no problems. Unfortunately, given the circumstances, the warmhearted Prior of the Cordeliers has few openly avowed parallels in the history of the sixteenth century, but he has been derived, in part, from certain saintly figures of the period who have had their full share of secular experience before entering upon a career in the Church, or before taking a monastic habit. In the Prior's discourse against the use of torture, the reader will recognize an argument profoundly Christian in spirit but borrowed by me slightly in advance from Montaigne. The learned and politically shrewd Bishop of Bruges has been conceived along lines of other prelates of the Counter Reformation, but is not incompatible with the little we know of the actual incumbent of that seat in those years. Don Blas de Vela was fashioned on the model of a certain César Brancas, Abbot of Saint André at Villeneuve-lez-Avignon, an ardent cabalist whose monks drove him away about the year 1597, on the charge of "judaizing." The figure of Fray Juan, purposely kept in the background, suggests Fra Pietro Ponzio, the friend and follower of young Campanella.

The portraits of men in commerce and banking follow closely upon real models, actual participants in the financial history of the time, which itself underlies history as we know it: Simon Adriansen before his conversion to Anabaptism, the Ligre family and their rise in society, Martin Fugger, imaginary, like the others, but grafted, as it were, upon the historic family of that name which governed sixteenth-century Europe from behind the scenes. Henry Maximilian is one of a whole battalion of cultivated, adventurous gentlemen equipped with a modest portion of the humanist's wisdom, a type common to the France of that time, but regrettably nearly extinct by the end of the century.* And finally, of lesser estate, Colas Gheel, Gilles Rombaut, Josse Cassel, and their comrades have been created, as far as possible, from the meager documents concerning the life of the common man at a time when chroniclers and historians depicted upper-middle-class life almost exclusively, when they were not treating of Court life itself. One could venture a similar reflection as to

* Fragment 99 of Petronius, as Henry Maximilian quotes it, is increased by a gloss from the inventive Nodot of the seventeenth century, but here, for the requirements of the story, these additional lines are supposedly composed by some ardent humanist of the Renaissance, perhaps by Henry Maximilian himself. *In summa tranquillitate* is a fabrication, but a noble one.

the scarcity of information available for the feminine characters, since the women of the period, apart from a few princesses and queens, are usually less fully delineated in the histories than are the men.

In any case, a good quarter of the minor characters in this book are taken unchanged directly from history or from local chronicles: the Papal Nuncio della Casa, the Prosecutor Le Cocq, Professor Rondelet (who created a scandal at Montpellier in having his son's corpse dissected in his presence), the physician Joseph Ha-Cohen, and, of course, among many others, Admiral Barbarossa and the charlatan Ruggieri. As for the drama at Münster, the principal actors, Bernard Rottmann, Jan Matthyjs, Hans Bockhold, Knipperdollinck, come from contemporary chronicles; although accounts of that Anabaptist revolt have been written only by its adversaries, we may accept as credible most of the details of the atrocious story, since we have witnessed so many examples of fanaticism and mass hysteria in our own times. The tailor Adrian and his wife Marie are memorialized in the *Tragiques* of Agrippa d'Aubigné; the Italian beauties in Siena and their French admirers are portrayed in Brantôme's *Dames Galantes* and in Montluc's *Memoirs*. The visit of Marguerite of Austria to Henry Justus Ligre is imagined by me, as is Henry Justus himself, but the transactions of this princess with such bankers are well known; her tender affection for her parrot, the Green Lover (bewept at its death by a Court poet), and her attachment to Madame Laodamia are both mentioned in Brantôme (*Les Dames Illustres*). The curious commentary on love between women which is given here in the portrait of Marguerite of Austria is taken directly from another page of the same chronicler. The homely detail of the mistress of a great household nursing her child in presence of a royal visitor comes from the *Memoirs* of Marguerite of Navarre, who was received in Flanders a generation later.

Documents contemporary with Zeno's lifetime provide information used here about Lorenzo de' Medici (Lorenzaccio), his service in Turkey as ambassador for the French King, his passage through Lyons in 1541 with his suite, which numbered at least one Moor, and the attempt there upon the life of that Florentine prince.* The scenes of plague at its height are justifiably placed in Basel and Cologne because of the frequent outbursts of that pestilence, almost endemic in sixteenth-century Europe; but the year 1549 was chosen to fit the needs of the story and not because of a known recrudescence of the fatal malady just then in the Rhine region. Zeno's reference in October 1551 to risks run by Michael Servetus (condemned and burned at the stake in 1553) might seem premature, but it is made in view of the dangers threatening the Catalan physician over many years, from Catholics and Protestants alike, who agreed at least in consigning this unlucky man, genius though he was, to the flames. There is no historical basis for alluding to a mistress of the Bishop of Münster, but the surname chosen for such a figure in this text echoes that of a mistress to a sixteenth-century Bishop of Salzburg of some celebrity. With only two or three exceptions, in fact, the names of the imagined characters come from archives or from genealogies, at times from those of the author herself. Certain well-known names, for example, that of the Duke of Alba, are given here in their Renaissance spelling.

*   *   *

The charges brought against Zeno by civil and ecclesiastical authorities alike, and the procedural details of his trial, are borrowed (with allowance for the different circumstances in each case) from a half dozen lawsuits, some of them notorious, others little known, but all from the second half of the sixteenth century or the beginning of the seventeenth. More particular use, perhaps, has been made of the first two trials of Campanella, in which offenses of a secular nature were alleged

* Pierre Gauthier, *Lorenzaccio* (Paris, 1904).

along with those of impiety and heresy.* The smoldering conflict which brings the civil prosecutor into open opposition with the Bishop of Bruges, thus complicating and delaying Zeno's trial, is invented, as is the entire case, but it can readily be deduced from the violent hostility then existing in the Flemish cities with respect to administrative prerogatives of the new bishops, installed by order of Philip II. The facetious remark of the theologian Hieronymus van Palmaert, dispatching Zeno to explore his "infinity of worlds," was actually made at the execution of Giordano Bruno, by one Gaspar Schopp, a German espouser of the Counter Reformation. Likewise from Schopp comes the jocose proposal that the prisoner (in that case, Campanella) be enabled to fight the heretics on flying bombers of his own construction.

Most of the details of penal procedures specific to Bruges which are mentioned in the last two chapters are taken from Malcolm Letts, *Bruges and Its Past* (A. G. Berry, London, 1926), which is particularly well documented in what relates to the judiciary archives of that city-state. For example, the horrible execution which Zeno describes to Canon Campanus as a sinister memory from his childhood was one which occurred in Bruges in 1521, for a crime not designated in the record; the penalty for infanticide in Bruges was death by fire; transgressors convicted of illicit sexual practices had to be burned outside the city walls. The brief Mardi Gras episode is based upon what took place nearly a century earlier in that same city, when the local authorities tortured and executed those councilors of Emperor Maximilian who supported him in his claim to Bruges. The story of the judge asleep at the hearing, who awakens thinking that the death sentence has already been pronounced, comes almost unchanged from an anecdote current at the time about Jacques Hessele, a judge at

---

* For these complex questions of semiecclesiastic, semicivil procedure, see the vast body of recorded testimony assembled by Luigi Amabile, *Fra Tommaso Campanella* (Naples, 1882).

the Tribunal for the Tumults (known to its victims as the Council of Blood).

Certain historical incidents, however, have been slightly modified in order to fit them within the frame of the present narrative. Thus, the autopsy performed by Dr. Rondelet on a son who died as a young child has been placed some years later than the actual event in order to present this son as a young adult, and as that "fair specimen of the human machine" on which Zeno is meditating. In fact, Rondelet, early celebrated for his work in anatomy (he also dissected the corpse of his mother-in-law!), was, in real life, only slightly older than his fictitious student. As to Gustavus Vasa, although he was known to frequent his castles at Uppsala and Vadstena, the dates implied for certain of his sojourns there, and the assumption that he was still able to attend the Diet of 1558 are chiefly due to the desire to give, in a few lines, some idea of the monarch's moves with his Court in attendance, and of his tasks as a statesman. The date of the first commissions granted to captains of the "Sea Beggars" is authentic, but the exploits and prestige of those partisans are perhaps slightly antedated. My account of the brutal treatment of Count Egmont's "steward" combines the execution of Jean de Beausart of Armentières, a member of Egmont's Guard, and the torture inflicted upon Pierre Col, steward to the Count of Nassau, who is on record as having refused to surrender a painting by Bosch, not to the Duke of Alba, as the Prior of the Cordeliers says in the novel, but to Juan Bolea, Chief Justice and High Provost of the Spanish army in Flanders. The hypothesis that this picture was destined for the collections of the King is of my making, and seems at least tenable, since Philip's predilection for Bosch is well known. The episode of Monsieur de Battenbourg's capture in flight, with all his gentlemen, and of their execution at Vilvoorde, is slightly compressed in time. The chronology of intrigues in the Turkish Court during the reign of Suleiman the Magnificent has also been somewhat modified.

And finally, two or three times the state of mind of the character who is speaking introduces an element of apparent inaccuracy into the story: Zeno at twenty, en route to Spain, defines that country as the home of Avicenna, because it was through Spain that Arabic philosophy and medicine were traditionally transmitted to the Christian Occident; it mattered little to the young scholar that that great man of the tenth century was born in Bokhara and died in Ispahan. Cardinal Nicholas of Cusa was for long, if not to the very end, more conciliatory toward the Hussite heresy than the Bishop of Bruges admits, but the Bishop, in his conversation with Zeno, more or less consciously attributes to that ecumenical prelate of the fifteenth century the less tolerant views of the Counter Reformation.

A more considerable change, in some respects, relates to the date of two prosecutions for sodomy made against two groups of monks, Augustinians of Ghent and Cordeliers of Bruges, and ending in the execution of thirteen of the former and ten of the latter. These two trials did not take place until 1578, ten years after the time I set for them, and at a period when the adversaries of the monastic orders (assumed all to be staunch supporters of Spanish rule) had the upper hand, briefly, in these two cities.* Although I antedate the trials in order to make the scandal in Bruges serve as one cause for Zeno's catastrophe, I have tried nevertheless to show, against the local political background which is necessarily different but equally somber, the same partisan fury of the enemies of the Church and the same fear on the part of ecclesiastical authorities of appearing to conceal a scandal, the two forces combining to lead to the same legal atrocities. It does not follow, however, that the accusations against the monks were necessarily unfounded. I share the views of Bartholomew Campanus on the suicide of Pierre de Hamaere, which oc-

* For this affair, as for several of the incidents mentioned in the preceding paragraph, see *Mémoires anonymes sur les troubles des Pays-Bas*, edited by J. B. Blaes (Bruxelles, 1859–60), in two volumes.

curred as I recount it, though not in Bruges, since this victim belonged to the group of monks in Ghent. Voluntary death was extremely rare at that time, and according to Christian morality was an almost irremissible sin, so the act suggests that the accused must have broken other prescriptions also before defying that one. Not counting the authentic Pierre de Hamaere, I have reduced the group of monks in Bruges to seven characters, all fictitious, as is the Damsel de Loos, with whom Cyprian falls in love. Likewise invented is the hypothesis of some connection, merely suspected by Zeno but sought out by the judges, between the self-styled "Angels" and survivors of sects supposedly exterminated nearly a century earlier, and accordingly forgotten, like the Adamites and the Brethren and Sisters of the Free Spirit, who were thought to indulge in similar sexual promiscuity, and traces of whom are to be found in the work of Bosch, so certain scholars claim, perhaps too arbitrarily. Such sects are referred to in the novel only for the sake of indicating that beneath the doctrinal alignments of the sixteenth century ancient sexual heresies were eternally welling up, perceptible also in other trials of the period. Furthermore, it will have been remarked that the drawing sent in derision by Brother Florian to Zeno is only a fairly exact copy of two or three groups of figures taken from the *Garden of Earthly Pleasures,* by Hieronymus Bosch; the painting is now in the Prado, but is listed in the catalogue of works of art once belonging to Philip II, under the title *Una pintura de la variedad del Mundo (A Picture of the World's Diversity).*

Printed in the United States
30094LVS00006B/85-90